### Ares spun Cara around so her back was to the sea.

"Who are you?" He gripped her shoulders firmly, his fingers digging into the blue flannel pajama top. With penguins. She wore *penguin* pajamas.

"I'm not a demon."

"What is your name?"

She blinked as if she didn't understand the question, and finally murmured, "It's Cara... This isn't real..."

Ares gripped her shoulders and bent to look directly into her eyes. Which were the exact color of the sea. Crystal blue with flecks of green.

"This is all real."

A sinking suspicion made his gut plummet. Had the hound given her Hell's Kiss? He leaned in... She smelled like a spring meadow. His cock stirred, the stupid bastard.

"W-what are you doing?"

He didn't reply. He touched his lips to hers. A shocked gasp escaped her, and damn, she tasted sweet. He stroked his tongue across her satin lips.

Her mouth was soft, her body ripe with curves, and he hadn't kissed a real human woman in thousands of years. Head swimming, he tugged her against him...

"Wicked... decadently sinful... prepare to be burned!"
—GENA SHOWALTER,
*New York Times* bestselling author

"Ione's best yet...a fast-paced read that kept me flipping the pages as fast as I could. I couldn't wait to find out what happened next!...Each Demonica book just keeps getting better and better. The momentum of the story and pacing keeps you drawn in until way past your bedtime." —FictionVixen.com

## Passion Unleashed

"4½ Stars! The third book in Ione's supercharged Demonica series ignites on the first page and never looks back... Adventure, action, and danger leap off every page. The best of the series to date!" —*RT Book Reviews*

"Fast-paced from the onset and never slows down until the exhilarating climax...Readers will be enthralled by the action and the charmed lead couple." —*Midwest Book Reviews*

"Larissa Ione pulls no punches...The love scenes are scorching hot and grab at your heart with their emotional intensity. Dark moments are written with just the right touch of hope that leaves the reader begging for a happy ending. I couldn't have loved *Passion Unleashed* more and hated for it to end. Raw, gritty, and tremendously passionate...It was awesome!" —RomanceJunkies.com

"5 Stars! Larissa has outdone herself with the story of Wraith. I was pulled into this story from the first page. The action is intense and nonstop. I was engrossed and enthralled...and highly recommend adding this series to your library." —BittenByBooks.com

"Plenty of steamy love scenes...nicely balanced with a high-octane plot...Larissa Ione is fast becoming a master at telling dark, edgy, and highly complex paranormal tales." —BookLoons.com

"Absolutely fabulous! Wraith is the ultimate bad boy who is just begging for salvation and Serena is his perfect complement. Ms. Ione will have paranormal fans begging for more." —**TheRomanceReadersConnection.com**

## *Desire Unchained*

"4 Stars! Rising star Ione is back in this latest Demonica novel...Ione has a true gift for imbuing her characters with dark-edged passion...thrilling action and treacherous vengeance...a top-notch read." —*RT Book Reviews*

"A fabulous tale...The story line is fast-paced from the opening sequence...fans will relish a visit to the Ione realm." —*Midwest Book Review*

"Warning! Read at your own risk. Highly addictive...Rising star Larissa Ione takes her already well-crafted and unique demon world to new heights. The sex is darker, hotter, wickeder, and wonderfully erotic; the vengeful enemy is diabolical, and the story line is unparalleled. Ione is a master at creating tortured, sexy bad boys who are full of flaws and make you melt...*Desire Unchained* may only be book two in her Demonica series, but I'm completely head-over-heels in love. I have never been so enthralled with a series before. With the end of each book, I'm left desperately wanting more." —**FreshFiction.com**

"Imaginatively riveting...Emotional intensity is the driving force behind every Larissa Ione book. Scenes may be packed with suspenseful peril or steamy passions or even quick humor and clever banter, yet it is the emotions behind the reactions of the characters that really grab the reader." —**SingleTitles.com**

"Five Stars! Larissa Ione has become one of my favorite authors, and I crave more of her books. The first book in her Demonica series was fantastic, and this one is even better...I wish I could go back and read *Desire Unchained* again for the first time. It was just that good."—**FallenAngelReviews.com**

## *Pleasure Unbound*

"What a ride! Dark, sexy, and very intriguing, the book gripped me from start to finish—totally recommended."
—**Nalini Singh, *New York Times* bestselling author of *Mine to Possess***

"4 Stars! [Ione's] hard-edged style infuses the story with darkness while taking it to sizzling heights." —*RT Book Reviews*

"5 Stars! Fascinatingly innovative...full of fervent encounters and shocking disclosures...compelling scenes and dynamic characters." —**SingleTitles.com**

"Fast-paced...never slows down...Romantic fantasy fans will appreciate the first Demonica tale." —*Midwest Book Review*

"Intense, engrossing, and titillating, *Pleasure Unbound* is a story not to be missed. I can't wait for the next story."
—**RRTErotic.com**

"4½ Stars! Wow, wow, wow! This is one hot demon love story! The pages are riddled with action, sex, and danger. The intensity is palpable. I was moved by this love story and will think about it for some time."
—**TheRomanceReadersConnection.com**

"Sexy, dark, and emotion-filled...Took me on a rip-roaring ride through every emotion I have...Go out and buy a copy today." —**JoyfullyReviewed.com**

# ETERNAL
# RIDER

## ALSO BY LARISSA IONE

# ETERNAL RIDER

## LARISSA IONE

**GRAND CENTRAL**
**PUBLISHING**

NEW YORK   BOSTON

Copyright © 2011 by Larissa Ione Estell.
Excerpt from *Immortal Rider* copyright © 2011 by Larissa Ione Estell.
All rights reserved. Except as permitted under the U.S. Copyright Act of 1976, no part of this publication may be reproduced, distributed, or transmitted in any form or by any means, or stored in a database or retrieval system, without the prior written permission of the publisher.

Grand Central Publishing
Hachette Book Group
237 Park Avenue
New York, NY 10017
Visit our website at www.HachetteBookGroup.com.

Grand Central Publishing is a division of Hachette Book Group, Inc. The Grand Central Publishing name and logo is a trademark of Hachette Book Group, Inc.

The publisher is not responsible for websites (or their content) that are not owned by the publisher.

Printed in the United States of America

First Printing: April 2011

10 9 8 7 6 5 4 3 2 1

Sometimes I have to pinch myself to believe that my writing dream has not only come true, but has far surpassed even my loftiest visions. With this first book in a new series, I've realized just how far I've come. So this is for the authors who inspired, encouraged, and taught me. (And yes, Lynn Viehl, that dictionary was damned lucky!)

And for all my awesome readers out there, with a special shout-out to the Writeminded Readers, the Underworld General Hospital RPGers on Facebook, and all my Twitter, Facebook, and Goodreads buddies. Your support, enthusiasm, and ability to entertain keeps me going. Happy reading!

# Acknowledgments

Books don't come together by themselves, and I'm always amazed and humbled by how many people are willing to help at the drop of a hat and even without a bribe.

So huge thanks to Jennifer Rowland, April Renn, Larena Wirum, Yvette Lowe, Melissa Bradley, Ann Aguirre, and Lea Franczak for their incredible generosity.

Thanks, too, to Fatin Soufan and Lillie Applegarth for all the work you do at Writeminded. Huge hugs to you!

More squishy hugs go out to some people who have put time, effort, and their very hearts into their passions and have been good to me...Maggie Atchison, Heather Cass, Jackie Spencer, and Tricia Picky Schmitt.

And, as always, to the entire team at Grand Central Publishing. You've been behind me and my books from the beginning, and I can't thank you enough. Amy Pierpont, your guidance (and patience!) has been a blessing. Lauren Plude, you make my life so much easier, even though I probably drive you nuts!

Finally, thanks to Irene Goodman, for believing in and supporting this new project. It's great to have you by my side!

# Glossary

*The Aegis*—Society of human warriors dedicated to protecting the world from evil. See: Guardians, Regent, Sigil.

*Agimortus*—A trigger for the breaking of the Horsemen's Seals. An agimortus can be identified as a symbol engraved or branded upon the host person or object. Three kinds of agimorti have been identified, and may take the form of a person, an object, or an event.

*Daemonica*—The demon bible and basis for dozens of demon religions. Its prophesies regarding the Apocalypse, should they come to pass, will ensure that the Four Horsemen fight on the side of evil.

*Fallen angel*—Believed to be evil by most humans, fallen angels can be grouped into two categories: True Fallen and Unfallen. Unfallen angels have been cast from Heaven and are earthbound, living a life in which they are neither truly good nor truly evil. In this state, they can, rarely, earn their way back into Heaven. Or they can choose to enter Sheoul, the demon realm, in order to complete their fall and become True Fallens, taking their places as demons at Satan's side.

*Guardians*—Warriors for The Aegis, trained in combat techniques, weapons, and magic. Upon induction into The Aegis, all Guardians are presented with an enchanted piece of jewelry bearing the Aegis shield, which, among other things, allows for night vision and the ability to see through demon invisibility enchantments.

*Harrowgate*—Vertical portals, invisible to humans, which demons use to travel between locations on Earth and Sheoul. A very few beings can summon their own, personal Harrowgates.

*Khote*—An invisibility spell that allows the caster to move among humans without being seen or, usually, heard.

*Marked Sentinel*—A human charmed by angels and tasked with protecting a vital artifact. Sentinels are immortal and immune to harm. Only angels (fallen included) can injure or kill a Sentinel. Their existence is a closely guarded secret.

*Quantamun*—A state of superaccelerated existence on a plane that allows some supernatural beings to travel among humans. Humans, unaware of what moves within their world, appear frozen in time to those inside the *quantamun*. This differs from the *khote* in that the *khote* operates real time and is a spell rather than a plane of existence.

*Regent*—Head(s) of local Aegis cells.

*Sheoul*—Demon realm. Located deep in the bowels of the earth, accessible only by Harrowgates and hellmouths.

*Sheoul-gra*—A holding tank for demon souls. The place where demon souls go until they can be reborn or kept in torturous limbo.

*Sheoulic*—Universal demon language spoken by all, though many species speak their own language.

*Sigil*—Board of twelve humans known as Elders, who serve as the supreme leaders of The Aegis. Based in Berlin, they oversee all Aegis cells worldwide.

*Ter'taceo*—Demons who can pass as human, either because their species is naturally human in appearance or because they can shapeshift into human form.

*Watchers*—Individuals assigned to keep an eye on the Four Horsemen. As part of the agreement forged during the original negotiations between angels and demons that led to Ares, Reseph, Limos, and Thanatos being cursed to spearhead the Apocalypse, one Watcher is an angel, the other is a fallen angel. Neither Watcher may directly assist any Horseman's efforts to either start or stop Armageddon, but they can lend a hand behind the scenes. Doing so, however, may have them walking a fine line, that, to cross, could prove worse than fatal.

# Prologue

Her name was Lilith, and she was an evil succubus. His name was Yenrieth, and he was a good angel.

After hundreds of years of seducing humans, Lilith got bored. So she set her sights on Yenrieth, the ultimate challenge. He resisted. She pursued. He resisted some more. This went on for decades, until the inevitable happened. She was, after all, beautiful, and he liked his wine a little too much.

No one knows what happened to Yenrieth after their night of passion, but nine months later, Lilith gave birth to four children, three boys and a girl. She named them Reseph, Ares, Limos, and Thanatos. Lilith kept the girl, Limos, with her in Sheoul, and she planted the males in the human world, exchanging them for the infants of wealthy, powerful families.

The boys grew into men, never suspecting the truth about their origins. At least, not until demons rose up, *spreading terror and seeking to use Lilith's sons against the humans. Limos escaped from Sheoul, found her brothers, and revealed the truth about their parentage.*

*By this time, the brothers had seen their lands and families destroyed by demons and, blinded by hatred and the need for revenge, Lilith's children encouraged (manipulatively and forcibly, sometimes) humans to help them fight violent, never-ending battles against the underworld abominations.*

*This didn't go over well in the heavenly realm.*

*Zachariel, an angel of the Apocalypse, led a legion of angels to Earth, where they met in battle with demon hordes. When the earth and waters ran red with blood, and humans could no longer survive on the poisoned land, Zachariel struck a deal with the devil.*

*Lilith's children were to be punished for slinging mankind to the brink of doom in their selfish bid for revenge. Because they had nearly brought about the end of days, they were charged as the keepers of Armageddon. Defenders or instigators; the choice would fall on their shoulders.*

*Each of them was given a Seal, and with each Seal came two prophecies. Should they protect their Seals from breaking until the prophecy laid out by the Bible came to pass, they would save their souls—and mankind.*

*But should they allow the Seals to be broken prematurely, as written in the Daemonica, the demon bible, they would turn evil, and would forever be known by the names Pestilence, War, Famine, and Death.*

*And thus were born the Four Horsemen of the Apocalypse.*

*Six Months Ago...*

"Mmm...I love the story about how you came into existence. Doesn't it give you shivers when you hear it?"

Ares, seated at the bar in an underworld pub, tried to ignore the female behind him, but the rub of her breasts against his back and the slide of her dainty hands from his waist to his inner thighs weren't easy to tune out. Her heat burned right through his hard leather armor.

"Yeah. Shivers." Some idiot read the legend aloud from the plaque that hung on the wall every time he was in here...which was often. The tavern, kept in business mainly by Ares and his siblings, was his second home, was even known as the Four Horsemen, and for the most part, male demons melted into the background or scurried out the back door when Ares arrived. Wise. Ares despised demons, and that, combined with his love of a good fight, led to...*bad things*...for hell's minions.

But the opposite sex was a little braver—or maybe hornier. Female demons, shifters, weres, and vamps hung out twenty-four-seven in hopes of getting their hands, paws, or hooves on Ares and his brothers. Hell, Ares couldn't swing his dick without hitting one. Usually he was a little more receptive to drinking, gambling, and general mischief, but something wasn't sitting right today. He was on edge. Twitchy.

He was never like that.

He was even in danger of losing the chess game he was playing with the pudgy pink Oni bartender, and Ares hadn't lost any game of strategy in...well, ever.

"Oh, War." The female Sora demon, Cetya, ran her tongue along the top of his ear. "You've got to know it makes us hot."

"My name," he gritted out, "is Ares. You don't want to be around on the day I become War." He moved his rook, tossed back half his ale, and was about to signal for another, when the female's hand dropped between his legs.

"I still like War better." Her voice was a seductive trill, her fingers nimble as they sought the opening at his groin. "And Pestilence... such a sexy name."

Only a demon would think "Pestilence" was a turn-on. Ares peeled her red hand away. She was one of Reseph's regular bedmates, one of hundreds of Horsemen groupies who called themselves Megiddo Mount-me's. They even subclassed themselves according to who their favorite Horseman was; Ares's groupies liked to be called Mongers. *War Mongers.*

The bartender made a foolish move with his knight, and Ares hid a smile in his mug.

The female, who looked like a cartoon devil, traced a long, black nail over the stallion tattoo on Ares's forearm. "I love this."

The horse was as much a part of him as his organs, whether Battle was on his skin or under his seat, and Ares stiffened at the sensation of both his arm and scalp being stroked. Any contact with the glyph sent a shock of sensation to the corresponding parts of Ares's body, which could be a real pain in the ass. Or it could be inappropriately pleasant...

Ares spun his mug down the length of the bar top and slid his queen into striking position. Triumph sang through him, filling that space in his soul that was always hungry for victory. "Checkmate."

The bartender cursed, the Sora laughed, and Ares

came to his feet. At nearly seven feet tall, he dwarfed the demon, but that didn't faze her, and she plastered the entire length of her tank-topped, miniskirted body to his. Her tail swished on the hay-strewn floor, her black horns swiveled like pointy satellite dishes, and if her gaze grew any hotter his breeches were going to get real uncomfortable.

He despised his body's reaction to demons, had never truly warmed up to females who didn't at least appear to be human.

Some grudges lasted a lifetime.

"I'm outta here." Despite the chess coup, his unease was becoming an itch under his skin, the way it did when a global war escalated. He needed to get back to the hunt for an ex-bedmate of his, a demon named Sin who had started a werewolf—or, *warg*, as they liked to be called— plague. Ares and his siblings had only recently determined that she was the key to a prophecy that, if it came to pass, would break Reseph's Seal and turn him into the very thing Cetya wanted: Pestilence.

Sin had to die before a werewolf civil war broke out.

Unable to remain still any longer, he flung a gold Sheoulin mark at the three-eyed bartender. "A round for the house."

With a firm grip, he dislodged the Velcro-demon and strode out of the tavern and into perpetual twilight. Muggy, hot air that reeked of sulfur filled his lungs, and his boots sank into the spongy terrain that defined the Six-River region of Sheoul, the demon realm in the Earth's core.

Battle writhed on his skin, impatient to run.

"Out," Ares commanded, and a heartbeat later, the tattoo on his arm turned to mist, expanding and solidifying into a giant blood bay stallion. Battle nudged him with his nose in greeting—or, more likely, for sugar cubes.

"You forgot this."

Always ready to live up to his name, Battle bared his teeth at the Sora, who stood in the tavern doorway, her tail wrapped around the hilt of a dagger, which she dangled playfully. The blatant invitation in her sultry smile told him she'd plucked the weapon from Ares herself, but he knew that. He didn't leave weapons behind.

Of course, he never got weapons lifted, either. The female was good. Real good. And even though he wasn't normally into demons, he had to admire her talent. No wonder Reseph liked this one so much. Maybe Ares would make an exception to his *no-demons-that-look-like-demons* rule...

Grinning, he started toward her...and stopped dead.

The hairs on the back of his neck prickled in warning. With a furious scream, Battle reared up, and from out of the forest of shadowed trees a buffalo-sized hellhound leaped through the air. Ares zeroed in on the beast's left side, seeking—and not finding—the jagged scar that would have identified the vile creature as the one Ares had been hunting for thousands of years. Disappointment rocked him even as he shoved the Sora out of the way, a stupid move that nearly landed him between snapping jaws.

Ares and his sibs were immortal, but hellhound bites were poison to the Horsemen, causing paralysis, and then the suffering *really* began.

He dove to the ground as Battle struck out with a powerful hoof, hooking the other animal in the ribs and sending it tumbling into the tavern door. The hound recovered so quickly that Battle's blow might as well have been a fleabite, and it targeted the Sora, who scrambled backward on her hands and knees. Her terror was palpable, like little whips on Ares's skin, and he had a feeling this was her first experience with a hellhound.

Hell of a way to pop *that* cherry.

"Hey!" *Distract.* Rolling to his feet, Ares drew his sword. *Provoke.* "I'm over here, you piece-of-shit mongrel." *Terminate.*

Anticipation gleamed in the hellhound's crimson eyes as it swung around, melting into an inky blur of evil. Ares met it head-on, with three hundred pounds of armored weight behind his blow. The satisfying crunch of steel meeting bone rent the air. An impact tremor shot up Ares's arms, and a massive jet of blood spewed from the hound's chest.

A bloodcurdling snarl ripped from the hound's throat as it launched a surprisingly effective counterattack, slamming one huge paw into Ares's chest. Claws raked his breastplate, and he flew backward, plowing into a stone summoning column. Pain lanced his upper body, and then the hellhound was on him, its jaws snapping a millimeter from Ares's jugular.

Foul breath burned Ares's eyes, and frothy, stinging saliva dripped on his skin. The beast's claws tore at his armor, and it took every ounce of Ares's strength to keep the hound from ripping out his throat. Even with Battle striking at the canine's body, the creature did its damnedest to get a mouthful of flesh.

As hard as he could, Ares jammed his sword into the animal's belly and yanked the blade upward. As the beast screamed in pain, Ares rolled, twisted, and brought the sword around in an awkward arc.

Awkward or not, the stroke cleaved the hound's head

from its shoulders. The thing fell to the ground, twitching, steam hissing from its gaping neck. The spongy ground drank the blood before it could pool, and hundreds of blackened teeth sprouted from the dirt, clamped onto the hound's body, and began to chew.

Battle whinnied with amusement. The horse's sense of humor had always been perched on the gallows with the crows.

Before the earth could claim the beast, Ares wiped his blade clean on its fur, giving repeated thanks to whoever was listening that the hound hadn't bitten him. The horror of a bite was never-ending—the paralyzation didn't stop the pain . . . or the ability to scream. Ares knew that firsthand.

He frowned as a thought spun up. The vile canines were predators, killers, but they generally hunted in packs, so why was this one solo?

What was going on?

Ares glanced over at the tavern door. The Sora had disappeared, was probably pounding shots of demonfire in the bar, and hey, wasn't it great that no one had bothered to come out and help. Then again, no demon in his right mind willingly tangled with a hellhound no matter how much love he had for the slaughter—and most demons *loved* to slaughter.

Light flashed, and twenty yards away in a copse of black, twisted trees, a summoned Harrowgate shimmered into existence. Normal Harrowgates were permanent portals through which underworld creatures could travel, but the Horsemen had the ability to summon them at will, which made for easy surprise attacks and quick escapes.

Ares sheathed his sword as Thanatos emerged, throwing menacing shadows where there should be none. Both he and his pale dun mount, Styx, dripped with gore, and the stallion's nostrils bubbled with blood.

It wasn't an unusual sight, but the timing was too coincidental, and Ares cursed as he swung up onto Battle. "What happened?"

Thanatos's expression darkened as he took in the dead animal. "Same thing that happened to you, apparently."

"Have you heard from Reseph or Limos?"

Thanatos's yellow eyes flashed. "I was hoping they were here."

Ares threw out his hand, casting a Harrowgate. "I'll go to Reseph. You check on Limos." He didn't wait for his brother's reply. He spurred Battle through the gate, and the warhorse leaped, his big hooves coming down on a rocky shelf that had been scoured smooth by centuries of harsh wind and ice storms.

This was Reseph's Himalayan hideaway, a giant maze of caverns carved deep into the mountains and invisible to human eyes. Ares dismounted in one smooth motion, his boots striking the stone with twin cracks that echoed endlessly in the thin air.

"To me."

Instantly, the warhorse dissolved into a cloud of smoke, which twisted and narrowed into a tendril that wrapped around Ares's hand and set into his forearm in the brown-gray shape of a horse tattoo.

Ares barged through the cave entrance, and he hadn't gone a dozen steps when an electric current of ten-thousand-volt alarm shot up his spine.

*Time to dance.*

He was already in a dead run when he drew his sword, the metallic sound of the blade clearing its scabbard like a lover's whisper during foreplay. It didn't matter that he'd just engaged an enemy; he loved a good battle, craved the release of tension that hit him with the force of a full-body orgasm, and he'd long ago decided he'd rather fight than fuck.

Though he had to admit that after a good brawl, winding down with a lush, sultry female couldn't be beat. Maybe he'd head back to the tavern after this and find a *War Monger* after all.

Adrenaline pumping hotly through his veins, Ares took a sharp corner so fast he had to skid into a change of direction, and then he burst through the doorway to Reseph's main living area.

His brother, hand wrapped around a bloodied ax, stood in the middle of the room, which was painted in a fresh, dripping coat of blood. Reseph was panting, his shoulders slumped, head bent, white-blond hair concealing his face. He was motionless, his muscles locked up hard. Behind him, a hellhound lay dead, and in the corner, a very much alive hound let out a gravelly snarl, its gaping maw lined with razor-sharp teeth.

"Reseph."

Ares's brother didn't move a muscle.

*Fuck.* He'd been bitten.

The beast swung its shaggy head toward Ares. Red eyes glowed with bloodlust as it gathered its hind legs under it. Ares calculated the distance to the target in a millisecond, and in one quick motion launched a dagger that impaled the hellhound in the eye. Ares pressed his advantage, heaving his sword in a horizontal side swing that caught the creature in the mouth, slicing its jaw clean off. The hound howled in agony and fury, but Reseph had already injured it and, weakened, it stumbled and fell, allowing Ares an opportunity to run his blade straight through its black heart.

"Reseph!" Leaving the sword impaled in the animal, Ares ran to his brother, whose blue eyes were wild, glazed with pain. "How did they get in?"

"Someone," Reseph groaned, "had to have...sent them."

That much was becoming clear. But very few beings could handle or control a hellhound. So if someone had sent the beasts, he was serious about putting Ares and his brothers—and maybe Limos too—out of commission.

"You should feel special," Ares said, with a lightness he didn't feel. "You got two hellhounds, and I only got one. Who'd you piss off?" Gently, Ares wrapped his arms around Reseph's chest and lowered him to the ground.

Reseph sucked in a gurgling breath. "Last night... my...Seal."

Ares went cold to the core, and with trembling hands, he tore away Reseph's T-shirt to expose the chain around his neck. The Seal hanging from it was whole, but when he palmed the gold coin, a vibration, dense with malevolence, shot up his arm.

"The warg plague..." Reseph spoke between gritted teeth and rattling breaths. "Worse. This is...not...good."

*Not good* was an understatement. As Ares held the medallion, a hairline fracture split it down the middle. All around them, the cave began to shake. Reseph screamed as his Seal cracked into two pieces.

The countdown to Armageddon had begun.

⌒

"The first Horseman of the Apocalypse has been loosed."

Sergeant First Class Arik Wagner, one of two

representatives for the U.S. Army's paranormal unit, the R-XR, missed a step as he paced the length of the conference room inside The Aegis's Berlin headquarters. The two agencies had worked independently for decades, but had recently joined forces to combat the ever-increasing underworld threat. Arik never took intel from The Aegis lightly, but he still had to run Kynan's words through his brain a couple of times before he could make sense of the situation, let alone believe it.

As he inhaled a shaky breath, he concentrated on pacing without falling on his face as he slid glances at Kynan and the other eleven Elders who were sitting around the conference table. It was obvious that some were already in on the news, but the others...not so much, if the shock and fear in their expressions was any indication. The shock was expected; it was their fear that put Arik on edge. The Aegis was an ancient demon-fighting organization that had weathered end-of-the-world scenarios time and time again, so to see its leaders frightened...disturbing as hell.

"Damn." Regan, a stunning, bronze-skinned woman who was way too young to be in any way called an "Elder," flipped her long ponytail over her shoulder and played with the dark ends, a habit Arik knew she ran to when she was nervous.

Arik's normally unflappable partner, Decker, had lost all the color in his face and was now relying on the doorframe to keep his big body upright. "When? How?"

"I just found out this morning." Kynan's denim-blue eyes flashed as he shoved the Daemonica, the demon bible, to the center of the table and opened it to expose a page near the back. "It's all about this passage. *She of mixed blood who should not exist, carries with her the power to spread plague and pestilence. When battle breaks, conquest is seal'd.*" Tension put lines in his face as he looked around the table. "*She of mixed blood* is my sister-in-law, Sin. She started the plague that spread through the werewolf population and led to the conflict that broke out within the species a couple of days ago. As the prophecy indicates, when *battle breaks, conquest is sealed.* The warg battle is what broke the Horseman's Seal."

Arik kept up the carpet-wearing routine, his combat boots thudding like muffled gunshots. "So you're saying that this is a demon prophecy?"

There was a long pause before Kynan delivered an ominous "Yes," in his gravelly voice. He'd had his throat nearly ripped out by a demon back in his Army days, and he wore the scars and trashed voice like a badge of honor.

"How is the demon prophecy different from human prophecy?" Decker had regained some color, which was good, because with his gray-blue eyes and blond hair, he'd resembled a reanimated corpse.

Kynan, in worn jeans and gray fitted tee, kicked back in his chair and folded his hands over his abs. "Apparently, if the Daemonica's prophecy goes down, the Horsemen will embrace their demon halves and turn pure evil. If the prophecy from the Bible comes to pass, the Horsemen will take after their angel father and fight on the side of good."

That stopped Arik in his tracks. "What? The Horsemen *are* evil. Have you read the Book of Revelation? They're supposed to usher in the end of days, with disease, war, famine, and death."

"That's the most common interpretation of the Bible's passages." One of the senior Elders, Valeriu, who also happened to be distantly related to Arik by marriage, drummed his fingers on the oak tabletop. "But some scholars, including myself, think that the Horsemen's Seals will be broken by Jesus himself, and the Horsemen will lead the way to the end of days, but that's not necessarily a bad thing."

"Of course not," Arik drawled. "Every Apocalypse is a party. Bring your own beer, pretzels, and semiautomatic weapons." Regan shot him an annoyed glance. Apparently sarcasm wasn't appreciated in Aegis headquarters. It wasn't appreciated in the R-XR either, but mainly because Arik was still in the dog house for going AWOL a few days earlier instead of revealing his werewolf sister's location. "So what does the first broken Seal mean to us? Can we repair it? Prevent the others from breaking?"

"I don't know." Kynan let out a frustrated breath. "We're going to have to dig deep for theories, prophecies, any scrap of information we can scrounge up."

Shit, Arik was going to need a stiff drink after this. "Do we know what will cause the next Seal to break?"

"All we have is what the next line in the prophecy says." Valeriu flipped through the stack of paper in front of him and pulled out a single page. "*An angel's mistake shall bring about War, and her death shall break his sword. But be wary, a hound's heart may yet defeat.*"

Arik ran his hand over his military-issue haircut, and wasn't it an odd time to note that he needed a trim. "What the hell is that supposed to mean?"

"It's about the second Horseman, War." Valeriu shoved his glasses up on his nose. "We don't understand all of it, but we believe War's *agimortus* is an Unfallen."

An Unfallen... an earthbound fallen angel who hadn't

yet entered Sheoul and become irreversibly evil. Interesting. "Wait." Arik shook his head. *"Agimortus?"*

"Yes," Valeriu said. "A trigger for breaking a Seal. It can be a person, an object, or an event."

"Pestilence's Seal was broken by an event," Kynan explained. "Sin was an *agimortus* whose actions put into motion an event that triggered the Seal to break. Killing her before the plague she started led to war would have *prevented* the broken Seal. But we believe War's *agimortus* is a person. Killing this being will *break* his Seal."

Arik paused in his pacing. "If you knew about the first prophecy, that Sin was an *agimortus*, why didn't you kill her?"

Kynan inhaled a shaky breath. Sin was sister to his best friends—demon best friends. "In hindsight, it's obvious. But at the time, we didn't know. We were too close to it."

*"You* were too close to it." Regan stood, her tall, curvy body drawing Arik's appreciative gaze. Not that he was interested—he liked his women a little softer and less I'll-kill-you-where-you-stand—but she did remind him that he hadn't seen any mattress action in a long time. Hard to hook up when you had to lie about everything from your name, to your job, to your entire life history.

Red splotches colored Kynan's cheeks. "Yeah. I was. I'd read the prophecy a million times, so I should have seen that she was the *agimortus* as soon as the plague started. The thing we need to remember is that prophecies *are* obscure for a reason."

Arik considered everything he'd been told. "The prophecy mentions hounds. Would *hell*hounds have anything to do with any of this?"

Ky's dark eyebrows drew together. "Why?"

"The R-XR has received an unusual number of reports of hellhound sightings."

The Guardians exchanged looks, and Val finally said, "We've noted an increase in sightings as well. Our Guardians have encountered more in the last week than in the entire year before." Before Arik could ask, Val shook his head. "We don't know why."

"Okay, so we have to find a way to prevent War's Seal from breaking. What about the other Horsemen? Can the Seals be broken out of order?"

"According to the Daemonica, Pestilence's Seal had to break first, but the others can break in any order. And it gets worse," Val said miserably, and oh, joy, all of this somehow got *worse*. Arik's drink was going to be a double. With a chaser. "If any two Seals break, the others will fall as well, without any trigger. Once all four Seals are broken, we're chin deep in Armageddon."

Arik felt his thoughts being scattered like confetti in a windstorm. He had so many questions, and he had a feeling there weren't nearly enough answers. "Are we looking at imminent breakage of the other Seals? Or is this something that could go on for centuries?"

"Technically, it could go on." Regan's gaze was somber, her husky voice grim. "But Pestilence being loosed is bad enough. All over the world, disease is springing up, water sources are contaminated with bacteria, and demonic activity is off the charts. Do we really want that going on for centuries?"

Val cleared his throat. "It's written that the destruction of one Seal weakens the others. In effect, it causes events to occur that will hasten the breakage of the other Seals. An object needed to break a Seal, for example, might be found after thousands of years of hiding. And, no doubt, Pestilence, as pure evil, is actively trying to break his siblings' Seals. The Horsemen are the most powerful underworld beings in existence, next to Satan himself. They will virtually rule the Earth if the Final Battle goes in favor of evil."

"That's just great," Arik muttered. "So what's the plan? Sounds like we need to either contain or kill these Horsemen so that if their Seals break, they can't wreak havoc, or we need to work with them to keep any more Seals from breaking."

"We don't know that they *can* be contained or killed." Regan shoved her coffee mug under the coffee dispenser. "We don't know nearly enough about anything."

"I'll see what my in-laws know and can find out," Kynan said. "They have a unique perspective on demonic lore."

"Excellent idea." Regan's voice was more full of saccharine than her coffee. "Get demons to help."

"We need all the help we can get." Kynan laced his hands behind his head and gazed at the medieval painting behind Arik, the one depicting a battle between angels and demons. "And we need it from the Horsemen."

"Is that wise?" Decker asked. "Do we really want to get cozy with these guys? If they're evil, we don't want to be on their radar."

Kynan shook his head. "According to the Aegis histories, they used to work closely with us."

"Why'd they stop?"

"Modern stupidity. Around the time of the Middle Ages, The Aegis went a little fanatical with religion. Hell, The Aegis is behind the witch persecutions. There was a huge shift in thinking, which led to the belief that everything supernatural is evil, including the Horsemen." Kynan gave everyone a stern look. "It's only been in the last couple of years that we've started to return to the original path."

Arik bit back a grin at Kynan's tacked-on, in-your-face last sentence. Though he'd met with a lot of resistance from the Elders, Kynan was largely responsible for The Aegis's new line on underworld creatures. Not only was he married to a half-demon, but he also carried angel blood in his veins. Then there was the fact that he'd been charmed by angels and was fated to play a role in the Final Battle, and Ky wasn't afraid to use his status to get the Elders to see things his way.

"So basically," Arik said gruffly, "we need to ask for help from guys who might hold a grudge against The Aegis and who have the power to usher in the end of the world."

Kynan's smile was pure twisted amusement. "Welcome to everyday life in The Aegis."

# One

⌒

**"War is hell."**
　　　　**—William Tecumseh Sherman**

**"Sherman was totally my bitch."**
　　　　**—War**

*Present day...*

Ares, also known as War, second of the Four Horsemen of the Apocalypse to much of the human and demon world, sat astride his stallion on the outskirts of a nameless village in Africa, his body and mind vibrating with energy. A battle raged here; two local warlords, their brains ravaged by an insect-borne disease, were clashing over what little water had puddled in the bottom of the village's well. Ares had wandered the area for days, drawn to the hostilities like a drug addict to heroin, unable to pry himself away until the blood stopped flowing. It was a catch-22, though, because his very presence ramped up the violence, feeding into the bloodlust of every human in a five-mile radius.

Damned Reseph.

No, not Reseph. Not anymore. The most easygoing and playful of Ares's siblings, the brother who had held them all together over the centuries, had been gone for six months. Now he was Pestilence, and with the name and transformation came unholy powers that threatened mankind. Pestilence was roaming the globe, causing disease, insect and rodent infestations, and mass crop failures with nothing more than a bite or a touch of his finger and a thought. As the disasters spread, more wars like this one broke out, and Ares was drawn to the battles and away from his most pressing task—locating Batarel, the fallen angel who held Ares's fate in his hands.

As the current holder of Ares's *agimortus*, if Batarel died, Ares's Seal would break, unleashing War upon the Earth.

Chased relentlessly by Reseph, as well as by any demon who wanted to usher in the Apocalypse, Batarel had fallen off the grid, which, unfortunately, left Ares unable to protect her.

But then, even if Ares found her, his ability to defend her was limited, thanks to a fun addendum to his curse, which caused him to weaken in close proximity to his *agimortus*-bearer.

The battle before him finally began to wane, and the electric high that had held Ares hostage eased, replaced by the usual numbness. Women and children had been slaughtered, the few goats that had survived the blight had been taken for food, and fuck, this was just one of scores of similar scenes that were playing out on this continent alone.

His leather armor creaked as he fisted his pendant,

closed his eyes, and concentrated. He should feel a distant buzz through the Seal, some clue as to Batarel's location.

Nothing. Somehow, Batarel had masked her vibe.

A hot breeze blew the foul stench of blood and bowels across the parched earth, ruffling Battle's black mane against his reddish-brown neck. Ares gave the beast a firm pat. "We're through here, boy."

Battle pawed the ground. The humans didn't see any of it, not as long as Ares remained inside the *khote*, a spell that allowed him to travel invisibly around the human world, but the tradeoff was that he moved like a ghost, unable to touch them. Reseph had gotten off on popping out of the *khote* to flash humans and freak them out. Unlike Ares, Reseph's presence hadn't affected humans. Except the females. Reseph had definitely had a way with *them*.

Ares didn't glance again at the gruesome remnants of the conflict. Instead, he summoned a Harrowgate, and Battle leaped through it, bringing them to the entrance of his brother Thanatos's Greenland keep. The ancient castle, shielded by elemental magic that rendered it unnoticeable to human eyes, rose up from the craggy, barren landscape like a breaching whale.

Ares dismounted, coming down on the hard ice. "To me."

The warhorse settled into Ares's skin, and he strode into the richly decorated manor, waving away the bowing, scraping vampires who had served Thanatos for centuries. He found his brother in the gym, beating the hell out of a punching bag. As usual when he was home, Thanatos wore black workout pants, no shirt, and a black bandanna over his shoulder-length, tawny hair. With every punch, his tattoos danced on his deeply tanned skin, from the cracked, bleeding bones inked on his hands, to the various weapons that decorated his arms, to the depictions of death and destruction on his back and chest.

"Thanatos. I need your help. Where's Limos?" He frowned at the dark stain on the floor behind his brother. "And what is that?"

"A succubus." Than wiped sweat off his forehead with the back of his hand. "Reseph sent another one to tempt me."

"He's not Reseph anymore." Ares's voice rang out in the cold air like an avalanche breaking loose. "Call him what he is." Easier said than done, since Ares hadn't yet gotten used to it either.

Thanatos's pale yellow eyes drilled into Ares's nearly black ones. "Never. We can get him back."

"Seals can't be restored."

"We'll find a way." Than's tone was hard, final. He'd always been as uncompromising as the death he represented.

"We have to kill him."

All around Thanatos, shadows swirled, moving faster the more agitated he became. He'd always been the quickest of the four of them to lash out, but then, thousands of years of celibacy would do that to a guy. It was also why he lived in the middle of nowhere; a flash of temper could kill every living thing in the human realm for miles around.

"Do you not remember how Reseph was always traveling the world to find the sweetest apples for our horses? How he never came over without bringing a gift? How, when any of our servants were injured or fell ill, he searched for medicine and nursed them back to health?"

Of course Ares remembered. Reseph might have been

an irresponsible playboy with the females, but with those he considered family, he'd been attentive and thoughtful. He'd even worried about their two Watchers when they didn't pop in every few months. Reaver, an angel who represented Team Heaven, and Harvester, a fallen angel who played for Team Sheoul, hardly needed Reseph's concern, but he'd always been relieved to see them.

It had been that way ever since their original Sheoulin Watcher had done more than simply "watch" the Horsemen. Eviscerator had suffered for months before dying in a manner befitting his name for revealing the material used in the making of Limos's *agimortus* without permission.

"None of that has any bearing on our current situation," Ares said.

"We won't kill him."

There was no point in arguing. Not only did they not have the necessary tools to put an end to their brother, but Than would never budge on the issue, and Ares's jaw still throbbed from the last time they'd discussed it. It wasn't as though Ares *wanted* to kill Pestilence, but he also wasn't going to let him lead the charge to Armageddon.

"So you would rather see the Daemonica's prophecy be the one that comes to pass?"

The human prophecies, though they varied, still favored humans in the Final Battle and left room for the Horsemen to fight on the side of good. Should the demon prophecy reign, evil would hold all the cards.

And evil dealt from the bottom of the deck.

Than gave the punching bag a final, knockout blow. "I'm not a fool, brother. I've been hunting Reseph's minions, and I've managed to...convince...one of them to talk."

"Convince, torture, whatever." Ares crossed his arms over his chest, his armor's hard leather plates cracking against each other. "So what have you learned?"

"That I need to find a minion who's privy to more information," Than grumbled. "But I did find out that Reseph has sent teams of demons to search for Deliverance."

"Then we need to beat him to it," Ares said.

Thanatos grabbed a towel off the weight bench and wiped his face. "We've been looking for the dagger since the 1300s with no success."

"Then we look harder."

"I told you—"

Ares cut off his brother. "Having Deliverance doesn't mean we have to use it. But it's better to have it and not need it than the other way around. If Res—Pestilence locates it first, he'll make sure we never get our hands on it."

Thanatos strode toward Ares, and Ares braced for battle. It didn't matter that they were brothers; Ares lived to fight, and even now his adrenaline was singing in his blood, obliterating that damned numbness.

"When we get the dagger," Than growled, "*I* hold on to it."

Frustration put an edge in Ares's voice, because dammit, *he* wanted possession of Deliverance. It was the one thing that could kill Pestilence, was *the* weapon for the war of wars, and like any good commander, he wanted complete control over his arsenal. "We'll discuss it when we have it."

"What," came a deep, amused voice from the doorway, "are you two arguing over now?"

Ares whirled to Reseph, who stood in the doorway, his tarnished armor oozing a black substance from the joints. He held a severed female head in his gauntleted hand.

Ares's stomach plummeted to his feet. "Batarel." He fumbled for the coin around his neck. Relief that it wasn't broken collided with fury and confusion and the need to kick his brother's ass.

It was a real fun stew of what-the-fuck.

"Obviously," Reseph said, "since you aren't sporting shiny new fangs that make all the ladies hot, your Seal hasn't broken. The idiot fallen angel transferred the *agimortus* to someone else."

Reseph dropped the idiot fallen angel's head to the floor. Batarel's body should have disintegrated upon her death, which meant that she'd been killed either in a demon-built or an Aegis-enchanted structure, or on land owned by supernatural beings.

On Ares's arm, Battle stirred in agitation, his emotions tied to Ares's. "Where did you find her?" Ares ground out.

"Cowardly bitch was holed up in a Harrowgate," Reseph said, which explained why Ares hadn't been able to sense her. "I had to send out spiny hellrats to find her."

Of course. Reseph could communicate with and control vermin and insects, which he used to spread plague and pestilence throughout the human population. And, apparently, he used them as spies.

Thanatos moved toward their brother, his bare feet silent on the stone floor. "Who did Batarel transfer the *agimortus* to, Reseph?"

"No idea." Reseph grinned, a real cat-that-ate-the-canary, revealing his "shiny new fangs." "But I'll know soon. Maybe after I let rip a few new plagues. The cool kind, with boils and incontinence." He opened a Harrowgate, but paused before stepping inside. "You all should stop fighting me. I have the backing of the Dark Lord himself. The longer you stall the inevitable, the more those you care about will suffer."

The Harrowgate snapped shut and, cursing, Ares spun, drove his fist into the punching bag, and damn, what he wouldn't give for that to be Pestilence's face right now. Reseph had never been cruel or callous, had lived in fear of succumbing to his evil side. And if *he* was that bad now that his Seal had been broken . . . Ares was screwed.

"Give me your hand."

Ares swung around to Thanatos, who handed him Batarel's eyes. Just the eyes. And an ear.

Ares had stopped being grossed out by his gift a long time ago. Closing his palm around them, he let the vision come.

"What do you see?" Than asked.

"Reseph's sword." The huge blade had filled Batarel's vision, the last thing she'd seen. Ares waited as the visions worked in reverse, until . . . *there*. Batarel's ear vibrated, and audio joined the visuals. "A blond male. Name's Sestiel. He's screaming. He doesn't want the *agimortus*."

"Duh. Who'd want a bull's-eye on their ass?"

The *agimortus* wasn't a bull's-eye, exactly, but yeah, it did make whoever hosted it a target for Pestilence's blade. Strange, though, that the host was male. Was the prophecy wrong? Had it changed?

One of Than's vampire servants hustled to clean up Batarel's remains, and he bowed before Ares. "May I take those body parts from you, sir?"

So polite. Of course, most beings were pretty kiss-ass to the Four Horsemen of the Apocalypse.

Probably wise. No, not probably. Definitely.

*Suck up now, world, because once the Seals broke, it would be time to bend over.*

Nothing good ever came of a knock at three o'clock in the morning, and as Cara Thornhart shuffled down the hallway to her front door, she had a very, very bad feeling.

The pounding became more urgent, every blow on the wood kicking her heart into a stuttered rhythm.

*Breathe, Cara. Breathe.*

"Thornhart! Open the fuck up!" The slurred voice was familiar, and when she put her eye to the peephole in the door, she instantly recognized the man standing on her porch as the son of one of her former clients.

Ross Spillane was also one of the many twenty-something jobless delinquents with six kids by six different women. Apparently, the one drugstore in town didn't sell condoms.

Cara shoved up the sleeves of her flannel pajamas and stared at the two deadbolts, the chain, and the regular door lock. A flicker of dread skittered up her spine. She lived in the country, the middle of nowhere, and while she doubted Ross was an ax murderer, she'd always had a reliable sixth sense, and right now, she was sensing trouble.

*Or maybe you're just being paranoid.* Her psychologist had said it was normal to have moments of panic, but that had been two years ago. Shouldn't she be able to open her door without trembling like a frightened rabbit by now?

"What's wrong, Ross?" she called out, because she still couldn't bring herself to work the locks.

"Open the goddamned door! I fucking hit a dog."

A dog? Crap. "I'm not practicing anymore. Take it to the clinic."

"Can't."

No, of course he couldn't. Ross sounded drunk, and the town vet just happened to be married to the town's chief of police. The vet was also a corrupt bastard who overcharged, took shortcuts with care and materials, and he'd been known to refuse help to any animal that was rude enough to be sick or injured after office hours.

"Dammit, Thornhart. I don't have time for this."

*Help the dog. Suck it up, and help the dog.* Sweat dampened her temples and palms as she flipped all the locks and opened the door. Before it swung all the way in, Ross shoved the pitch-black canine into her arms, knocking her back a step.

"Thanks." He started down the porch stairs.

"Wait!" Awkwardly, she shifted the dog's weight, which had to be a good seventy pounds. "You shouldn't drive."

"Whatever. It's a mile."

"Ross—"

"Bite my fine ass," he muttered, as he headed down her gravel walkway toward his old Ford pickup.

"Hey!" She couldn't stop him, she knew that, but he had a passenger, a petite blonde who looked like she might still be in high school. "Is your friend able to drive?"

He opened the driver's-side door and tossed the keys at the girl. "Yup."

As he stumbled around the front of the truck, and the girl climbed out, Cara called, "Why did you bring me the dog?" *Subtext: Why didn't you let the dog die on the side of the road?*

Ross stopped, hooked his thumbs in his belt loops, and

looked down at his cowboy boots. When he spoke, Cara had to strain to hear him. "No mutt has ever stabbed me in the back."

Cara stared. Go figure. She'd always been judged harshly by people who didn't know her, and she'd just gone and done the same thing to someone else.

Then Ross whooped, slapped the young blonde on her Daisy Dukes, and spat a wad of tobacco on the ground, once again reinforcing a stereotype, but hey... at least he liked dogs.

Cara closed the door, awkwardly locking it, and carried the limp bundle of fur to a room she'd shut up tight two years ago.

"Dammit." Her curse accompanied the creak of unused hinges as she wedged open the door with her shoulder. The stale air reeked of failure, and no matter how hard she tried to tug up her big-girl panties and be brave, her hands still shook as she laid the dog on the exam table and flipped on the light.

The dog's black fur was matted with blood, and one hind leg was twisted awkwardly, the broken end of a bone piercing the skin. The dog needed a real vet, not her. Not someone who healed through *vibes* that even she sometimes doubted were real. The only physical medical experience she had was as a veterinary technician, and that had been eight years ago, when she'd been a teen working in her dad's practice.

She did a U-turn before she went too far down that dark road, snapped on gloves, and when she turned back around, she recoiled. The pup—at least, it had the rounded, cuteish features of a young puppy despite its size—was looking at her. And its eyes were... red.

*Blood, it's got to be blood*. Which didn't explain the eerie glow behind the irises.

"Um...hey, fella."

The pup's lips peeled away from extremely sharp, extremely *large*, teeth. What breed was the thing? It looked like a cross between a wolf and a pit bull, with maybe a little great white shark thrown in, and by her best guess, it was approximately four months old. Except that it was the size of a full-grown Siberian husky.

*And those teeth. Those eyes.*

There was a military base nearby, and since the day she had moved to this rural South Carolina town, she'd heard rumors of experiments, of strange creatures the government was breeding. For the first time, Cara considered the possibility, because this dog was not...natural.

The pup shifted on the table, yelping in pain at the smallest movement, and suddenly, it didn't matter where it had come from or if it was a lab creation, a genetic mutation, or an alien from outer space. She hated seeing an animal in pain, especially when there was so little she could do.

"Hey," she whispered, reaching out her hand. The pup regarded her warily, but he allowed her to stroke his cheek. And yes, it was a *he*. She didn't have to look...she just knew. She'd always been able to sense things about animals, and although the vibes coming from this creature were odd...disjointed...she was still getting them.

Slowly, so as not to startle the dog, she slid both hands down his body. Right now, the most she could do was triage, keep him alive until she could get him to Dr. Happs. The jerk would only put the dog to sleep if no one would pay for its care, which meant that Cara would have to choose between paying the vet bills and paying her mortgage.

Her fingers dipped into a puncture wound, and the pup screamed in pain, his body trembling. "I'm sorry, boy." God, it was a bullet hole. Someone must have shot the dog before he was struck by Ross's truck.

Whimpering, the pup writhed in misery, and Cara felt his pain all the way to her marrow. Literally. It was part of what made her different from everyone she knew, this talent that had been both a blessing and a curse.

She'd sworn to never use her ability again, but seeing the dog suffer was too much. She had to do it, no matter how hard her mind was screaming against it.

"Okay," she murmured, "I'm going to try something. Just hold on."

Closing her eyes, she placed both hands over his body, her palms hovering an inch from his fur. She forced herself to relax, to concentrate until her emotions and energy centered in her head and chest. She'd never been formally trained in the arts of spiritual or energy healing, but this had always worked for her.

Until it had killed.

She shook her head, clearing her thoughts. Gradually, a tingle condensed and expanded inside her, until it pulsed with its own heartbeat. She visualized the energy as a purple glow that streamed from her chest and into her hands. The pup calmed, his breaths slowing, his whimpers tapering off. She couldn't fix broken bones or ruptured organs, but she could slow the bleeding and manage pain, and this poor guy needed everything she had.

The energy built, vibrating through her entire body as though it was eager to be let loose.

Just as it had done *that night*.

The memory tore through her brain like a shotgun blast, hurling her back in time to the night when her gift had warped into something sinister and surged not into a dog, but a man. His terror-filled eyes had bulged as blood spurted from his nose and ears. His screams had been silent, but those of his buddies had not.

*Stop thinking!* Her power cut off, snuffed by her fear. The room spun and her legs wobbled, all carnival fun-house. Without the fun. A whine yanked her out of the trance, and she stumbled to the antique chest where she kept all the traditional medical supplies that had belonged to her father.

"Sorry, boy," she rasped. "We're going to have to do this the old-fashioned way." She hadn't gone to vet school, but she'd worked with her father for years, and she knew damned good and well that this dog was going to die if she didn't act.

As quickly as her shaking hands could manage, she loaded a cart with tools and supplies and rolled it over to the dog, who was lying still, his breaths more labored than they'd been just moments before. In the area of the gunshot wound, the flesh was swelling rapidly, and when she looked closer, she gasped. Before her eyes, the muscle and skin was dying. If she hadn't seen the progression herself, she'd have estimated that the wound had festered for a week. Gangrene had set in, and the stench of dead flesh filled the room.

"My God," she breathed. "What's happening?"

Afraid to waste even another second, she grabbed the scalpel and hoped the dog wouldn't bite, because this was going to hurt.

Carefully, she made a small incision at the site of the bullet hole. The pup whimpered, but remained still as she mopped up pus and blood and then palmed the forceps. "Hold still, baby."

Cara held her breath and prayed for a steady hand. *Do it. Do it now . . .*

She worked the forceps into the wound, cringing at the squishy sound of the metal passing through rotting flesh. Though she hadn't summoned her power, a trickle she couldn't stop ran down her arm and into her hand. *Don't panic.* Somehow, she kept it together until she felt the forceps bump against the bullet. Though the dog yelped when she clasped the slug, he didn't move . . . or bite.

As gently as possible, she eased the bullet free. Odd . . . it was silver. She placed the forceps on the tray, grabbed the bandages, and turned back to the dog.

And screeched.

The pup was standing on the exam table, head cocked and tongue lolling out as if he had been happily romping in a park and not minutes from death. The only sign that he'd ever been injured was blood matted in his fur and pooled on the floor and table.

Reeling from the impossibility of the situation, Cara's legs gave way beneath her, and the cold floor rose up to meet her body. Her skull cracked on the tile, and the next thing she knew, the pup was beside her, his crimson eyes glowing. His tongue slathered across her face and mouth, and oh, yuck, his saliva tasted like rotten fish. Weakly, she pushed him away, but he came back and slammed his heavy body down on her.

He panted, his breath so toxic it worked like smelling salts, and she gagged even as she became alert.

"Ugh." She wheezed, waving her hand in front of his mouth to ward off his stench. "We have to do something about your halitosis from hell." God, she was talking like this was real.

It wasn't. Couldn't be. She was probably still in her bed, and this was a dream.

Suddenly, Halitosis was on his feet, crouched over her, a growl vibrating his deep chest. Not a normal growl, either. It was smoky, serrated, something she'd expect to hear from a dragon. Or a demon. *Freaky.*

The door burst open in a crash of splinters, and four men filed through the doorway.

A scream welled in her throat, but lodged there, blocked by terror. *Not again, not again.* Memories of the home invasion that had ruined her life collided with current events, and she froze up, so paralyzed that her lungs couldn't expel her held breath.

There was a gunshot, a snarl...and then godawful screams. Blood splattered on the floor, the walls, on her... and she broke out of her paralysis to scramble to her feet.

Hal slammed one of the men to the floor, his claws— which somehow had extended like a cat's—tearing into the man's chest as the other two slashed at him with strange bladed weapons.

Cara scanned the room for a weapon of her own, anything at all. She lunged for a heavy glass jar of cotton balls but reeled back at an explosive, blinding flash of light. A beautiful blond man appeared in the middle of the room. Flames erupted from his fingertips as a ball of fire flipped into the air, bursting into a gold net that fell on Hal, who went down in a tangle beneath it.

"No!" She dove for the dog, but someone grabbed her

from behind. Hal went crazy, a mass of teeth and claws as he struggled to get out of the net.

Curses flew, and someone fired a shot at the newcomer, who took the bullet in the chest with no more reaction than if he'd been stung by a bee. He scooped up the net, Hal with it, and in another flare of light, he was gone.

The man tightened his arms around Cara, and one of the men limped toward her, his left arm dangling, his face mottled with rage. "What are you?"

She blinked. "W-what?"

"I said," he snarled, *"what are you?"*

"I don't understand."

His hand lashed out so fast she didn't see it until her cheek stung from the blow. "What kind of demon are you?" he screamed, his spittle spraying her face.

Oh, God, these men were crazy. This whole situation was crazy. This was Crazyland, and she was the queen.

"Why..." She sucked in a ragged breath and tried to stay calm. It wasn't easy when the man holding her in a vise grip against him was squeezing the air out of her lungs. "Why would you think I'm a demon?" Maybe they were religious fanatics, like the ones who had accused her of practicing witchcraft before she learned to hide her healing gift.

Her theory was blown out of the water when the third guy, the one who had been kneeling next to the dead man on the floor, stood and picked up the bullet that had been lodged in the dog. He held it out to her. "Because," he said, in an eerily calm voice, "only a demon would heal a hellhound."

# Two

Hellhound?

These people were insane. "It was just a dog."

"Really?" The red-haired, freckled one with the bullet, who reminded her vaguely of Carrot Top, spoke in a deceptively soft voice. "And was the guy who flashed into the room and took the dog just a man?"

She opened her mouth to answer, but what could she say? The guy had disappeared into thin air. "I . . . what else would he be?"

"Oh, maybe a demon. Like you."

Keep them talking. And calm. Excellent plan in theory, but who was going to keep her calm? False courage gave her a voice, at least. "Who are you people?"

The one who had struck her whipped a strange, S-shaped, double-bladed weapon from a harness on his chest, and held the gold end to her neck. "Are you that stupid, or are you just playing that way?"

"Garcia." Carrot Top put his hand on the weapon-wielder's shoulder. "Look at her, man. She's terrified. She doesn't know who we are."

"Stupid then." Garcia dragged the tip of the blade down her throat, and she felt a sting and a warm drip. "I know you've heard of Guardians."

"Guardians?"

He spun the weapon around and scraped the silver end down the other side of her throat, eliciting another sting, another drip. "The Aegis? You know, demon slayers?"

Seriously? These guys had issues. Maybe they'd played too many role-playing games. Or they were on drugs.

"I'm not—" She broke off to clear her throat of the hoarseness. Didn't clear away the terror, though. "I'm not a demon. I'm human. The dog was hit by a car. And shot..." She trailed off when Carrot Top peeled back his jacket, revealing a pistol in a holster.

"We know." The guy holding her spoke into her ear, his hot breath and cold voice sending a chill down her spine. "We're the ones who shot the fucker and then tracked the hick who brought it here."

"Then why would you think I was a demon? I didn't do anything but take the dog from the man who brought him to me."

"I already told you. Hellhounds heal quickly, but not that quickly." Garcia frowned at his odd gold and silver weapon. "Neither of these metals affect you. We can try something else."

Not affect her? She had two streams of blood running down her throat, thank you very much. She realized she must have spoken out loud when Garcia slapped her across the face. Her mouth had always gotten her in trouble.

"Dude," Carrot Top said, sarcasm lacing his voice. "Here's a thought. She might be human. A witch or shaman or some demon's minion. So, duh, neither metal would affect her."

*Crazycrazycrazy...*

Garcia appeared to consider that, but she had no idea whether what Carrot had said was a good or bad thing for her. "What kind of magic did you use to heal the hound?"

*That* she couldn't explain. Because even though only a trickle had accidentally escaped her, what she'd done to the dog *had* been magic. Evil magic. Oh, some more open-minded people called it a gift, and some explained that what she did was really an intense form of Reiki. Whatever. She'd never found any literature that referenced the strength of the power she wielded.

When she said nothing, Garcia waved the weapon in front of her face. "We can make you talk."

Deep inside her, the gift she despised began to flow through her veins. *Breathe...keep it together...*

Once again, Carrot lay a restraining hand on Garcia's shoulder. "You know the rules. If she's human or human-based, we need to call a supervisor."

"Fuck that. The new *softer, gentler* rules are for treehuggers."

"Idiot." The guy holding her shifted, bringing his heel down on her bare toes, and she bit down on a cry of pain even as her power throbbed at the walls of her vessels, wanting out. "Treehuggers are environmentalists."

"You know what I mean. Fucking demon sympathizers." Garcia grinned at her. "Even if she's not a demon, she's working with them. That makes her no better than them, and fair game."

Her lungs grew tight as her breath became labored with some serious freakout. "Please," she whispered. "Just go. I won't tell anyone about this." *Wuss*. Yeah, but she'd have to kick herself about it later.

If she survived.

Could one person get lucky enough to live through the same thing twice?

"Go?" Garcia leveled the tip of the weird weapon against the sensitive skin just beneath her left eye. "Not until we get some answers."

Cara shrank back, but her head bumped into the chest of the guy who held her, and she froze before the blade pierced her eyeball. Tingles spread through her fingers. Her hand lifted, almost on its own, to touch Garcia. *No!* Dear God, what had she been about to do?

There had to be another way, but she had to think fast. These guys were going to kill her, and not without causing her a whole lot of pain first.

The phone, coated in dust and hanging on the wall behind Carrot, came into focus. If she could get to it... what? They'd kill her before she could dial the 9, let alone the 1-1. Still, she had to try. *Give them what they want, within reason*. Her self-defense instructor's voice was a whisper in her ear and a welcome injection of steel into her spine.

"I'll tell you anything you want," she said, though she was unsure how much she meant that—or how much she actually knew. "Just let go of me." She wriggled in the man's grip, biting back a cry when he jammed his fist into her breastbone to still her.

"Oh, you'll tell us everything," Garcia said. "You don't need your eyes to talk."

"Garcia!" Carrot stepped forward as if to stop his buddy, and she took advantage of the interruption.

Remembering the instructor's advice, which amounted to *kick your attacker in the balls and run like hell*, she brought up one knee, catching Garcia in the crotch, and at the same time, she rammed her elbow back, sinking it into the belly of the guy behind her. His grunt wasn't nearly as satisfying as the way Garcia doubled over, but it gave her a chance to dive for the door.

"Fuck," Garcia wheezed. "Get her!"

Arms closed around her, and Carrot spun her back to the man she'd elbowed, who wasn't nearly as gentle in his handling this time.

Another flash of light flooded the room, and the nightmare got a whole lot worse.

Standing where the guy who disappeared with Hal had been was a huge man in leather armor, his ebony eyes hard, his expression uncompromising. In his hand was a sword as long as she was tall. As terrifying as the three *demon slayers* were, this stranger left them in the dust. She actually shrank back against the man who held her, as if he could—or would—help her.

The big guy in armor seemed to assess the situation in less time than it took for her heart to beat. He moved like a viper, lashing out with his massive arm and knocking Garcia and Carrot across the room. When the man behind her shoved her aside, the leather-armor guy struck with a closed fist, adding her captor's body to the pile.

Cara didn't even have time to scream. Or run. Or faint. In a single stride the newcomer was in front of her. She backed away, but was blocked by the exam table. He stalked her, his presence overwhelming, as if he owned the very air, and she had to struggle for every breath.

"You," he said in an impossibly dark, deep voice, "have some explaining to do."

⌒

Damned Aegis idiots.

Ares generally supported their efforts, had, in the past, fought alongside them in battles against demons. But the demon slayers tended to think that anything they didn't understand was evil.

He glanced at the three Guardians—no, four. One was dead. The live ones struggled to their feet, pain twisting their expressions and murder gleaming in their eyes. The human female was backed against an exam table, her terror a tangible odor that was mixed with the scent of her blood, of the Guardians' blood, and . . . of hellhound.

But there was no sign of Sestiel, the fallen angel Ares had tracked to this very room, and now, suddenly, Ares couldn't sense the angel at all.

He gauged the situation, decided it wasn't necessary to kill the Aegi, but he did need to know what had gone on here. It was critical that he find Sestiel before Reseph did, but the fact that the fallen angel might be in possession of a motherfucking hellhound was an added complication; the beasts acted like radar-jamming equipment, and as long as Sestiel was near the hound, Ares would be unable to locate him.

Then there was another, worse scenario to consider— that Sestiel wasn't in possession of a hellhound, but rather that a hellhound was in possession of *him*. Which meant that Ares needed to glean every crumb of information he could get from the human female, and he'd get his answers one way or another.

Too bad for her. Seizing her arm, he tugged her to him, opened a gate, and stepped through the shimmering veil, unconcerned by the fact that humans came out on the other side of a Harrowgate dead. Nope, one of the cool advantages of a summoned Harrowgate was that humans could travel with the Horsemen. Not that it happened often. Not since their break with The Aegis.

A warm salt breeze hit him as they exited, their feet coming down on rock and ivory sand. A hundred yards away was his Greek manor, a sprawling white structure that sat atop an island in the Aegean Sea. The island was unmapped—invisible to human eyes and technology—and Ares had lived here for three thousand years, since the day he'd wrested it from the demon who'd built it. It was a great place, especially since he'd brought it up to modern standards and comforts.

But they weren't going inside.

He spun the woman around so her back was to the sea, her bare feet close to the cliff edge. "Who are you?" He gripped her shoulders firmly, his fingers digging into the blue flannel pajama top dotted with penguins. She wore *penguin* pajamas.

"P-please..." The wind whipped her sandy-blonde hair into her face, and some weird impulse made him want to brush it away.

He resisted. *"Who are you?"*

"I'm not...not a demon." Her breath sawed in and out of her so violently that he half-expected her to pass out.

"What is your name?"

She blinked as if she didn't understand the question,

and when he repeated it, she finally murmured, "Cara. It's Cara. I'm not a demon. I swear, I'm not a demon."

"You keep saying that." He inhaled, once again catching the bitter scent of her terror, but also, the faint, smoky tint of hellhound. She'd been in direct contact with one. "Why were you handling a hellhound? Were you attacked?"

A tiny squeak came from her, as if fear had closed up her throat. Hellhounds could do that to a person. But he didn't have time to coddle a delicate female through her trauma. He needed intel, and he needed it now.

He snapped his fingers in front of her face, startling her out of her freaked-out trance. "Did The Aegis save you?"

"The men? They...they tried to kill the pup."

Ares couldn't decide if she was a little...slow...or just scared out of her gourd. Maybe both. Even so, she should be a little more agitated in his presence, and he wondered what was up with that. He took a deep breath and spoke slowly, even though he didn't have the time or patience for this shit. "Yes, I'm sure they tried to kill it. It's their job."

"To kill dogs?"

"*Demon* dogs. You know, hellhounds?"

"This isn't real," she whispered. "I want to go home..." She shook her head, backpedaling wildly. "No, not home! Those men are there. This isn't real..."

Shit. He was losing her. Before she could go into a complete meltdown, he gripped her by the shoulders and bent to peer directly into her eyes. Which were the exact color of the sea below when the sun hit it just right. Crystal blue with flecks of green and gold. Stunning.

"Listen to me. I need to know if you saw another man in that room. Long blond hair. Angelic."

She nodded, her wide-eyed gaze locked onto his as if she were afraid to look away. As if he was a lifeline and if she let go, she'd plunge into an abyss of insanity. "Where is Hal?"

"Hal?"

"The dog."

She'd named the hellhound? The things were mean as fuck, ravenous, horny...suddenly a sinking suspicion made his gut plummet. Had the hound given her a Hell's Kiss? Nah. They never, *ever* did that to humans.

And yet...he leaned in, and as he got closer, the odor of fear and beast gave way to a more feminine scent. She smelled clean, like a spring meadow, with soft floral undertones. His cock jerked, the stupid bastard. The woman was terrified, human, and possibly shackled to one of the most vile creatures to ever have been spawned in Sheoul.

"What are you doing?"

He didn't reply. He touched his lips to hers. A shocked gasp escaped her, and damn, she tasted sweet. There was a faint mint tang of toothpaste on her breath, and as he stroked his tongue across her satin lips, he got the telltale numbing tingle of the hellhound's kiss. Which explained why she wasn't combative with him—by bonding with Cara, the hound had brought her over into the supernatural world. She was still human, but with...enhancements.

He should have retreated, right then and there, but her mouth was soft, her body ripe with curves, and he hadn't kissed a woman—a real human woman—in thousands of years. Head swimming, he tugged her against him. This was unexpected, amazing—

Sudden, stabbing pain lanced his groin. He grunted out a curse, doubled over, and clutched his balls, which she'd cracked with her knee.

"Bastard!" Cara followed up on that by jamming that killer knee of hers into his nose.

While he reeled in surprise that she'd caught him off guard, she tried to launch past him, but she was too close to the cliff's edge. Her foot slipped, and her shriek cut off as the ground fell out from under her.

*Son of a—!* Ares dove, skidded on his belly and barely snared her hand as she disappeared over the side. Rocks and dirt broke away beneath him as he struggled to hang on. A giant chunk of earth crumbled under his chest, and suddenly, he was hanging by his hips, his leverage lost, and in about two seconds, they were going to go over.

Waves crashed on the rocks below, the plumes of spray shooting up as though trying to grab at them, to drag them down to a watery grave. Well, grave for her, maybe. Ares would merely suffer in agony until he regenerated.

"Battle," he called through clenched teeth. "Out!"

Cara clung desperately to his hand, but as she watched the smoke unwind from his arm, he thought she might actually let go. The wisp swirled up over his shoulder, and then he heard a snort, felt the stallion's bite clamp down on his calf. Agonizing pressure shot up his leg, but the hard armor prevented the warhorse's teeth from tearing into flesh.

Battle dragged him backward, and Cara with him. He tugged her over the edge and rolled with her to safety, coming to rest on top of her. For a moment, she stared, her wide, haunted eyes swimming with disbelief.

Then it all went to hell.

Screaming, she pummeled him with her fists and rocked her head up to bite him. He reared back, barely avoiding her teeth, and when Battle stomped one enormous hoof next to her head in a protective warning, her screams deepened, so full of raw terror that Ares felt the vibrations in his chest.

"Okay," he murmured. "Cara, calm down..."

But there was no calming her, and he knew it. She'd been pushed beyond reason, beyond her ability to cope, and the only thing he could do for her now was knock her out or turn back the clock.

Well, he could pluck out her eyeballs and plug into her visions, but as ruthless as he could be, he preferred to use drastic measures only if necessary and, if possible, only against other warriors. Which meant that if any Aegi were still in her house, they were in for a little all-is-fair-in-war.

Unfortunately for Cara, she wasn't going to get away unscathed either. If she was bonded to a hellhound, he needed her. The beast would come to her, either physically or in the dream world, and he could lead Ares to Sestiel. Cara would be the bait for Ares's trap. All he had to do was return her to her home and wait.

"Battle, to me." Ares swore Battle growled before he wound around his arm again, which, of course, set Cara off with a fresh round of screams. Tightening his arm around her, he summoned a gate, rolled them into it, and came out on the soft, green grass outside her home.

Before she could renew her hysterics, he waved his hand in front of her face. Her expression went slack, her eyes glazing over. He took a minute to readjust her memories...he couldn't create new ones, but he could erase the most recent events. Being a Horseman came with some pretty cool tricks.

Once he was finished, he carried her into her house. The place reeked of blood and hellhound, and though it appeared that the Aegi had gone, he didn't take chances. Silently, he laid her on the couch and performed a sweep of the rooms. All clear. A disaster, but clear. The Guardians had damaged the back door, probably when they'd broken in, and before they gathered their dead and left, they'd gone through some of her drawers and closets. Blood was splashed all over the room he'd found Cara in, some sort of veterinary office. She'd be confused as all hell tomorrow when she woke up.

Well...hell, he could at least give her a reasonable explanation for her memory loss. He scrounged around the kitchen until he hit paydirt in the form of a shot glass and a dusty bottle of vodka. After dumping the contents in the sink, he wetted a washcloth and returned to her.

She was curled up on her side, her long hair covering her face. At some point, she'd knocked papers off the coffee table—mostly overdue bills, from what he could tell. For a long moment, he looked at her, wondering if he should shed the armor that helped shield him not only from weapons, but from strong emotion. The hard leather, fashioned from Gerunti demon hide, was a favorite of several demon races that made their living as slave traders, assassins, and mercenaries, none of whom could afford weakness of any kind—and emotions were weakness. But Ares had learned long ago that sometimes a warrior gained a unique perspective by losing the armor.

When you understood what your enemy was feeling, you understood how to hurt him most effectively. Or, in circumstances like this one, if you let yourself see the world the way your target did, you could revise your strategy to take advantage of her situation.

Tossing the bills aside, he feathered the pads of his fingers over the crescent-shaped scar just under his jawbone on the left side of his neck, and his armor melted away, leaving him in black BDU pants and a black tee. These were his everyday clothes, what felt most comfortable to him. But for some reason, he felt naked now, as if he needed the leather armor.

For what? Protection against the sleeping human female?

He shook his head to clear it. Pestilence's mind-fucks must really be messing with him.

Cara stirred, turning her slightly rounded face up to him. Her eyes were swollen, and an angry bruise in the shape of a handprint marred her cheek. Anger he wouldn't have felt had he been armored up made his skin flush hot.

Those Aegis sons of bitches. He should have taken the time to tear them apart. Ares understood the need for ruthlessness: War was not pretty, and The Aegis was engaged in a mission to save mankind. But torturing non-combatants, especially women, was not in the field manual. Not when there were much easier and better ways to get information.

He silently cursed them as he used soft, light strokes to wipe away the smudges of dirt from Cara's face and hands. He lingered on her fingers. Slim, strong, with square nails coated with clear polish. He'd always had a thing for nice hands, and images bloomed in his mind, improper ones involving her touch on his body. He sensed that she'd have a light touch, her caresses tentative, and for some reason, that appealed to him.

Something different, he supposed. His dick was on board with the something-different thing, and he shifted to make space in his pants as he finished with her hands, turning her gold pinky ring around so the tiny ruby sat properly. So feminine, like everything about her. Even her pajamas, while not the sexiest things he'd ever seen, made her seem softer, more fragile, and he cursed The Aegis yet again as he used the washcloth to mop up the streaks of blood that had dried on her throat. The wounds themselves, obviously made by a sharp blade, had sealed, and thanks to the hellhound bond, would be healed within hours. So would her bruises and scrapes. But he couldn't be certain how complete the mind-wipe had been, and he couldn't do anything about the dirt and grass stains on her pajamas.

When the last drop of blood and dirt had been swabbed away, he withdrew—and froze when her hand shot out to grasp his wrist. Her eyes were open, but they lacked the terror he'd expect to see in someone who had just woken up to a stranger hovering over her.

She was still asleep.

She tugged at him, drawing him closer, as if she wanted comfort, or protection.

"Shh." Ares smoothed his fingers through her hair and used his thumb to close her eyes, and in a few seconds, she was snoring daintily. He turned on the TV in case she was the type to fall asleep while watching, and allowed himself a smile as he nodded in a silent farewell.

After locking her doors and windows, he headed back to the vet office. Reaching under his shirt, he palmed his Seal, hoping to get a bead on Sestiel. Nothing.

Normally, this would be the point at which Ares would curse up a storm. But he had an ace up his sleeve in the form of that little human female. Taking one last look at her, he opened a gate and flashed out of there.

But he'd be back.

# Three

Pestilence had always liked Mexico. When he'd been Reseph, he and Limos had partied for days in various towns, from tourist traps to remote villages where the locals had called them *brujos*, viewing them as magicians of sorts, even though he and his sister never revealed any of their secrets...except for their longevity. Reseph and Limos had been visiting the villages for decades, had known many of the elders when they were toddlers.

Now he stood in the center of one of those mountain villages, watching as the last of the locals, a twenty-something male, writhed at his feet, trying desperately to suck air through his constricted windpipe.

"Nice work." Pestilence looked over his shoulder at Harvester. The female fallen angel, one of the Horsemen's two Watchers, studied Pestilence's handiwork with a critical eye. "How long did it take these people to realize you weren't here to bring them gifts?"

"Not long." When Pestilence arrived, the children had come running, expecting candy, and the adults had set about preparing a feast fit for a king. Reseph had never appeared without offerings for the poor farming community, from gifts of livestock and crates of medicine, to books and shoes for the children.

So when he'd shot the first arrow through the first heart, shock had frozen the entire population.

Until he'd grabbed a teenage girl, sunk his fangs into her throat, and injected a demon strain of hemorrhagic fever that spread through the village in a matter of minutes. The guy at his feet was the last one to die, his final, gurgling breath coming as his eyes dissolved in his head.

Harvester knelt next to the body and dragged her fingertip through the mud formed in the dirt by the man's leaking bodily fluids. "This is what, your fourth plague in Mexico alone?" The fallen angel's expression was hidden by her long black hair, but Pestilence could read displeasure in the stiff set of Harvester's shoulders. "All tiny, isolated villages. Just like in Africa, China, Alaska."

"I'll hit larger populations soon," Pestilence said, unable to keep a note of defensiveness out of his voice. "I do have a plan."

Harvester unfurled to her full six and a half feet, coming eye to eye with Pestilence. "Lies. You're wiping out everything that reminds you of your old life. Punishing humans for your kindness." The angel sneered. "Now that your Seal is broken, you need to get your ass in gear while the underworld is swelling with momentum."

"Aren't you and Reaver supposed to be impartial?"

She snorted. "Hardly. Each of us is here only to make sure the other plays fair. Reaver wants to stop this Apocalypse, and I want to see it begin. I might not be able to help you directly, but I can work behind the scenes, and I can certainly root you on." She studied her black-lacquered nails. "I can also get pissed at your dicking around. There's talk of adding more Watchers to keep an eye on you and your siblings now, and I don't plan to share my job with anyone, so get moving."

"I'm working on it. I slaughtered Batarel—"

"Not before she transferred Ares's *agimortus*!"

Pestilence fisted Harvester's tunic and yanked her so close that their breath mingled. "I have my minions hunting Unfallen to the ends of the earth. I've slaughtered six in the last two days. Scores have entered Sheoul to escape me. Even if I don't find Sestiel soon, he won't have anyone left to transfer the *agimortus* to."

It sucked that the *agimortus* couldn't be transferred to fallen angels who entered Sheoul and went from a toe-the-line Unfallen to an evil True Fallen. A True Fallen would likely sacrifice his life to break Ares's Seal.

Harvester's skin grew mottled, shot through with inky veins, and her green eyes swirled with ruby streaks. Leathery, black wings rose from her back. "Fool," she spat. "The *agimortus* can be transferred to a human. If Sestiel grows desperate, he has billions of potential hosts at his disposal."

"And you didn't mention this before...why?" he ground out.

"That," she said, "is not for you to question." Her wings lifted even higher and spread wide, the effect no doubt calculated to make Pestilence quake in his boots before her awesome evilness. As if.

He wondered how much force it would take to rip a

wing off a fallen angel. "I hope he *does* transfer the *agi-mortus* to a human. I can kill a man as easily as a fly." He tightened his fist, gathering the fabric of Harvester's tunic and turning it into a noose. "Won't be as enjoyable as killing a fallen angel, though."

She hissed. "Of the four of you, you were always my least favorite. I was sure that once your Seal broke and you became Pestilence, you'd stop being a wastrel and would put some effort into making a name for yourself. Clearly, I was wrong."

Pestilence gnashed his teeth. "I intend to prove myself to the Dark Lord as the worthiest of my siblings. When the Earth and Sheoul become one, *I* will have first choice of the realms." Yep, it was written that following the Apocalypse, the demon realm would spill over into the human one, and the whole kit and kaboodle would then be divided into four quadrants, with varying amounts of water, food, land, and populations of humans and demons. The Horseman who proved to be the best would get first pick and turn his region into a paradise of misery and pleasure.

Pestilence would be that Horseman.

Harvester grinned, her fangs glinting wetly. "You can't truly believe that. Ares will win, just as he wins everything."

With a roar, Pestilence slammed the fallen angel into the side of one of the shanties. The impact blew a hole through the wood, and they both staggered into the building. "I'm not allowed to kill you," he snarled, shoving her against a support beam, "but I can make you wish you were dead."

"The truth hurts, doesn't it?" She whipped one veiny wing around his back and sank the clawed tip into the back of his neck. Pain shot up his spine and ricocheted around the inside of his skull, but he didn't give her the satisfaction of a sound. "You've always been jealous of Ares."

Not always. It wasn't until after Reseph's Seal broke that the *great Ares* had gotten under his skin. Ares had been a masterful commander as a human. Ares had never lost a battle. Ares was the original of the Greek god of the same name. Blah fucking blah.

It was Pestilence's turn. He was going to hurt Ares where it mattered—those servants he cared so much about. Hell, yes, Pestilence was going to make a name for himself. He would be the most feared of the Horsemen. Long after the Apocalypse ended, his name would be spoken with reverence. With awe. With *fear*.

He reached behind his back and caught Harvester's wingtip. With a twist of his wrist, he snapped the bones in her wing. He cut off her screech by ripping into her throat with his teeth. Blood spilled down her chest, coating him with sticky warmth.

No, he couldn't kill her. That was against the rules. But he could stop just short of it.

And he could make sure that the initial tales of his reign of terror came from a firsthand account.

*Help me.*

The voice came to Cara as she floated in a dark, cold room, her body a misty shadow. Below her, a dog howled from inside a cage, its glimmering red eyes watching her every move. She moved closer, unsure how, since she was hanging in the air, but in any case, she was suddenly eye to eye with the canine.

*Find me.*

She started. The voice had come from the dog. Not an actual voice, but more of a thought inside her head.

"Who are you?"

*I am yours. You are mine.*

*Mine? Yours?* This was so weird. She put her face right up to the cage, oddly unafraid of the creature inside. It was clearly a puppy, but something about it radiated lethal power and danger. Its fur was so black it seemed to absorb what little light entered the room from behind closed shutters on a single, tiny window, and its teeth looked as if they should be inside the mouth of a shark rather than that of a dog.

She searched for a lock...heck, a *door* on the cage... but found nothing except odd symbols etched into the bars. The entire cage sat inside a painted circle on the cement floor. "How do I release you?"

*You must find me.*

So...this dream dog-thing was a little dimwitted. "I've found you."

*In the other world.*

He was definitely not right in the head. *Says the person talking to the dog.*

"Who put you here?"

*Sestiel.*

Who was Sestiel? She floated up and looked around what appeared to be a basement. The walls had been built with layers of stone, suggesting older construction. She drifted to a set of dusty shelves, which held only a few label-less cans, a broken pencil, and a glass flask half-full of clear liquid. Oddly, the flask wasn't dusty. She reached for it, only to have her hand pass through the bottle and the shelves.

Maybe this wasn't a dream. Maybe she was a ghost. But how had she died? Her memory was a black hole.

A distant pounding startled her, and she spun around to the dog. "What was that?"

*What was what?*

The pounding came again, a dull knock, growing louder, and she felt herself being pulled toward the sound, her body stretching like taffy. Something soft cradled her body, and light flooded her eyes. She blinked, her surroundings coming into sharp focus, and she sat up.

Her living room. She was in her living room, on her couch. The weird dream faded, replaced by real-life confusion. She'd obviously fallen asleep on her couch, but... why was there a glass and an empty bottle of vodka on her coffee table? She didn't drink, not a drop since the break-in two years ago. She'd learned that life was fragile, full of surprises, and she didn't want any of her senses—or reflexes—dulled by anything, including medications or alcohol.

Unease rolled down her spine as she ran her hands over her face. Her skin felt tender, and as she dragged her fingers down to her mouth, the unease doubled. Her lips were swollen, inflamed.

As if she'd been kissed.

A sudden image of an impossibly huge man holding her against him popped into her head, and whoa, that had to have been part of a dream, because *no one* was that big. Or handsome. A vision unfolded in her mind of him lowering his perfectly shaped mouth to hers. She could practically feel his warm tongue stroking her lips, and it was so real that her body flamed hot.

A pleasant flush spread over her skin, but when the

hairs on the back of her neck prickled, she suddenly went from oddly aroused to feeling as though someone was watching her. Forgetting her swollen lips and the dream man, she whipped her head around, but there was no one there. Damn, she was sick of this paranoia, but that didn't stop her from scanning every corner twice.

Satisfied that there was no one in the room, she ignored the lingering sensation that eyes were on her to focus on the TV, which was blaring some breaking news about a deadly malaria outbreak in Siberia. Since Siberia wasn't exactly a malaria hotspot, the disease was a big deal, made bigger by the fact that experts had never encountered this particular strain.

*"The Siberian outbreak is only one of dozens of odd occurrences of highly lethal plagues striking populations all over the globe,"* the anchor was saying. *"Religious leaders everywhere are citing end-of-the-world prophecies, and scientists are advising people to use common sense. As one researcher at the World Health Organization puts it, 'People screeched about Armageddon during the last swine flu outbreak. And before that, it was the bird flu. What we're seeing is nature rebelling against insect control chemicals and antibiotics.' "* The journalist's expression was grim as he looked into the camera. *"And now we go to the Balkan peninsula, where rising tensions—"*

Cara turned off the TV. It seemed like lately the news was all bad, full of disease, war, and growing panic.

She stood, feeling a little wobbly...and what the heck? Her pajamas were filthy, as if she'd rolled around in a barnyard. Two different colors of dirt smeared her pjs, and there were grass stains on her sleeves. And was that...*blood*...on her top?

Heart pounding wildly, she patted herself down, inspecting for injuries, but other than a kink in her neck she could probably blame on the lumpy couch, she felt fine.

If losing her mind could be considered *fine*.

The sound of a vehicle engine broke into the cacophony of her jumbled thoughts. Grateful for the distraction, she drew aside the front window's heavy curtains. The mailman's Jeep pulled away, which explained the pounding that had woken her up. She went to the door, relieved that all the locks were in place. But still, why was she filthy? Had she sleepwalked? And sleep-slammed a dozen shots of vodka?

Caffeine. She needed caffeine to figure this out. The spiderwebs in her brain seemed to be catching all her thoughts and tangling them up so they couldn't form a coherent explanation for any of this.

She worked the locks, being careful to check the peephole before unhooking the chain, and then grabbed the box and rubber-banded mail the mailman had left. The letters turned out to be bills. Lots of them, and all of them with yellow or pink slips inside.

Well, electricity and running water were luxuries, weren't they?

The box, containing her only indulgence—gourmet coffee—she left unopened. She'd have to send it back. Now that she'd been laid off from her part-time job at the library, she could no longer afford even that one small thing, not with bills piling up, no job prospects in the tiny town, and no buyer for the house in sight. Heck, she might have to give up even the generic grocery store grind.

Shuddering at the thought, she tossed the mail onto the

little table next to the door, flipped the locks, and shuffled toward the kitchen, hoping the few scoops of coffee she had left could be stretched into a full pot. But as she turned the corner to the hallway, she came to an abrupt halt.

The door to her office was open.

She hadn't been inside that room since she'd closed down her practice. Oh, God, what *had* she done in her sleep? A muted sense of anxiety shimmered through her as she crept down the hall to the open door.

She'd done a lot more than drink vodka and roll around in the dirt while sleepwalking.

Boxes of supplies lay scattered on the floor, their contents spilling out. A dark substance that looked suspiciously like dried blood was spattered on the walls and pooled on the tiles, and when she stepped fully inside the room, she got an eyeful of tumbled furniture and smashed cabinets.

What had happened in here, and *whose blood was that?*

And why, dear God *why*, did she feel like someone was watching her?

Spying could normally be considered a skill. Unless you were a supernatural being who could hang out in a *khote*. So yeah, Ares didn't exactly feel like he was doing anything but being a Peeping Tom, as today's population called it.

But he couldn't exactly pop out of thin air and ask Cara what she'd dreamed about last night. Not when she'd just discovered the mess in her veterinary office. She might appear outwardly calm, but the color had drained from her face, and when she backed out of the room, she stumbled.

And Ares nearly stepped out of his *khote* to catch her.

Idiot. He watched her trudge down the hallway to the kitchen, where she made coffee, poured herself a bowl of generic bran flakes cereal, and ate with mechanical, precise motions. She had to have known that her pajamas were filthy with dirt and dried blood, but it didn't faze her. Shock. Definitely.

The hardened, battle-edged commander side of him wanted to tell her to snap out of it. To *grow a set and get over it, soldier.* But another side of him wanted to... what? Comfort her? Fold her into his arms and whisper sweet, mushy things into her ear?

*Fucking* idiot. He brushed his finger over his throat, and his armor snapped into place. It had been foolish to come here without it.

Ares had been raised to be a warrior—and he'd been a damned good one, had learned the art of war from the human he'd believed to be his father, which honed the instinct he'd been born with, thanks to his demon mother and battle-angel father. But then, when the Seals were doled out according to "best—and worst—fit" for each sibling, he'd also been supplied with a massive dose of insta-expertise.

The desire to fight a good battle had always been there. No blaming *that* on the stupid prophecy.

Time to kick his own ass and do what needed to be done. The fate of all mankind rested on his shoulders, and if he traumatized one little human female to save the world, so be it.

He was about to let down the *khote* when Cara grabbed the phone, dialed, and said in a droning voice, "Larena, it's Cara. I need to know what dreaming about a black dog means. It was howling, in a cage. And if the name Sestiel means anything to you, that would help, too. Thanks."

Caged? That meant that Sestiel was in possession of the beast and not the other way around. Was he hoping to bond with it? Even though fallen angels belonged to a small handful of beings who could tame hellhounds, now that the beast was bonded to Cara, no one else could control it, tame it, or bond with it. Sestiel must not be aware that his hopes for a hellhound protector, at least from this specific hound, were dashed.

But Ares's hopes were still alive. The hound could be the one he wanted, and Ares's blood sang with anticipation that he might finally have his revenge. That Cara would become collateral damage didn't matter, and Ares had a feeling that even when he took off the armor, the hatred for the beast would far outweigh any prick of conscience he'd have for the consequences to the human.

Cara hung up and ambled into the bedroom, clearly on autopilot. Curious, he followed, and when she began to strip, he decided that popping into the open now might not be a good idea.

He'd been raised during a time in which nudity wasn't given a second thought, and he rarely batted an eyelash at an unclothed body. Sure, like any red-blooded male, in the heat of the moment he appreciated a naked woman, but it took a hell of a lot more than simple nudity to stir his loins even a little bit.

And yet, as Cara peeled off her pajama top, he definitely found himself stirred.

As if she felt she was being watched, she angled away from him, but too late. Her high, full breasts and dusky rose nipples were already seared into his memory. And he had to admit that the view from behind was just as tantalizing.

Cara's skin was pale, as though she didn't spend much time outside, but aside from a few freckles, it was flawless, milky and smooth, and he had an intense urge to touch it, see if it was as supple and warm as it looked. Her toned muscles flexed with every movement—she was stronger than she looked, as his still-tender balls could attest.

Bending over, she shoved down her pajama bottoms and underwear, and Ares, who had always preferred battle over sex, who had grown bored of sex because it offered no challenges, nothing new...nearly swallowed his tongue. He was a breast man, but Cara had one *fine* ass.

And wasn't ogling a woman who was still suffering from shock real fucking noble. Not that he'd ever claimed to be noble.

She padded to the bathroom, and again, as if she could sense his presence, she closed the door. And locked it.

Through the flimsy plywood, he heard the shower start, and though he could cast a Harrowgate to get into the bathroom, he had a better idea.

He summoned a gate to take him to his Greek stronghold, changed into khaki cargo pants and a white linen button-down that he left untucked. He wanted to appear casual and nonthreatening, and for half a second he even considered throwing on his leather flip-flops. No male looked like a badass in flip-flops.

But they also weren't made for saddle stirrups, and he wanted to be prepared to ride, so in the end he shoved his feet into a pair of combat boots, grabbed a wad of American money, and called it good. He figured he had a few minutes to spare before Cara finished showering, so he checked his email, hoping for intel or gossip from his spies and underworld sources. Any information about Pestilence's location, his activities, movements...*anything*...could be a major breakthrough.

"There's a new meningitis outbreak in Uganda and a bubonic plague flare-up in the Philippines."

Ares rubbed the bridge of his nose between his thumb and forefinger before shooting an annoyed glance at Reaver. The blond angel loved popping into rooms unannounced. He stood in the doorway to Ares's office, his arms folded over his broad chest, his sapphire blue eyes glowing with intensity.

Ares scanned CNN's website. "It hasn't made the news yet."

Reaver waggled his brows. "The DBS always scoops everyone else."

Ares was tempted to argue that the underworld often had its finger on the pulse of bad news before Reaver's so-called *Divine Broadcasting System* did, but it wasn't worth his time. Angels didn't like to admit that demons ever got one up on them. Then again, Reaver wasn't your usual halo. The guy had spent some time as a fallen angel, and he'd worked at the demon hospital, Underworld General, for years before he'd earned his wings back. Because of that, he had a unique perspective on demons, and he even remained friendly with some of them.

Weird.

"I'm sure Thanatos is assessing the outbreaks for signs of Reseph's hand." Thanatos, as the Horseman who would become Death should his Seal break, was naturally drawn to scenes of mass casualties, just as Ares was drawn to large-scale battles. They often haunted the same scenes.

"And what are you doing?"

Ares leaned back in his chair, stretching his long legs out and crossing them at the ankles. "You know, you would be a lot more helpful if you maybe—here's a novel idea—helped."

"You know the rules."

Yeah, yeah. "The rules are fucked."

"That's what I love about you warrior types," Reaver drawled. "You're so articulate."

"We don't need to be. Our swords speak louder than words."

The angel just shook his head. "Have you found the bearer of your *agimortus* yet?"

"I keep getting brief buzzes through my Seal, but by the time I follow the lead, he's disappeared again. Do you know where he is?"

"He's hidden even from me."

"You wouldn't tell me if you knew," Ares growled. "But I have his name. Does Sestiel ring a bell?"

"Sestiel?" Reaver rubbed his chin thoughtfully. "He fell a few hundred years ago. He succumbed to human temptations and neglected his duties one too many times. Last I heard, he was trying to earn his way back into Heaven."

"Who does he hang with?"

Reaver made a golden ball of light appear in his palm, bouncing it lightly. Ares hated when he did that—one slip of the Heavenly Illum, and the entire island would be engulfed in bright daylight twenty-four-seven.

"You are familiar with Tristelle?"

Ares nodded. The female Unfallen had been around for as long as Ares could remember, seemingly content to walk the line between good and evil.

"Sestiel has been trying to redeem her for decades." Reaver winked. "And no, this information isn't *helping* you, since it's common knowledge."

Excellent. Tristelle might be able to provide some clue to Sestiel's whereabouts.

His scalp prickled, and Harvester took form next to Reaver, who let the light go out as he looked her up and down. "What happened to you?"

"None of your business," she snapped, and...*okaaay.* The evil Watcher had always been testy, but her bitchiness was usually couched in sarcasm. But then, in the two thousand years she'd been a Watcher, he'd never seen her so...beat up.

Strike that. Not just beat up, but *beaten.* Her black wings, too wrecked to fold against their anchors, drooped so low that they dragged on the floor, her head hung as though her neck pained her, and Ares swore that for just a second, her eyes looked haunted. Thing was, angels healed quickly, so whatever she'd tangled with had to have been of equal or greater power—and there were very few beings in either category.

Reaver shot a tight smile at her. "Humiliated that someone finally gave you what you deserve?"

Oddly, Harvester didn't fire back. Instead, she moved toward the computer screen, still showing CNN's website. "Human governments are keeping the majority of Pestilence's handiwork quiet. Have you noticed?"

Ares had noticed. He also noticed how she was favoring her left leg. "Why are you here, anyway?" He glanced at Reaver. "That goes for you, too."

"Because I can tell you what Pestilence has been up to," Reaver said. "He's been sparking miniepidemics all over the world and killing every Unfallen he can find. I think he's frustrated that he can't locate Sestiel."

Maybe, but Reseph had never been a hothead. When Ares, Thanatos, and Limos had been rampage-furious about something, Reseph had always been the one to step in and calm them all down. Maybe turning into Pestilence had changed that, but Ares didn't think so. No, he was smarter than that. If Ares were in Reseph's place, he'd cut off Sestiel's escape routes, not waste time on petty vengeance...

"I know what he's doing. He's taking out anyone who could potentially become the *agimortus*." Ares cursed. "And he's using the pockets of epidemics to trap them."

Harvester's wings twitched. "How so?"

"The Unfallen are attracted to the suffering," Reaver mused. "Angels always are, and Unfallen are no exception. They may hope that by comforting the dying, they can earn their way back into Heaven."

Ares studied the giant world map on the wall. Pushpins marked Pestilence's known handiwork. The sucker was running out of room. "Pestilence is setting traps. It's what I'd do."

The door to the office opened, and Vulgrim, one of Ares's Ramreel demon servants, entered with a tray of iced tea, which he placed on the desk. After Vulgrim left, Reaver pinned another location on the map. "Let's just hope that Sestiel doesn't panic and do something stupid if he runs out of options to transfer."

"Stupid?"

Harvester snatched a glass off the tray the way she always did; as if she was afraid someone would take it before she got it. "The only other species that can be an *agimortus* is human."

*Son of a*—Ares shoved back from the desk. "Maybe you could have mentioned that earlier? You know, like about two thousand years earlier?" He cursed, not waiting for her or Reaver to say something idiotic like, *you know the rules.* "Humans are fragile. Easy to kill. If one of them takes on the *agimortus*—"

"That's not the main problem," Reaver said.

"Being easy to kill sounds like a big fucking problem to me. So what else is there?"

"Humans aren't meant to host it. It'll kill them. A human would, at most, have forty-eight hours to live." Harvester smiled, and it was almost a relief to see her back to her sinister self. "And FYI? Pestilence knows. Expect him to step up the killing of Unfallens so Sestiel is forced to use a human. And then watch your world crumble, Horseman."

# *Four*

⌒

Reaver stood alone outside Ares's house staring blindly at the distant olive grove, his helplessness eating at him. There were so many freaking rules when you were an angel, and Reaver was more aware of that fact than most.

He'd broken a strict Heavenly rule once, and he'd paid the price, had spent a couple of decades as a fallen angel. Then, during a near-Apocalyptic battle a couple of years ago, he'd sacrificed himself to save humanity, and he'd earned his wings back.

For a while, being fully winged and no longer scorned by his Heavenly brethren had been awesome. He was a battle angel, one of God's warriors, and he'd spent his days slaughtering demons. He'd also been assigned as the Horsemen's *good* Watcher. That had been cool, too, even if he was forced to deal with Harvester on a regular basis. Watcher was a prestigious position, and Gethel, the angel who had previously been assigned, hadn't seemed to mind being rotated out of the duty.

Reaver hadn't known why he'd been given the task, but now, with a new Apocalypse on the horizon, he was beginning to suspect that this was a test. A test to make sure he could be trusted not to break any rules no matter how dire things got for the human world.

Leaving behind the tang of the warm salt breeze, Reaver flashed to Reseph's lair in the Himalayas. It was difficult thinking of the easygoing Horseman as Pestilence now, especially when Reaver strolled through the cave and the remnants of Reseph's life: bean-bag chairs, a margarita blender, open bags of chips, and clothes strewn about the place.

Reaver wandered through the cave, seeking any evidence that Pestilence had been here recently. Hellrats the size of woodchucks scurried under his feet, their gaping mouths lined with multiple rows of needlelike teeth, their forked, black tongues flicking in the air. These were Pestilence's little spies, and they would report back to him that Reaver had been here.

But not if Reaver could help it.

Smiling grimly, Reaver made a sweeping gesture, and power sang through him, creating an invisible wave of holy fire. The rats disintegrated, their squeaky screams echoing off the walls. Holy fire was awesome. Too bad it only worked on low-level evil.

Still, as an angel, he had an arsenal of weapons at his disposal. The Horsemen did, as well, and if they could locate Deliverance, they would have two weapons in one . . . because the dagger had a use they didn't even know about. Problem was, neither he nor Harvester could reveal what they knew. To do so would be a violation of divine law. And Reaver was never going to break a rule again— even if not doing so meant an end to the world.

Gathering his thoughts, he circled the living room, trying to find a way to help Ares, Thanatos, and Limos without actually helping. They were running out of time, and he didn't need to read all the celestial, biblical, and prophetic signs to know that. He felt it in the tremor shaking his soul.

*Tremor.* Frowning, he stopped pacing, but impact shocks continued to shoot up his legs. A dense malevolence thickened the air, the ground shifted beneath him, and suddenly pebbles were raining down from the ceiling. He looked up as a massive crack tore through the rock, and then the entire cave collapsed inward. A recliner-sized boulder crashed down, slamming into Reaver's shoulder. Pain was a whitehot bolt of agony as he summoned all his concentration and flashed out of there before he was crushed and entombed for eternity inside a mountain.

Spreading his wings in the sky above the mountain range, he scanned the area, immediately zeroing in on the source of the sinister vibes...and the violent cave collapse.

Harvester.

Snarling, he dove for her, hitting her as she stood on a nearby mountain peak. She screamed as they both tumbled down the icy cliff face, hitting the bottom in a tangle of limbs and wings.

"Demon scum!" he snarled, as he wrapped his hand around her throat.

Her green eyes fired crimson, and her nails became talons that she swiped across his face. "What is your malfunction?"

He squeezed, taking satisfaction in her gasp for air.

"What, you thought I'd be happy that you tried to encase me in stone forever?"

She blinked, and for a moment, he almost thought she didn't know what he was talking about. Then she sank her claws deep into his ruined shoulder, and the pain that swept through him was enough to make him sway and loosen his grip.

She was up in an instant, her booted foot crunching into his ribs. "If I'd wanted you out of the way, you wouldn't have gotten out of there. Do you know what it's like to be crushed flat and unable to die? Oh, that's right, you don't, because even if it had happened to you, you wouldn't remember, would you?"

The bitch. He had no idea how she knew about his memory loss, but she loved needling him about how he couldn't remember his life beyond events that led to his fall. Oh, he'd *known* things about Heaven and history and people, but he couldn't remember the details of his existence before he'd met Patrice Kelley, the woman who had eventually convinced him to break such a critical rule that he'd been cast from Heaven.

Neither could anyone else. Even the Akashic records, the ultimate Heavenly database that contained the knowledge of *everything*, revealed nothing. It was as if Reaver had been erased.

"That was just a warning," Harvester continued, her voice a deep purr. She was enjoying this. "Your love of breaking rules is well known. Don't even think about finding loopholes to help the Horsemen." She smiled, flashing fangs. "See, I have some Heavenly contacts, and I'll make sure that the next time you fall, there will be no redemption. Only fire and pain."

With a delicate wave, she flashed away, leaving Reaver alone on the ice, bleeding and shaken. He couldn't afford to fall again. Doing so meant bypassing the earthbound, in-between stage and going straight to Sheoul, do not pass go, do not collect two hundred dollars.

So no, Reaver wouldn't break rules. But he would find a way to pay Harvester back. And when the Final Battle came, she would be the first demon he destroyed.

⌒

Harvester flashed herself to her opulent apartment in the Horun region of Sheoul...and screamed. Screamed until her throat went raw. Screamed until her blood slave, a huge male werewolf she called Whine, covered his ears and went to his knees.

When her voice finally went out, she took a few calming breaths, poured herself a shot of Neethul marrow wine, and downed it. The outrageously expensive liquor, made by the demon slave traders, burned like liquid fire and then sat in her belly like a lump of coal. The agony only lasted a moment, and then came the payoff, several minutes of orgasmic ecstasy so intense she had to lean on Whine as she shuddered through the pleasure.

When it was over, she sank down next to him, partly because her legs wouldn't support her, and partly because she needed to feed. Silently, because he wasn't allowed to speak unless she told him to, he tilted his head to the side, exposing his jugular. The shackles around his ankles clanked as she shifted to sink her fangs into his neck, and it occurred to her that her chains might be invisible, but she was just as much a prisoner to her fate as he was.

Frustration made her rougher than she normally would

be with Whine, and he jerked with each of her vicious pulls on his vein. But dammit, the last two days had been hell...no pun intended. Her fury—and thirst for revenge—was why she'd destroyed his cave. She'd needed to strike back, even if the blow was a minor one.

The problem? Reaver. She hadn't known the do-gooding angel was in the caves when she'd collapsed the mountain. She could have told him the truth when he'd attacked her, but he wouldn't have believed her, and worse, she'd have been left trying to explain why she'd wanted to demolish Pestilence's old residence in the first place.

And now, if Reaver didn't keep his big mouth shut, Pestilence would find out that she'd been the one to destroy his cave.

She shuddered, remembering how, after he was through with her in that Mexican villa, he'd crouched over her naked, broken body and whispered roughly in her ear.

*That was just a taste of what I will do to you next time. You answer to me now, not the other way around. Remember that. Piss me off again, and I'll rip you a new asshole and then fuck it. And that's just the foreplay.*

Oh, she hated him. Right now, she and Reaver couldn't do much more than monitor the Horsemen's activities and report back to their bosses, and anything they did do to help or any information they provided had to be cleared first by said bosses. Information such as how Ares's *agimortus* could be transferred to humans...that tidbit had been okayed for revealing just yesterday. Why, she didn't know. She'd learned long ago that she, along with most every other being in the universe, was nothing but a game piece.

Now she just had to figure out how to play. Because as

terrified as she'd been at times over the thousands of years
she'd been in Sheoul, it was nothing compared to how
afraid she was right now. Armageddon was right around
the corner, and for the first time, she wasn't sure if her life
in hell would be worse if evil lost . . . or if it won.

# *Five*

Still torqued from the conversation with Reaver and Harvester, Ares knocked on Cara's front door and waited. And waited. Just as he raised his fist to knock again, he heard footsteps, and then a muffled, "Who is it?"

"Name's, ah, Jeff." That was a common human name, wasn't it? "I wanted to check on the dog I dropped off last night." She wouldn't remember the dog, thanks to his memory deletions, but it would be interesting to see how she handled this.

Silence. More silence. Then, finally, came the metallic clicks of the multitude of locks being manipulated. The door cracked open, but only as far as the chain would allow. Those chains were ridiculous. Any normal-sized male could force the door, and Ares wasn't normal. He could break it with his pinky.

"Dog?"

*Put her at ease. Smile. Create explanations for every-*

*thing that seemed odd this morning.* "Yeah. You know, the injured dog I brought you last night."

Her eyes flared in what he suspected might be recognition. He hoped to hell not. His mind-wipes might not be as effective as Than's or Limos's—she could actually replace memories—but they still did the job. Maybe the hellhound bond had affected his ability.

"Who are you?" she asked. "You're not from around here."

"I'm thinking about moving here. Staying with cousins in town until I find a place. They told me you're a vet." He hoped he'd gotten that detail right, and that all the stuff in her office was actually hers.

"I'm not," she said with a strange hitch in her voice. "Not really."

What was that supposed to mean? He shoved his hands in his pockets and tried to look nonthreatening. Should have gone for the flip-flops. "Look, it's not my dog, so if it died, you can tell me. I just figured I'd pay you for his care and apologize for waking you and leaving him on the lawn. I didn't think you were going to open the door to a stranger in the middle of the night."

"Yes, thank you. Um... I'm afraid the dog didn't make it. I'm sorry."

"S'okay. Didn't think he would. He was bleeding pretty bad." He pulled a wad of money out of his pocket. "What do I owe you?"

Cara eyed the cash as if it were food and she was starving. Remembering the bills on her coffee table, he prepared himself for an outrageous quote. "You don't owe me anything," she sighed, surprising the shit out of him. "Thanks for coming by."

He shrugged. "I appreciate you trying." He shoved the money back in his pocket and recalled what she'd said on the phone. "Weirdest thing. I dreamed about that damned dog last night. He was in a cage, howling like he wanted to tell me something." He turned, took one step off the porch, and smiled when he heard the chain clank on the door.

"Wait. You . . . dreamed about a dog? A black dog? The dog you brought to me?"

He swung back around. "Yeah. Why?"

"Because," she said softly, "I did, too." The door creaked wider, but she still stood behind it and peeked around, as if using it as a shield. "In my dream he was in a basement. You, too?"

He widened his eyes in mock surprise. "Yeah. What else do you remember?"

Reluctance bled into her body language, the way she gripped the door so hard her knuckles turned white and worried her bottom lip. "The cage was in the center of some sort of big circle. With symbols."

Restraining glyphs to keep him from flashing out of the cage and from crying out for help from his pack. "Were there symbols on the cage, too?"

She nodded, her wet hair falling forward to conceal her cheeks. He wished she'd step out from behind the door so he could see what she was wearing. Not that it mattered. But she seemed like the jeans and sweatshirt type, and he wanted to see if he was right. That, and he'd love to know what her extremely fine ass looked like in denim.

"So we both dreamed the same thing," she mused. "What do you think it means?"

"No idea. But with any luck, we won't dream of caged

dogs again tonight." It was a lie, because he needed her to dream. At this point, she alone could lead him to Sestiel.

"That would be nice." She had a musical, soothing tone to her voice, and Ares found himself hoping she'd keep talking. "Hey, do you have a phone number where I can reach you? Um, you know, in case I have any questions about the dog or anything?"

Bullshit. She wouldn't have questions about the dog. But he'd established a connection with her, had given them common ground in the form of a mystery, and any normal human would want to solve why two complete strangers would have the exact same dream.

He covertly fished a hundred-dollar bill out of his pocket and tucked it under a business card with his cell number. Why, he wasn't sure, except that he knew she needed the money and he had plenty of it.

She finally came out from behind the door, and he allowed himself a long, slow visual ride down her body. Hell yeah, he'd been right about her clothes, and the plain gray oversized sweatshirt and well-worn jeans looked great on her. She had hips made for a good grip, thighs meant to crush a male between them, and sexy, dainty feet that would lock tight behind that male's back. He'd bet his left nut that she had sensitive ankles.

"Thanks." She took the card, but scowled at the money. "I said—"

"Take it. If you don't, I'll leave it on your porch with another hundred." He might do that anyway. And fuck, when did he become a walking, bleeding-heart charity? Maybe when he'd been sizing her up for sex and all his blood drained out of his head.

She offered him a tentative, hesitant smile that jacked

his temperature a few degrees. He'd had his mouth on those lush lips, and damn if he didn't want to do it again. It had been his first taste of a woman in forever, and he wanted more.

"Thank you." She scratched her phone number on a scrap of paper and handed it to him. He made sure his fingers brushed hers, a lingering, yet "innocent" touch that made her lips part on a gentle, startled inhalation of breath.

Her hands were so damned soft. He had no doubt she'd be soft everywhere.

"Feel free to call me anytime." He feigned a shy smile. "Maybe sometime we could go out for a drink or dinner?"

Wrong thing to say, because she skittered backward, deeper inside the house. "I, uh, I don't think that would be a good idea, but thank you."

"You married? Have a boyfriend? Girlfriend?" All good things to know, since he was going to have to get a little more involved in her life at some point, if he wanted information from her. He didn't need interference or questions from a jealous lover.

"No," she said, and the answer pleased him more than it should. "I'm just not feeling social."

He had to wonder what had happened to her to make her so reluctant to accept his offer. Granted, he was a stranger, but no female had ever resisted his advances. One of the few bennies he'd gotten from his sex demon mother was an irresistible sexual magnetism that only succubi could resist. Even human women who became violent in his presence threw themselves at him. They just did it while wanting to kill him.

Cara's resistance was trauma-related...the evidence

was in her mannerisms and speech, but mostly, it was in her eyes. What had put those tortured shadows there?

Fuck it, there was nothing Ares could do about it anyway. He started down the steps again. "If you change your mind, you have my number."

She frowned down at the card he'd given her. "Where do you live?"

"Greece." He shot her a wink, and he swore she blushed. "If you ever want to visit, I have lots of room. You'd love it. White sand, blue sea...it's so beautiful you'll swear you've been there before."

Because she had.

Cara watched Jeff saunter away, her belly fluttering madly, her palms sweating around the business card and money, but for once, it wasn't fear that made her so jittery. The man was hypnotically gorgeous...and without a doubt, he was the person kissing her in the weird dream/memory she'd had.

So even though she didn't remember him bringing the dog to her, clearly, her brain cells had taken detailed notes. You just couldn't completely forget a guy who stood well over six-and-a-half feet tall and radiated confidence, power, and sex. Oh, yes...sex. She might not have had sex in years, but she remembered it, and feminine instinct told her that one night with Jeff would be better than all other nights in her past combined.

And his smell, the masculine, spicy fragrance that had wafted from him might as well have been an aphrodisiac. Common sense told her she should be terrified, but her hormones were trying to beat her fear into submission.

A shiver of appreciation wracked her as she gazed after him, unable to tear her eyes away from his graceful, rolling gait. His tan cargo pants hugged his butt in an obscenely nice fit, and his back muscles formed a symphony of movement under his shirt. In the sunlight, his brown hair glinted with reddish highlights, and she could only imagine the number of women who had run their fingers through those messy locks while arching beneath that spectacular body.

Regret was a bitter lump in her throat that no amount of swallowing was going to clear. The hottest man she'd ever seen had asked her on a date, and she'd reacted like he'd offered to murder her. Would it really have been that bad to accept? To maybe meet him somewhere public, so she'd have her own vehicle and there would be no pressure?

As if Jeff sensed her eyes on him, he slowed, and her heart kicked into a higher gear. In an agonizingly unhurried motion, he turned his head to look over his shoulder at her, a long lock of hair falling over his forehead and one eye. Their gazes met. Tangled. Awareness washed through her in a hot, liquid rush of oh...my...God. No man had ever affected her like that, especially not from just a look.

His mouth tipped up in a cocky, sensual smile, as if he knew what she'd been thinking...and *knew* he could give it to her like she'd never had it before. Sweet baby Jesus, she nearly choked on her own tongue.

And what in the world was she doing standing in her doorway ogling a complete stranger when she needed to be...what, *not* paying bills?

Before she made an even bigger idiot of herself, she started to close the door, and then she blinked. Jeff had disappeared. She hadn't seen a car, and she hadn't even considered that he might be walking back to town, and now he was...gone.

*Chalk it up to all the other weirdness.*

Yeah, good plan, except that Jeff had accounted for almost everything. The dog, the grass stains, the blood.

But that didn't explain why she'd drunk so much vodka that she couldn't remember any of it. Or why they'd both dreamed the same thing.

Or what she'd done with the body of the dog—it had to have died, or she would have put it in one of the kennels next to the house, and they were empty.

At least the feeling that someone was watching her was no longer with her, but Cara still felt the unwelcome buzz of fear slithering over her skin. Something had happened last night to make her drink, but what? She'd never defaulted to the bottle, and if her father's death and the night of the break-in hadn't done it, nothing would.

She did her best to not think too hard about either the mystery of last night or Jeff and his incredible body as she cleaned her office. When she finished, she sank bonelessly to the couch, where the television was blaring the same old, same old. Mysterious diseases were cropping up like wildfires, water in at least four rivers and three lakes had become polluted with poisonous organisms, and six countries had declared war on each other, completely out of the blue. The United States government was trying to decide how involved it wanted to get, and the military was gearing up for possible deployment.

The world was going to hell in a handbasket, as her dad would have said, even as he packed his bags in preparation to move out with animal rescue groups to war-torn areas.

Slamming her hand down on the remote with more force than was necessary, she shut off the TV. She used to love the idiot box, had bought a top-of-the-line Sony theater system back when she still had money. And ambition. Almost everything in the house, in fact, was "the best." Her drive to succeed and never settle had been a source of pride for her.

But all of that had died two years ago, along with the intruder.

Numbly, she plodded to her bedroom, where she curled up on her bed. The moment her head hit the pillow, sleep took her.

*Help me!*

"Hal!"

Cara shook her head. Rubbed her eyes. Wondered if she should be as aware as she was that this was a dream. Once more, she was floating around the dark basement with the caged dog, but this time, everything was more familiar. She even knew the pup's name was Hal. Short for Halitosis.

*Find me.*

And again, the animal seemed to be one bark short of a dog. "I've found you."

Hal's red eyes glowed brighter, and his hackles snapped up. He looked like some prehistoric monster ready to tear right through the fabric of reality and destroy everything in his path. *Go.*

"I just got here—"

She broke off, dazzled by a bright light and the sudden appearance of a familiar blond man. When he saw her, his eyes went wide, and he lunged. His hand brushed her arm as she twisted away.

*Go! If he catches you, you will be trapped here without your body. Go through the ceiling!*

Without her body? Okay, that didn't sound good. The world blurred and her body seemed to break apart as she shot upward and passed through stone, cement, and wood, and then suddenly, she was outside in the blinding light of day, and the house she'd just come out of was behind her.

Where was she?

She had to leap out of the way of a vehicle . . . a vehicle driving on the wrong side of the road. It had an odd license plate . . . She floated a little farther down the road to a sign that said Newland Park Drive, which told her nothing.

She continued along the sidewalk, and then, as if she'd struck a wall, she couldn't go any farther. She could see beyond where she was, but she couldn't move. She could go backward, but not forward.

*Find me or we both die.*

Hal's desperate voice clanged through her head, and suddenly, she was in her house, in her bed, and not wherever she'd been in that dream. This time, she didn't sit around in confusion. She bolted out of bed and ran down the hall to her spare bedroom, where her ancient computer hummed softly. The chair squeaked as she plopped down in it, and then she was hitting Google with a vengeance.

*Newland Park Dr.* Well, that search turned up about a million results, few of which were helpful, though many popped up as being in York, England. Fingers clicking, she went to Maps, and then typed *Newland Park Dr. U.K.*

Her heart nearly stopped when a satellite map came on the screen. It was the neighborhood she'd seen. She'd never been to England in her life, but she recognized the street, the houses. Newland Park Drive was long, and she couldn't zoom in enough to pinpoint the house she'd come out of in her dream, but that was definitely the area where she'd been. She wondered if Jeff had dreamed the same thing. Maybe she should call him.

*Find me or we both die.*

She stared at the screen, her brain repeating the dream that seemed so real. It had to have been real. There was no other way she could have such explicit details about Newland Park Drive in her head.

So either she'd become psychic or she was communicating with a strange dog she didn't even remember treating.

Who had somehow gotten to England in a matter of hours.

The things that made sense mingled with the impossible, until she felt like her sanity was stretched thin enough to snap.

*Find me or we both die.*

# Six

⌒

"Tell me you know where Sestiel is." Pestilence stood on a bridge that spanned the Inferno River in the Dread region of Sheoul and stared at the scarred hellhound—one of the largest fucking hounds he'd ever seen. Drool hung in a thick rope from its gaping mouth and puddled at its feet. Disgusting.

Serving as translator was a vampire member of the Carceris—demon jailers—who kept kennels of the hounds for tracking demons. He stood perilously close to the edge of the stone bridge, no doubt prepared to leap out of the way of danger if the hound—or Pestilence—decided to not play nice. "Eater of Chaos is still seeking both Sestiel and Ares, as per your agreement."

Eater of Chaos. Stupid name for a hellhound. Not that Pestilence was going to say anything. He might hate the bastards, but he wasn't an idiot. He was still vulnerable to their bites, and he wasn't about to put himself at risk for potentially endless paralyzation and pain.

"Our agreement was that he incapacitate either Ares or Sestiel, and he's done neither."

The hellhound snarled, and beneath his enormous paws, the bridge's basalt slabs began to steam. The creatures were extremely volatile. Even the vamp inched backward.

"Chaos indicates that there's been a complication." The vamp shifted his weight a couple of times. "He and his offspring were pursuing Sestiel. The Aegis interrupted..." He frowned. "I'm not sure I'm translating this right, but I think Chaos's pup was injured, and Sestiel captured him."

"So that's how Sestiel is masking himself," Pestilence mused. "He has himself a hellhound."

"It appears so. Chaos can't sense him. But he wants Sestiel's heart between his jaws. He'll get a twofer—revenge for his offspring, and Ares's Seal broken. I think he wants to see Ares ruined as badly as you do."

Pestilence doubted that, but he'd take what he could get.

"Find Sestiel, you mangy hound," Pestilence said. "Find him, and when I kill him, we'll get your kid back."

The vamp cocked his head, listened, and nodded. "He wants what you promised him."

"Yeah, yeah, I'll let you have Ares for thirty days." Pestilence grinned. "He'll be all yours."

Pestilence couldn't think of anything worse. He'd rather spend a year being skinned alive and having his eyes gouged out over and over than spend a single hour being defiled and eaten by a pack of hellhounds. As he watched Chaos dematerialize off the bridge, Pestilence smiled. As Reseph, he'd been repulsed by torture. As Pestilence, he craved it.

He'd definitely have to hang out for the hellhound gang-bang-slash-feast at which Ares was the guest of honor.

The Temple of Lilith.

It was a temple Ares rarely visited, but he was on a hunt, and he'd been tipped off that he'd find his quarry here.

Except "he was tipped off" would be more accurately stated as, "He had killed a false angel, a species of demon that pretended to be angels in order to lead humans astray, and gathered visions from the demon's eyes."

Ares descended the steps into the secret cave buried deep in the Zagros Mountains, the sounds of chanting and sex already reaching his ears and rousing his cock. Not that it took much—the damned thing was already worked up from listening to Cara's twenty-four-hours-old voice message before he stepped in the Harrowgate to get here, and Ares was, after all, half sex demon. He was definitely not immune to the seductive energy cast off by multiple erotic acts. Hell, the temple itself was literally infused with sex, from the pornographic etchings on the walls, to the spells cast by sorcerers during orgies as the shrine was being built. Everyone who entered experienced immediate arousal that intensified with every step down into the main chamber.

This was the second temple constructed to his mother. The first, originally erected to worship Lilith as a goddess of protection, had fallen into the ruins of ancient Sumeria. Yep, she'd fooled humans for hundreds of years, soaking up their adoration, gifts, and sacrifices. She was a real piece of work, his mother.

The temple Ares was now entering recognized her for what she was: the first succubus and a seriously evil bitch.

In centuries past, people had left gifts of food at the original temple. Ironically, before Ares learned the truth about his existence, he'd gone with his human brother, Ekkad, to worship Lilith. Ekkad had asked for protection for Ares and his family. Ares had requested protection for his army, not because he didn't believe his family needed the goddess's help, but because Ares truly believed that he alone could safeguard them. Ekkad had laughed, calling Ares a soldier to his bones. Ekkad, whose own bones had been twisted from birth, leaving him crippled and in need of Ares's protection despite the fact that Ekkad had been nimble of mind and one of the brightest men Ares had ever known.

Ares's defense of Ekkad had started at an early age— Ares had been five years old when he'd begged his father to let the newborn babe live, when the man had been determined to drown the deformed infant. Ares had continued to champion his brother through the years, earning beatings when he showed too much affection, because caring for someone affected judgment.

That had proved true in the most horrific way, and not even thousands of years could scour away the pain of losing his sons and Ekkad. Ares's love had cost them their lives, and not a day went by that he didn't regret his decision to keep them close instead of sending them away.

Ares hit the main chamber in a clomp of boots that made everyone gathered around the life-size statue of Lilith turn toward him. Most of the two dozen worshippers were humans engaged in sexual acts meant as offerings to Lilith, and as he strode toward his prey, the side-effect of his presence took root. It always began with verbal insults among the humans, but would soon escalate into bloody fights. The longer he remained with the humans, the worse the fighting would become, until no one was left standing.

No doubt, his mother would be amused to see both sex and death taking place in her temple.

"Ares." Tristelle, a female Unfallen, pushed away the male human kneeling between her thighs. Less than thrilled by the rejection and feeling the effects of Ares's proximity, the human launched at another man, nailing the guy in the face with his meaty fist. Tristelle didn't seem to notice, pulling her black robe closed as she hurried toward Ares. "I've been offering to your mother for days, praying that she would bring Pestilence to heel and stop the Apocalypse in its tracks."

"For fuck's sake." Ares ran his palm over his face. "My mother *wants* the Apocalypse to start. She would have sacrificed you right here in her shrine, and her worshippers would have used your blood as lube."

Ares stepped aside as two women engaged in a catfight nearly collided with him. "Come outside or these people will tear each other apart."

"You care about these insects?"

The fact that she'd called the humans insects probably explained why she hadn't earned her way back into Heaven. Granted, they were demon worshippers, so... yeah, insects... but angels were supposed to work on the assumption that all humans were redeemable. Ares knew better.

"No." He started up the stairs. "But it's hard to talk when blood is flowing around you." Plus, his entire body quivered with the desire to do battle with a couple of the larger males, one of whom was a *ter'taceo*, a demon in human skin.

"How did you know I was here?" she asked, as they stepped out into the moonlight beneath the Iraqi sky.

"I remembered your penchant for forcing false angels to serve you. It wasn't hard to locate one who had recently been your slave." He spun around and gripped her upper arms. "You've always played for both teams . . . working to get your wings back while sucking up to Lilith in hopes of earning a place at her side should you enter Sheoul."

She gasped in outrage. "I would never. How dare you—"

"Shut up. I'm far from stupid. Now, tell me why you're really here. You don't care about the Apocalypse. Humans don't mean that much to you."

Genuine fear flashed in her eyes. "It's your brother," she admitted. "Pestilence is tearing up the Unfallen community to prevent another transfer of your *agimortus*. Many have entered Sheoul and become True Fallen so they can no longer bear the symbol and he won't destroy them. We need your mother to tell him to stop killing us."

*Tell him to stop.* As if it would be that easy. Tristelle must know that, too, and this was a Hail Mary move if he'd ever seen one. "You're wasting your time, but you're not wasting mine. Tell me where I can find Sestiel."

"I don't know—"

Ares grabbed her by the robe's lapels and slammed her against the cave entrance. "Tell me."

"He made me promise."

Ares released her. "Then I can't help you. When my brother comes to rip your heart out through your mouth, give him my regards." He opened a Harrowgate.

"Wait!" Tristelle stepped in front of him. "I can't tell you exactly where Sestiel is, but he mentioned Albion."

"*Great Britain*," he muttered. Angels were always calling locations by their ancient names...Ares had no idea why they couldn't catch up with modern times. But it couldn't be a coincidence that Cara had mentioned flying to England in the voicemail. Dammit. He wished he'd gotten her message sooner, but he'd been traipsing around the globe and Sheoul in remote locations that had made it impossible to get a cell phone signal.

"Yes, there. He has a hellhound to mask his location, but he said he can't remain with it all the time. He's been part of the movement to stop you."

Ares frowned. "Stop *me*?"

"Not you specifically. All of you." She tugged her robe more tightly around her. "A few months ago, before Reseph's Seal broke, all of you were attacked by hellhounds, were you not?"

He stiffened. "Yes."

Her gaze darted nervously around them. "Sestiel is responsible. He and a couple of other Unfallen. They sensed trouble in the fabric of the world, and when the demon, Sin, started the werewolf plague, Sestiel formed a plan to render all of you immobile. He sent the hellhounds after all of you."

"So that if our Seals broke, we wouldn't be able to wreak havoc on the world," he murmured, more to himself than to Tristelle. As much as being paralyzed by hellhounds for all eternity would have sucked, Ares had to hand it to Sestiel. It had been a good plan, and one that might have earned the ex-angel his place in Heaven had it worked. "Will he try that tack again?"

"Perhaps."

Ares ran his mind through dozens of scenarios, and

yes, now that Sestiel had a hellhound in his possession, he could use it as leverage to gain the cooperation
of the animal's pack. If so, he'd have to visit the only
summoning circle outside Sheoul that was dedicated to
hellhounds.

Looked like Easter Island would be Ares's next stop.

Battle kicked impatiently on Ares's arm. *You'll get your
fight soon enough, buddy.* "How many of you are left?"

"A dozen, maybe," she said. A *dozen*? Jesus. Fully a
hundred must have been killed or given over their souls
to Sheoul. Tristelle gazed up at him with pleading eyes.
"You said you can help?"

"I lied."

Panic drained the color out of her face. "What can
we do?"

"Pray." Ares gestured to the entrance to Lilith's
temple. "And this time, don't waste your time praying to
a demon."

---

Blood streamed in fat rivulets down Sestiel's arms and
legs. His throat had been slashed, his torso flayed open.
None of the wounds would kill him, but death was coming for him nevertheless.

The sound of hoofbeats clanged painfully inside
his head, as if someone was tapping a hammer against
his skull. Sestiel stumbled down the rock face of the
mountain he'd flashed himself to after Pestilence found
him on Easter Island. He'd hoped to find Tristelle at the
Temple of Lilith, but according to a worshipper, he'd just
missed her.

He inched along a sloping ledge, praying Pestilence

wouldn't follow, but he knew better. Pestilence had drawn blood, and his demon stallion could now track Sestiel wherever he went, even if he was clinging to the hell-hound pup in his basement.

Weakened by battle and blood loss, Sestiel lost his footing and tumbled over a cliff. He caught air, and for a lingering, weightless moment, he could pretend he still had wings. Could almost feel them stretching in a grace-ful arc behind him like phantom limbs.

But angels ousted from Heaven had their wings docked, and unless he redeemed himself, ghost feathers were all he had. There was one other way to get wings, but completing his fall by entering Sheoul, the demon realm humans called hell, had never been an option. Ses-tiel might have fallen, but his faith in the good and holy would not be shaken.

He held on to that thought as he hit the ground, the impact snapping bones and wrenching a cry of agony from his lips. He could barely breathe, but he dragged himself to a boulder and used the crevices as handholds to pull himself up.

He couldn't fail. He had to perform one final service to mankind. To his Lord.

But thanks to Pestilence and his army of minions, Ses-tiel had nearly run out of Unfallen to transfer the *agimortus* to, and now he couldn't afford the time it would take to hunt down one of the remaining few. Which left only humans as hosts. Humans, who would die within hours of receiving it.

It was possible, however, that if the human had been supernaturally enhanced, he would be stronger, last lon-ger under the *agimortus's* life-draining burden.

While he still had time, he closed his eyes and gulped

the tiny vial of blood he'd taken from the hellhound after he'd flashed into the basement where he kept the pup and saw the human female's disembodied spirit fleeing, a clear sign that she was bonded to the beast. His gut wrenched as the poison entered his belly, but awareness filtered through the nausea, hazy and distant. The human woman, Cara...he could feel her...

Light flashed before him, and the hoofbeats in his head became a raging thunder in his ears. Dressed in dull armor that creaked as his white warhorse galloped, Pestilence loosed an arrow.

Sestiel lurched to the side, but the arrow adjusted course like a guided missile and pierced him in the heart.

"You can run, but you'll just die tired." The Horseman's shout reverberated off the mountain and brought stones and clumps of dirt raining down. "That's a human military saying, but it's so appropriate, don't you think?"

Sestiel's vision swam as a blood bay stallion leaped onto the scene through a veil of light, its rider guiding the beast with nothing but pressure from his knees and muscular thighs. *Ares.* In one hand, he bore a giant wood and iron shield, and in his other fist he clutched a sword. Rage smoldered in his ebony eyes.

"Stand down, brother!" Ares's voice was a guttural roar. He swiveled his head to Sestiel. "Go. Now!"

The two stallions clashed, and Ares swung his great blade, but Sestiel didn't wait around to see what happened.

Summoning his last gasp of energy, he flashed away, offering up a silent prayer for the poor soul who was about to receive his gift.

# Seven

So this was York.

Cara had always wanted to see England, but not like this.

To finance the trip, she'd talked Dr. Happs into buying all of her veterinary equipment. Then she'd left Jeff a message that she might be on a wild goose chase, but that she was heading to England to find the source of their dreams.

Now she was wandering the walled city, having just finished dinner. It was too late to start the search for the house on Newland Park, but she wasn't ready to head back to the B&B. Instead, she decided on a little sightseeing. Which was why, when she first saw the bloody man with the arrow impaled in his chest, she snapped a picture. But as the handsome blond actor stumbled down the middle of York's famous Micklegate Street, something struck her as odd.

He looked very similar to the man she'd seen in her dream, the one who had tried to grab her when she was in the basement with Hal. Even odder, no one around her seemed to notice him. Soupy fog choked the streetlights and darkness had fallen, but it wasn't *that* dark.

Gripping her cell phone tighter, she took a step back, alarm growing as the man came closer. In an awkward but lightning-quick move, he surged forward and grasped her shirt. Fear closed in on her, suffocating and ice cold as he slapped his palm against her chest. A burning sensation nearly ripped her apart, but she couldn't scream through the pain.

Somehow, she wrenched herself away and slammed her fist into his face. As if he weighed no more than her own hundred and thirty pounds, he flew backward several yards, hit the pavement, and skidded into a light pole. She didn't ponder how easy it had been to toss him like that, nor did she wait for him to get up. Spinning around, she scrambled toward the nearest pedestrian, but . . . something was wrong. Very, very wrong.

The pedestrian wasn't moving. No one was moving. Every vehicle, every person had frozen.

In midstride.

A blinding light flashed . . . a camera? Had she wandered onto the set of a movie? Or some kind of reality TV prank? Her mind flipped through several scenarios, none of which really made sense, and then her mind went utterly blank when a massive white horse appeared from out of nowhere, its eyes blazing a reddish-orange fire. On its back was a knight, his armor streaked with black, the joints oozing blood.

For a crazy moment, Cara was glad to see him—a

knight. It meant this really was some sort of production . . . right?

Sure, the special effects were abnormally great. The blood looked real. The pain on the arrow-guy's face was spot on. The evil and cruelty in the knight's ice-blue eyes couldn't be more genuine.

And when the knight put a second arrow into the man who had grabbed her, the thud, the spray of blood . . . all so incredibly real.

"Will you die already?" The knight almost sounded bored as he nocked another arrow. His long platinum hair fell forward to conceal his expression, but dark amusement rolled off him in an oily wave Cara felt on her skin.

*Please let this be a movie set. Or a dream.*

The pincushioned man stumbled onto the sidewalk, bumping into the motionless people and scattering them like bowling pins. They fell hard, their bodies so stiff they might as well have been mannequins.

The knight released the arrow, nailing the guy in the back. Grunting, the unarmed man went down to his hands and knees, but kept crawling, leaving a trail of blood. Cara barely restrained a cry of horror.

Another horse and rider appeared from out of a giant oval of light in the center of the road. And this time, there was no vague sense of familiarity about the man sitting atop the horse. She knew exactly who it was.

*Jeff.* Her first, oddball, thought was that he'd gotten her voice message. Her second thought was that it was weird that he and his bay stallion wore some sort of leather armor, and though Cara couldn't be certain, she thought they were both even larger than the first horse and rider.

The blond horseman grinned at Jeff as his stallion reared on its hind legs. Jeff's *"No!"* rang out, but with an ear-shattering scream, the white beast came down on the arrow-pierced guy's head. Bits of bone and gore sprayed the animal's legs, a light pole, the front of some old lady's dress.

Cara cried out, but neither man seemed to notice. Jeff swung his sword at the blond, who drew a blade of his own.

Stark terror coursed through her, making her tremble as she backed away. Desperate to avoid their attention, she eased down the sidewalk. All around her, the normal world was eerily silent except for the violent sounds of battle; curses, metal striking metal, the snorts and screams of stallions drawing blood.

Cara risked a glance back, but the sight of the horses dancing in the dead man's remains as they slashed at each other with teeth and hooves curdled her stomach.

Nausea sluiced through her, bringing her to a halt in an alley between a tea shop and a bakery. Her dinner of pork pie, mash, and carrots was in serious jeopardy. Swallowing repeatedly to keep it all down, she forced her feet to move again.

Once her stomach was stable, she ran in an uncontrolled, blind sprint. She had no idea how far she'd gone when she rounded a corner and nearly bowled over a man with a walking cane. Already on edge, vision blurred by panic and unshed tears, she overcorrected, whirling into the street and slamming into a car.

The driver honked, and though Cara had nearly been turned into roadkill, she laughed. Sure, it was hysterical laughter, but *the world was moving again.*

"You all right, missy?" A middle-aged man stepped off the curb and came toward her, eyeing her with concern. Eyeing her as if the only thing wrong with the universe was her.

*Not even close.* Her smile was as shaky as her voice. "Yes. Thank you."

He nodded and continued on. Everyone continued on. As if nothing had happened. Her cell phone rang, startling her enough to jump.

It was her therapist. Perfect timing. "Larena. It's good to hear from you."

"Sorry I didn't call you back sooner. I got your message, though, and I can tell you what I think the black dog and cage mean."

"Dog and cage?" Cara's brain was still skipping like an old record, and it took a moment to translate Larena's words. "Oh, right. I asked you about the dream." Larena might be a therapist, but she'd also become a friend. A totally unconventional one, but it worked for Cara, and Larena was the only one she trusted with all her deepest and darkest.

Well, not *all.* Larena didn't know the extent of Cara's unnatural ability. People—even friends and family—had a tendency to keep you at arm's length when you were a freak.

"Are you all right? You don't sound so good."

Cara dragged her hand through her tangled hair. "I—" *just saw a man killed, two knights appeared out of thin air, and time stopped. But other than that, I'm fine!* Someone must have slipped acid into her tea at dinner. That was the only explanation. But what could explain all the other stuff that had happened at her house?

*Insanity*, a chipper voice in her head chimed in. That would explain it.

"It's nothing a hot bath won't cure. Okay, so what's up? Larena?" she prompted, when her friend hesitated.

"You said the dog was growling. That could mean you've got some sort of inner turmoil going on. You feel caged and trapped. The fact that it's a black dog suggests danger."

Danger. No kidding. Larena's words drew her sharply back into focus. She'd come here chasing a freaking *dream*, and had gotten herself into a nightmare.

A rowdy group of twenty-something men exited the pub behind Cara, and she moved aside to avoid being trampled. "What about horses? And knights fighting? Any significance to that?"

"Ah...I'm not sure. I'd have to research it," Larena said. "Maybe you should make an appointment."

One of the men bumped her, didn't acknowledge it with either a "Sorry," or a "Screw you," and Cara glared. The jerk...oh...*oh, Jesus*. She lurched backward, nearly dropping the phone.

Stubby black horns pushed up out of the man's dark hair, and he had no skin. Only exposed muscle and bone was visible in places his clothing didn't cover. Cara blinked, and the man appeared normal again, laughing with his buddies and disappearing into another pub.

"Cara? Hey, you there?"

"Yeah," she croaked. She closed her eyes, counted to three, and opened them again. Time was moving and no one looked like a demon. Life was good. "Sorry. I'm just tired. I'll call for an appointment next week."

"Do that. I'll talk to you soon."

Cara shoved the phone into her bag and got her bearings. The B&B was only a few blocks away, thank God. Drizzle had begun to fall, her head was pounding, and her nerves were shot. Time for a sleeping pill and twelve hours of shut-eye. Maybe tomorrow all of this would prove to be one big nightmare. In fact...

She clicked the photo icon on her camera to view the pictures. She wasn't sure if she hoped to see the now-dead man or not. Confirmation that the battle she'd seen had been real, or confirmation that she was crazy? Seriously, which was more preferable?

Holding her breath, she waited for the last photo she'd taken to pop onto the screen, and nearly cried with relief when the picture revealed only a street full of cars, buses, and people. No bleeding man with an arrow sticking out of his chest. No Jeff dressed like a Dark Ages warrior.

She tucked her cell in her jacket pocket, and by the time she'd walked the six blocks to the B&B Cara had convinced herself that nothing she'd seen was real, that she wasn't loony, and that she was never drinking anything she hadn't poured with her own hands again. Inside the nineteenth-century home, Cara waved to the sweet fifty-something lady who owned it and mounted the stairs to her room. It was tempting to fall into bed with her clothes on, but she managed to peel out of her jeans and sweater. Wearing nothing but her underwear—she rarely wore a bra—she dug through her suitcase for her pajamas.

Straightening, she caught sight of herself in the mirror. And screamed.

In the center of her chest, between her breasts where the arrow-pierced man had touched her, was a brand. Welted, bright crimson lines formed a shield and sword... the tip of which lay over her heart.

*It had all been real.*

---

"Damn you, brother," Ares breathed. "*Damn you.*" Ares widened his stance and raised his sword—broken off at the tip—and braced for another round of who-can-hurt-who-the-most. Fortunately, his armor and weapons had rehardened now that Ares's *agimortus* was no longer nearby. For a few tense moments, he'd been sure his sword would shatter under Reseph's blows, or worse, that his brother would land a lucky stroke that would cut through his weakened armor as if Ares were wearing nothing more protective than a Hanes wife-beater and tighty-whiteys.

Reseph grinned, revealing blood-streaked teeth. "Touchy. When's the last time you got laid? Just wait until your Seal breaks... demon females will fall at your feet in worship."

Ares gripped the sword hilt tighter. He'd known that the destruction of a Seal would be catastrophic, but he truly wasn't prepared for the evil that had been unleashed—especially not in Reseph.

"You can fight this," Ares said. "Let me take you to Reaver—"

Reseph's laughter rumbled up from deep in his chest. "The angel can't help. You know that what's done is done." He ran his tongue along the length of his blade, catching a drip of Sestiel's blood. "Being evil is way more fun than walking the boring-ass line we straddled for five thousand years."

Ares glanced down at the smashed—and now

decapitated—fallen angel on the street. Normally, only another angel could kill an angel, but the Horsemen were exceptions to the rule. Fury tripped through him as Sestiel's body began to dissolve. There would be no second chances for Sestiel—as an Unfallen, his soul couldn't return to Heaven, and instead, he'd now suffer in Sheoulgra, the demon-soul holding tank, for all eternity.

Furious as Ares was at Sestiel's fate, he kept his voice even, unwilling to give his brother the satisfaction of seeing him riled. "You must be so disappointed that you didn't break my Seal."

Reseph's eyes flashed unholy crimson. "It's only a matter of time. I'll find that human whore Sestiel transferred it to, and then you'll join me on the side of win." He swung up onto Conquest, his stallion. Battle snapped his teeth, but Conquest danced out of the way of the strike. "Because evil *will* win, Ares. Good has far too many limitations."

A portal opened, and in a whoosh of air displacement, Conquest and Pestilence were gone.

Shit.

Ares glanced around the city—York, England. He'd recognize it blindfolded. Bloody battles had been fought here over the centuries, and he'd been drawn to them all.

He inhaled the layers of odor, from the ancient stench of chamberpot sewage and slaughter house waste to the modern scents of auto fumes and Earl Grey tea. Swirling throughout was the faint funk of hellhound that had clung to Sestiel.

Automatically, Ares fingered his Seal. Sestiel had transferred the *agimortus* before he died, and Ares had no doubt it had been transferred to Cara—she had been the only human able to see what was happening, which was a side-effect of being bonded to a hellhound... but the big clue had been how his armor and weapons had returned to normal strength after she took off. But where had she gone? He wondered if she'd located her hell beast.

And if she truly understood what had happened to her.

He swung around in the direction she'd gone. All around him, the membrane separating Ares's plane from the human one began to crack as the concentration he needed to maintain the *quantamun* fragmented. Select beings like angels and the Horsemen used the supernatural plane to move amongst humans at a different frequency, a million times faster than their eyes could see. Once it collapsed, he'd be visible to the humans.

A portable Harrowgate opened, and smoky shadows billowed out, followed by Thanatos. "What happened?"

"Reseph killed Sestiel, but not before the angel transferred the *agimortus*."

"That's good news. Why so glum?"

"Because he transferred it to a human." A vision of Cara, shot through with one of Pestilence's arrows, flashed in his head. And that was a best-case scenario. "Our Watchers said the *agimortus* isn't meant to be borne by a human. It'll kill her."

Thanatos adjusted the weapons harness criss-crossing his plate armor. "What the hell was Sestiel thinking?"

Ares swallowed a curse. He'd been so busy hunting Sestiel that he'd not filled in his brother and sister on the hellhound crap. Quickly, he brought Than up to speed.

Than let out a low whistle. "Hellhounds don't bond with humans. In all our time, I've never heard of one."

"Tell the hellhound that," Ares said sourly. "You got

anything helpful, because I could use some good news."
He supposed it was good that Pestilence couldn't sense
Cara, but then, neither could Ares.

Styx tossed his head, and Than reached down to pat
the stallion's neck until he settled. "I did squeeze some
information out of another of Reseph's minions. He
hasn't located Deliverance, but he's got demons digging
up ancient burial grounds all over the world, and in a lot
of places we've already been over while seeking Limos's
*agimortus.*"

Fan-fucking-tastic. It had taken centuries to even figure out what Limos's Seal-breaker was. They'd finally
determined that somewhere in the world was a small cup
or bowl that, if drunk from, would break her Seal. They'd
never found it.

Thanatos was the lucky one—his virginity *was* the Seal.
Though if that could be called lucky...Ares shuddered.

"We're too fractured," Ares said. "We don't have the
manpower to search for Limos's *agimortus*, locate Deliverance, and protect Cara. We've got to focus."

"Cara then?"

He nodded. Even though her very presence would
weaken him, he had to find her and keep her close. "She's
the priority, but I have a way to locate her. After that, we
need to do everything within our power to protect her."
Ares exhaled on a long breath that was visible in the icy
air. "I know myself too well, Than. If she's killed and I go
evil, nothing on this earth can stop me from wiping out
every last remnant of the human race."

# *Eight*

Cara didn't sleep. She couldn't. In a daze, she'd called down to the B&B owner for an extra blanket, showered, tried to scrub the weird mark off her chest, and when that didn't work, she'd put on pajamas and tried to call Larena again, but it figured that she was unreachable.

She sat on the creaky bed in her rented room and stared at the TV. BBC was covering rivers in Africa that were running red with poisonous algae, but Cara barely heard any of it. She was too numb, her mind disconnected from her ears. The last time she'd felt like this was after the break-in.

After she'd killed the man.

The official coroner's report had cited heart attack, but she knew the truth. She'd seen a heart attack firsthand, when her father had collapsed in front of her.

God, she missed him. He'd loved her even if he'd been wary of her ability. All she'd have had to do was call, and he'd have been on the next plane out of the States.

His death, just one month before she'd moved to South Carolina, had crushed her. She'd only started to get her life back together when, four months after that, the men had broken in.

And now this. She'd finally lost her hold on reality.

Her cell phone rang, and she grabbed it off the night-stand. "Larena?"

"No."

The deep, resonant voice echoed through her ears and brought an instant surge of both relief and anxiety. "Jeff?" she whispered.

"Where are you? I need to see you."

See her? "This is going to sound crazy, but I saw you . . . or thought I saw you. Earlier. On a horse—"

"Cara, listen to me." His voice was no-nonsense, sharp, commanding, and she couldn't have put down the phone if she wanted to. "You're in danger, and I have to find you. Your message said you were in England. Where?"

She shouldn't say anything. She knew it. But at this point, she was desperate, with no one to turn to, and he was the only link she had to whatever was going on with the dog. "I'm at a B&B in York." She fumbled through the bedside drawer for the brochure and gave him the address.

"Thanks." He hung up before she could ask any more questions.

Now what? Even if he caught a plane right now, it would be late tomorrow afternoon before he could get to York. And did she truly expect any answers from him?

A knock on the door had her leaping off the bed. *Calm down, just breathe. It's just the extra blanket.*

She opened the door. And stared in disbelief.

"Jeff—"

"Ares." He stepped inside, ignoring the fact that she hadn't invited him in. It didn't escape her notice that he had to duck to avoid cracking his head on the doorframe. Or that his broad shoulders brushed the sides.

*He couldn't have gotten here that fast.* And . . . Ares?

Unless he *had* been here. On the horse.

He closed the door quietly behind him, trapping her.

"Stay where you are." She scooted around the bed, putting it between them. "Don't touch me."

Ares held up his hands in a nonthreatening gesture, but it didn't help. If he wanted to, he could have her in two strides.

"I'm not here to hurt you, Cara. I'm here to help."

"Can you wake me up? Because the only way you can help is if you wake me so this nightmare is over."

"It's not a nightmare. What you saw tonight was real."

Her hand went to her chest, where the weird mark was throbbing. "So . . . some bloody guy branded me with his palm, and then you and some other guy came out of thin air, on horseback, and fought? Time stood still? I saw people turn into monsters? You really want me to believe that?"

"It would be helpful. Sooner would be better than later."

She shook her head, even though denial was becoming something that wasn't worth the effort anymore. This was all real, and she knew it.

Ares cocked an eyebrow. "You have another explanation for the mark you now have between your breasts?"

Of course she didn't have an explanation. If an alien spaceship landed outside the window, she wouldn't have an explanation for that either.

"Who *are* you?" She took in his combat boots, black leather pants, and black AC/DC tee beneath a black leather biker jacket. "Why would you be riding a horse and wearing armor?"

"We can discuss it after I get you to safety."

"Are you mad?" She stared at him in disbelief. "I'm not going anywhere with you."

His hand sliced through the air in a silencing motion, and he stalked to the window. "Have you seen any rats?"

Her mind spun at the sudden shift of subject. "Rats?"

"Rodents that resemble large mice."

"I know what rats are," she gritted out. "Why?"

"They're spies." He peered through the curtains into the darkness. Thick fog diffused the yellow lamplight, creating an eerie glow on the street below. "Have you seen any?"

Rodent spies? The man might be hot as hell, but he was a loon. As inconspicuously as possible, Cara inched toward the door. "I didn't see any furry little James Bonds." When he leveled a flat stare at her, she added, "Yes, there were things scurrying in the shadows, but I saw a lot of weird stuff tonight." More inching.

"You won't make it."

"Won't make what?"

His voice was a curious mix of bored and amused. "You won't make it to the door."

Yeah? Well, she could try. She measured the distance, figured she could sprint the rest of the way, but she froze solid when his massive body went taut. "What is it?"

"I heard a horse."

She swallowed, remembering the scary white stallion with the malevolent ruby eyes. "A . . . bad horse?"

"Pestilence," he hissed. Wheeling around in a blur of motion, he came at her. "We're out of here."

He threw out his arm, and a strange doorway of light appeared in the center of the room. His hands clamped down on her arms, and just as an ear-shattering boom rocked the building and an explosion of heat and fire roared at them, Ares dove with her into the light.

Chased by demonic flames of infernal fire, Ares hurled himself and Cara out of the Harrowgate and into his great room.

*Shit, that was close.* Too close. His instincts should have warned him sooner than they had, but thanks to his limitations when in close proximity to the *agimortus*, he'd been hobbled like a brood mare waiting to be mounted by a randy stallion.

Heat seared his ankle, the fingers of fire nearly closing on him before the gate sealed. Ares hit the marble floor on his shoulder, rolling to take the brunt of the fall. Cara clutched him tightly, preventing her limbs from flailing and striking the hard surface.

Unlike the last time he'd had her on the ground, this time she ended up on top of him, her arms wrapped around his waist, her face buried in his neck. She smelled like flowers and vanilla, and it probably wasn't appropriate to notice, but it had been a long time since he'd had a woman's soft body wrapped up with his.

The erection that popped in his pants was even more inappropriate, especially given that they'd almost had their skin seared off like suckling pigs in one of Limos's Hawaiian barbecue pits.

*Oh, yeah, great time to throw wood, asshole.*

"This nightmare really bites," Cara muttered against his throat, and he hoped to hell she wasn't saying that because she felt his hardening cock prodding her.

Ares pushed her off him and came to his feet. She sat there in her pink flannel pajamas that were spotted with puffy white sheep. Ares hated pink. And soft, fluffy crap. It was a miracle this woman had survived even the human world—she wouldn't last five minutes in his. Though he had to give her credit for a couple of sharp comebacks and trying to sneak out of the hotel room.

He'd have had her pinned to the wall before her fingers touched the door handle.

"It's not a nightmare," he barked, and no, he didn't feel bad at all when she flinched. She needed to toughen up, and fast. "I'm not going to tell you again."

"Then maybe you could tell me what's going on." Her chin came up defiantly. Good girl. "You said you brought in the dog. You said you were visiting cousins—"

"I lied." He crouched beside her, waved his hand in front of her face, and unlocked the memories he'd buried in her brain.

She gasped, her eyes going wide as she scrambled backward. "What did you do? Oh, my God, what...who are those men in my house?" She grabbed her head, the memories hitting hard, a flood of data that would lock up even the most advanced computer.

"They were human warriors." He moved toward her, slowly, herding her in a pink, fluffy cloud toward the corner. "Demon slayers. I suspect they were tracking the hellhound you treated." He practically spat that last part, unable to believe anyone would help one of those nasty-ass things.

"That's what they kept saying. Hellhound." She peered at her bare feet, her sandy brows pulling into a frown. "Wait. The man who came out of thin air in my office. He took Hal, and later, I saw him in the dream." Her hand went to her chest. "He's the one who gave me this mark."

"His name was Sestiel. He was a fallen angel."

"F-fallen angel?" She swallowed, licked her lips, and naturally, his gaze was drawn to her mouth. She might be soft, but when it came to females, sometimes *soft* was desirable. "Why did he want a...hellhound?" She stumbled over the word, licked her lips again. He wished she'd stop doing that. "Um, Hal."

"He took the hound because proximity to them can mask a fallen angel's whereabouts." They were also an effective weapon against the Horsemen, but she didn't need to know that. "I think he was hoping he could tame it and get it to bond with him. He must not have known that it had already bonded to you."

"Bonded?"

Cold, stale hatred fisted Ares's heart. "Hellhounds are vile, evil creatures. They live to slaughter and maim, and they feel no remorse. So whatever you did to him, saved his life or something...it made him grateful." The very idea made Ares ill. He'd rather eat ghastbat guano for the rest of his life than be bonded to a grateful hellhound. "You've been dreaming about him, except they aren't dreams. Hellhounds can communicate through the bond using astral projection. You go to him while you're sleeping, but it can be dangerous, because in that dream world, angels and demons can capture you, keep you with them until your physical body dies."

Cara backed up a little more. Her eyes had gone unfocused, her brain swamped with information beyond the scope of anything she could possibly understand. "And you—you grabbed me from my house. You kidnapped me."

"I saved your life," he pointed out. "The Guardians were going to torture and kill you."

She buried her face in her hands, and then her head snapped up, her cheeks mottled with red. "You *kissed* me!"

His gaze dropped once more to her mouth, those lush lips he'd sampled. She'd tasted of mint and hellhound then, and he wondered about her flavor now. "It wasn't a kiss, human, so don't get excited."

She sputtered in outrage. "I don't know what putting your lips on someone else's mouth means for your people—whatever they are—but *humans* call that a kiss."

"Congratulations, then. You made out with a hellhound." He raked his gaze over her body, which, though hidden under oversized pajamas, was curvy. He'd never forget the unintentional strip show she'd put on before getting into the shower. "I would avoid that in the future. Hellhounds fuck what they kill. Usually while they're killing it. No telling what they'll do to someone they actually *like*."

Her mouth worked soundlessly for a moment. "You're disgusting."

He snorted. "I'm not the one who sucked face with a hellhound."

A tremor rocked her, and for a brief—very brief—moment, he experienced the tiniest bit of remorse for taunting her, and he considered armoring up to counter it. Then she shot him a glare of utter revulsion, and so much for the rare pang of conscience. "Where are we?" When he didn't reply within the two seconds she apparently allotted for an answer, she huffed. "Well?"

Impressive, how she could flip from looking as if she was going to collapse into a quivering puddle to demanding answers to her questions. "Greece. This is my house."

"You mentioned Greece when you gave me your phone number," she mused.

To her credit, she didn't freak out again. Like any competent warrior, she surveyed her surroundings, taking note of the environment, and he had no doubt she'd logged every exit. *Good girl.* When she was done, she attempted to get to her feet, but he'd caged her between his body and the wall. He stood, offered her a hand, which she ignored.

So she was skittish *and* stubborn. Talk about a frustrating combination.

She scrambled to her feet on her own and slid along the wall to put a yard of distance between them. "This is all so crazy. Demons? Hellhounds? Fallen angels? Why am I involved in this? What did I do?"

Good questions. Too bad he didn't have any good answers. "Wrong place, wrong time. When the hellhound gave you Hell's Kiss—"

"He didn't kiss me," she ground out. "He's a *dog.*"

"He's more than a dog, and at some point, he licked you on the mouth. Do you remember that?"

Frowning, she nodded slowly. "I'd just helped him. He'd been shot and hit by a car. He healed remarkably fast once I removed the bullet, though."

"Because he's a hellhound. They're hard to kill, but

The Aegis shot him with an enchanted slug. He would have died if not for you. They don't give their bond over to just anyone. You made a major impression, and he gave you his life."

"Gave me his *life*?"

"Hell's Kiss bonds your life forces. Any time you're injured, you'll draw from him and vice versa. You'll both heal with supernatural speed. The catch is that if he's injured, you'll feel the drain on your energy. The more severely he's hurt, the worse it'll be for you. It's possible that he could completely drain you to death."

She tugged down one of her sleeves that had ridden up to expose her forearm. "Aren't you the bearer of fun news."

He shrugged. "If it makes you feel any better, being bonded to a hellhound lengthens your lifespan." At least, it would if she wasn't hosting an *agimortus,* which would likely drain her faster than the hellhound's life force could recharge her. "He must have been seriously grateful, because hellhounds are immortal, but by bonding to a mortal, he lost his longevity. He'll still be hard to kill as long as you're healthy, but when you die, so will he."

She pondered that. "Are you immortal?"

"Yes. But with most immortals, there are ways to kill them—vampires will live forever unless they're exposed to sunlight, beheaded, or staked in the heart. But I'm indestructible. I can't be killed." Except by Deliverance, the dagger forged specifically to take out the Horsemen.

"Vampires are real?" Cara wrapped her arms around her midsection as though trying to hold herself together. He hadn't had the same luxury when he learned the supernatural world was real—his arms had been shackled behind his back as he watched his wife tortured and killed. "Okay, so how did my helping the...hellhound... get me involved in all of this?"

"I told you Sestiel took the hound to keep his own whereabouts hidden. He'd been targeted for assassination and needed protection."

She looked down at her feet again, which were pale even against the white marble. "Why did someone want him dead?"

Now things were going to get tricky. He gestured to the black leather three-piece sectional sofa that Limos had made him buy. Because every guy needed to seat twelve full-grown men on a freaking couch.

"Sit. I'll send for some food if you're hungry."

"I'm not hungry. I don't want to sit down." She crossed her arms over her chest in stubborn defiance. "I want to know what the hell is going on."

Ares was not accustomed to taking orders, and he made that clear with a firm, "You know what you need to for now."

"Really?" An angry flush reddened her face to her hairline. "I know *everything*? You said before we left the hotel that I was in danger. What about the people at the B&B? Did it blow up? Is that what happened? Did people die because *I'm* the one in danger?"

"Cara—"

"Tell me! I'm still on the fence about how much of this to believe, so I need some answers, and I need them now."

His feathers ruffled at her command, and okay, if she wanted it, she was going to get it, uncensored and uncut.

"Yes. Those people died because you were in danger. The B&B was engulfed in infernal fire." Which was forbidden to use in the human realm, but no one was going to police Pestilence. "Spirits straight out of hell hunted down every human within range of the heat and burned them alive while sucking the souls out of their bodies. They would have been seared from the inside out. It's a fucking hellish way to die, and worse, their souls are now trapped in hell with no hope of ever getting to Heaven." Her sea-water eyes teared up, and although he had the oddest urge to try to comfort her, he went in a direction he was far more comfortable with; drill sergeant. "Listen up, human. It sucks that you got caught up in this, but you did, and you're here. There's a lot at stake, and you're going to need to do some serious toughening up if you want to survive. A lot of people are going to die before this is over, so dry the tears and deal. Right now you're the most important human on the planet, so act like it."

"You bastard," she rasped.

"Yes, I'm a bastard. Literally. And you are the recipient of Sestiel's *agimortus*." He closed the distance between them in two strides and tore open her pajama top, flinging buttons everywhere. Cara shrieked and tried to get away, but he caught her with one hand around the back of her neck. He jabbed his finger into her chest, over the symbol there, ignoring the way it seared his skin and watered down his muscles. "This is an *agimortus*. This is something that only a fallen angel is strong enough to bear."

"Let go, you perv."

Not happening. Not until he'd drilled his point home. "Think about what I've just said, Cara. *Only* fallen angels are supposed to be marked with this, and all you can think about is your exposed hooters?" And what nice hooters they were. It took every ounce of military conditioning

Ares had not to stare. He was a bastard, but he wasn't a sicko who got off on scaring women.

Cara shoved at his shoulders. "Get your hands off me, and I'll ask the damned question you want me to ask."

Stepping back, he watched with amusement as she yanked the shirt back together, the little sheep rippling angrily on the cotton candy flannel. "Go ahead. Ask. Prove you've got some brains in that pretty little head."

"Jerk," she spat. "I'll play your game. So tell me, if only fallen angels can have this *agimorty* thing, why do I have it?"

*Smart cookie.* He'd have smiled if the answer wasn't so dire. "Because fallen angels are currently on the endangered-species list. So the only other being Sestiel could transfer it to is a human. Unfortunately, humans can only bear it for a matter of hours, but because you are bonded to the hellhound, Sestiel must have wagered that you'd have a little more stamina."

She lost a little color, but her expression remained nice and pissed off. Excellent. No wailing or vapors. "Was he right?"

"Yes, but it won't last. You're drawing on Hal's life force to stay alive. If we don't find a fallen angel to transfer the *agimortus* to, you'll both grow weaker, until eventually, he dies." Ares had to hand it to Cara, because although he saw in her eyes the exact moment what he'd said sunk in, she remained calm.

"And when he dies," she said flatly, "I do, too."

Slowly, deliberately, he reached for her, and this time she didn't protest when he tugged open her top to reveal her breasts. Between them, the brand cut starkly into her skin, the red lines raised like fresh whip lashes. "Look at it. As crimson as fresh blood." She didn't flinch as he traced the tip of his finger along the top edge of the shield. "It's going to fade as the hours pass, as you begin to die. When it's the same color as your skin, time's up. It's a stopwatch, Cara." He pressed against the very tip of the blade, watching as the flesh turned white and began to refill with blood. "And time is running out."

# Nine

~

Cara stood there like a deer in headlights, her mind spinning, her heart pounding. "I think I need to sit down after all."

Her feet were leaden as she moved over the marble floor to a thick throw rug, on top of which sat a huge coffee table designed like a chessboard. She knocked over two game pieces the size of soda cans as she sank down in an overstuffed leather chair.

"You like chess." Her voice was hollow, her observation plain moronic.

"Yes."

"You're good at it, then?" Another moronic statement. She was discussing something as mundane as chess when Ares was talking about fallen angels, demons, and her death.

He righted the pieces. "No one has ever beaten me."

"Remind me not to challenge you to a game," she muttered.

"It would be wise not to challenge me to anything." He swung toward one of the exits on the far side of the room and shouted for someone named Vulgrim.

His arrogance, while probably justified, irritated her, and she welcomed the annoyance. Anything was better than being afraid and confused. But before she could say anything, a hulking creature with ramlike horns and a broad snout stalked into the room, his hooves clacking on the floor. He—at least, she thought it was a he—wore some sort of leather tunic over chain mail that must have something else underneath it, or his thick, tan fur would have gotten pinched in the links.

She'd thought nothing could possibly freak her out more than she already was, but she assumed her best imitation of a stone statue, trying to be as invisible as possible as Ares spoke to the thing.

"My lord?" the thing rumbled.

Ares inclined his head. "Vulgrim, bring orc-water for the human. Instruct the others that she is to be given anything she wants." He slid her a meaningful glance. "Except freedom. She is to be guarded with your lives."

*Orc*-water? Surely he said *orchid*-water. Like rosewater. Only with orchids. God, she wanted to laugh like a maniac right now, because there was a monster in the room, and she was thinking about flower water. She eyed Ares and revised her thought. There were two monsters in the room.

Vulgrim bowed, wheeled around crisply on his hooved feet, and disappeared down the hall.

"What—" she cleared her throat to get rid of the humiliating hoarseness "—what was that?"

He peeled off his jacket and tossed it over the back of

the couch. "Ramreel demon. I have thirty on staff as servants and guards. They won't harm you."

Of course not. Because why would *demons* harm her? "Do all demons look like goat-things?"

He inhaled deeply, as though gathering patience to answer her questions. "There are as many species of demons as there are mammals on earth, though many appear as human as you and I. We call them *ter'taceo*. You'll be able to sense or see some of them now that you're part of this world."

She remembered the man who had come out of the pub in York, the one who had turned into a hideous creature for a few horrific seconds. Something furry darted across the room, and she forgot the pub guy. "Is...that thing behind you a demon?"

Ares swiveled around, a broad grin softening his rugged features. "Yep." He made some purring noises, and the beagle-sized thing, a miniature, roundish, bushier version of Vulgrim, sprinted over on four legs. She watched, amazed by Ares's unexpected tenderness, as he gave it an affectionate tickle. "Go home, Rath. Your father is probably worried." The little goat-thing bleated and bounced away, and Ares smiled until he turned back to her. "Vulgrim's grandson. He's only a few months old, and curious as hell. Mother is dead."

Man, she had a bazillion questions for him, but she didn't even know where to start. Maybe the reason she was here would be a good place. She settled back in the chair, and when Ares's gaze raked her boldly, she brought her knees up to her chest and arranged the ruined pajama top to keep herself covered, though at this point, she supposed it didn't matter. He'd already seen it all.

"Polite men don't ogle," she snapped, because dammit, he'd seen it, but he didn't have to drool.

"Oh, they ogle," he drawled. "They're just more subtle about it."

Whatever. "Why did you bring me here?"

He began to prowl the length of the room, his long strides eating up the floor, his severe expression frozen in concentration. "To protect you from my brother."

"Your brother? He's the one trying to kill me?"

"He was the male on the white horse, and he's not the only one who wants you dead. Half the underworld will be after you. That's why you need to be here. My brother can find the island, but few others can. He'll suspect that I brought you here, but he'll have no specifics—I've had the island cleaned of vermin and bats, and my Ramreels have hawks chasing birds out of the airspace." At what must have been a questioning look on her face, he added, "My brother can communicate with disease-carriers and use them as spies."

Eew. So that was why Ares had asked if she'd seen any rats. "Your brother sounds charming."

There was a long pause, silence that was filled only by the strike of his boots on the floor. "He used to be."

Somehow she couldn't picture the psychopath on the demon horse being *charming*. "Maybe it's time you told me exactly who you and your brother are, because frankly, I'm having a hard time processing any of this."

He shook his head. "Knowing isn't going to make it any easier."

"Is it really going to make it *harder*?"

"It's not going to be easy to believe."

"Ah...hello." She gestured in the direction the ram-horned demon had gone. "After what I've seen, you could say you're Darth Vader, and I wouldn't be surprised."

One corner of his generous mouth tipped up in a smile before settling back into a firm, forbidding line. But for that one second, she actually felt herself drawn to him the way she'd been when she'd first seen him on her porch.

"My brother's name is Reseph," he said roughly. "*Was* Reseph. He's now the being you might recognize as Pestilence, first Horseman of the Apocalypse."

Okay, she'd been wrong about not being surprised. Doing her best to not hyperventilate, she sat in stunned silence for a moment. Brother. Ares's brother was Pestilence. She finally managed to speak, but the sound was more of a croak. "And that makes you . . . ?"

"War. Second Horseman of the Apocalypse." The demon, Vulgrim, arrived with a bottle of water, which Ares brought to her. "Drink."

Numbly, she did as he bade. The cold water relieved her parched tongue, and she downed half the contents before his hand came down on hers and gently nudged the bottle away. The word "gentle" seemed odd when paired with him, but right now, all that frightening power was contained, and even the hard-cut angles in his face, the forbidding set of his mouth, had become less severe.

"Easy, female," he murmured. "You're going to shock your system."

Too late. She couldn't be much more shocked than she was right now. "It doesn't taste like flowers." Wasn't she the queen of moronic statements today. He eyed her as if she was feverishly insane and he could catch the crazy virus. "You said it was orchid water."

He frowned, silently repeated what she'd said, and then

he laughed. And wow, he was downright beautiful when he did that. "Orc-water. I had Vulgrim add an orcish herb that'll help you relax."

She should be pissed that he'd drugged her, but the orc stuff must already be working, because she just didn't care. In fact, an effervescent warmth was spreading through her veins, and her muscles grew pleasantly relaxed. "So what now?"

"We have to find your hellhound before Pestilence does. If he knows you've bonded to it, he'll torture it to kill you." He reached up to rub the back of his neck, his flexing biceps testing the limits of his T-shirt sleeves' strength. "You were in York to find the mutt, were you not? Do you know where he is?"

"Not exactly. But in one of those dreams, I saw the name of a street. Newland Park Drive."

"Then I'll start the search there. No doubt Pestilence already has his minions combing the city."

*Don't ask...don't ask...* "Why does he want to kill me? Why would the underworld want me dead?"

"Why?" Ares's voice was so deep it vibrated all the way to her insides, and oddly, she liked the sensation. "Because the underworld is full of demons." He looked down at his arm, where the horse tattoo seemed to move, as though a breeze was fluttering its mane. She recalled seeing his real stallion shift into smoke and turn into that tattoo, and yep, that was one more thing to ask him about. "Most demons who live in the human realm like things the way they are now. But the ones who are stuck in Sheoul want out, so they're joining Pestilence's cause to kill you. And Pestilence wants you dead because your death will break my Seal."

"And that's bad?"

He laughed, but this time the lack of humor in it chilled her blood, which already felt sluggish, thanks to the orc stuff. "Bad? Cara, your death will bring about the Apocalypse. Utter destruction. The end of the world as we know it. So yes, your death is bad."

"That would be a bummer." At some point, she'd grasped his hand. She should be mortified, because she was stroking his palm lightly with her fingers. But she'd also just said that her death causing an Apocalypse would be a bummer, so what the hell? "Orc-water is awesome."

One brown eyebrow shot up. "I think Vulgrim might have made it a little strong."

"Oh! Speaking of strong...the vodka. I didn't drink any vodka, did I? That night I took care of Hal and you kidnapped me."

His long fingers curled around hers, and her entire body went all liquid and warm. "I staged it after I wiped your memory. I wanted you to think you had a reason for not remembering what happened."

"Might have worked, except I don't drink. Ever." She sat forward. "Can I have more orc-water?"

His lips quirked as he pushed the bottle out of her reach. "I don't think that's a good idea."

Probably not. Especially since her eyelids were starting to feel heavy. But her insides had gone in the opposite direction. They were positively dancing, doing a jig with her hormones, which seemed to have awakened from a deep sleep since meeting Ares. "You smell really good. And you're extremely handsome. Your face is a little cruel, though." His scowl proved her point. "Your brother was scary. You're scary, too. Are you evil?"

"Not yet. But that's why we have to keep you alive, Cara. If you die, I'm going to go very, very bad."

"Like when you kissed me? That was bad."

"It wasn't a kiss. And it wasn't *bad*." He sounded so put out that she smiled.

"Your mouth was on mine." Her vision had begun to blur, but she could see his lips clearly. They were so perfect. And if she remembered right, they were also very firm, but smooth. She reached out, touched the pad of one finger to his lower lip.

His mouth parted on a harsh inhale, and something fluttered in her stomach. Maybe the orc-water. Slowly, she traced his lips with her finger, and yes, they were soft. Velvety. She wanted to feel more of them.

Somewhere in the recesses of her mind a voice screamed that this was wrong, but she was sleepy, loopy, and a little bit...horny. "I'll show you," she murmured, as she angled her body forward. "Will show you what a kiss is."

He reared back, but she caught his mouth with hers, and he locked up as if she'd hit a switch. A giggle rose up in her, but it never made it past her lips. Nope. They were too busy mashing themselves against Ares's.

She had never been the aggressor in any relationship. Had to be the orc-water. She slanted her mouth over his, the way she remembered him kissing her. His tongue had swept out, traced the seam of her lips, so she did the same.

"This," she whispered, "is what you did to me."

A needy, masculine sound rumbled in his chest, a cross between a moan and a growl, and then Ares was on her. He pressed her into the chair, his body crushing hers, his hips cradled between her spread thighs. Again, the voice deep in her skull screamed that this was a mistake, but her body was relaxed, languid, and after the hell of the last couple of days, all she wanted to do was forget.

Ares planted his fists against the armrests and pushed his upper body off Cara. *Ah, damn.* That shit was *not* cool. She'd been drugged, was drunk on orc-weed, and he'd known the instant she'd touched his mouth with her finger that he should stop her.

Instead, he'd been curious to see what she'd do. He hadn't thought she'd kiss him. And when she had...it had been the sweetest kiss he'd experienced in, well, ever. Her mouth had been hungry, her tongue slick and hot, and it had lit a fire inside him he'd thought had been long since doused.

And when her fingers dug into the back of his neck, the fire had flamed out of control. His warrior instincts had demanded that he move in, go on the offensive, and conquer. He had her under him in a heartbeat, his body hard, straining, his mouth tasting willing, sexed-up female.

Now he was covering her, his arousal pressing against her core, his chest tight with uneven breaths. And she was asleep.

*Get off her, dumbshit.*

The back of his neck prickled with the sensation of being watched, and he whipped his head around to the source. Vulgrim stood in the doorway between the dining area and the great room, his tiny, piggish eyes bright with speculation and curiosity. No doubt. Ares rarely brought females here. And when he did, they didn't spend time making out in the living room. They weren't usually drugged to unconsciousness, either.

Yeah, this looked real good.

"What?" he snapped, as he shoved off Cara. He resisted the urge to explain that this wasn't a roofie-in-the-drink thing. Ares could have any female he wanted. He didn't need to drug them, and it wasn't his servant's business, even if he *had* done it to have sex with the human.

"I see you're...busy," Vulgrim said, his usually flat voice dripping with amusement. "I'll clean up later."

"Do that. And tell Torrent to keep a better eye on Rath." Not that he minded the little furball in the house, but if Pestilence found the baby Ramreel by himself... God, Ares didn't even want to go there in his thoughts.

He scooped Cara into his arms. Her top splayed open, the ripped-off buttons and torn fabric completing the per-verted fuck-her-while-she-sleeps scenario. Excellent.

"I hear Rohypnol is even better than orc-weed, sir," Vulgrim called out as Ares carried her down the hall.

"I have a torture room in the dungeon," Ares shot back, and he was only half-kidding. Damned demon.

Problem was, the demon wasn't half as afraid of Ares as he should be, and as much as Ares wanted to regret allowing Vulgrim and family into Ares's inner circle, he couldn't. He didn't like demons, but Vulgrim was differ-ent and had been since the day Ares had rescued him from certain death as a kid.

In his arms, Cara stirred, snuggled against his chest, and wrapped her arms around his neck. A curious warmth filtered through him, something he couldn't quite identify, but it was...nice.

*There is no room for tenderness in our world. Warriors fight. They fuck. They kill. That is all.* His father's voice— the voice of the human male who had raised him—still clanged around in Ares's skull after all this time. As a toddler, Ares had been beaten for showing too much kindness toward animals and slaves. His gentle side had literally been battered out of him by the time he was ten. He'd gotten the message loud and clear. Don't get attached to anyone or anything, because possessions were easy to lose, power was fluid, and living things died easily.

No shit. He'd forgotten that lesson eventually, and his family had paid for his failure. In blood.

Cara began to snore, delicate rumblings he tried to find unattractive. Not cute. Nope, not cute at all. He told himself that over and over as he carried her to one of his five bedrooms, choosing the master suite. It had a bathroom, the biggest bed, and in the corner, a chair where he could sit and watch her if he needed to. It also sat at the edge of the cliff and boasted the best view, best sea breeze, a patio, and was nearly inaccessible from the outside.

He laid her on the mattress, had to peel her fingers off his neck, and did his best to avert his gaze from her gaping shirt as he drew a sheet over her. Okay, maybe not his *best*. Ah, hell, the effort was pathetic. He needed to get her new pajamas. Immediately.

With a soft sigh, she curled on her side and snuggled into the sheets. A twinge of jealousy pricked at him. He didn't remember ever nestling into a bed like that—it was such a human thing to do. But then, even when he'd believed he was human, he'd felt disconnected, as if he didn't belong. He'd gone through the motions of getting married, having a family, and enjoying life, but he'd always known deep down that something wasn't right. That he was meant for something bigger, and he didn't need or deserve human comforts or feelings.

He realized he'd been hovering over Cara, lost in his thoughts, his hands cradling her head because he had no pillows on the bed, his fingers stroking her smooth cheek. Hissing, he jerked away with such force that he threw himself off balance and had to catch himself on the chair before he landed on his ass. Son of a bitch. Both the stumble and the drifting thoughts were clumsy, uncharacteristic, and as much as he wanted to blame the *agimortus*... okay, yeah, he'd blame it. No way was a woman making him addled, no matter how beautiful she was.

Snapping himself back into warrior mode, he assigned guards to the patio, the roof, and within sight of each of the windows. Once he was satisfied that nothing, not even one of Pestilence's rats, could sneak into the room, he texted Limos and Thanatos. Both arrived within an hour, and he met them in the great room.

"Tell me you have the human," Thanatos said, by way of greeting.

He was dressed for battle in his demon-bone plate armor, and his boots boomed like thunderclaps as he strode across the floor. He'd pulled his pale hair back with a leather thong, but the two thin braids on either side of his temples tapped loosely against his face as he walked. In his hand was an icy can of Mountain Dew. He was addicted to the stuff.

Limos entered behind him in orange board shorts, a yellow, orange, and blue Hawaiian print tank top, and floral flip-flops. She even had a yellow flower tucked into her black hair. She was *such* a girl.

"Hey, bro." She patted Ares on the chest as she walked past him. "What's up?"

"I have the human. She's sleeping."

"Good." Than tossed back half his soda. "Are you having trouble with her?"

*More than you know.* "If you're asking if she's combative in my presence, no."

"What about the effect the *agimortus* has on you?"

Ares clenched and unclenched his fists. Of everything he'd been saddled with when he'd been cursed to be a Horseman, the loss of powers and potential weakness was the one that chafed the most. "When I fought Reseph in York, my armor and sword failed, but I haven't needed to make use of any of my skills since grabbing Cara."

*Liar.* His reflexes had been slow in the hotel, the proximity to her dulling his ability to sense impending danger. But he couldn't admit his failings, not even to his brother and sister. He could list all the logical arguments— that it wasn't his fault, that it wouldn't have happened with anyone else, yadda-yadda. But bottom line? It was humiliating.

Li shot him a skeptical look, as if she wanted to offer him supernatural Viagra for his *agimortus* issues, but wisely, she kept her trap shut. "How's she dealing? She can't be happy to suddenly be the underworld's most wanted dead."

"She's dealing about as well as she can." He moved to the wet bar near the fireplace. Tequila had a way of replacing the raw burn of shame with its own brand of fire. "For now, at least."

"Is she showing signs of weakness?" Li's violet eyes lit up as Ares ducked behind the granite counter. "Yes, please. Something fruity."

"You want an umbrella, too?" She flipped him the bird. One of these days, his sister would learn to like proper drinks, not sugary girly crap. "No weakness that I can tell yet. The bond with the hellhound is going to keep her strong for a little while. We need to find the animal, though, because if it dies, so does she. I have a place for us to start— a street in York, and we can go door to door if we have to. We also need to hunt for a fallen angel so Cara can transfer the *agimortus*, and we'll have some breathing room."

Limos sighed. "I'll go home and pack some things. You need at least one of us here to help you protect the girl."

"Good. I'll go after the mutt. Than, you hunt for an Unfallen. I'd start at the Temple of Lilith. I found Tristelle there." Ares hoped she had been stupid enough to stay.

"Done."

"I hope so. She said that there were only a dozen or so fallen angels left. They've all either been killed by Pestilence or entered Sheoul to escape his blade." When Than let out a raw curse, Ares couldn't agree more. "Any other news?"

Thanatos tossed his can into the garbage. "Reseph tried to convince one of my vamps to slip an aphrodisiac into my drink."

"Ares is quite fond of the orc-weed," Vulgrim called out from the kitchen, and yeah, there was a set of chains in the dungeon with his name on them.

Limos scowled. "What did your demon say?"

"Nothing," Ares muttered. He lobbed an ice cube at Than, who was frowning, clearly trying to puzzle out what the Ramreel was blabbing about. "Obviously, Reseph's plan didn't work?"

"I suspected he'd try to get to me through my staff, so I warned them that I had a stake waiting for anyone who betrayed me."

Li studied her alternating pink and yellow nails. "You'd better avoid the Four Horsemen pub. Apparently, Reseph stopped in and promised an eternal place at his side after the Apocalypse to anyone who could get you on your back. The females are already looking for chains that can hold you. There are even a few males who plan to get in on the action."

"Nice." Thanatos's eyes glinted like canary diamonds.

Ares splashed rum in the blender for Limos's girly drink. "Do you see now that we have to destroy him?"

"I said no." A brief flicker of shadow darkened the area around Than's feet. "We'll find another way. Reaver offered to help."

Limos rolled her eyes. "I'll believe it when I see it."

"I hear that," Than muttered. "But technically, he won't be *helping*. He suggested bringing representatives from The Aegis to meet with us."

"Meet with us? They probably want to kill us." Limos had had a nasty run-in with a group of Aegi a couple of hundred years ago, and they'd informed her that killing Horsemen would prevent the Apocalypse. Somehow, they'd known about the effects of a hellhound bite and had shot her with an arrow coated in hound saliva. They'd kept her paralyzed for a full week before Reseph rescued her, and though what they'd done to her couldn't match Ares's own experience with hellhound paralyzation, it had still taken her weeks to shake it off.

Yeah, Aegi were, technically, the good guys, but they were definitely not friends.

Ares added fresh strawberry daiquiri mix and ice to the alcohol. Yuck. "If they are still up on our vulnerability to hellhound bites, we could be walking into a trap."

"Or they could help us," Than said. "I hate to agree with Reaver, but at this point, we can't afford to turn down any offer of assistance. Besides, they might be able to help us get our hands on Deliverance before Reseph gets the dagger."

"I don't like it." Limos tapped her foot, making her flip-flop slap on the floor.

Ares considered their options, and unfortunately, they didn't have many. "We need to talk to them, but we'll do it on our terms. Than, tell Reaver we'll meet with them at your place."

"What," Limos said, "a whole freaking squad of them?"

Ares shook his head. "There are three of us, so we'll allow no more than three of them. Cara will be with us, and I can't risk her safety."

"How will they get there?"

"That's Reaver's problem." Ares flipped on the blender.

"I still think this is a mistake," Limos said, after the noise stopped.

"Li, we've been searching for your *agimortus* for thousands of years, with no success. If we haven't found it by now, we never will. But The Aegis has assets we don't. We don't have a choice. Reseph has the backing of evil now, including their resources. If he finds your *agimortus* before we do—"

"Yeah, yeah. I get it. But I don't like it."

"I don't either, but—" A scream cut Ares off.

*Cara.* He tore off down the hall, Than and Li on his heels. He burst through the double doors into the bedroom, where Cara was sitting up in bed, her eyes wild, face drawn. Her fingers clutched the sheet so tightly to her chest that her knuckles were white.

"Ares," she gasped, and then her mouth dropped open

at the sight of Than, his sword in hand, and Li, who had armored up in her Croix viper-skin samurai-style tunic and breeches. Ares had, at some point, suited up as well, and his armor creaked as he strode across the room.

"These are my siblings." Instinctively, Ares scanned every inch of the room before putting his back to the wall next to each window, where he peered out into the night. His Ramreels were standing at attention, undisturbed. "What happened?"

"Someone took Hal." Cara inhaled raggedly. "They hurt him."

Thanatos sheathed his weapon, the slice of a blade sliding into its housing cutting through the tension in the room. "Hal?"

"The hellhound she's bonded to," Ares explained, his voice as sharp as Than's sword. "Who took him?"

Cara tugged the sheet up to her neck, her gaze darting between Thanatos and Limos. "There were six of them. Five men and a woman. He didn't want to go. They jabbed him with spears...he was inside the cage and couldn't get away." A tear squeezed from her eye, and he had the absurd urge to wipe it away. It was a feeling he shouldn't experience while wearing his armor, but being this close to Cara had turned the hard leather to supple doeskin, and emotions that would normally be blocked were annoyingly close to the surface.

"Can you tell us anything about what they looked like?" Than propped himself against the dresser, getting too comfy in the bedroom for Ares's liking as he grilled Cara. "Their weapons? What they were wearing?"

Cara replied, but to Ares. "Jeans, mostly. Some were in leather. One had a crucifix and a bottle of liquid."

"Holy water," Ares muttered. "What else?"

She reached up to her throat, fingered where she'd been bleeding when Ares took her from the Guardians the other night. "They had the same weird, S-shaped things that cut me. They have blades on each end. One is gold, the other is silver."

"Stangs," Li snarled. "Aegis weapons. Fucking human scum."

"Dammit," Ares breathed. "Thanatos, talk to Reaver and set up that meeting with the Aegi *now*. We're going to get some answers, and we're going to get that damned hellhound away from them before they kill it."

Limos's amethyst eyes glittered. "They won't kill it right away. They'll experiment on it first."

"And I'll weaken while they do it." Cara's eyes lifted and clung to his until he felt as if he was drowning in them. Willingly, the way a human male could be lured to his death by a water nymph. "Isn't that right?"

"Yeah." He could sugarcoat the rest, but she already knew. And he'd never sugarcoated anything in his life. "You'll weaken until you die and trigger the end of the damned world."

*You'll weaken until you die and trigger the end of the damned world.*

Cara wondered how many times she'd have to hear that before it truly sank in that the fate of mankind rested with her.

Blindly, she reached for Ares's hand, not knowing fully why. Maybe because the guy with the pale yellow, hawklike eyes and an eyebrow piercing was staring at her and the raven-haired, violet-eyed woman had snarled about human scum, and right now Ares was the only ally she had.

If he could truly be called an ally.

She slid covert glances at the newcomers. The guy wasn't as broad in the shoulders as Ares, a little slimmer all over, and his hair was much lighter and longer, but the similarities in the commanding way they held themselves, their angular features, and their intense expressions were striking. The girl was one of those women Cara had always hated; flawless skin, long, black lashes framing stunning eyes, and drop-dead gorgeous without a touch of makeup.

"So this is your brother? And sister?" *Another Horseman And a . . . Horse*woman?

"That's Thanatos." Ares gestured to Yellow Eyes. "The female is Limos. They won't hurt you." Reaching down, he tugged the sheet up to cover her exposed chest. He shot a glance at his brother and sister. "Could we get a minute?" He sounded irritated, which was nothing new, Cara supposed.

"Yeah." Thanatos eyed her, and she suddenly felt very naked under the sheet. A growl-like noise rumbled out of his throat, and his voice went deeper. Rougher. "I need to . . . go. I'll summon Reaver."

"And I need to pack a few things if I'm going to babysit your human." Limos adjusted the flower in her hair, and with a swipe of her fingers over her throat, the armor disappeared, leaving her in shorts, flip-flops, and a Hawaiian print top.

This situation just kept getting weirder and weirder. Strangely, Cara wasn't freaked out by things that would have had her hyperventilating a couple of days ago. Just yesterday, actually.

A moment later, she and Ares were alone, and she peered around the sparsely decorated bedroom. "How did I get here? I don't remember falling asleep."

"I gave you a mild sedative."

Mild? It felt more like he'd clobbered her with a bottle of whiskey. She rubbed her eyes, but it did little to clear away the sleep-haze. She realized she was still holding his hand, but she didn't let go. In fact, she squeezed harder, needing an anchor. He stood there, looking vaguely confused, as if he wasn't sure what to do.

"Thank you."

"For what?" He tried to pull away, but she wouldn't let him. He might still be a virtual stranger to her, but he was the most familiar thing around.

"For being here." Idly, she smoothed her thumb over his. His hands were so rough, and yet, for all the times he'd manhandled her, he'd never hurt her. "Your brother and sister scare me."

"They should."

She sighed. "You really aren't very good at giving comfort, are you?"

"I'm a warrior, not a nursemaid." His tone was completely void of sympathy.

"No kidding," she mumbled. "So why do they hate me? Your brother and sister."

"They don't hate you."

"Right," she said dryly, as she studied a scar in the web between his thumb and forefinger. How odd. If he was immortal, why would he have scars? "I must have slept through the warm hugs."

Ares peeled her hand away and stepped back, flexing his fingers as though trying to rid them of her touch. "They don't trust you. You're human. Easily corrupted and brainwashed. Weak of mind and body."

Weak. The word was a spear through the heart, completely obliterating the mild annoyance at the reminder that she'd been drugged without her knowledge. She'd been weak once, but she'd spent two years building herself back up. Therapy. Weightlifting. Self-defense classes. Not that any of her training had come in handy when she'd been attacked by the demon-slayer people. Fear had taken over, and in the midst of the terror, she'd forgotten most of what she'd learned about self-defense.

Well, she remembered now.

The mark between her breasts throbbed as she swung her feet over the side of the bed and stood, not caring that her pajama top had fallen open. "I might not be some sort of biblical legend warrior guy, but I'm not completely helpless."

"Against the beings in my world, you are." His gaze raked her, pausing a little too long on her chest, and a sound broke from his lips, a whispered curse, she thought. "So you'll listen to me and do what I say."

"So that's it? You drag me to your island, drug me, shove me in a room, and hold me prisoner?"

"That about sums it up." He pivoted on his heel and started toward the door. "Go back to sleep so you can contact your hell mutt. We need to find out where The Aegis took him."

Oh, no. She would not be held against her will again. Fury and frustration at her helplessness, her situation, and Ares made something inside her snap, and she launched herself. He spun and caught her easily as she struck out, and in a heartbeat, she found herself backed into the wall, his body pinning her, one hand gripping her shoulder, the other cupping her chin so she couldn't so much as turn her head.

"I am the only thing standing between you and death," he said through clenched teeth, "so I'd be a little more grateful if I were you."

"Are you completely delusional?" She wriggled, but she might as well have been trying to move a boulder. "You want me to be grateful? Okay, how's this? I'd be grateful if you'd find someone else to transfer this...this...*agi-whatever* to. I'd have been grateful if you had protected the fallen angel who had it so he didn't *need* to give it to me. And I'd be *really* grateful if you released me." She struggled more, and this time, his big arms bucked under her struggles, and after a brief flash of surprise in his expression, his grip grew firmer.

"Listen to me carefully, Cara." His voice had gone quiet. Chillingly quiet. "Don't ever use violence against me. Violence...excites me. You do *not* want to be part of that."

His dark gaze narrowed, his jaw tightened, and for a moment, she thought she'd gone too far. After all, she didn't know anything about the Horsemen beyond what she'd seen in the movies, read in books, or heard in Bible school so many years ago, and none of it was very flattering. Her heart pounded as her anxiety level rose, and then a subtle shift in his expression made her heart pound for a different reason.

He'd softened. Even his grip had loosened, and yet, he somehow had gotten closer. The brand between her breasts drummed, and as she studied the pulsing vein in his temple, it occurred to her that the rhythm was the same as her own.

She became achingly aware of a dozen different sensations, including erotic energy radiating off him, and though the room was already warm, his weight, his heat...sent a fluid surge of lust to her very center.

And his mouth...she remembered putting her lips on him. Yes...when they'd been in the room with the ram-demon thing. They'd been talking, she'd had some water, and then...then she'd felt funny. A sudden clarity made her pulse roar in her ears.

"You said you put a sedative in the water!"

"I did."

"Then why did it make me..." Heat blasted her cheeks.

"Horny?" he finished. "Orc-weed is an aphrodisiac for some species. For others, like humans, it's a sedative. For you, apparently, it's both."

"Oh, isn't that wonderful," she snapped. "And you keep this date-rape drug handy...why?" Probably not the smartest thing to say to a man who was three times her size, and whose name was *War*, but she was tired of being a victim. Of being helpless. Helpless... "Oh, my God, you didn't—"

"No, I didn't," he said, and was it wrong to notice again how good he smelled? Like leather and horse, warm sand and rich spice. "I wouldn't have had to. You molested me on your own."

"Because you drugged me!"

He shrugged, a slow roll of one massive shoulder. "Would have happened eventually. Females always yield to me."

*Yield?* What. A. Jerk. "Female what? *Demons?*"

His thumb stroked her cheek, and she hated herself for liking it. "I prefer human females, but—" He gnashed his teeth so hard she heard the crack.

"But, what?" she pressed. "They're too smart to put up with your crap?"

"I make them combative."

"Well, gee, with your personality, I can't imagine why that would be."

Something sad flickered in his expression, but then it was gone, replaced by that ruthless cruelty again. "It's my curse. When I'm around humans, they want to fight."

She squirmed in his grip. "You think?"

His smile was both sensual and wicked. "This is normal fighting. You seem to be immune to my effect."

"Really? Because you seriously piss me off." He did other things to her, too, things he shouldn't, but it seemed that when it came to him, her body and brain were divorced.

"Yeah. Really." Amusement glittered in his eyes. "If you weren't immune, you'd be insanely pissed for no reason, and you wouldn't have any moments of rational thought."

She wasn't feeling very rational right now, that was for sure. "Am I the only human who isn't affected? Is it because of the *agimoney* thing?" The mark grew hotter, and an intense energy spread over her skin and seeped into her veins, where it seemed to circulate through her entire body.

"*Agimortus.* And yes. Though Guardians are immune as well. They wear enchanted jewelry to ease the effect. I'm the reason they started enchanting their bling in the first place."

He seemed proud of that. "Good for you." She frowned, remembering how she'd thrown Sestiel across the York street so easily. "What else does the *agitatus* do that I should know about?" Yes, she knew she was pronouncing it wrong, but she was out of her element, and she wanted to have control over something, even if it was one little word.

"Nothing."

"Is it possible that it could somehow make me stronger?"

"Why?"

"Because...I can't really explain it, but I feel like I could lift an extra hundred pounds."

His face darkened. "It's killing you, so if anything, you should be weaker."

God, how she hated that word. "Well, I'm not weaker. Now, tell me if there's another way I can get rid of it besides transferring it to an angel."

"There isn't a way."

"Do you have a computer? Books?"

He regarded her as if it was a trick question. "Why?"

"It's called research, ancient biblical legend guy. I'm not going to sit by and do nothing. Maybe there's something you've overlooked about getting rid of the *agithing* and getting unbonded to hellhounds."

One eyebrow crawled up his forehead. "On the internet?"

She sniffed. "You can Google anything." She ignored his snort. "Can you release me now?"

"I don't know." He leaned into her, and whoa...he had an erection to go with that low, husky voice. Her brain wasn't sure if she should be seriously nervous or seriously aroused, but her body had made up its mind. Heat built between her thighs, her breasts tightened, and her breath quickened. "Will you promise to do what I say? Because here's the thing. You die, the world ends. You listen to me from here on out, because you're nothing but a...a—" He scowled as if searching for the right word, and when he spoke again, his voice was little more than a snarl. "A pawn. You're nothing but a pawn in this game, and I play to win."

A pawn? A goddamned pawn? So much for the arousal. She'd concede that she needed him, and that without him, she was lost in this world. But, according to him, she was, right now, the most important human on the planet.

"I'll listen to you, but you need to treat me with a little respect. Because it doesn't sound like I'm a pawn. Sounds like I'm more of a queen." A vein in his temple began to throb, and she grew bolder, the sense of power emanating from the mark on her chest filling her with the mettle she'd lost after the break-in two years ago. Lowering her voice to a tense whisper, she nipped his earlobe. "Checkmate."

# *Ten*

For the second time in two days, third time in six months, Arik was back at The Aegis's Berlin headquarters, which normally wouldn't be a problem—Arik loved German food, beer, and women. But he hadn't had time to indulge in any of those things, and he was starting to get cranky.

Worse, in order to get in on Aegis inner workings, he'd had to swear in as an official Guardian. The organization was a little too radical, secretive, and unorganized for him—he preferred the stricter, more structured management of the military. But once it became clear that The Aegis wasn't going to budge on this, he'd handed over the only piece of jewelry he wore—his Army ring—so The Aegis could engrave it with their shield symbol and imbue it with protective magic.

He wiggled the fingers on his left hand, feeling the heft of the ring on his middle finger. Somehow it felt heavier than it had before, as if the Aegis spells that enhanced his night vision and gave him a number of other handy abilities, had added weight.

Regan greeted Arik in the antechamber, which was decked out to resemble an accounting office. Anyone who came in to deliver mail, food, or whatever thought the building belonged to a firm that kept personnel records for large corporations. The Guardian riding desk duty was from a local Aegis cell, trained to act like a secretary. She pressed a button, and one wall slid back, revealing a seemingly endless hallway lit by flickering fluorescent tubes.

Regan led Arik down the hall, past the main offices, the conference room, the labs, the stairs that led to the containment cells...aka dungeon. The Aegis didn't experiment on demons the way the R-XR did, but they did extract information from them. No doubt The Aegis was as good at intel-gathering as the R-XR was.

Finally, they arrived at a secured door that required Regan to enter a password into the keypad on the wall.

What the hell did they have in there? Arik was used to extreme security measures in the R-XR, but The Aegis seemed to rely more on magic and their own inflated sense of invincibility, so passwords inside an already secure area seemed odd.

"Kynan's inside," Regan said. "Don't touch anything."

"First time I've heard *that* from a woman," he drawled, mainly to annoy her. But it was also true.

"Asshole," she muttered, as she spun on her chunky-heeled boots and sauntered away, her long ponytail bouncing against the back of her neck.

Smiling to himself, he entered the room...which was more of a warehouse than anything. Rows of numbered shelves laden with boxes, bags, and tagged items stretched for what seemed like miles. Along the ceiling, cameras mounted at regular intervals formed a grid that no doubt covered every inch of the room, which was temperature- and humidity-controlled. To his right was a washing station and surgical gloves.

"Arik!"

Kynan raised his hand from where he sat in a recessed area that resembled a library study. Dozens of books and scrolls formed a mountain on the table where Kynan was working with a laptop computer.

"What do you guys keep in here?" Arik asked, as he pulled up a chair across from Ky.

"Ancient and religious artifacts, magical items, demonic objects…you name it." Ky cocked his thumb at another space that was crammed with bookshelves. "That's our entire history. Everything ever written about The Aegis, no matter how small the account, is there. What we know of, anyway." He sat back in his leather chair. "Heard anything from the R-XR?"

"An Australian plague is affecting sheep with a hundred percent mortality rate, and it's spreading faster than one of their wildfires. Twenty percent of the native population of Madagascar has been wiped out by some demon strain of bubonic plague. And in the Marshall Islands, everyone on Lib Island has been blinded by what the WHO suspects is a parasitic infection. The military has been deployed to four continents to suppress growing violence over the flu pandemic and to assist the UN in quarantining as many affected areas as possible. Problem is that there are too many, and dozens more pop up every day." Arik blew out a long, tired breath. "What about The Aegis? What's new with you guys?"

"Some Guardians have disappeared. We lose them every once in a while...they get killed by demons and dragged away, but we've suddenly lost two dozen within a matter of weeks, snatched right out of their homes. And tension is firing up between the born and turned wargs again. The truce I negotiated after the battle in Canada finally fell apart."

Arik studied his friend, noted the dark crescents framing his eyes. "You look like hell."

"That's because all I've been doing is research. Gem hasn't been feeling well lately, and I have to fucking be stuck in Aegis headquarters going over crap that makes no sense."

"What's wrong? Is it the baby?" Gem was about eight and a half months pregnant, and Kynan was so devoted to her that being away couldn't be easy even if, thanks to Kynan's ability to use Harrowgates, something normal humans couldn't do, he was only minutes away from her no matter where he was in the world.

"Gem's exhausted. The unrest in the underworld is creating a lot of patients for Underworld General, and she's working overtime. The baby's fine." He grinned, and the dark circles vanished. "We can't wait."

"Do you know if it's a boy or girl?"

"Nope. Like Luc and Kar, we wanted it to be a surprise."

Luc, a warg paramedic at UGH, and his mate, Kar, had delivered their baby girl just last week. "I'm guessing you're not doing up the nursery in neutral pastels?" Gem was a Goth chick, half-Soulshredder, a species of demon that made other demons piss themselves, and as far as Arik could tell, there was nothing soft about her.

"Hell, no. Gem's all about the primary colors. The

baby's room looks like someone regurgitated a box of crayons."

Arik laughed, and then sobered. "Okay, so I don't think you called me here to talk about babies."

Ky's expression got four-star-general serious. "No." He pushed the laptop at Arik. "Can you speak Silan?"

"As in, the language of Silas demons?"

"Yes. We intercepted some chatter, but we can't understand it, and we can't find anyone who speaks this particular dialect. Not even my in-laws."

"Why do you think talk between a bunch of demon mercs is important?"

"Because they were recruited by one of Pestilence's men, a former Aegi we've been watching since we kicked him out a few months ago." Kynan's gaze met Arik's. "This has to stay between you, me, and Regan. Not even the other Elders know."

"Why?"

"Because the former Aegi traitor is Valeriu's son, David."

Arik whistled, loud and long. "Val? An Elder's own son is teaming up with demons?" Arik supposed he shouldn't be surprised—David had betrayed The Aegis before. But working with Pestilence to bring about the Apocalypse... that went beyond *betrayal*.

"Yeah. Nice, huh?" Kynan rubbed his eyes with his thumb and forefinger. "We don't want to take him into custody yet. Right now, he's doing more good for us than he knows. Val's been trying to mend the relationship with him, and if he knows what David has been doing..." Kynan shook his head. "I don't know what he'll do."

"Why is he free in the first place? I thought he was a prisoner."

"Val convinced us to release him into his custody."

"Well, shit." Arik attempted to calculate the kind of damage David could do, but the mental math left him exhausted. "So what's up with the computer?"

"Hit Shift-P."

Arik did, and voices drifted out of the speaker. It was all gibberish at first, but Arik had an uncanny ability to listen to any demon language, and after only a few words, learn it. Cool, sure, but it had come via a disease he'd contracted from a demon, and sometimes he wondered if any other, less useful abilities were going to rear up.

The R-XR ran a monthly battery of tests on him, and so far there had been no alterations in his DNA, no changes in his appearance, no demonic signs of any kind at all.

"There are three of them. They're talking about eating . . . ah, man, demons are *nasty*." Arik leaned in, listening carefully. "Okay, so . . . they're supposed to be on the lookout for a human woman. Pestilence wants her dead. They think she's probably with War. Now they're going off about something . . . some great lord wants his bride." Arik separated the blah from the blah, wondered if there was a soda machine close by . . . "Oh, got it. Looks like Satan wants to settle down and have some unholy little spawns. How sweet. Lucky woman, whoever she is."

The recording got scratchy and ended.

Kynan braced his elbows on the table, his expression contemplative. "I couldn't care less about Satan's love life, but the human? We have to find out who she is and why Pestilence wants her dead. Anyone he wants dead could be our new best friend."

"This is needle-in-haystack shit. And the haystack is made of needles. On a needle planet."

"Which is why we need to find a way to neutralize the Horsemen, and I think I've found it." Ky opened one of the tattered tomes to a page he'd bookmarked. "Seems that in 1108, a group of Aegi were battling a hellhound, and losing. Two of the Horsemen—doesn't specify which—dropped by to help. Apparently, one of them yelled to the other, something about avoiding a bite. The surviving Guardian noted it because he found it odd that a Horseman would fear anything."

Arik leaned back in his chair, crossing his legs at the ankles. "So you're saying these big bad immortal Horsemen are crybabies when it comes to dog bites?"

"That's the thing...it's not the bite itself." Kynan tapped the page. "See, two hundred years later, a Guardian searching for a weapon against the Horsemen found the account of the battle and theorized about the potency of hellhound saliva. Then, in 1317, the Great Famine was at its worst, people in Europe were starving, eating their work animals, abandoning their children, engaging in cannibalism. Everyone thought the end of the world was upon them, and the third Horseman of the Apocalypse, Famine, was blamed."

"Naturally." Didn't matter if it was hundreds of years ago or just last week, humans were always blaming someone, whether it was a Horseman, the devil, or God, for natural and man-made disasters.

"The Aegis performed a ceremony to call Famine," Kynan continued. "When she arrived, they nailed her with an arrow coated in hellhound saliva, and it totally incapacitated her."

Arik developed a severe case of the uh-ohs. "What did they do with her?"

Kynan winced. "Let's just say that things were bad between The Aegis and them already, and after that? It's a wonder the Horsemen haven't wiped out every one of us." Ky's voice grew troubled. "One of the passages also indicates that they took something from her, but it's not clear what."

"Okay, so hellhound spit is our magic weapon against them? Don't suppose The Aegis has a kennel full of them."

Kynan cocked a dark eyebrow. "Hardly. But about thirty seconds before you got here, an Aegis cell in York, England, procured one."

Arik sucked in a sharp breath. "No shit? How?"

"People in a suburban neighborhood complained of howling, and police entered, found a strange black dog in a cage in the basement. The containment symbols on the cage and floor freaked them out, and when they made calls about it, The Aegis got wind, and we went in and got the hellhound pup."

"You said it's a puppy?"

"Yeah. Stroke of luck. I don't know how we'd have pulled off the transport of a full-grown one."

Abruptly, a sparkly flash of light appeared behind Kynan. Arik instinctively leaped to his feet and reached for his sidearm, but when Kynan merely sighed, Arik relaxed.

A little.

"Reaver, do you not know how to knock?"

"Angels don't knock."

"Do angels explain why they haven't been available for six months?" Kynan asked. "I've been trying to summon you."

Reaver shrugged. "Shit happens." He cast a glance

at Arik. "Heard you signed on with The Aegis. Good move—they can use you."

Arik didn't bother to ask how the angel knew he'd joined. Even if he'd wanted to ask, he couldn't. He was standing in a room with a freaking angel and utterly speechless.

"Have the Horsemen agreed to meet with us?" Kynan asked, and Reaver nodded.

"They'll see up to three Aegi, but I only want you two."

Arik finally found his voice. "Why me? There are more senior members of The Aegis, and I'm not *really* a Guardian."

"You're sworn in," Reaver replied. "And you're a member of the R-XR. The military needs to be kept up on everything. And the fact that your sister is a werewolf and your in-laws are demons might help convince them that you're not a fanatical Aegi who is out to kill them."

"Is that why you want me, too?" Kynan asked.

Reaver's sapphire eyes darkened. "I want you because you're charmed. If the Horsemen decide that killing Aegi instead of working with them is preferable, you should survive."

# *Eleven*

⌒

The hot shower—in the white marble bathroom with six shower heads and heated benches—did not help Cara feel normal at all. The reality of her situation had sunk in, but now she wasn't sure how she fit into this new actuality that was full of demons, legends, and gates of light that could take you anywhere in an instant.

Then there was the...whatever it was...happening between her and Ares. She'd kissed him. He'd kissed her back. He definitely couldn't hide his attraction to her, not when she'd felt it jabbing into her belly when he held her pinned to the wall.

So yes, there was something physical making the air between them crackle. But at times it seemed like there was more. He could be hard, a total jerk, but he'd also feather a soft touch over her skin, or allow her to cling to him when she was scared out of her wits. And the fact remained that he had saved her life and given her safe harbor. Granted, keeping her safe was in his best interests. But he could make her captivity so much more miserable.

Then there had been that fun little announcement about how violence excited him. Some twisted part of her had continued to push him, and she wasn't sure why. Maybe because if he was right, her lifespan had an expiration date that was coming up soon, and she wasn't going to go down without a fight.

Though she'd never been religious, she'd prayed for a full return of the strength she'd had before the home invasion. She'd spent two years hoping to be rid of the constant paranoia, the jumpiness, the terror that would reach up and grab her by the throat every time she heard a strange sound or someone knocked on her door.

*Be careful what you wish for.* Because, yeah, she'd finally tapped into her inner well of strength, but only because she'd been attacked, kidnapped, branded, and hunted. She wasn't sure the tradeoff was acceptable.

No, she was sure. It wasn't.

Dripping wet and with only a towel around her, she padded into the bedroom, and it dawned on her that the only thing she had to wear was pajama bottoms. *That's what you get for not planning a kidnapping better.*

Having no choice, she pawed through Ares's dresser until she found a shirt to sleep in. Because as much as she hated to admit it, he was right; she needed to find Hal. Now that her life was tied to his, it was more important than ever that she locate him and get him to safety. Still, the idea that her role in helping was to sleep pissed her off, to be frank.

She'd been sleeping for two years, doing just enough to survive, and she was sick of it. She wanted to be the person she'd been before the break-in, someone who made goals and then went after them. It was why she'd moved to South Carolina and started a holistic veterinary practice. She might have been hiding her ability, but that hadn't meant she couldn't use it as part of nature-based healing.

Frustrated, she jerked the white and red shirt over her head. The hem caught her midthigh, and the sleeves came past her elbows. Frowning, she tugged the front out to read it. Detroit Red Wings. Figured Ares was a hockey fan. A nice, violent game.

*Violence excites me.*

His words drew a shudder from her even as a forbidden thrill wove its way through her veins. She'd been a pacifist from birth, raised to believe that the pen was mightier than the sword, that physical force was a last resort and even then, there should be rules and fairness and minimal bloodshed. Her father had believed that war was *never* acceptable.

"*Better to die yourself than dirty your soul by killing another*," he used to say, and she wondered how he'd feel about the intruder she'd . . . yeah. She wondered.

"*Violence is for those who don't have the intelligence to find another way.*" Another of his favorite sayings, and one that made her smile, because her dad had never met Ares. The Horseman was far from stupid. Arrogant, brash, and oozing authority, maybe, but not stupid.

Absently, she reached up and ran her finger over the mark that had throbbed when he touched her, which was even now tingling. The tingling was different though, was more . . . urgent. It burned. What the . . . ? She peered down the inside of the neckline. The mark was even brighter than before, its raised lines pulsing angrily.

So...this couldn't be good. No, definitely not good, she thought, as a familiar odor drifted to her nose. It smelled like her veterinary office the morning she'd found it torn up.

It smelled like Hal.

A muffled growl from behind her brought every hair on her to attention. Icy terror made her clumsy as she slowly turned in an unsteady circle.

And came face to face with a rhino-sized hellhound.

---

Checkmate? She fucking *checkmated* him?

Ares paced like a tiger in a cage, steam building in his body, and not only from the frustration of Cara's getting one up on him.

She was in the bedroom with the door closed and locked, and he was in the hallway, wanting in. He'd damned near worn a hole in the stone floor, and his earlobe throbbed from her bite. It hadn't hurt, but it had left an impression all the way to his cock, which wanted the same treatment.

*Violence excites me.*

What a fucking stupid thing to say. Mainly because it was true. There was a reason for the term "bloodlust." Hell, it was Ares's middle name.

Not that he got all worked up from watching senseless violence. But being in the thick of battle, with the adrenaline pumping, the testosterone raging...nothing beat that rush.

Nothing except being chest to chest with Cara.

Shit, he'd wanted inside her. But then something extremely fucked up had happened. He'd felt as though his heart was connected via a pipeline to the *agimortus* on her chest. The sensation had been mildly erotic... until his heart had made like a gas pump, delivering fuel from his body to hers. Before his eyes, her skin developed a rosy glow, and though he could write some of it off to anger, and maybe a little arousal, he'd felt strength rising in her. She'd begun to emanate power like a damned nuclear power plant, and all the while, he'd felt himself draining.

Maybe not draining, exactly, because it hadn't been painful. Just... freaky. He'd lost his ability to sense conflict. And worse, his thoughts had gone linear, so singleminded he doubted he could strategize his way out of a shopping mall.

Footsteps approached, and he knew by the cadence that it was Thanatos. Knew by the heavy strikes that his brother was armored up.

"I visited Lilith's temple and there was no sign of Tristelle... and what the hell are you doing?"

Ares cursed, long and loud. "I'm an idiot."

"Duh." Than grinned, because yeah, he was a real barrel of laughs. "But what are you *doing*?"

"Fucked up. This is so fucked up." Ares slammed his fist into the wall and hissed through the pain. He never did shit like that, because if you ruined yourself, you couldn't fight. Sure, the bones he'd just broken would be healed in an hour, but still. "She beat me."

"Did you like it?"

"You're still not funny." Ares's jaw was clenched so tight he could barely understand his own words. "She knows how important she is, and she called me on it." Man, she'd shocked the shit out of him. Up until now, she'd been as timid as a mouse, afraid of someone saying boo to her, and suddenly, she'd sprouted some teeth.

Probably because the *agimortus* had ripped his balls out and transplanted them into her.

Thanatos laughed, and speaking of teeth, Ares wanted to knock his brother's out of his head. "It's about time someone got one up on you. And a female human at that."

"Fuck you."

"I can't have sex."

"This isn't a joke, brother." Every one of Ares's muscles twitched. "I want her."

Than arched a tawny eyebrow, the silver piercing catching the light. "Then take her."

"It isn't that simple. She can't stand me." Ares kept pacing, his gut churning, his dick aching. "But then she looks at me with..." Lust? Too strong a word. Longing? Too wimpy. But shit, he could smell her desire, and the way her body would curve into his...

Thanatos laughed again, and Ares's hands curled into fists. "You can have any demon female in the underworld just by crooking your finger, and now you want a human, but you don't know how to have her. This is good." He cocked his head and studied Ares for a second. "Do you think you want her *because* she's human? Is that the draw?"

It was a valid question. Ares hadn't been with a human woman since before he was cursed, had been forced to sate his lusts with demons who appeared human. Half-breeds were best; at least they were only part demon.

"Does it matter?"

Than's eyes narrowed, and he sobered. "This isn't a simple case of being horny, is it? You're juiced."

"Yeah." Between the arousal, the vibes of world

violence that were slamming into him, and the anger at the way his body and equipment were failing him in Cara's presence ... he was ready to blow. And not in the fun way.

"Shit."

"Yeah."

Thán braced one shoulder against the wall, his rangy body slipping into a deceptively relaxed pose. "You need to find a Monger to spend yourself on."

Ares ran both his hands through his hair. "I know." His body craved release ... from fighting, fucking, or both. The longer he went without getting it, the more danger he put people in. Even now, people in nearby towns on the mainland would be engaging in violence, their tempers out of control. The longer Ares went like this, the farther the violence would spread.

"I can stay here while you go to the Four Horsemen."

That would be the smart thing. He could find a demon female who was into the rough stuff, because right now, that was the only thing that was going to bring him down.

"Damn," he breathed. "I haven't been this bad off since we were first cursed." For about fifty years after they'd become Horsemen, Ares had been unable to control his demon half, and he'd gone on fierce rampages of killing and sex. It had been a dark time for them all, so dark that they rarely discussed it. Than never did.

"You need to go. Hook up with Saw or Flail. Or both."

Ares growled. Saw and Flail were Neethul demons, sisters named after implements of torture. The Neethul were a violent, cruel race of slavers, and though they didn't look human, they didn't look entirely demon, either. They were beautiful, with fine elven features, and Ares could handle that.

But he didn't want to. He wanted to handle Cara.

"Okay, yeah. I'd planned to go anyway. See if I can get any intel on Pestilence." He stared at the bedroom door. "I'm going to check on her first."

"That's not a good idea."

He had to. Had to convince himself that he didn't want her. Make her hate him or something. Anything to ease this insane lust. It wasn't only about his physical hungers— it was about making sure he could function. A distracted soldier was a dead soldier...but a distracted commander soon found himself in charge of nothing but an army of dead bodies. He couldn't afford to be distracted now, not when all humanity depended on him.

"I'll be fine," he insisted.

"Ares..."

"Stand down." Ares shouldered past his brother, and when Than laid a restraining hand on his biceps, Ares's temper flared even hotter. "Get your fucking hand off me."

Than decked him. Knocked him right into the wall. With a roar, Ares struck back, nailing his brother in the jaw. Blood exploded from Thanatos's mouth, and his eyes glowed furious amber, but he didn't attack.

"For fuck's sake, Ares, I'm trying to help. You're too far gone to see your own recklessness." He put his hand to the back of his mouth, stared at the wetness that came away. "You might not remember the trail of death you left behind the last time you had your head up your ass like this, but I do. I followed your roadmap of destruction like a junkie after a dealer, and fuck if I'm going to do that again."

Thanatos's words broke through Ares's haze of need, but only barely. Than's draw to death bothered him, but he couldn't help it. Large-scale death energized Than like nothing else, gave him the climax he couldn't have in any other way.

Closing his eyes, Ares took a deep, calming breath, which was about as effective as spitting on a forest fire. "Fine. I'm out of here. Tell Limos to—"

The smoky stench of evil hit him so hard his eyes watered, and he and Than spun toward the bedroom's twin doors. Ares blew through them, tearing one off the hinges. And stopped dead, his heart hammering like a fist against his rib cage.

The hellhound that had murdered his family was inches from Cara.

And its teeth were centimeters from her throat.

# *Twelve*

Hellhound breath was *foul*.

Cara had no idea why, as she was staring at razor-sharp teeth that belonged to a beast that looked ready to eat her, she could only think about its breath.

"Back toward me, Cara." Ares's command came from behind her. "Slowly."

The hound's sinister snarl told Cara exactly what he thought of that idea, and she planted her feet so firmly on the floor that she might as well have grown roots.

In her peripheral vision, she saw Ares and Thanatos prowl along opposite walls to flank the hound. With another snarl, he snapped his paw out and hooked her around the waist, his serrated claws ripping into the jersey. She cried out, more from surprise than pain, though the beast's claw tips were now digging into her skin.

"Release her." Ares's deep voice was warped with rage.

A sudden vision of herself, decapitated and disembow-
eled, the hound feeding on her corpse, flashed in her head.
She'd always possessed an empathic ability to sense an
animal's emotions, but this went beyond feelings. She was
reading the animal's thoughts, what he wanted to do to her.
Another flash went through her brain, of Ares, screaming
silently, his body mutilated, his bones shattered as a pack
of hounds fed on him. Around his neck, his Seal was broken, and across the dark space was Pestilence, smiling.

The hellhound's plans for her and for Ares kept coming. Swallowing bile, Cara fought to keep from vomiting.

The mark on her chest flared hot, and her gift, usually
buried deep, rushed to the surface. It wanted to kill, was
somehow connected to the *agimortus*, and she had a sick-
ening feeling that as powerful as her ability used to be, it
had now gone atomic.

"Release her," Ares growled, "or I swear to you, I'll
skin you alive and spend weeks making you die."

It wasn't a threat. He'd do it, and a wave of dizziness
came over her at the savagery winging through the air.
She had to do something. Anything. Her hand tingled as
her power condensed in her palm.

*Violence is for those who don't have the intelligence to
find another way.*

Right. Okay...think. She sifted through what she
knew about hellhounds...which was nothing. But she'd
saved one's life. Could she tell this beast that? She'd never
communicated with an animal before, at least, not with
words, until Hal. But that had been in her dreams. Would
it work with a hellhound she wasn't bonded to?

Tentatively, she smoothed her hand over the wiry fur
on his shoulder. "Hey, big fella. Let's calm down, okay?"

She heard the buzz of Ares's voice and the deadly rumbles in the hound's throat, but she ignored all of it to focus, praying he'd tune in to her wavelength. Almost instantly, the beast stilled, and his memories ran through her head like a movie on fast-forward. So much data downloaded into her brain that she couldn't process it, could only take in the scenes involving Pestilence, Ares, and even Hal. So much death and destruction...

A howl pierced her eardrums in a painful boom. He flung her across the room, and the floor came at her in a rush. Thanatos moved like a cat, scooping her up before she hit the tile. The sound of furniture breaking and bodies thumping against walls broke through the ringing in her ears.

Thanatos had barely set her on her feet when she twisted around to see Ares on the floor, his armor crumpled, his broken sword beneath the hellhound's hubcap-sized paw. Thanatos shoved Cara behind him and lunged for the hound, his blade coming down in an arc.

The blow would have severed the beast's head if the hound hadn't suddenly disappeared.

Thanatos tore out of the room, shouting for Vulgrim and calling for a search of the property. When Ares didn't immediately stand, Cara offered her hand to him. "Are you okay?"

He ignored her offer and exploded to his feet. He let loose a tirade in a language she didn't know as he gripped her shoulders and yanked her close. "Did he hurt you?" His voice was harsh, clipped, and Cara moderated her own in hopes of calming him.

"He wanted to at first, but no."

"How did he find me?" He released her, jamming

both hands through his hair over and over. "How the fuck did he—"

"Your brother," she murmured. "Pestilence told him how to find you. And me."

"How do you know?" His question was more of a demand, his cold gaze that of an interrogator.

"He told me. I'm not sure how, but he told me. He—his name is Chaos—wants you dead."

"I'm aware of that," he barked. "The feeling is mutual. So why didn't he kill you?"

"Because Hal is his son."

His expression turned thunderous. "He's what?"

"They were chasing Sestiel when The Aegis shot Hal. That's how he ended up at my house. I didn't get much more than that from him, but I think he'd planned to kill me . . . until he learned that his pup is bonded to me."

"Son of a bitch." Ares swept up his broken sword and hurled it against the wall. When he swung back around to her, every part of his body reflected his anger, from the way his brows punched down over flashing eyes to his clenched hands to the way his feet were spread wide in an aggressive fighting stance.

And yet, there was a sensual electricity in the air, and the longer they faced off, the more intense it became, until the air grew thick and hot, and her body flushed with sudden fever.

His gaze darkened dangerously . . . and then it dropped, traveling down her body as if mapping every curve. "You're wearing my shirt. Take it off." His voice was low, husky, little more than a rumble of thunder.

She stiffened. "Maybe I should have asked, but you were gone, and I didn't have anything else to wear."

"Take. It. Off." Ares's nostrils flared, and a muscle jumped in his jaw. "I need you naked."

Oh. A serious case of cottonmouth stole her voice. But anger gave it back. "Don't order me around. You'll get nothing from me like that."

Too late she realized she'd thrown a gauntlet, and this was not a man to back down. Her challenge lit up his eyes, and he moved toward her, big shoulders rolling with every silent step. Her heart went ballistic, and with it came a zing of excitement, a growing desire to let him do what she thought he was going to do.

*I need you naked.*

Wait. *Need.* Not *want.*

*I need you to shut up and strip.* Her attackers had said that. One of them, anyway. She could never remember which.

The *agimortus* throbbed, and though she was getting a load of that pleasant sensation she'd gotten the last time Ares was near, a suffocating tightness clamped around her chest. What if her power surfaced at the wrong time? Ares said he was immortal, unkillable, but she'd seen what her ability could do. Terror shrunk her skin.

"Stay away from me!" Blindly, she swept up a clay bowl off his dresser and heaved it. Ares was nothing but a blur as he knocked it aside with his forearm and lunged with the grace of a pouncing panther.

A scream escaped her as she scrambled backward. Her foot caught on the towel she'd dropped to the floor. She stumbled into a wooden chest, and the floor fell away beneath her. Arms closed around her and jerked her up just before her head hit the floor.

"*Ares!*" Thanatos's roar vibrated the very air, and with a snarl, Ares tucked her against his chest and whirled to face his brother, two powerful, lethal animals readying for combat.

Cara might as well have been a rag doll with the way her feet hung off the floor. The jersey had ridden up uncomfortably high, allowing her bare butt to feel the impressive bulge behind the fly of Ares's pants and probably exposing a lot more than she wanted anyone to see, but the two brothers were too engaged in their stare-off to notice.

"Let her go, man," Thanatos said, his voice now a soothing, silky drawl. "You need to get to the pub. Or find yourself a brutal, bloody war."

Ares's muscles twitched, his grip loosening slightly.

"That's it," Thanatos continued. "Go take care of yourself. Limos is fetching a sorcerer to lay wards around the house. No hellhound will get inside again."

There was a heartbeat of hesitation, and then Ares peeled away from her. "Sorry . . . I wouldn't have . . . fuck." His skin glistened with a fine sheen of sweat and his eyes were wild, reminding her of a trapped animal, or of one in pain, terrified, and not understanding what had happened to it. She couldn't have imagined Ares being terrified or trapped, but there was something going on inside him, a vulnerability she doubted he could name, and it bit right into her heart.

"Ares," she murmured, in the voice she used with Hal, "it's okay."

He focused on her, and gradually, the feral light in his eyes faded, darkening to a smooth ebony. At the same time, the *agimortus* buzzed more urgently, becoming a tether that compelled her toward him. It tugged on her skin, walked a line between pleasure and pain as she stepped closer to Ares. He jerked as if she'd slapped him.

"I have to go." He stalked out of the room without looking back, leaving her with Thanatos.

She wanted to go after Ares, but all she could do was breathe deeply, unable to shake the notion that they'd been skirted by a hurricane. "What...what was wrong with him?"

Thanatos's expression gave away nothing, but he stared at her with a predator's interest, and it struck her that maybe the hurricane hadn't passed. Maybe only the eye had. "His demon half was pulling his strings."

Demon half? She didn't want to know. "Why?"

His pale eyes dropped to her bare legs, and she resisted the urge to tug the jersey down. There was a tormented hunger in his gaze she didn't understand and wasn't sure she wanted to. "How much has he told you about us?"

"Pretty much nothing."

The tendons in his neck strained, making the tattoos dance. "Cover yourself." He turned away.

"Gladly." While he was examining the wall, she stepped into her pajama bottoms. "So what's the story?"

He didn't turn back around. "Short version: Our mother was a succubus demon, our father was an angel. With the exception of Limos, we were raised on Earth as humans until we learned the truth. We didn't take it very well, and our actions led to mass human casualties. As punishment, we were cursed to be the keepers of the Seals of Armageddon. And with that honor came side-effects, hints of what we will be once our Seals break."

"And Ares's side-effect is..."

"Humans get aggressive and fight in his presence. In turn, he's affected by human turmoil. When mankind is at war, or there are large-scale conflicts going on, he's drawn to them. He's compelled to fight, needing the physical release. Fight, or...because mommy dearest was a sex demon, he needs to have sex. And when it gets bad, he has a hard time controlling himself."

Didn't it figure that the thing she feared and hated the most was violence, and the Horseman she was stuck with was violence personified. "So where did he go?"

"To find a female or a fight."

Oh. A twinge in her chest at the thought of Ares with a woman freaked her out a little. She wasn't jealous...had no right to be. So why did the image of his naked body entwined with another woman give her heartburn?

*Change the subject.* Fast. "And, ah, who are you? What Horseman, I mean."

Thanatos swung around. "Death."

Cara swallowed. Audibly. "As in, the Grim Reaper?"

He snorted. "That poser. He deals with evil souls. He guides them to Sheoul-gra, which is sort of a demon holding tank, until they can be reborn. I won't be escorting souls anywhere. I'll be doing the killing that releases the souls from their bodies."

She considered that. She also noticed that she hadn't batted an eyelash at the fact that the Grim Reaper was real. "So, Ares has all those issues to handle. What is it that you have to deal with?" Besides tattoos that seemed to move in 3-D.

"That's none of your concern."

"I see." She studied Thanatos, trying to get a read on him, but the tall warrior was even harder to pin down than Ares. His face wasn't quite as cruel, his eyes not as calculating, both of which probably made him more handsome. But there was definitely a darkness in him, and she sensed that it ran so deep that no amount of excavation could uncover it all. "So it's okay to spill your brother's secrets, but not your own."

Inky storm clouds brewed in his eyes, and all around him, shadows she swore hadn't been there before writhed. The brand between her breasts flared hot, and it took everything she had to not step back. "I told you because you're going to be stuck with him, so you need to understand why he behaves the way he does. You don't need to understand me." He stalked toward the door, but halted at the threshold. "What I've told you tonight isn't for outside ears. If you tell anyone, you'll answer to me, and not as Thanatos. As Death."

A lick of fear lashed at her heart, but she met his gaze, refusing to flinch. "I can't be allowed to die."

"That's the thing about living for as long as I have and being drawn to great suffering," he said in a voice as cold as a grave. "I don't need to kill to cause misery. I excel at making people beg for death."

Ares was fucking *wired*. He sat astride Battle, his entire body cramped with tension, his panting breaths burning hot in his throat. What the fuck had just happened?

Before he'd burst into the room to find the hound about to rip Cara's throat out, he'd been crazed with lust. Then he'd been crazed with rage that had only intensified when, in Cara's presence, he'd been vulnerable to the hellhound. His armor had softened, his sword had shattered, and he'd lost his ability to predict his opponent's next move.

The hound had gotten one up on him, and if not for Thanatos...

Mother. Fuck.

Not since his "human" days before the curse had Ares felt so helpless. Oh, he'd been pretty damned helpless when he'd been paralyzed for weeks by the hellhounds, but that was different. No one had been relying on him for protection. But this time...had Thanatos not been there, Ares would have been bitten, and Cara could have been killed. She'd said the beast didn't harm her because she was bonded to his pup, but hellhounds were deceptive, not to be trusted, and he wouldn't believe any information gained from the bastard.

Especially not if he was working with Pestilence.

As Battle cantered across the island, spraying sand in his wake, Ares thought about Cara and wondered how this had gotten so complicated. The pity in her eyes when she'd asked if he was okay had snagged his trip wire, and that, combined with his utter humiliation over being spanked by the hellhound, had lit him up. Oh, and then there had been the fact that he was already running on a full tank of lust, so when he'd gotten a full frontal view of Cara wearing his hockey jersey, his control had disintegrated. Those legs. Holy shit, she was gorgeous. Fresh from the shower, her dewy skin had made his mouth water, her wet hair had made him want to run his fingers through it, and her long, toned legs had made him want to part them and park himself between them.

Something seriously primal had come over him at the way she'd been covered by his clothing, and his brain had gone caveman and started screaming, *mine*, over and over. There had been no thought after that, just a driving need to claim her.

It was a damned good thing Thanatos had interrupted,

though in truth, Cara's scream had pierced Ares's fog of lust, and he'd been about to release her when his brother barreled into the room. That had set off another fucked-up reaction, one of fierce protection...as if Than was as much a threat to Cara as the hellhound had been.

Fuck.

The danger she'd been in kept circulating in his head. He kept seeing those teeth at her throat. Those claws wrapped around her waist. She'd been terrified, but she'd also been incredibly brave. The way she'd smoothed her hand over Chaos's fur and spoken to him in a calm, soothing voice had stunned the hell out of Ares. The terror rolling off her had been incomprehensible, and yet, she'd pushed past it to save them all.

In all his years, he'd never seen anything like it. Her bravery in the face of danger had been something to behold, and the biggest turn-on of his life. She might not know it, might not *want* to know it, but hers was the soul of a warrior. Oh, it was still leashed, suppressed by the weight of polite society, morals, and probably her upbringing. The problem, he knew, would be that when her inner warrior was loosed, it could prove to be dangerous, destructive, and uncontrollable. He spurred Battle past the vineyard and toward the southern end of the island. The stallion threw his head, jerking the reins so violently they nearly flew out of Ares's hands. Talk about uncontrollable. The horse was agitated, sensing Ares's mood.

Ahead, the Harrowgate loomed between two ancient stone pillars. Battle pranced inside, and the dark room expanded to allow for their size. As the shimmering veil solidified, two maps appeared on the obsidian walls; one of Earth, and one of Sheoul. Ares tapped the Sheoul map, and it instantly expanded into a dozen levels. He fingered the third level from the top, outlined in blue light, then kept tapping as the maps rotated and grew more focused until he finally located the Harrowgate that opened up about a hundred yards from the Four Horsemen pub.

Battle leaped out and onto the squishy ground. Ares let the stallion have his head, and Battle, who knew exactly where they were going, took off at a dead run. This was why he'd chosen to use a stationary gate instead of a summoned one—the horse needed to let out some energy, and so did Ares.

Battle's hooves pounded the ground with massive force, sending powerful shocks up his legs and shoulders, and into Ares's body. Ares loved this, the rush of the charge, and the only way it could be better was if he was charging into a bloody fray.

Dammit, Cara had worked him into a frenzy, and now his blood pumped hotly through his veins, his adrenaline felt like nettles in his muscles, and his vision sharpened as his body primed for a challenge. The Neethul females would give him a fight, blood would be drawn, and teeth would find flesh.

A shiver of desire went through him. Would Cara give him all that? When he was at his most jacked up, would she give him the battle he craved? Images of him taking her against a wall, on the rocky cliffs, in the temple ruins that littered his island sifted through his mind. In some of them, she was scratching, clawing, biting, even as she screamed with pleasure. In others, she was caressing his shoulders, kneading his muscles, kissing her way down his body.

What would that be like? There'd been no tenderness

in any sex he'd had since his wife died. Even with Nera, it hadn't been a love match. There'd been passion, but no true tenderness. So why the hell was he picturing all the gentle crap with Cara?

With a nasty snarl, he reined Battle to a halt in front of the tavern. He didn't bother to call the stallion to him. Right now, they were both too worked up, and the writhing marking would only distract and infuriate him. He flung open the door ... and walked into the biggest crowd of females he'd ever seen hanging around the pub.

Immediately, he was surrounded, had hands, paws, and hooves all over him. He didn't like it. In fact, he nearly turned around and got the hell out of there. But there was a malevolent tang in the air that made his scalp and his skin crawl. Something was off. Very, very off.

He captured the closest female, a slinky, humanoid succubus, by the arm. "What's going on?"

"Pestilence is here." The succubus's pupils dilated and constricted like a cat's. "He's hotter than ever, now that he's got that evil aura."

Ares's breath hissed through his teeth. "Where?"

The female rubbed against him, a purr rumbling in her throat. "Out back with Saw and Flail."

Ares scanned the room, focused on the back door, and bellowed, "Make way!"

Instantly, the demons backed away from him, and as he stalked toward the rear of the pub, they scattered like fish before a shark. As he reached for the door, he paused. The Sora female, Cetya, was sitting on a bench, head bowed, shoulders slumped, her normally bright red skin washed out to a grayish brick color. And her tail ... what the fuck? It was in a knot.

"Hey." He hooked her chin with a finger and tipped up her face, was startled by the tears streaming down her cheeks. "What happened?"

"He's not the same," she whispered. She flicked up her tail, her pain obvious in her wince.

"Reseph—Pestilence—did that?" Ares spoke sharply, his already unstable temper wobbling.

Cetya nodded, and his temple throbbed with rising fury. Reseph had never been sadistic. Even when his demon side surfaced, which was rare, women had never been the targets of his rampages.

"Go to Underworld General. They'll fix your tail—"

"My sister worked there," she said numbly. "She died."

"I know you miss Ciska, but you need to go or your tail will die. And stay away from my brother from now on."

He slammed out of the tavern and into a black forest partly concealed in reddish mist. Silently, Ares drew his sword and moved through the dense foliage and fog.

He smelled blood long before he reached the scene, but he was still startled when he stepped into the clearing. Flail lay lifeless on the ground, her nude form nearly unrecognizable and her throat mangled all the way to her spine. Reseph, his naked body shot through with black veins, held Saw against a tree, his fangs in her throat. Blood covered both of them, and though most of it appeared to belong to the demons, Reseph bore his own fair share of injuries.

The females had fought back.

"You sick fuck," Ares growled.

Reseph swung around, fangs still buried in Saw's neck. His eyes glowed evil crimson, and with a smile, he tore out the demon's throat with his teeth. He dropped her corpse to the ground and stalked toward Ares. His dripping fingers flickered over the glyph on his throat, and plate armor suited his body. The armor, crafted by trolls, was practically impenetrable, self-repairing, and had to be given blood to keep it functional. No doubt it had been well-fed lately.

"War. Why so appalled? You act like you've never killed a female—"

"I've never had fun doing it," he roared.

"You will. When you've turned, we'll party. Thanatos can feed on our leavings." Reseph licked his lips, catching the stream of blood in the corner. "Did your buddy find you?"

A hot breeze ruffled the thorny leaves in the trees and brought the scent of death to Ares's nostrils. "If you mean the hellhound, yeah. You gave good directions."

"He has a name, you know. Eater of Chaos. Or Chaos Eater. Something like that. Nice dog. Don't know why you two have been fighting for so long." Reseph grinned. "Oh, right. He ate your best friends, your beloved brother, and your sons. Tough break."

"I can't believe you went there," Ares ground out. "I can't believe you allied with him—"

"And I enjoyed doing it."

"You know what I'm going to enjoy?" Ares raised his sword. "Opening you from crotch to chin."

Reseph halted two yards away. "Think hard about that, bro. Because you're the one who is going to take a beating. And after I pound you to a quivering pudding of organs and bone, I'm going after the human." His grin was all fang. "I hope she doesn't die *too* quickly."

The image of Cara being subjected to what Ares had

seen when he entered the clearing was like Drano in the brain. It burned like a mother, scoured away all rational thought. Snarling, he struck. His sword landed a glancing blow to Reseph's shoulder as his brother spun away. And then Reseph was holding his bow, and in the span of a heartbeat, he'd launched an arrow. It punched into the unprotected juncture of Ares's shoulder and throat, and pain lanced him, shooting through the top of his skull.

"Out!" Reseph launched another arrow as Conquest formed at his side.

Ares whirled out of the path of the second arrow, but it changed course and slammed into his neck next to the first one. The ground shook, and the rhythmic pound of hoofbeats was like an earthquake, and then Battle was there to take the other stallion's blows. Panting, Ares ripped the arrows from his flesh and froze at the sound of flapping wings. Hundreds of them. Thousands, maybe.

*Oh, shit.*

They descended like a cloud of locusts. Man-eating demon locusts the size of buzzards. Ghastbats dove at him and Battle, their gaping mouths full of razor-sharp teeth, their claws like needles, a bone spike on the end of each wing. In seconds, Battle was covered, screaming as they tore at him. Conquest kept striking, his hooves hacking at the other stallion and scooping out chunks of flesh.

Ares's armor shielded him, but the creatures were tearing at his face and shoving their spikes between the leather joints. Battle's hooves and teeth crushed scores of ghastbats, but there were too many.

"Give up the human, and I'll call them off," Reseph called out.

"Fuck you."

"Incest, brother?" He shrugged. "Well, hell, I've tried everything else since my Seal broke..."

Ares hurled his sword, catching Reseph in the jaw. Teeth, flesh, and blood sprayed into the air, and Ares leaped onto Battle before his brother could recover. The ghastbats bit and stung, and he was half-blind from a claw in the eye, but he managed to open a Harrowgate. It sliced a dozen of the little fucks in half, and then Battle catapulted them into it, and they came out near the entrance of his manor house.

Guards charged toward them, swords drawn to destroy the creatures that were still clinging to Ares and the stallion. Battle stumbled, and Ares swung down, relieving the horse of his weight. While the Ramreels were dispatching the ghastbats, Ares led Battle into the house via the arched entrance to his great room.

Battle limped, trailing blood and bumping into walls and furniture. Aw, fuck, the horse was blinded.

Thanatos jogged into the great room from the kitchen. "What the hell happened?"

"Our brother happened," Ares growled.

Than let out a low whistle. "Reseph did this?"

"Not Reseph. Pestilence. He's more powerful than ever, and if there was any question left in you before, I can assure you that he's no longer our brother."

Ares waited for Thanatos to argue about not giving up on Reseph, and for a heartbeat, his brother's expression was glacial, a hard challenge. And then Battle began to tremble, and with a crash, he went down.

"Shit!" Wiping blood out of his eyes, Ares sank to his knees and shouted for Vulgrim. "Get towels, water. Needle and thread."

He assessed the massive, gaping wounds through which muscle, tendon, and bone erupted. Battle looked as if he'd been tenderized by a troll's giant spiked mallet, and his pain was gutting Ares more than any blade Pestilence could wield. He was stronger than a normal horse, his supernatural connection with Ares giving him similar regenerative powers...but he *could* die if his wounds were severe enough. Limos had lost her first mount a hundred years into their curse, when a demon had sheared its head clean off. Her replacement had been a gift—one she'd been unable to refuse—and now she was stuck with a carnivorous hell stallion with a disposition that would make a hellhound seem friendly.

Behind him, Ares heard footsteps, too light to be any of the demons, and the constant vibrations that alerted him to worldwide conflicts became muted.

"Oh, my God." Cara darted toward them.

"Than, get her out of here."

She skirted Thanatos, twisting out of his reach with surprising nimbleness. "What's going on?" She kneeled beside Ares. "Dear...*Lord.*"

Ares didn't have the time or patience for this. She'd probably start crying or screaming or some crap. He also didn't need her presence draining him. "Go to the bedroom and stay there."

"I don't think so."

"You don't *think so*?" He stared incredulously. *No one* disobeyed his orders.

"I told you not to order me around." Cara rolled up the hockey jersey's sleeves in blatant defiance of his command. "I can help. I've been working with animals for years."

"Then help." Cursing irritably, he flicked his thumb over his throat and rid himself and Battle of their armor, which had softened already, and then he gripped her wrist as she reached for Battle's flank. "But he isn't your usual animal."

"Why," she muttered, "am I not surprised?"

# *Thirteen*

⌒

Palms damp with cold sweat, Cara prayed she wouldn't regret this. There was a real possibility that her gift would surface...and morph into something that killed instead of healed. Then Ares would kill *her*.

Nonchalantly, she wiped her hands on one of the rags the demons had brought.

"Do you need anything else?" Thanatos flicked his thumb over one of the many tattoos on his throat, and his armor melted away, replaced by black jeans, black shirt, and a black, long neoclassic coat that buttoned from the neck to the waist and then flared open to allow for movement. For him, apparently, black wasn't a color; it was a lifestyle. "I can raid a veterinarian's office."

Tempting as it was to send him to Dr. Happs's place to steal stuff, Cara shook her head and reached for the pile of towels. "We need to stop the bleeding."

"No kidding?" Ares applied pressure to one of the worst wounds, a massive laceration that was oozing dark blood. "You learn that in Vet Med 101?"

"Sarcasm isn't the way to get me to help."

"He's ... my horse," Ares said roughly, and she got it; he was hurting for the animal, and his fear was putting an edge on his already teetering temper.

She'd give him a pass on his less-than-polite behavior. The *agimortus* tingled, and her healing gift surfaced. Nuh-uh. No way. Concentrating, she kept it at bay ... worked so hard at it that her blood thundered in her ears and her breath burned her throat. Before, she'd been able to control it, but it seemed like the *agimortus* gave her gift a mind of its own. Her hands shook as she ran them over the stallion, probing for the worst of the damage. The horse groaned and kicked, and suddenly, blood sprayed in a geyser from his thigh.

"Shit!" Thanatos lunged to cover the gusher, but Cara beat him to it, and his hand came down on hers.

Unbidden, a blast of her healing gift ripped down her arm and into the horse. Instantly, the blood flow slowed, and before her eyes, the most minor of the injuries sealed. Than jerked away from her, and she rocked backward, as shocked as he was. Her ability had never shot through her so strongly before.

Not the healing ability, anyway. The killing ability ... she didn't want to go there.

"I ..." She sucked air, giving herself a second to gather her thoughts.

Ares's eyes narrowed, which must have hurt, given the cut that ran from the middle of his forehead to the base of his left eye. "That's why the hellhound gave you Hell's

Kiss. You *healed* him. You didn't just remove the bullet . . . you have a gift."

Thanatos pegged her with those yellow lasers. "You're a totem priestess."

"A what?"

"One who communicates with animals." Thanatos's voice was laced with what she could only call awe. "I was raised among druidic people, and totem priests and priestesses were revered. Today's humans call them animal psychics. They sometimes have the power to heal. Can you make it work with nonanimals?"

*Oh, it works with nonanimals, all right.*

Twenty-six years of buried secrets had built like steam in her chest, and now it was as if a fissure was forming at the epicenter, right over her heart. She'd denied her abilities for so long, even as she'd used them. That there was a name for what she was made it real. Personal. Throat closing up, she leaped to her feet and backed away.

"Cara?" Ares kept his hand on the horse, but his big body twisted around, his gaze tracking her.

"I don't . . . I don't know if I can control it. The *agimortus* made it stronger and less predictable." She swallowed dryly. "And it has an . . . evil side I don't understand."

Ares swore, a nasty, base curse. "I don't give a shit if it's shot out of the devil's ass. Battle is in pain and he could die. If you can help him, do it."

Battle groaned, and her heart clenched. How could she not do something? The argument with herself wasn't a new one. When she'd been a teen working in her father's veterinary practice, he'd begged her not to use her ability, for fear that the ultraconservative township would find out and brand her unfairly. And he'd been right.

He'd also been afraid of it, something she knew only because she'd overheard him talking to her stepmother.

"I've killed with it." God, her stomach clenched with revulsion at those words—words she'd never spoken out loud.

"A human?" Ares smoothed his hand over Battle's shoulder.

"Yes."

"Huh." Thanatos shifted, giving her a glimpse of a wicked-looking dagger tucked into his boot. "That was rarely spoken of in my time. Anyone who used the ability to kill was shunned as being evil. In fact—"

"Thanatos..." Ares's warning tone shut his brother up. He turned to Cara. "I don't care about the human. Make your choice. Help, or go. Battle doesn't have time to wait for your mental breakdown to end."

Harsh. But Ares was right, and it was the kick in the pants Cara needed. With a nod, she went back to Battle, placing herself at his head. His eyes were swollen shut and bleeding, and this was much worse than anything she'd dealt with in the past.

"Hey, boy. I'm going to help you. Is that okay?" She didn't know if he'd understand the words, but animals usually understood the sentiment.

Closing her eyes, she opened herself to his thoughts. They came in a rush, a blast of concern for Ares. Even as torn up as the horse was, he was worried for his master.

She felt eyes on her as she focused her energy. Cool air from the fan overhead diffused the heat that always made her feel sunburned when she was doing this, and she welcomed it as she ran her hands over Battle's body. Healing waves closed his wounds, but it wasn't long before his pain became hers. Sweat beaded on her brow, and her breaths became brief gasps between swells of agony.

It went on for an eternity. Someone called her name. The voice was distant, an echo inside her skull.

*Cara!*

Groggily, she opened her eyes. She was lying on the floor with Ares crouched over her, his hands on her shoulders, his expression pinched with concern. He was still wearing the leather pants and tee he'd had on earlier. Battle stood next to her, his velvety nose nuzzling her throat.

"What happened?" she croaked.

"You passed out." He reached up to pat Battle's shoulder, where a wide scar split the brown, blood-caked hair. "He's better, obviously. The scars will be gone by tomorrow. Now, why did you faint? Is that normal?" When she didn't reply, because she was still processing everything, he shook her gently. "Answer me."

So demanding. She was beginning to recognize a pattern; when he was worried, frustrated, or angry, he went into command mode. She tried to sit up, but when she fell back, Ares caught her, his muscular arm slipping behind her back to prop her up. His hand lingered on her hip before pulling away.

"I've never fainted before, but Battle was so big and the injuries were so severe." She shuddered, nearly falling over again when a wave of nausea crashed through her. Once again, Ares's arm went around her, and this time he left it firmly in place. Grateful for his support, she sank into him. It was weird, leaning on someone, but instead of making her feel weak, it gave her a sense of security.

Thanatos crouched in front of her, forearms braced

on his knees. He'd taken off his coat to reveal a T-shirt, and now that she could see skin...wow. Intricate tattoos extended from his fingertips to where they disappeared under his shirt sleeves, and then up his neck to his jaw. Sans armor, he was lankier than Ares, but his lean build was no less powerful. He was a tiger to Ares's lion.

The scorpion on his throat writhed as he spoke, the stinger appearing to jab him in the jugular. "You take the victim's pain into yourself when you heal, don't you?" She nodded, and Thanatos reached out to cup her cheek. "And what about when you kill? Is it the opposite? Do you get off on it?"

"No," she gasped, jerking away from him, her body trembling. Dear God, how did he...oh, God, he knew. He knew that as horrifying as killing the man had been, there had been an underlying...high. A rush of power so evil it felt as though her soul had been permanently bruised.

She'd never even admitted it to herself. Not really. Not until now.

"Enough." The warning in Ares's voice was unmistakable. "She just saved Battle's life. Now isn't the time to grill her." Ares folded her protectively against his chest. "Don't touch her again, Than."

"I only meant to help." Thanatos shoved to his feet and stalked away, and Cara got the impression his feelings were hurt.

"I'm sorry." She rested her forehead against Ares's breastbone. "I didn't mean to cause trouble between you and your brother."

"That?" Ares's palm caressed her back in slow circles. "That was nothing. Relax." With each slow pass of his hand, she did just that, shoving Thanatos's question and the ugly truth back into the locked box where she'd kept it for so long. "Are you hungry?" Her stomach rumbled in answer, and he chuckled. "Food it is."

Huh. Save a man's horse, and he got all nice. She'd have to remember that, the next time she came up against an immortal warrior-type. Which got her thinking. "Wait." She pulled back to look at him. "You're immortal . . . so do you need to eat?"

"Yes. And sleep. I wouldn't die from lack of either, but both Battle and I can weaken or rage out." He frowned. "Speaking of which . . ." His fingers tugged at the hem of the hockey jersey, lifting it up to expose her abdomen.

"Hey!" She grabbed his wrists before he revealed much more. "What are you doing?"

"Checking the *agimortus*. Remember that I said it will fade with time?"

Right. It was a virtual hourglass. A big, fat lump of dread plopped into her stomach, and suddenly, she wasn't hungry anymore. "I'll do it." Her hand shook as she hooked the neckline and pulled it out. But she couldn't bring herself to look down.

Ares knew, and as gently as if her hand were a hummingbird, he eased it away. The rasp of his knuckles was barely a whisper on her skin as he took the hem, but it made her heart beat faster, and when the cool air kissed her breasts, her pulse went out of control with both trepidation and excitement.

For a long time, he didn't look. He remained focused on her face, the intensity in his black eyes taking her breath. His lips parted, just barely, and she wondered what he'd do if she leaned in and kissed him.

Abruptly, his gaze dropped. His harsh inhale was the

only sound in the room. Even Battle, who had been snorting in the background, went silent. Ares's lids grew heavy, his nostrils flaring.

"You are magnificent." His voice was rough, raspy, and she forgot all about the mark that was a countdown to her death.

Ares tugged the shirt down, and with great care, he lifted her. In his arms, she felt small, feminine, and safe. Yes, he had a duty to keep her alive, but all this time it had been about protecting the *agimortus*, not *her*. Now she sensed a shift in him, as if he'd suddenly seen the person instead of the object on her chest.

Battle came forward and pressed his forehead into hers.

"You've made a hell of an impression," Ares said, his words still scraping gravel. "Battle hates everyone." He shouldered the beast out of the way. "Leave her alone, you big lunk."

"Where are you taking me?"

Ares didn't spare her a glance as he strode across the room. "To bed."

The way Cara went taut when Ares announced his intentions was both amusing and insulting. He planned to put her to bed, not bed her. Not that he didn't want to. The altercation with Pestilence had taken the edge off, but the desire to lose himself in female flesh was still burning like a pitch-soaked torch.

And with Cara in his arms, it wasn't just *any* female flesh. He wanted the human even more than before. What she'd done for Battle, knowing the cost to herself and after everything she'd been through recently, earned both his gratitude and his respect. She'd had a hellish introduction to his world, but after a shaky start, she was pulling it together.

How many humans could have accepted as much as she had in so little time? Hell, it had taken Ares decades to come to grips with the reality of the paranormal realm.

Though it was clear that Cara wasn't as new to it as she wanted to believe. The power she wielded was obviously something she'd been dealing with for a long time, so she'd had an inkling, even if it had been buried, that there was more to life than what most humans knew. And with Battle out of danger, he was curious about the human she'd killed.

But he couldn't ask about it now. She was too weakened from the healing, and she would have enough to deal with when she discovered that the *agimortus* had faded. Just a shade, but when every change was another shovelful of grave dirt, it was a blow.

He'd covered his reaction, had let himself admire her perfect breasts, her flawless skin, her narrow waist, and in a heartbeat, he'd felt a wrenching reversal in his emotions. It shouldn't have happened—he'd cut himself off from tender feelings a long time ago. But something about this woman was hell on his instincts, and he liked it as much as he cursed it.

Caring about her would be stupid. Either she was going to die soon, or she'd transfer the *agimortus* and still die. If Pestilence learned that Ares cared about her even a little, he'd kill her solely to cause Ares pain. Besides, just being close to her was a drain on his strength and senses, so what would full-on sex do?

"Don't worry," he said. "I'm going to do nothing more threatening than tuck you in." He scowled at the blood on her hands, arms, and legs. "You stained my jersey."

She sniffed. "With *your* horse's blood."

"You have my thanks. And Battle's heart, I think," he added wryly.

Her fragile smile made his own heart skip a beat. Pale and exhausted as she was, she was still beautiful, and her weight felt good in his arms.

Fierce admiration swelled in his chest as he set her gently on the bed. He could admire her without caring about her, right? But the way he'd torn into Thanatos, telling him to never touch her again, had nothing to do with admiration. He'd hated the sight of Than's hand on her, and Ares, who had never been jealous in his life, had wanted to rip his brother apart.

Yeah, this woman was definitely hell on his senses.

"Do you want to clean up?" he asked, anxious to get her settled in so he could get out of here.

She practically purred. "I would never turn down an opportunity to use your amazing shower."

"You can use it whenever you want," Ares said, his voice hoarse, because now he was picturing Cara there. Naked. Soap suds streaming in bubbly tendrils over her breasts, stomach, thighs... that private place between.

"Don't say that. I might just move into it." Once again, her smile did bizarre things to his insides. And outsides. This was bad. "And I like it when you smile. You don't do it often, do you?"

He didn't like that she'd ascertained that about him, even though it didn't take a rocket scientist to see it. "I haven't had much to laugh about since I learned I wasn't human," he said simply. Even before that, he'd been intense, at ease only with his sons and brother.

"How long has that been?"

"Five thousand years. Give or take a couple of centuries."

Her eyes shot wide, giving him another rare laugh. "You don't look a day over twenty-nine."

"It's my healthy lifestyle," he said lightly, because oddly, this conversation with her was the most normal thing that had happened to him in what seemed like forever. Usually females wanted one thing from him, and it wasn't talk. When they did talk, either it was to heap praise on him in a suck-up-fest, or they wanted to hear about his exploits. They didn't want to hear about *him*.

"Well, sign me up." She shifted on the bed. "Why are there no pillows?"

"Comfort makes a man soft."

"Hmm. I'd think comfort would make a man happy. You should try it."

She was teasing him, and he experienced the strangest euphoric feeling inside. It felt good, the way he felt after downing a bottle of Jack Daniel's, but without the loss of clarity. "So all I'm missing from life is a pillow?"

"Hardly." She patted the mattress. "You could use a softer bed, too." Before he could comment, not that he knew what to say about this female suddenly wanting to take over his bedroom, she gestured to the dresser. "Can I borrow another shirt from you?"

Hell, yeah, he wanted her to wear his clothes. There was something incredibly sexy about her wrapped in his clothing. But she needed more than his oversized T-shirts and sweats that would have to be duct-taped around her waist. "While you're showering, I'll pick up some things from your house."

"Thank you." She stood, swayed, and plopped back down on the mattress. "A little woozy."

Guilt wasn't something he felt often, but now it moved in and made itself at home like an unwanted roommate. Sort of like what *she* was doing. "Hold off on the shower. I'll bring warm water and a washcloth."

"And give me a sponge bath?" Cara graced him with a *yeah, right* look. "I don't think so. If I get dizzy, there are plenty of places to sit in there."

True, half the shower was lined with heated benches set into the marble. He sometimes turned on the steam and the stereo and lounged in there for hours. Cara could easily wash while sitting down. And there he went, picturing it.

And what a fine picture it was. A master-fucking-piece.

He offered his hand. "I'm going to make sure you get to the bathroom."

Cara rolled her eyes, but she allowed him to pull her to her feet, and she didn't protest when he gripped her upper arm to steady her. By nature, he wasn't a caregiver, but tending to Cara's needs gave him a sense of satisfaction. He hadn't been in a caretaker role since he'd taken Vulgrim in a few hundred years ago, but even then, he'd focused more on being a protector, and then a teacher. His intent had not been to raise a family—caring for Vulgrim had been a strategy to gain an ally in the demon community. Yet the demon and his son, Torrent, had woven their way into the fabric of Ares's personal existence, and sometimes, Ares wondered what kind of price had yet to be paid for that.

Shaking off the useless reflection on his past, he started the water for Cara. "If you want music or steam, there's a control panel on the right."

"Don't suppose you've got a fridge and microwave in here, too?"

"Thought about it, but can't figure out a way to insulate the electronics," he teased, and wow, that was way out of character for him. Maybe one of the ghastbats had caused brain damage. "I'll leave you alone."

It took fewer than ten minutes to get in and out of Cara's house with a duffel full of clothes, a pillow, and the toiletries she'd had on her bathroom counter.

One thought dominated his mind as he gated himself back to Greece: *She wore Victoria's Secret boyshorts.*

He could so easily envision her lush curves contained in the sexy underwear. Yeah, thongs and lacy panties and crap were nice, but for some reason, the mix of masculine and feminine of the boyshorts worked for him. *Really* worked.

He'd love to hold her against him while his hands slipped down the back of the boyshorts to cup that tight ass . . . and fuck, he was obsessing over freaking *panties*.

Feeling like the Webster's definition of loser, he stalked through his house, halting at the bedroom door. His heart did something weird against his sternum, a spastic flutter of anticipation. Was he actually looking forward to seeing Cara again? The goofy way his lips were curved into a smile said yes, and horror of horrors, he realized he was experiencing some sort of crush.

He needed to kill something. Needed to get his head back in the battle, reacquire his target, and go on the offensive, because he was doing exactly what he used to berate other men for. Hell, he'd actually arranged for women to seduce enemy commanders, and then he'd waited for their dicks to lead them to distraction and destruction.

Cara must be the ultimate karma.

Mercifully, the shower was still running, so he figured it was safe to enter the bedroom, where he tossed the bag and pillow onto the bed. He moved to the door, but froze at the sound of a thump and a weak cry.

"Cara?" He was halfway across the room before her name was fully out of his mouth. Adrenaline spiked, his warrior instincts came to bear, and he charged into the bathroom, prepared to take out the threat.

He burst into the shower, found her trying to get to her hands and knees.

"What happened?" he barked, fear roughening his voice, and he silently chastised himself. Nothing should rattle him this much.

Startled, Cara screeched like a banshee—and Ares knew well what they sounded like—and tried to cover herself. The effort was useless—what he'd seen had already been saved to his memory card and tagged as a favorite.

Hot water drenched him from the multiple shower heads, but he didn't give a shit. He sank down on his heels to help her. "Cara!" His voice cracked like a bullwhip in the tiled space. "What happened?"

"It was nothing." Drawing her knees up to her chest, she wrapped her arms around them and huddled against the wall. "I slipped."

"What, you slipped on soap?" She was too pasty, with dark circles under her eyes, and he wasn't buying her excuse. "Bullshit."

"Don't talk to me that way," she snapped.

"Then tell me the truth," he shot back. "You passed out."

Her eyes roiled like the waters off his coastline after a storm. "I didn't pass out. I just feel so...weak."

"This is more than a side-effect of healing Battle, isn't it?"

"I don't know. I've never felt this way before. Is it the *agimorbid*-thing?"

"*Agimortus*," he corrected, though by this point, since she'd said it right before, he suspected she was deliberately mispronouncing it just to annoy him. Too bad he found it to be sort of endearing. *Endearing*. Holy hell. "Likely. Or The Aegis could be hurting the hellhound."

"Hal," she said, the sea-storm in her eyes gathering strength again. "His name is Hal."

"Yeah, whatever." The idea of naming a hellhound as if it were a dainty lap yapper irritated the hell out of him. He wiped water out of his eyes. "Let's get you out of here."

"I have to rinse first." Cara dragged her fingers through her hair. The action exposed the swell of her breasts, the deep cleavage between them, and for all of the water, his mouth went dry. "Full of shampoo."

"I'll help."

"I'll manage on my own." She shifted, giving him a tantalizing glimpse of honey-colored curls at the juncture of her thighs, and oh, hell, he didn't need to see that. Didn't need to see the imprint of the *agimortus* on her chest, either, but at least that cooled him down a little.

"This isn't negotiable. I can't let you fall and break your neck." At her horrified expression, he gnashed his teeth. "I'm old enough to have seen it all a million times over. Stop being a child."

"Well, I'm *not* old enough to have shown it off a million times over. So stop being an ass."

Impossible woman. "Would you feel better if I were as exposed as you?" He peeled off his soaked shirt and started to unzip his pants.

"No!" She grabbed his wrist. "Really, it's okay."

She looked like a cornered cat as he gently lifted her to her feet. God, her skin was soft. Smooth. Her body . . . yeah, he wasn't supposed to look, but shit, she was built like the women of his time—of his human time. They'd been lush, with curves that signaled that they were fertile and built to bear a warrior's lust and his offspring.

His body hardened, primed for that thought. So much for cooling off.

"I can stand on my own—" Her legs gave out, and he caught her, tucked her against him. "Or not."

He wrapped one arm around her waist and held her so her breasts were pressed to his chest and her belly cradled his erection.

If the way her face flamed red was any indication, she'd noticed his state of arousal. And the way her eyes darkened said she liked it.

# Fourteen

⌒

This had to be the weirdest thing that had ever happened to Cara. Which was saying something, considering that she was bonded to a hellhound, had been imprinted with a mystical symbol that made her a target for assassination, and she'd traveled instantly from England to Greece.

Now she was naked and in a shower, being propped up by a walking, talking legend. And said legend had an erection. She'd read somewhere that normal, healthy men got up to twenty erections a day. Um...yep, Ares was definitely healthy.

"Can we hurry?" She pressed her body as tightly against him as she could. The closer she was, the less he could see of her.

Not that being plastered to him wasn't nice. Ares was a rock-solid mountain of muscle, and she couldn't help but stroke his skin as she clung to him. And God, she wanted to lick the droplets of water that glistened on his powerful shoulders.

"Tilt your head back." His command was just that; an order, spoken gruffly. Yet his hold was tender.

"How many times do I have to tell you that I don't appreciate being barked at," she sighed.

His hand came up to her chin, and he lifted her face. His eyes were hooded, unreadable. She thought he was going to say something, but instead, he tipped her head under the stream of water. His palm was a light caress on her forehead and scalp, his ministrations deliberate, careful, as if he was afraid his touch would hurt her. In a way, it did. Her heart pounded crazily, almost painfully. No one had ever been so attentive with her.

And how could someone so comfortable with killing, who had done the things Chaos had shown her, be so tender?

Ares's fingers sifted through her hair in long, soothing strokes. Gradually, her lids grew heavy, and she closed her eyes, slumping against him as her muscles loosened. This was very calming, yet at the same time, her pulse was thundering in her ears and sprinting through her veins. The brand on her chest was tingling. And between her legs, heat was building.

Ares took his time rinsing her hair.

"There must be a lot of shampoo," she murmured.

"Yeah," he said, and was it her imagination, or had his voice cracked a little? "I'm thorough that way."

"Mmm."

He brought his palm to her cheek to wipe away the water. "Anywhere else you need to be washed?"

Her eyes flew open. A "no" formed on her lips, but

no sound came out. The way he was looking at her... this time, his expression was as readable as a large-print book. Hunger burned in his eyes. His gaze held hers captive, and she became achingly hyperaware of a growing anticipation.

She licked her lips, and his gaze dropped to her mouth, zeroed in on the tongue action. Inside her head, she pleaded for him not to kiss her. But she lifted her face and pushed herself up on her toes, surprised that her legs were no longer shaky.

"This is stupid," Ares whispered, even as he lowered his head, slowly, until only a whisper-thin layer of steamy air separated their lips. She could have pulled away. *Should* have. But for the first time in a long time, she finally felt safe. How crazy was it that she felt safe in the arms of a man who could break her in half with a flick of his wrist, a man whom the entire world regarded with fear and horror?

Oh, but his lips were soft when they finally made contact. At first, he merely brushed his mouth over hers. A shivery sensation spread from every point of contact between them, electrifying her entire body. Gone was the fatigue that had weighed her down. She felt as if she could run a marathon. Heck, she felt as if she already had, with the way her pulse was racing.

He increased the pressure on her lips, alternating light kisses with nibbles and soothing strokes of his tongue until she moaned. As if her sound of desperation had unlocked something, he got serious. His tongue delved between her lips, demanding entrance. God, no one had ever kissed her this way, so masterfully that she opened up without hesitation. Their tongues met, tangled as he deepened the kiss. His hand gripped a handful of her hair as the other wound around her waist to tug her even closer. She clung to him, her fingers digging into his arms.

With a great surge, he backed her into the wall. The kiss grew fiercer. He was stroking, sucking, and his breathing became as ragged as hers. He dropped one hand to her thigh and lifted her right foot onto the bench, putting her core in contact with his arousal. They both groaned.

In this position, water poured directly onto Ares's back and neck, cascading over his shoulders in wide rivulets that formed rivers in the deep valleys of his muscles. He was beautiful, perfect, and the way he undulated against her in the most primal of male responses brought a purr of pure female appreciation rising up in her chest.

His hand smoothed up her thigh to cup her butt, and oh, yes, that was good. His other hand slid up her rib cage until his fingers reached her breast, his thumb rasping back and forth over her nipple. He kept kissing her, his tongue flicking against hers, and those agonizingly wonderful little nips on her lower lip drove her to dizzying heights.

She ground against his rigid length, losing herself in the steam of the shower, the heat of his kiss, the luxury of his touch. This was so decadent, and she was so into it that she let her head fall back so he could kiss his way down her chin and jaw to her throat. When his hand left her breast to slide south, she dragged her own hands up his back, mapping the different textures, the taut layers of muscle.

"Cara." His hot breath fanned against her skin, and his voice vibrated through her in an erotic wave.

"Mm-hmm?"

His hand stopped its downward exploration. "Are you bleeding?"

Her lust-clogged brain took a second to process what he'd said. "I didn't hurt myself—"

"Not an injury." His fingers brushed across her mound. "Female bleeding."

Her face grew hotter than the steam around them. "Why?" Her ex had been squeamish about her time of the month, wouldn't touch her during it or for a few days afterward, as if she were contaminated. "Is it repulsive to you?"

A frown tugged at the corners of his kiss-swollen mouth. "There is nothing repulsive about a female's fertility cycle, and blood has never bothered me. I wondered because there were tampons on your counter. I brought them." His cheeks bloomed pink.

It was so cute the way he glanced away, his face bright with embarrassment. "Why are you asking about this now?"

"Because I want to touch you." His fingers drifted lightly, tentatively, over her sex. "But I don't know if those feminine things interfere. Or hurt."

Her throat closed up, clogged by a mixture of lust, shyness, and amusement at his inexperience with the subject. So instead of saying anything, she put her hand over his. Taking a deep, bracing breath to steady herself, she guided his fingers between her legs.

For a moment, his throat worked on a hard swallow, and then he closed his eyes and stroked her. Once more, her head fell back against the wall, the arch of her body pushing her hips forward and allowing him even more contact. Long, light passes of his fingers over the outer hills of her sex became firmer, and when he worked a finger into her slit, electric sparks lit fire to her blood. His thumb joined the action, circling her clit, and she began to pant, to pump her hips wantonly, needing him to find that perfect rhythm, that perfect pressure.

His other hand came up to cup her breast, and she shuddered at the dual sensations.

"That's it." His voice was a guttural rasp. "God, you're beautiful."

Oh, yes, she could come from just his words. She could feel his eyes on her, and she dare not open hers for fear that she'd lose this dreamy feeling. Reality was a strange place right now, and for a few stolen moments, she wanted to be somewhere nice.

Then it dawned on her that she *was* somewhere nice. She was on a Greek island in the middle of a crystal blue sea, in a shower outfitted for royalty, with a powerful man who epitomized the male animal. Sensation rocked her, the sex-on-the-brain as stimulating as Ares's fingers.

Liquid heat seeped through her center, and Ares made a harsh sound as he pushed two fingers inside her. He worked her, gently at first, and then harder, stroking a place deep in her core that had her rocking into him, riding his hand.

"Now," she moaned, quivering with the need to explode.

"Say please." His thumb circled her nub, the pressure perfectly calculated to keep her in a holding pattern. The orgasm coiled tight, ready to go the moment Ares touched just the right spot... which he seemed to know. His torture was masterful, the way he kept her teetering on the edge. "Yield to me. Say it."

*Females always yield to me.*

His arrogant words came back to her, but given what

was going on right now, she supposed that his arrogance was justified. She'd give him this, but only because he'd worked for it. And because the promise of the best climax of her life balanced on one little word.

"Please!" Her shout wasn't intentional, but she'd hate herself for it later. The climax hit hard, dropped her into a freefall of pleasure so intense that the floor gave way beneath her, and all she could feel was ecstasy and Ares's hard body as he absorbed her spasms. His fingers worked her through it, and as she came down, he did something sinfully twisty with his thumb, and set her off again.

"Yes," she gasped. "Oh...*God*." The orgasm went on and on, and where had he learned to drag it out like that? No, she really didn't want to know...

His cheek grazed hers as he bent his head to whisper roughly into her ear, "How long has it been since a man has taken you?"

Dazed, she had to repeat his question in her head a couple of times, and still, she didn't quite understand. "Taken me?"

"Fucked you."

Oh. Her cheeks heated, and she blinked up at him. "I've never been fucked, as you so delicately put it." She was still breathless, and though his crude words should have turned her off, they only added to the struggle to take in enough air. "I've made love. And it's been over two years."

"You *made love*." His fingers still feathered over the pad of her sex as one eyebrow cocked up in amusement, and the mellow postorgasm bliss veered sharply to irritation.

"There's no need to make fun of me, just because I'm not like you." She inhaled a couple of times, in desperate need of oxygen.

The lovely play of his fingers stilled. "Like me?"

"You aren't human. Your mother is a...sex demon." She tripped over that a little, because seriously, that was one of those things you never thought you'd say. "And violence and killing excite you." She tripped over that, too, but for a different reason. *And what about when you kill? Do you get off on it?* She *was* like Ares. A tremor of revulsion would have knocked her off balance if not for Ares's hold.

A frosty glower replaced the amusement in his eyes. "I apologize for subjecting your pure, nonviolent self to my repulsive lusts. Thank you for bringing me to my senses."

Cara jerked, lanced by shock—not by what he said, but by the reason he'd said it. She'd hurt him. For some reason, the idea that he *could* be hurt had never occurred to her. He was...*War.* Sure, she'd seen a vulnerability in him after Chaos had left, and when Battle was injured, but this was different.

Angry at herself for not seeing beyond his armor, she reached up and cupped his cheek. "I didn't mean to judge—"

"Yes," he growled, as he reared away from her touch, "you did. Let me guess, you're all missionary, all the time. Sweet and angelic. *Human.*" He practically spat that last word. "But me? I'm a demon with no morals."

"I didn't say that. And I'm not all missionary," she muttered, even though she sort of was. But only because her two lovers hadn't been all that adventurous.

"No?"

"No."

Wrong thing to say, because a wicked glint of I'll-prove-you-wrong competitiveness sparked in his eye, and he put his mouth to her ear, his lips a whisper on her skin, just like his voice. "Have you ever done it on your hands and knees, mounted from behind? How about in the shower, against the wall, being driven into while you slide up and down the tile?" His teeth caught her earlobe, and she arched against him with a moan. "Or sitting on the bench, while he goes to his knees and licks you between the legs? Maybe you on top, sucking cock while he tongues you? Ever use honey, Cara? Hot wax? A riding crop?"

The erotic images jumbled in her head, leaving her breathless, dizzy, and speechless.

"Didn't think so." Ares shut off the water and grabbed a towel off the heated rack. Before she could protest, he'd wrapped it around her and was leading her to the bedroom.

She stopped him just short of the bed. "Wait. I don't understand. Why did you ask me all those things if you weren't going to . . . you know."

"Fuck you?" His laughter rumbled deep and harsh in his chest, which she just noticed was smooth, hairless—utterly lickable. "Is that what you really want?"

*Yes.* "Of course not." Really, no. This thing between them had already gone too far, and she had enough problems as it was. The last thing she needed right now was to get involved with anyone, let alone an immortal half-demon whose brother wanted her dead.

"Of course not," he repeated, bitterness dripping from his words. "Doesn't matter. You're not strong enough to handle what I have to offer anyway."

Again, the talk of her weakness. "You don't know me. You don't know what I'm capable of."

"But I know what I'm capable of." He peeled back the sheets and nudged her toward the bed. "You were right,

Cara. I'm a demon. All I've known my entire life is fighting. Battle, sex, it's all the same to me. I fuck like I fight,
until the other person is begging for mercy. Trust me, you
don't want to be part of it. I was wrong to think anything
else." His hands came down on her shoulders, and he
pushed her onto the mattress. "Sleep. Locate your mutt."

She glared, stung by his rejection, and she didn't even
know why. She didn't want him. What she wanted was her
life back.

*And you want that life back... why?*

Because in her old life, she might be on the verge of
being homeless, but she hadn't been dying. Demons and
evil legends weren't chasing her.

No hot men were stroking her to orgasm in their showers.

Frustrated by the direction of her thoughts, she jerked
the sheet over her, rolled to the side, and smashed her face
into squishy softness. Her anger ebbed, replaced by confusion. "You brought me a pillow."

He gave a casual shrug, but a pink blush smudged his
cheeks. "You should be comfortable when you sleep. To
find the hound," he added quickly. As if his feet were on
fire, he swept out of the bedroom.

He'd been embarrassed about doing something nice.

Cara stared after him, a sense of disquiet stirring her
thoughts. Ares was a hard man—what she'd expect from
an ancient warrior. But she'd seen him care for his horse,
for the baby goat-demon thing. She felt his gentle touch,
his protectiveness. And he'd been thoughtful enough to
bring her a pillow.

So why did all of that bother her when she should be
happy to know that he was more than a cold-blooded killing machine?

*Because you don't want to like him. Everyone you love holds you at arm's length.* If Ares was capable of caring about her, he'd hurt her, the way her ex had. The way her family had, even if unintentionally, by treating her as if she was different.

The brand, which always tingled in Ares's presence, stopped, as if punctuating that point. Absently, she looked down, and stifled a cry. No longer angry crimson, it was the color of a dying rose.

Her first instinct was to leap out of bed, get dressed, and demand access to Ares's library and computer. Her second instinct was to curl up in a ball and sob. That second instinct? Something that had developed since the attack two years ago.

Screw that. She swung her feet over the side of the bed and grabbed the duffel full of clothes. She might have sworn to never kill again, but she hadn't sworn to give up on life. She was going to live.

When Pestilence was Reseph, he had, for the most part, avoided Sheoul. He'd descended into the demon realm to hang out at the Four Horsemen, but other than that, it had been too depressing. Reseph had liked parties and vacations and surfing. If it got the adrenaline pumping, the females purring, and the alcohol flowing, he was so there.

Reseph had been a pussy of epic proportions.

Pestilence ran his tongue over the sharp point of a fang as he crossed the threshold of his Sheoulin dungeon... which wasn't actually in Sheoul. Technically, it wasn't a dungeon, either. When his Seal had broken, he'd gained a massively cool ability...he could turn areas of the human realm into land claimed in the name of hell. Now, in the basement of the Austrian manor he'd commandeered, demons who normally couldn't leave Sheoul could hang out in the human world and enjoy luxuries they'd never known, which included the ability to torment humans.

And they'd turned the basement into a Disneyland of torture and misery.

Reseph would have been mortified. Pestilence was orgasmic.

Pained screams and moans joined laughter and pleasurable grunts. The mouthwatering scent of blood and lust teased Pestilence's nostrils, mingled with the stench of death, bowels, and charred bone and flesh. All kinds of earthly and demonic creatures hung from various hooks and chains on the walls and from the ceiling, and different species of demons skittered around, some of them playing, others performing tasks Pestilence had given them.

Starting an Apocalypse required a lot more help than he would have thought.

A graceful, elflike demon carrying a spiked club crossed the room when he saw Pestilence. A Neethul slave trader, Mordiin was Pestilence's right-hand man, his ruthlessness and uncanny ability to sense fallen angels making him indispensable.

Mordiin had located the two Unfallen that were currently chained down here. Mordiin had found them wandering the human realm, minding their own business, and Pestilence had grabbed them. Instead of destroying them, as he'd been doing to keep Ares's *agimortus* from being transferred yet again, he'd dragged them here.

Oh, they were still going to die, but first he had special plans for them.

"My lord," Mordiin rumbled. "We have destroyed four more hellhounds."

"Good work. Only what, a few thousand left to go?" He hated those fucking things. They were the one weapon that could be used against him, and he wanted them gone. Even Chaos, whom Pestilence had convinced to work with him. Once that mutt rendered Ares immobile, Pestilence was going to kill him. Double-crosses were part of being evil, after all.

"Slaughtering the hounds took a heavy toll on us," Mordiin said. "We lost several good fighters, more than we lost in the capture of the fallen angels."

Pestilence snorted at that. Demons were a dime a dozen. "Keep killing the hellhounds, but capture one alive. And tell me you've finished with the other tasks."

Mordiin inclined his head, and his white hair fell forward, catching on his pointed ears. "Your message has been prepared. The structure is built and ready for delivery."

Excellent. The two Unfallens were going to make memorable gifts for Ares. "What about the Aegi?"

Mordiin gestured to a bloody human strapped to a table. "Like the others, this one knows nothing. He's too low-ranking to provide any useful information."

Cocking his head, Pestilence studied the man, whose mouth was open in a silent scream as one of the imps worked him over with a hot poker. "Why can't I hear his agony?"

Mordiin shrugged. "His screams blew out his voice box."

Interesting. "Tell the turncoat Aegi that unless he provides us with more substantial results, he'll be the next victim on the table." He'd hate to have to permanently maim David, who had been a high-ranking Aegis member and had so far given up a lot of great intel, but Pestilence was getting desperate. He had to find Deliverance, and someone in The Aegis must know where the dagger was.

"Let's finish the angels and the Aegi. Time to deliver the message to Ares."

When Ares stepped out into the hall, face hot and still dripping wet and ready to explode out of his skin from the unspent sexual energy, he ran into Limos, who was propped against the wall, suitcase at her feet. She'd changed into a glaringly bright muumuu, and her impish smile told him everything he needed to know about how long she'd been there.

"Wow," she chirped. "Didn't take you long to get into her pants. And here I thought Reseph was the charmer in the family."

He brushed past her, water sloshing in his boots. "Don't start." Each squishy step took him blessedly farther away from Cara and brought back the return of his seismic battle senses. It was unsettling to be with her, for his body and mind to experience stillness, as if the world had stopped moving. The lack of distraction left him too focused on her—and on his desires.

Not acceptable.

But neither was how fast his inner tuning fork was starting to vibrate. Ever since Reseph's Seal had broken, the buzz of worldly violence had intensified, but this new buzz was different, a new, more potent frequency that was drowning out the hundreds of others. Something very, very bad was coming.

"You are no fun," Limos called out. "Oh, and you might want to change. Reaver got the Aegis assholes to agree to a meeting. They'll be at Thanatos's place in an hour. I'm sure you don't want to look like you've been drowned."

He swung around. "Why didn't Than call me?"

"Because he called me. I figured I'd tell you when I got here to babysit." She jerked her thumb toward the door. "You gonna take her with us?"

Damn straight. "Cara has to be with one of us at all times."

"My lord?"

Ares didn't bother to turn around. "What, Vulgrim?"

"Your brother left a message."

"I know. I'm heading to his place in a minute."

"Not that brother."

Ares pivoted around to the Ramreel, whose broad nose flared the way it did when he was stressed. Even his curled horns seemed to be drooping a little. Not good. Torrent, who stood beside his father, looked even more miserable, his grayish fur rippling nervously. "Tell me."

"If you'll come with me..." The Ramreels headed down the hall, hooves clacking.

"Dammit." Ares pointed to Limos. "Grab Cara. Join me in the great room."

"But—"

"Do it!"

Limos stuck her tongue out at him, but she moved to the bedroom door. Ares caught up to the two Ramreels at the back door. As Ares stepped out into the rear courtyard, his gut did a somersault, and his stomach threw in a double twist. The organ gymnastics were a perfect 10 of *oh, fuck.*

In the middle of the courtyard, next to the barbecue pit, was a giant wooden cross. And nailed to it were two headless bodies. Their intestines had been yanked up through their ruined necks and wrapped around their torsos like Christmas tree garlands. Their lungs had been arranged behind them to look like wings, and they each held a bloody heart in their hands.

Lying on the ground in front of what Ares suspected were fallen angels was a human. A Guardian, if Ares went by the Aegis shield that had been carved into his stomach.

Vulgrim handed Ares a note. Reseph's scribbles confirmed Ares's suspicions. *I'm sure you're looking for Unfallens, so I thought I'd deliver. Enjoy.*

# Fifteen

⌒

"That angel is an asshole."

Kynan laughed, and Arik wanted to deck him. Would have, too, if he hadn't been freezing to death in the middle of God-knows-where. Reaver had flashed them to some featureless expanse of ice and then disappeared without so much as a "Good luck," or a "Hope the Horsemen don't kill you."

"You should have seen Reaver when he was still fallen," Ky said.

"He was even more of an asshole?"

"Nah. He was just grumpier."

"I don't think I like angels," Arik muttered.

Kynan shot him a sideways glance. "You don't like anybody."

"True." Arik tugged his jacket tighter. He supposed he should be grateful that the angel had been able to flash them here instead of Kynan's using the Harrowgate.

Humans couldn't use them while conscious—they came out on the other side dead. But Kynan, thanks to his invincibility charm, could travel through them, and unfortunately, Ky would have to knock Arik out in order for them to leave here. The idea was not appealing in the least.

Arik squinted his eyes against the bright sunlight glinting off the snow. "You know we could be walking into a slaughter."

Kynan shrugged. "*I'll* be fine."

"That's comforting."

A blast of icy wind took the sting out of Kynan's chuckle, mainly because it numbed every part of Arik's body. "The Aegis and Horsemen have a long history of working together. You know, before we betrayed them. We should be able to talk it out."

"*Should.* Great." They tromped through the snow. Ahead, there was only vast wasteland on top of more vast wasteland. "Are you sure we're in the right place?"

"Yeah, human, you are." The deep, rumbling voice came out of nowhere, and both Arik and Kynan instinctively drew weapons—Kynan palmed an Aegis stang, and Arik pulled his pistol.

"Show yourself," Arik called out.

Suddenly, a giant dun stallion was rearing up, and Jesus, Arik damn near got his head smashed in by one flailing hoof. The beast came down, and his rider, a big male with sandy hair wearing some sort of ivory plate armor, raised a gauntleted hand in greeting.

"*I looked and there before me was a pale horse,*" Arik murmured. "*Its rider was named Death, and Hades was following close behind him.*" He stared in awe at the huge male described in Revelation. "You're Death."

The dude rolled his yellow eyes. "Thanatos. I don't become Death unless my Seal breaks." He wheeled the horse around and muttered, "Fucking humans always fucking up prophecies."

What a douche. Arik was totally over his awe. He glanced at Ky. "I guess we're just supposed to follow?"

Kynan shrugged, but Thanatos snorted. "I'd keep to one side of my stallion. You don't want to be behind him when he passes gas."

Yep, a douche. They trudged another fifty yards or so—hard to tell when there were no landmarks—and out of thin air, a massive castle shimmered into existence, rising up out of the snowy landscape like an iceberg in the ocean.

"You can only see it because I'm letting you." Thanatos dismounted and gave the horse a fond pat on the neck. "To me." The stallion dissolved into a thin line of smoke, did a loop-de-loop, and then shot inside the Horseman's gauntlet. Freaky.

Kynan's dark brows drew together as he stared at Thanatos. "What kind of armor is that?"

"Lava beast scale."

Jesus. Few humans had ever seen the massive demons that lived deep inside volcanoes, but they supposedly fed off the misery and death eruptions caused. Legend had it that their scale was fireproof and impenetrable by conventional weapons and that with every death its wearer dealt, it would become stronger. Arik would love to outfit a tank or APC with that shit.

They followed the Horseman across the inner bailey. An arched entrance sized for a T-Rex opened up into the keep and a chamber larger than a high school gymnasium.

Against the far wall, a blazing fire burned in a hearth, and tending to it were two beings Arik thought might be vampires. In front of the hearth was a trestle table built to seat at least two dozen people, but right now there were only two...a brown-haired male in leather armor and a black-haired female in a fuchsia, blue, and yellow...muumuu? They had been concentrating on a game of chess when Ky and Arik entered, but were now casting dark, intense glares their way.

*Fuck me, this is not my idea of a good time.* Nope. Arik wasn't good at negotiation. Not when it involved sensitivity and talking things out. His idea of negotiation involved firepower and who had the most and best.

In this case, the other guys had the biggest dicks. That never did sit well with Arik.

He scanned the room, taking note of the layout, exits, potential weapons. He was startled when he noticed a woman curled up in a recliner, dressed casually in jeans and a University of Missouri sweatshirt. She glanced up from the ancient-looking book she'd been reading to watch them with curiosity...nothing even close to the hostility they were getting from the other three.

The male and female at the table stood as Arik and Kynan approached.

Leather Armor Guy spoke harshly. "Your names."

Bristling at the male's abrupt demand, Arik gestured to Kynan. "That's Kynan. He's a Guardian. I'm Arik. R-XR." He figured they didn't need to know about his Guardian status, given that they hated The Aegis, and Arik liked his head on his shoulders.

"I'm Ares."

*Then another horse came out, a fiery red one. Its rider*

*was given power to take peace from the earth and to make men slay each other.* Arik stared at the Horseman who would be War.

Ares cocked his thumb at the female. "Our sister, Limos."

*I looked, and there before me was a black horse. Its rider was holding a pair of scales.* He'd known Famine was female, but he hadn't thought she'd be so hot.

Damn, this was real, wasn't it? Arik was standing in a room with three of the Four Horsemen of the Apocalypse.

"It's pretty awe-inspiring, isn't it," came Thanatos's deep, dry voice, and Arik blinked.

"What?"

"Your jaw was open and you were gaping like an idiot at them," Kynan said, a little louder than he really needed to.

"Tool," Arik said under his breath. He nodded at the seated female. "Who's she?"

"Not your concern," Ares said, his voice as icy and forbidding as the landscape around them.

Thanatos put a restraining hand on his brother's shoulder, and Arik wondered how close he was to getting his ass kicked.

Limos moved closer, her flip-flops slapping the floor, her off-the-shoulder muumuu swishing around slim, shapely ankles. "You two have a lot of balls coming here."

Kynan gestured to Arik. "*He* does. I'm charmed. Nothing can hurt me. Or my balls."

"Really?" Limos came at Kynan, swung, and Ky didn't even flinch. The female Horseman's swing went wild, and she stumbled, nearly fell. "What the hell?"

"Told you. I can't be harmed."

She jammed her fists on her hips. "That's annoying."

Limos was like nothing Arik would have expected. No, he'd been thinking more of a mannish Amazonian-type warrior. This female was ultrafeminine, had breasts that made her dress a fucking work of art, and she didn't look as if she could handle a weapon if she had to. Maybe she'd get scarier once her Seal broke.

"So why are you here?" Ares asked. "Reaver said you wanted to help, but The Aegis hasn't been on our side for centuries, and I don't even know what the R-XR is."

Arik studied the brown-haired warrior. His expression revealed nothing, and neither did his flat eyes. But somehow Arik knew he was lying about not knowing about R-XR.

Kynan cleared his throat. "We know that Pestilence has been loosed. We want to discuss how to stop him."

"If we knew how, we'd have done it already."

"So you don't want to usher in the Apocalypse?" Arik asked.

That earned him murderous glares from the three of them. Ares clenched his fists as though imagining Arik's neck in their grip. "We want to prevent our Seals from breaking and stop Pestilence's rampage. But even if we knew how to stop him, we wouldn't tell you."

"Because we could use the knowledge against you."

Limos snorted. "Aren't you a brain surgeon."

Arik ignored that. She might be hot, but he wasn't into smartass immortal women. "We can still help to prevent your Seals from breaking."

"How much do you know about our situations and Seals?" Thanatos folded his arms over his broad chest, code for, *say the wrong thing, I dare you.*

Kynan picked up on the body language as well, and he kept his voice even, businesslike. Arik hoped Ky knew more than he did about what might be the "wrong thing." "Honestly, not much. We have a copy of the Daemonica, so we've read the prophecies, but they're pretty obscure and aren't a lot of help."

"So you need information from us." Ares studied them, the cold calculation in his gaze measuring them for deception. And maybe for a coffin. "Why should we trust you? Why should we believe that you don't want to destroy us?"

"Because," Kynan said, "the ranking members of The Aegis know the history we've shared, and if you've paid any attention at all to the way The Aegis has changed in the last few years, you know that we've become more moderate."

"We don't need your help." Limos imperiously waved her hand in dismissal, her long pink and yellow-painted nails flashing. "Be gone."

Arik didn't think. He reacted. "You fools!" He seized her wrist to stop her from walking away. "We have resources and—"

Next thing he knew, he was flat on his back, with Limos straddling him while holding a dagger under his left eye. Ares and Thanatos were on either side of him, both leveling swords at his throat. Ares's huge boot was on his forehead.

"Ares." The hushed, shocked voice came from near the fireplace. The unnamed woman. "Please. Don't kill him."

"I'd appreciate it if you left him alive, as well." Kynan's words were casual, but Arik knew him well enough to recognize a rare note of concern.

"Here's the thing," Limos said, in an eerily chipper voice. "Don't touch me." For emphasis, she squeezed her knees, which were parked on either side of his ribs, and the air whooshed out of his lungs. Pain was a blistering firestorm in his upper body as his ribs cracked. He gritted his teeth, refused to make a sound, but yeah, he got the message.

The brothers backed off as suddenly as they'd attacked, sheathed their blades, and Limos leaped to her feet. Then, with a shit-eating grin, she offered her damned hand.

"S'okay," he wheezed. "Floor is surprisingly comfortable."

Kynan cleared his throat again. "If we're done with the ball-busting, maybe you could tell us what it'll take to earn your trust."

There was a long pause, and then Ares said, "Give us the hellhound."

Kynan tensed. "What makes you think we have a hellhound?"

Smart move, not denying that The Aegis had the beast. A lie would compromise the trust Kynan wanted to build.

"Doesn't matter." Ares's hand flexed over the pommel of his sword, as if he was still wanting to draw blood. "But we want it."

Arik sat up. Not without difficulty and a lot of pain, but he thought he managed to not look too pathetic. "Why?"

"Because they're so cuddly and cute," Limos purred, her violet eyes glinting with mischief. Chick was weird.

Kynan jammed his hand through his hair. "We can't give up the hound."

"Give us the fucking dog or we take it." Frost formed on Ares's words. "And we *will* take it."

"You're bluffing," Kynan said. "You don't know where we're keeping it."

Inky shadows billowed up from the floor around Thanatos's feet, and for a heartbeat, Arik swore he saw faces in the murky depths. "We will know soon enough."

Brittle tension winged through the air, thickening with each silent second. Arik pushed to his feet, clenching his teeth to keep from grimacing. Ares's hand now gripped his sword hilt. Thanatos had settled into a fighting stance, and Limos was standing there twirling a strand of glossy black hair. Somehow, she made the innocuous gesture seem dangerous. Like she could strangle him with that single lock.

The other female was gripping the book with white-knuckled ferocity and worrying her lower lip.

Unease wound its way through Arik's veins. This shit was going to go critical, and fast. "Maybe if we knew why the animal is so important to you, it would be less of an issue for The Aegis."

Ares locked gazes with Arik, and he got the impression the dude had been given the job of War for a reason. There was a general in that big body, someone who knew not only how to fight, but how to win at any cost.

"The hellhound is mine." Everyone swung around to the female who had been so quiet. "I'm connected to him."

"And who are you?" Kynan asked.

"She's the woman your Aegi were going to torture to get information about the hellhound they'd shot." Ares moved to stand next to her, and though he didn't touch her, there was a definite protective quality to his posture.

Kynan scowled. "I don't know what you're talking

about...wait." He zeroed in on the woman with such intensity that Ares bared his teeth. "In South Carolina? Three nights ago?" When she nodded, Kynan exhaled slowly. "A Guardian died that night. They said you were a demon—"

"Cara is no demon," Ares said. "Your Aegi are idiots."

"Hal—the hellhound...he killed your Guardian," Cara said. "He was protecting me from them."

Protecting her? A hellhound? Now Arik had heard everything. "I don't understand how all of this ties together."

Ares swung his head around to Arik. "How much do you two know about the *agimortus*?"

"We know it's a trigger," Ky replied. "An event. We know that Sin was the bearer of Pestilence's *agimortus*, and when she started the werewolf plague, it set into motion the events that broke his Seal. We believe that the bearer of your *agimortus* is a fallen angel."

Ares traded glances with his brother and sister, and after nearly imperceptible nods, Ares put his hand on the other female's shoulder. "This is Cara. She's the bearer, and she's human."

This time the exchanged glances were between Arik and Kynan. "So her death is what will break your Seal, and no doubt Pestilence wants her dead," Arik said.

"Which is why we're guarding her, Einstein." Limos didn't even bother looking at him. She was too busy studying her toes, which were painted the same pink and yellow as her fingernails. Apparently, she was the ADD Horseman.

"We have a little problem, though," Ares said. "Humans aren't meant to bear the *agimortus*. It will kill them. But she bonded with the hellhound you have in captivity. It lends his life force to her, which is buying time. But every time you hurt the animal, it weakens her."

Kynan let out a juicy curse. "I'll arrange for its release."

Arik eyed the vamps near the hearth. "I assume you've made sure your, ah, minions are no threat to Cara."

"Our staff is loyal," Ares said tersely. "They understand the consequences of betrayal. But every other demon in the underworld is a danger to her."

"Not every demon." Kynan's blue eyes became chips of ice.

A muscle twitched in Ares's jaw, as though he was fighting the urge to mouth off. "The majority then," he ground out. "They want out of Sheoul and they crave dominion over humans. You can't trust any of them."

Yeah, Arik felt about the same way. Even though his own sister was a werewolf who was mated to a demon, he hadn't ever gotten over his prejudice.

Kynan's body went bowstring taut, and before the guy went off in defense of his wife, his in-laws, and his unborn child, Arik stepped forward. Which hurt like fuck. Fuck with broken ribs.

"So what else can we do, besides letting the hellhound go?" Arik took a couple of shallow breaths. Still hurt like fuck. "We could help guard Cara."

"Having our demons and your demon killers in close proximity isn't ideal. What we could use is a fallen angel. One who hasn't entered Sheoul."

"Ah." Arik gave up trying to be all manly and wrapped his arm around his chest to keep his rib cage from splitting open. "We have tons of those to give out."

Limos tapped her flip-flopped foot in annoyance. "Pestilence has been slaughtering them left and right. I estimate that there are only about half a dozen remaining. He's determined to bring about the Apocalypse, in case you hadn't figured that out."

"Yeah," Arik drawled, "we were unclear on that. Glad you set us straight."

"We'll see what we can do," Kynan said quickly. "What about your Seals? How can we prevent them from breaking?"

Thanatos snorted. "Don't worry about mine. It will never break."

"Why not?"

"Because I have complete control of it."

Arik frowned. "So what could break it?"

"That's not for you to know." The shadows flitting around Thanatos seemed to grow more agitated. What *were* they? "Let it go."

Touchy. Arik nodded at Limos. "What about you, Bonecrusher?"

Limos grinned. "Still feeling the power of my thighs, are you? Keep taunting me, and I'll do it again. Only I won't stop until your upper body is nothing but lung marmalade."

Now there was a horrific image he'd take to his grave. "You going to answer my question?"

She shrugged one tan, curvy shoulder. "Nope."

Thanatos regarded his sister with amusement before turning back to Ky and Arik. "Limos's *agimortus* is an object. It's a small ivory bowl. Any Horseman who drinks from it will break her Seal."

"Seems like an odd requirement," Kynan said. "Why is that?"

"We don't know," Limos replied, but the way she said it, with a slight trail-off at the end of her sentence, left a question mark in Arik's mind. She might not know, but he had a feeling she had a theory.

"I'm assuming it's well guarded, at least," Kynan said.

There was a lot of weight shifting and sheepish expressions. "What?" Arik looked between the Horsemen, lingering for an extra second on Limos. It really was a great view. "It's not being guarded?"

"We don't know where it is." Thanatos's admission was delivered with a stare that dared Ky or Arik to snark back.

Arik snarked. "Oh, that's great. You lost it? Pestilence could be toasting to success with it as we speak."

Limos shook her head, making her long black hair swish in a shiny wave. "We didn't lose it. It's never been found."

Kynan scrubbed his hand over his face. "We need to get the hellhound situation handled. Do you guys have email? Can you shoot us all the info you've got on this bowl?"

"And how do you think you can find it if we haven't been able to?"

"We may have access to information, maps, histories, that you don't. It can't hurt." Arik paused. "So... are we going to work together? Or are you going to be stubborn until we're all doomed to Armageddon?"

There was a long, strained silence, and then Ares nodded decisively. "We work together. But no one else is to know the locations of our residences."

"Deal." Kynan handed Ares, Thanatos, and Limos cards with his information on them. "Unfortunately, no one in The Aegis but me can travel through Harrowgates, so we can't deliver the hound to you, and I can't transport a cage of that size on my own. Call me in an hour and I'll have coordinates to the Aegis facility where we're holding him."

Ares nodded. "There's one more thing." He slid questioning glances at both Limos and Thanatos. Limos inclined her head sullenly, but Thanatos tensed up. If his jaw got any tighter, teeth were going to break. "Besides Limos's bowl, Pestilence is seeking a dagger. We call it Deliverance. It resembles a miniature sword with a horse head as the pommel. Its eye is a ruby. The dagger was forged in metals from a rock that fell from the sky and was tempered in hellhound blood. We helped The Aegis craft it after we were cursed, and we entrusted them to keep it, but it was lost."

"It doesn't sound familiar," Kynan said, "but I haven't gone through even a tenth of our histories. Why is it important?"

"You asked how we could be stopped. The dagger is the only thing on Earth that can destroy us, and only if wielded by another Horseman."

Realization dawned, and Arik whistled. "That's why you wanted The Aegis to hold it. You didn't want one of you to go evil and destroy the dagger before it could be used."

"Yes. Deliverance was meant to be returned to us if one of our Seals was broken."

"And Pestilence wants it so you guys can't have it to kill him."

Ares gave a sharp nod. "I believe Pestilence is torturing Guardians to get it."

Kynan cursed. "That explains our missing Guardians."

"He delivered one of the bodies to me this night. I'll have Reaver take it to you."

"Thank you." Kynan inclined his head. "If there's nothing else, we'll get to work."

Arik and Kynan strode out of the keep. The second the heavy wooden door closed, Arik hugged his ribs and groaned. "Fuck, that bitch is strong."

Kynan's mouth twitched in mild amusement. "You know how to pick 'em." He slapped Arik on the shoulder. "Since I have to knock you out to move through the Harrowgate, I'll take you to Underworld General. Eidolon can heal you."

The idea of letting a demon fix him made him ill, but he was in too much pain to argue. Besides, Shade, Eidolon's brother, had already healed him once. Saved his life, in fact. And the damned demon never let him forget.

"Let's do it."

# Sixteen

After Kynan and Arik left, Cara took a seat at the table, and one of the vampires—holy crap, *vampires*!—brought her a ham sandwich and hot tea. Free of orc-weed, he assured, when she asked. She still had the leather-bound book Ares had given her before they left his place, *A Guided Tour of Sheoul*, which, though apparently written by a reasonably articulate, intelligent demon, was seriously creepy. But she was learning a lot, even if, so far, she hadn't found anything that might help her understand hellhounds or the *agimortus*.

As she nibbled at the sandwich, she listened to Ares and his siblings argue about The Aegis, hellhounds, daggers, Pestilence, fallen angels...they were all over the place, like marbles on glass. And even though Cara was in the middle of it all, she felt like a serious outsider.

"You guys can feel free to ask my opinion," she called out.

Ares strode over and pushed the uneaten portion of the sandwich closer to her. "We haven't had to include anyone else in any decisions in a long time." It wasn't much of an apology, but from Ares, it was a lot.

She glanced at his brother and sister, who were pretending—badly—to not listen. "Look," she said, lowering her voice, "I'm sorry for earlier. You've been trying to protect me, and I insulted you."

Flickering light from the fire played on Ares's face, throwing shadows in the hollows of his cheeks, and the flames danced in the black of his eyes. "You despise violence and those capable of it, don't you?"

Cara sipped her tea to buy time. How could she explain that what she despised was what *she* was capable of. "Yes," she said simply, because nothing else would come.

His hand dropped to his scabbard, his long fingers stroking his sword's pommel like a lover, and the *agimortus*, which had been tingling already, kicked up a notch. "You despise me."

"Not you." She liked him too much. Even now, her skin was tightening as if his fingers were caressing her instead of the sword. "I despise killing."

The sound of grinding molars joined the crackle of the fire, and then he drilled her with a stare so fierce she recoiled. "Tell me about the person you killed. Was it an accident?"

Whoa. He was as subtle as tank. "Y-yes."

"Self-defense?"

Her heart skittered in an erratic rhythm. "Yes."

"Then stop punishing yourself and everyone else who does what they have to do."

So easy for him to say. He'd had thousands of years to

stop punishing himself. If he ever had. "How many people have you killed?"

"Tens of thousands. And not all in self-defense." His eyes held her captive, when she would have stumbled backward. "Yeah, you're shocked. I'm a warrior, Cara. So go ahead and look at me with contempt, but you'll thank God that I'm there when the werewolf is at the door. Because I'll kill it, and I'll never regret it. You can sit back and be appalled, but at least you'll be alive, your hands will be free of blood, and it'll be because of me."

He wheeled away, but she snagged his armored elbow. The leather was surprisingly soft, and she wondered how it was supposed to protect him. "Wait."

His entire body went taut. "I live to serve," he said sarcastically, and God, that was it, wasn't it? No one had ever treated him as anything but a warrior, so how was he supposed to see himself as anything different?

"You're right," she admitted. "And I appreciate what you're doing for me. I don't mean to judge you, but I see more in you than a killing machine."

"How nice for you," he said. "But you're wrong. I can't afford to be anything else."

Her heart bled for him, that he believed that about himself. "Yes, you can."

He laughed, as if what she'd said was beyond ludicrous. "Are *you* going to give *me* life lessons? What the fuck does a human with the lifespan of a gnat know about a five-thousand year-old demon?"

"What is your problem?" She shot him an irritated glare. "Why do you have such contempt for humans?"

"They die." He bit out the words viciously. "You love them, and then they die. That's what's going to happen to

you, Cara. You're going to die, and then I'm going to—"
He snapped his mouth shut so hard she heard the crack of
teeth.

"You're going to what?" The question tangled on her
tongue, because she wasn't sure what she wanted to hear.

His gaze skipped away. "I'm going to go evil."

His answer chafed, for some reason. Had she wanted
him to say he'd be sad? Ridiculous. But...okay, yes, she
did. She wanted *someone* to be sad she was dead. The
mark on her chest buzzed as her anger sparked. Ares spun
around again, but oh, hell, no. She wasn't finished with
him yet.

Impulsively, she shoved him. Hard. Right into the
wall. "You do not get to walk away from me like that. Not
again. This is my life we're talking about. I'm not a delicate little flower, nor am I a child. I'm a woman with no
family and stuck in a strange world, so even if you have
to pretend to care whether I live or die, that's what I want.
And if I want to have sex, it's not your place to tell me I
can't handle it. And—"

"Cara."

"—How dare you discount my experience—"

"*Cara.*"

"What?"

Ares just stared at her in the silence. Slowly, she turned
her head, heat blooming in her cheeks at the sight of
Limos and Than watching her, both wide-eyed.

"Cara?"

Groaning, she turned back to Ares, her tirade coming back to her in crystal clarity. His eyes gestured to the
floor. She looked. Ares's feet weren't on the ground. With
a gasp, she looked up, and holy shit...she was holding

him against the wall and off the floor. Releasing him, she leaped backward, and he dropped to his feet.

"I guess the *agimortus* does make you stronger." His words were spoken with a certain grim approval.

"I don't understand. You said it was killing me."

"It is. But you're drawing on Hal in the meantime." There was a brittle silence. "And me."

She frowned. "You?"

There was a resigned note in his voice that she didn't understand. "When I'm close to you, it drains me. It's why my armor goes soft. And why I can't sense jack shit when you're around." He closed the distance between them, his hands coming down on her shoulders. "And why I feel things I shouldn't."

She swallowed against the sudden dryness in her mouth. "Like?"

"Like guilt for putting you in this position. Like wanting to keep you safe for more reasons than just because I'll go evil if I don't. Like lust that makes me want to throw you down and take you until we're both too tired to move. And like I'm a fucking idiot for feeling all of that."

Her mouth worked, but nothing came out. And Limos and Thanatos were still staring. Fortunately, a blond man materialized in the room and rescued them all from a whole lot of awkwardness. Cara thought she must be getting used to the weirdness, because she barely even blinked. Nope, she was just thankful for his timing.

Limos squealed in delight and threw herself into his arms. The man's grin lit up the entire room. And was he . . . glowing?

"Who is he?"

"Reaver." Ares raised his hand in greeting. "He's an angel."

"Fallen?"

"Nope. A real live Heavenly angel."

Well, there was something you didn't see every day. She wasn't sure what she expected an angel to look like, but she'd always pictured them wearing white. Not Reaver. He looked as if he'd stepped out of a modeling shoot for *GQ*. His black slacks and gray shirt couldn't fit better over broad shoulders that tapered to a slim waist and long legs, and he sported a gold watch that even from here looked as if it cost more money than she'd made in her entire life.

Limos beamed up at Reaver, who returned the expression of affection. "Does Limos always greet him like that?" Cara asked.

"Yes," Ares grunted. "He indulges her, for some reason."

"Ares." Reaver separated himself from Limos. "I stopped by your place. Saw Pestilence's handiwork. I was concerned."

"Aw, Reavie-weavie is worried about us," Limos chirped, and the angel rolled his sapphire eyes.

"I took what was left of the Guardian's body to The Aegis," Reaver said, and Cara was suddenly very glad Ares and Limos had kept her from witnessing the scene in Ares's backyard. "Did you accomplish anything in your meeting with Kynan and Arik?"

Limos, looking proud of herself, bobbed her head excitedly. "I broke Arik's ribs."

Reaver exhaled on a deep sigh. "Anything else?"

"They're going to research the dagger and Limos's bowl," Thanatos said. "And they're going to arrange for the release of the hellhound..." He drifted off, his stare going blank.

"Than?" Limos grabbed his wrist. "Than! What is it?"

Thanatos swayed, and his eyes sparked with an unholy fire. "Death. So...much...death." He reached out as if trying to grab hold of something.

A gate opened, and then he was gone. Just...gone. As if he'd been sucked into the light against his will.

Alarmed, Cara stepped back. "What just happened?"

Ares's next breath came out on a hiss. "Thanatos is drawn to large-scale death—if it's big or sudden enough, he's taken against his will."

"A battle?" Limos's armor snapped into place, Transformers-style. When Ares remained silent, Limos whacked her forehead with her palm. "Right. Insensitive much? You can't sense anything with Cara around. I'll track him down." She opened a gate and was gone.

"How can she track him?" Cara asked.

"We can land our gate in the last place our brother or sister's gate opened. And no, we can no longer track Pestilence." He gestured for Cara to return to her seat. "I need to call Vulgrim." He fished his cell phone from his pocket as Reaver sank down at the table across from her.

"So. How are you doing?"

"Um...fine?"

"You don't seem surprised to be talking to an angel."

"I'm sitting in a room with the second Horseman of the Apocalypse." She'd *made out* with the second Horseman of the Apocalypse.

"Good point." His shrewd gaze flickered over her, and she got the feeling he was looking right inside her. "How much of your situation have they explained to you?"

"You mean, that my death will bring about the end of the world, and I probably only have a few days to live if we don't find a fallen angel?"

Reaver dragged his hand through his hair. "Yeah. That. Do you know that even if you're able to transfer the *agimortus* to a fallen angel, you're still bonded to a hellhound? Which means you're stuck in our world? You can't exactly go back to living with humans when your dog is the size of a hippo and is capable of eating your neighbors."

"He doesn't have to live with me, does he?"

"No, but you can't predict when he'll pop in to see you. The bond is powerful. He won't want to be far from you."

Okay, she hadn't thought that far ahead. There was no point, not when she barely knew what was going to happen in the next hour, let alone the next week or next month. Reaver reached out and absently toyed with one of the pieces on the chessboard.

"Ares will take care of you. But keep in mind that he *is* a Horseman. If his Seal breaks, he will be the very definition of evil. And even now, he has an inborn need to win any challenge, no matter how minor, and no matter what the cost."

She'd noticed his competitive nature, for sure. "What are you saying?"

"I'm saying that he doesn't have a sense of fair play." Reaver flicked his fingers and leveled all the chess pieces. "He follows no rules, because to him, the end result is what matters—not how you get there."

A tremor of unease went through her. "And you're telling me this, why?"

"Because you need to be prepared to do the same. If you want to survive, you may need to make sacrifices and do things you never thought you'd do. Things that go against everything you've ever believed." His tone was dark, ominous, all the more frightening because it came from a being she had always associated with a soft... goodness. As if he knew what she was thinking, he took her hand. "Angels are warriors, and some of us, like me, are what you might think of as Special Ops. We play on the side of good, but make no mistake—we *are* soldiers, and we'll do what we have to in order to win."

"You...kill?"

"There is very little we *won't* do in the fight against evil."

She swallowed. "So you have no rules either?"

Reaver's sudden laughter had a deep, uplifting bell-tone quality to it. "We have rules. Oh, we have lots of rules."

Ares approached, and Reaver shot her a wink as he stood. "Kynan texted the coordinates to the hellhound. We can go as soon as I hear from Li or Than."

"I'm being summoned anyway," Reaver said. "I'll be in touch." He punched Ares in the shoulder, and in the next instant, was gone.

Cara blinked, feeling a little loopy, as though she'd just gotten off a carnival ride. "I have to say...he's not what I expected of an angel."

Ares laughed. She loved it when he did that. "What did you expect?"

"That maybe they'd be a little more...rigid. Or righteous."

Ares snorted. "He's not like other angels. They all have superiority complexes and sticks up their holy asses. Reaver's different. Probably because he spent some time as a fallen angel."

"Really? He fell? And he was able to go back?"

"An angel can fall, but if he doesn't enter Sheoul, he can be redeemed. But once a fallen angel enters Sheoul, he becomes irreversibly evil. Reaver earned his way back into Heaven by helping save the world not long ago."

Not long ago? She wasn't even going to ask.

One of those gate things opened up behind him, and a massive black horse leaped out—but it was like no horse Cara had ever seen. Its eyes glowed red, its teeth were more like fangs, and its hooves scorched the floor. Limos, her armor splashed with blood, was in the saddle, expertly guiding the stallion with her knees. Gone was the ultra-feminine beach-girl, and suddenly, Cara saw the warrior she was.

"Get Cara out of here," she yelled. "Than's coming."

Ares took Cara's hand in his and tugged her against his hard body. "What happened?"

"Reseph. Fucking asshole started a plague in Slovenia that's mowing people down by the thousands, almost instantaneously." Her stallion danced beneath her, as agitated as its master. "Something else is going on in that area. I can sense need and desperation, but I can't pinpoint it."

"I've felt something similar," Ares said gravely, and Cara wondered if that was why he'd been wound so tight. Then again, he seemed like the type that was always a bowstring waiting to be released. "Was Pestilence there?"

"And Harvester. She was feeding on the dying." Limos's eyes flashed like hot amethysts. "Reseph was—" Her gaze flickered to Cara. "It was bad."

Cara looked between the two. "Who is Harvester?"

"Our other Watcher. Reaver's evil counterpart." Limos made a sound of disgust. "She's a major bitch."

Another gate opened, and Thanatos, on his dun horse, stormed through. Jesus, he looked like something out of a horror movie... teeth bared, nostrils flaring, veins bulging in his throat and temple. The shadows that sometimes surrounded him had taken form, were circling, mouths gaping. One broke from the pack and shot toward her with an earsplitting screech.

Ares threw out his hand, opened a gate, and dragged her through it. She now understood why Thanatos was Death.

He'd had murder in his eyes.

The place Ares instinctively fled to when he needed a quick escape was his island. Specifically, the cliff where he'd taken Cara the first time he'd grabbed her.

"What was that all about?" Cara took a step back from the cliff, her eyes wild as she looked down at the rocks below.

Ares moved closer to the edge, putting his body between it and Cara. "When Thanatos is exposed to mass-casualty, he... changes."

"Like how violence excites you?" She inhaled harshly. "Sorry."

Shit. Not a comfortable conversation. "Yeah. Like that. He needs to kill."

"What are those shadows?"

Ares looked out over the water, focusing on a fishing boat. That was the difference between him and Cara: He got up in danger's grille but looked beyond. She backed away from danger but kept her eyes on it. "They're souls."

"As in... *souls*?"

"His armor collects them. Every time he kills a demon, human, or animal, the soul is sucked into his armor."

Her horror penetrated his own softened armor. "Oh, my God. They're trapped with him?"

"For a time. When he gets angry or goes into battle, or if he calls them out, they have a shot at freedom, but only if they kill something."

"Does the victim's soul replace the shadow after it earns its freedom?"

"No."

"Can he get different armor?"

Ares shook his head. "None of us can. It's part of us, like our horses and our curses."

"What's Limos's curse?"

Ares turned to Cara, his breath catching at the sight of her standing there in the breeze, her lips rosy, her silky hair blowing around her shoulders. It was hard to believe she'd lifted his heavy ass off the ground, especially given the dark crescents under her eyes. She looked exhausted, and at the same time, so very alive that he had to remind himself she was dying, no matter how strong she appeared to be.

*They die. You love them, and then they die. That's what's going to happen to you, Cara. You're going to die, and then I'm going to*—God, he couldn't believe he'd lost it like that. He never exposed himself, but Cara had dismantled his defenses, and he wondered how much of it was due to his proximity to the *agimortus*, and how much of it was just...her.

He had to clear his throat to continue. "Limos becomes a danger to herself. When she's drawn to famine of any kind—a lack of food, medicines, water—she falls into a deep depression and becomes self-destructive." It had always taken Reseph to get her out of it.

"And Reseph?"

"He was drawn to disease, plague. He would... become that disease. In order to rid himself of it, he had to kill someone with it. If he didn't, he'd spread the disease wherever he went. Now that he's Pestilence, he can cause whatever disease he wants, more potent and faster-spreading than its natural counterpart." His cell buzzed, and he checked it, cursed at the note from Kynan.

*Where are you? You'd think Horsemen would be a little more prompt.*

Hard to believe, but Aegi had actually gotten more annoying over the centuries.

Smiling tightly, he took Cara's hand. "You ready to do this?"

"Yep." Cara's big eyes took him in...she looked like that damned Puss-in-Boots cat in *Shrek,* all cute and heart-melting. The way she'd looked when she'd told him that she saw more in him than a killing machine. But how could she? No one had seen him as more than that. Even Ares's sons had looked up to him as a great warrior they wanted to be like when they grew up.

He made a disgusted noise. As much as he really wanted to take her in his arms, he couldn't. They were at war, and she still needed a lot of toughening up if she was to survive. *You're one to talk. You're softening as much as your armor when she's around.*

"Ares," Cara said, just as he opened his mouth to summon Battle. "Who did you lose?"

"What?"

"You said humans die." She squeezed his hand, might

as well have squeezed his breath out of his lungs. "Who died?"

Damn her. He didn't want to answer, but words spilled out of his mouth. "My wife. My brother. My two sons." When those Puss-in-Boots eyes went liquid, he ended it, right then and there. "Don't you pity me. Don't you dare."

Her chin came up. "Don't you tell me how to feel."

Okay, so he wanted her to toughen up, but her bravery might just veer into foolhardy territory with the wrong person. "You know I could crush you."

"I know you won't."

"Why, because I need to protect you?"

"No." She poked him in the breastplate. "Because you gave me a pillow."

He blinked. This female's logic was whacked, as Reseph would have said. "You're gambling your life on a pillow?"

"I don't doubt that you'll do what you have to do to save the world. You'll make hard choices. But you don't grab a pillow for someone you would have no problem killing." She snagged his wrist and flicked her finger over the lines that defined Battle's flank, and Ares sucked air at the sensation of his hips and ass being caressed. "You going to let him out or not?"

On his arm, Battle kicked, as if hearing her. Shit. "Battle, out."

Battle appeared, and wouldn't you know, instead of nudging Ares in greeting, he nuzzled Cara. "Hey, buddy," she purred, and the stallion rubbed against her even more. Stupid horse.

"Come on," Ares growled. "Cara, I'll help you up—"

Battle kneeled. He fucking *kneeled*. Cara shot Ares

a taunting grin and climbed into the saddle. Battle went back up on his hooves, and as Cara scooted forward, Ares swore Battle smiled, too.

Muttering obscenities, Ares swung up onto the horse, wrapped one arm around Cara's waist, and opened a Harrowgate. "I'm going to materialize a few blocks from the coordinates." He inhaled, took in her clean, floral scent, and instantly, his body reacted in a way that only happened when he was heading into a conflict. His heart pounded, his adrenaline surged, and damn, he wanted to throw down with her. *If I want to have sex, it's not your place to tell me I can't handle it.* He stifled a miserable groan. "I don't want to leap into a trap. I also want Battle available if there's trouble."

Especially since being this close to Cara meant that his armor and weapons would be all but useless. Sort of like his brain.

"Trouble?"

*She* was trouble. "I don't trust Aegi. And I wouldn't be surprised to find Pestilence lurking."

"You have a real fun family, you know that? I thought *mine* was odd."

Battle started toward the gate, but Ares tugged on the reins. She'd said she was alone, with no one to care if she lived or died. Why had he not asked about family before? Maybe because he was a callous bastard who'd forgotten what it was like to be human.

"I thought you said you had no family."

"My mom died of cancer when I was young, and my dad passed away a couple of years ago." Cara twisted around so she could see him, her eyes taking on the color of the water around his island, and he wanted to dive in. "I have an older stepsister from my dad's second marriage, but we fought a lot, and I haven't seen her or my stepmom since the funeral."

"And you said you don't have a boyfriend?"

"If I had, you wouldn't have touched me in the shower."

Inexplicably pleased by that, he urged Battle into the Harrowgate. The stallion stepped out into a foggy evening that came straight out of *The Hound of the Baskervilles*. Fitting, seeing how they were fetching a hellhound. Car lights sped toward them, and Cara yelped.

"They're going to hit us!"

"We're on another plane. We're not only invisible to humans, but we're formless."

"I thought you made it so people froze."

"I can do that, too. Or I can enter the world and exist just as humans do."

"But then they can see you."

"Yes, but I told you my presence makes people want to fight."

"And I told you that I can completely understand that," she said, and he had to smile. He smiled even wider when she leaned into him. Even through his armor he could feel her heat. He wanted to feel more of her. Less of her. Dammit, he didn't know what he wanted, and he'd never been indecisive.

Losing the teenage-crush grin, he spurred Battle into a canter, and they rode to a country estate that wasn't visible from the road. The property was fenced by a low stone wall, and Ares would bet his left nut that the perimeter was warded against evil or supernatural creatures. No ward affected him, but certain ones could propel him out of the *khote*.

Not that he was worried about it. His concern was about traps. He wouldn't put it past The Aegis to want to contain both him and Cara in the name of "keeping them safe." The Aegis always did have an overblown sense of its power and abilities, thinking only *they* were capable of making the big decisions. Those egotistical bastards would suck their own dicks if they could.

Ares guided Battle around the perimeter, and though he located concealed stones etched with protective, magical symbols, he found no evidence of a trap. With a command, he released the *khote*.

"I felt that," Cara murmured. "We're visible now, aren't we?"

"Yeah. No doubt we're being watched." As they approached the wrought iron gate, it creaked open. "Definitely watched."

An eerie howl drifted through the mist, and Cara sat forward in the saddle, which shifted her ass firmly against his groin, and he bit down on his tongue. Holy Heaven, he burned for her.

"It's Hal."

The reminder that they were going to rescue a hellhound she was bonded to turned his inner fire down a notch.

Ahead, a vine-choked manor materialized out of the fog. Outbuildings dotted the grassy field behind it, and in front, standing at attention, were a dozen or so humans, including Kynan. A cage had been placed on the drive, centered on top of a salt pentagram.

Instant, raw hatred scoured Ares's veins, as if they ran with hot sand instead of blood. Every bone in Ares's body wanted to slaughter the thing and send it to

Chaos in pieces—the way Ares had found his brother and sons.

Stomping his hooves, Battle tossed his head. He hated hellhounds as much as Ares, and the hostile vibes being thrown off by the Guardians weren't making the stallion any calmer.

"Easy, boy," he murmured. "We're not going to fight today." Too bad, too, because Ares was as juiced as his horse, though he had to credit Cara for some of that. He brought Battle to a halt ten yards from the Guardians.

"Ares." Kynan stepped forward. Most of his crew were watching with awe, but they also were wary, their fingers flexing as if preparing to go for the weapons tucked in their leather shoulder harnesses. That would be a huge mistake. He swept his hand behind him. "These are our Yorkshire cell Guardians."

Ares swung down from Battle. "They look thrilled to meet me."

"Trust me," Kynan said with a wry smile, "they'll be talking about you for months."

He snorted. "Years."

A very pregnant female waddled out of the house, her black Goth clothing matching her black and blue striped hair. Kynan reached his hand out to her while keeping an eye on Ares. "This is my wife, Gem. I brought her with me because she's due any minute."

The female rubbed her belly. "That minute is now."

Kynan's sharp intake of breath was audible even over Hal's whining. "Are you sure? We have to call Eidolon. And Shade. He's your pain management, right? And Tayla. Have you called Tay?"

Ares had always thought the fatherly panic was

fiction—when his own sons were born, he'd been told by messenger weeks after the births. But had he been there, he doubted he would have freaked out. During that time, men had little to do with pregnancies and birthing and babies, and as long as everyone survived the ordeal, it was all good.

Gem's smile turned into a wince. "I just got off the phone with her. I told her my water broke, so the guys are heading to the hospital."

"Your water broke?" Kynan patted down his pockets, maybe searching for a phone or keys. "We have to get you to UG."

UG? She was a demon, then. One of the leaders of a demon-hunting organization was married to a demon? Maybe The Aegis *had* changed.

"We'll be getting the hound and leaving, then," Ares said, and nearly had a heart attack when he looked over at the cage, where Cara was already on her knees and hugging the animal through the bars. Didn't matter that the canine was bonded to her—it could still kill her. Maybe. Ares didn't know. Shit, he had to get his emotions under control. Think like a soldier.

Which wasn't easy, given Cara's proximity.

"Uh...lady, you might not want to get that close," one of the Guardians called. All of the Aegi watched, bug-eyed and freaked out. Even Gem, who was in labor, wasn't budging no matter how hard Kynan tugged on her.

Finally, he scooped her into his arms. She wound her arm around his shoulders and nuzzled his ear, and deep in Ares's gut, something kindled. Longing? Envy? His wife hadn't been affectionate at all. Attentive, yes, but they had never shared intimate moments like that, and as Kynan peered down at his wife's swollen belly, his expression was a mix of worry, joy, and love.

Ares's eyes shifted to Cara, and he actually had to swallow a lump in his throat.

*Get your head out of your arse.* He could hear his father's bark, could swear a blow struck his cheek from his father's backhand. The bastard had long been in the grave, and he still had the power to reach out and try to put Ares in his place.

For the first time, Ares welcomed his father's interference. He couldn't afford to let Cara matter to him. She was going to die. Even if she didn't die because of the *agimortus*, she'd die long before he did, even with the hellhound bond. A couple of hundred years was a fruit fly's lifespan for immortals.

And what the fuck was he running through the scenarios for? Love was not an option for him. It never had been. Caring for someone made you weak. Made you make stupid decisions. He'd seen it all over the centuries; men losing property, wars, their very lives over the love of a woman.

Idiots.

"William, you handle this." Kynan awkwardly fished keys out of his pocket. "I'll leave the Rover near Woodacre."

There was a Harrowgate there, but it was still ten miles away. "Kynan." Ares threw open a gate just outside the property fence. "Take it. You'll come out at Underworld General."

Gem peeked over Kynan's shoulder to admire Ares's handiwork. "That is so cool. I want that power."

Kynan eyed the Harrowgate with distrust, until Gem

socked him in the shoulder. "Hello! Do you want me to drop this kid right here? The baby is charmed, remember? As long as it's in my belly, nothing can hurt me."

Kynan shot Ares a look that said, "If you land us in a Sheoul blood pit, you're dead," and then he sauntered to the gate, stepping through after only a second of hesitation.

Ares moved closer to Cara, but when the fucking mutt went insane, snarling and snapping at him, he halted. Battle didn't. He charged the cage, and before Ares could stop him, he reared up to smash the crate and hound to bits.

Cara leaped to her feet, put herself between the two-thousand-pound warhorse and the iron cage.

"*No!*" Ares's shout came out in a deep, horrified rumble as Battle came down hard enough to make the ground tremble.

He'd stopped mere inches from crushing Cara. She stood there, not even flustered, and took Battle's face in her hands. The horse calmed immediately, but Ares was shaking like a leaf, and his fear morphed abruptly into anger.

"Goddammit," he snapped. "What the fuck were you thinking, Cara? He could have killed you."

"Don't talk to me like that." She glared at him while stroking Battle's cheeks. "Obviously, I'm fine."

The Guardians shrunk back, twitchy fingers poised over their weapons. Great. They now thought he was not only incompetent, but an asshole as well. Snarling, he held out his arm. "Battle, to me."

The horse let out a furious whinny that lingered in the air even after he'd settled on Ares's skin.

"That," Cara huffed, "was unnecessary."

"No," he ground out, "it wasn't. When you released the mongrel, there would have been trouble."

"I could have handled it."

"*I* handled it. Now let's do this." He turned to the Guardians. "You had best watch from inside the house."

They retreated, and he gave Cara the go-ahead. "Lever on top should open the cage." Casually, he rested his hand on the hilt of his sword, even though he couldn't injure the animal for fear of affecting Cara.

She gave the lever a shove, and the door rattled open. The hellhound bounded out, pounced, and took Cara to the ground. Ares's heart jammed into his throat, but when Cara let out a delighted squeal and the dog bathed her face in sloppy kisses, it became clear that there was no danger here. No danger to her, anyway.

Hal lifted his head momentarily to peel back his lips in a silent warning aimed at Ares, and Ares returned it, hoping his hatred came across loud and clear. Dealing with this bastard was not going to be fun.

"Cara, let's go. I don't like you being this exposed."

She told Hal to let her up, and he tore off across the lawn. "He needs to run. Maybe we could walk to the gate instead of ride? Give him a chance to stretch his legs?"

"Cara—"

"Please?"

It went against his better judgment, but Cara had been through so much, with little of it in her control, that he could do this one thing for her, he supposed.

Two heartbeats later, his own words, barked out at soldiers, rang through Ares's head like a death knell. *Never let a woman sway you. Never. Or I promise you'll regret it.*

# Seventeen

~

Cara and Ares strolled across the grounds toward the gate, his pace purposeful, hers more leisurely, and he kept having to slow down and wait for her. But dammit, this was the first time she'd felt a little normal in days, and walking across a huge expanse of grass while Hal bounded around chasing birds just felt good. Relaxing, even.

"Why don't you like hellhounds?" she asked, and Ares let out a soft growl.

"I don't *not* like them." Even loaded down with armor and weapons, he moved like a predator down the drive, his sharp eyes in constant motion, nostrils flaring as though seeking the scent of danger. "I hate them with every cell in my body."

"That's a little harsh."

He swung around to her, his big body pulsing with menace, but she was instinctively aware that his mood wasn't directed at her. "One of them killed my brother and sons."

"How awful." A lump clogged her throat, and she had to swallow a couple of times before she could speak. "What did you do?"

"I chased that motherfucker through the centuries. Slaughtered some of his packmates, but never managed to kill him. Eventually, he and his pack got one up on me, paralyzed me with a bite, and then spent days eating me alive."

Oh, God. "They...*ate* you?"

"Thanks to my ability to regenerate, yes. I fed them well, and I felt every bite. When one of them ripped my leg off at the hip joint, I couldn't even pass out from the agony. And then I got to watch them gnaw on it, right beside my head."

Nausea bubbled up in her throat. She couldn't imagine Hal, that sweet puppy who was rolling around in the grass, doing that.

"Yeah, he'd do it," Ares said, somehow knowing what she was thinking. "He's just a pup, but when he's full grown, he'll be as big as a damned buffalo with an appetite for cruelty to match his size."

"Like the one who attacked you at your house? Hal's sire?"

"Hal's sire is the very hound who killed my sons and brother."

Oh...*damn.* "Hal...he wouldn't...I mean, look at him."

Hal leaped into the air, his jaws snapping as he caught a bird he'd flushed. The poor bird was gone in an instant, an explosion of feathers floating around Hal's head.

"Sure," Ares said wryly. "Look at him."

"Bad dog," she scolded. Hal wagged his tail and cocked his head, all flopping ears and drool. How could a puppy like him become the demon beast Ares was talking about?

Ares snorted. "Just wait until he's catching people instead."

"Is that..." She swallowed sickly. "Is that what they eat?"

"Not usually. They're Sheoul-dwellers. They rarely travel to the human realm unless they're summoned or brought here."

"So he can travel back and forth? Do his hunting in Sheoul?"

Ares inclined his head in a brisk nod. "They don't need Harrowgates, and usually they're invisible to humans when they're aboveground. He might be invisible now, in fact. We can see him because we're part of the supernatural world."

She trailed her fingers over her chest, feeling the raised lines of the new mark through her sweatshirt. "Because of this."

"And the bond to Hal." His gaze dropped to where she was rubbing the marking, and the energy coming off him shifted from menacing to erotic.

Back at Than's place, he'd said he felt things he shouldn't. That he wanted to keep her alive for more reasons than protecting his Seal. And that he wanted to throw her down and take her until they were exhausted.

She shouldn't want any of that. Well, maybe the sex. Opening her heart up again could be a colossal mistake. But every time she caught a glimpse of the man behind the sword, every time he wrapped her in his protective arms, it tapped into the part of her that wanted to be cared for and kept safe. Ares knew about her ability, knew what she'd done with it, and he didn't treat her like she was a freak, and that alone scored him a lot of points.

"What is this, Ares?" She probably shouldn't have asked, but she'd never been good at subtlety, and with all the uncertainty in her life right now, she wanted to be clear on this, at least. "I can't read your signals, and I don't know who you are."

"I'm a warrior."

"Yes, I know who you say you are, but why do you say that? Are you a warrior by birth? By choice? By circumstance?"

"All of the above." He cocked his head toward the exit. "We should go."

She grabbed his wrist, and he stiffened, but he didn't shake her off. "When were you born?"

"Dammit, Cara, we don't have time for this." The words were angry, but he let out a long-suffering sigh, and she knew she had him. For a moment, at least.

"Humor me. I've done everything you've asked. Give me this."

One eyebrow arched. "The orgasms weren't enough?"

A pleasant fluttering filled her belly. "Women like pillow talk to go with them, and you denied me that."

"I at least got you a pillow." At her flat stare, he rolled his eyes. "I was born around the thirty-second century BC."

"Did you know what you were?"

He looked up at the gray sky. "For twenty-eight years I thought I was human. My demon mother snatched human babies out of their cribs and replaced them with us. She used some sort of enchantment to arrange for our human parents to name us what she'd chosen."

"What happened to the babies she stole?"

He hesitated. "You don't want to know."

No, she probably didn't. "Where did you grow up?"

"Egypt." He looked past her at Hal, his gaze sharpening with hate. "Now, we're going."

Pretending she didn't hear him, she continued. "You had kids. Did you have a wife?"

"I've humored you for too long as it is—" He whirled so suddenly she yelped. "Who are you? Show yourself!"

Cara heard the crunch of gravel, as a man peered around the estate's iron gate. "I-I'm David. I'm a Guardian."

A deep, rumbling growl came from behind her as Hal, crouching flat on the ground, eased up to them. She dropped her hand to his head, soothing him with her touch. "It's okay, Hal. Shh." The last thing they needed was the hound tearing apart one of The Aegis's demon slayers.

Ares took her hand and led her to the road. Hal followed, though his ears were still back, and his teeth were bared in a silent snarl. The Guardian wisely backed away, hands up.

The moment they stepped outside the Aegis property, the forest erupted to life. A scream caught in Cara's throat as creatures appeared from out of the woods, out of the ground, and out of thin air.

In a graceful surge, Ares simultaneously drew his sword and threw open a Harrowgate. "Cara, go!" He leaped and spun, taking off a demon's head as she scrambled toward the opening.

Something wrapped around her throat and jerked her backward. Gasping, she reached up to yank on the rope, digging in her heels as a gray-skinned demon reeled her toward him. A flash of black fur, teeth, and claws sailed past her, and the demon who had captured her screamed as Hal tore him apart.

"Cara!" A creepy demon with hooks for hands swung at Ares, one hook burying itself in his armor. Ares fell backward as he struck out with a dagger. It didn't even scratch the creature. "Your presence is—" He broke off to slam his fist into another demon's flat face. "—Affecting my ability to fight."

She made a run for the gate, but two feet from the entrance, a green-skinned, scaly demon tackled her. She hit the ground hard enough to knock the wind from her lungs. Fire replaced air as she struggled to breathe, and then terror iced down her blood at the sight of a wicked, serrated blade slicing in a downward arc toward her throat.

A roar blasted through the air, and then Ares was there, his foot smashing into the demon's head. The blade flew out of his clawed hand, and Cara rolled out from under the now-bloody demon. She grabbed the dagger, shoved it upward as another demon swung at her. It caught the spindly creature in the gut. It screeched and fell, and another replaced it. Once more, Ares took the demon's head off, and if that was how he fought while handicapped, she couldn't imagine what he could do normally.

Hal ripped into another demon that launched itself at her, and blue blood splattered on the ground. A rain of arrows fell, and she looked up at Guardians running toward them, some firing crossbows and others wielding bladed weapons.

"Gate!" Ares shouted, and yes, she was trying. In the midst of the bloodbath, she crawled, finally reached the shimmering curtain of light, and went through.

She came out on Ares's Greek island. Hal followed, landing on top of her. He was covered in blood, and she immediately put her hands on him, seeking injuries. He had a few minor cuts, and without even summoning her ability, it flashed hot and channeled into him. She hissed in both surprise and brief pain as Ares's staff came running, and how crazy was it that demons were coming at her, and all she could feel was relief?

"Cara!" Limos ran toward her, still in her armor. "Where's Ares?"

Cara pushed to her feet. "Demons attacked us. He's fighting them—"

"Okay, let's get you inside." She grabbed Cara's arm, and Hal let out a vicious snarl. Dancing aside, Limos went for the dagger at her hip.

"No!" Cara seized Limos's hand. "Don't provoke him. Hal, it's okay. Be good. These are friends."

A blast of annoyance came off him, but he stopped growling. *Where are we?*

"Safe," she replied, blinked when she realized she'd understood him. Just like in the dreams. "This is Ares's island."

*I patrol. I keep you safe.* He slipped away, skirting the Ramreel demons and disappearing into the brush.

Cara allowed Limos to take her inside. "Will Ares be okay? There were a lot of demons. Maybe you should help."

Limos snorted. "Trust me, he'll be fine."

"But there were a lot of Aegi. Ares was worried about a trap."

"Listen up, human." Limos brushed her fingers over her throat, and her armor melted away, leaving her in the Hawaiian gown again. "He's immortal. As long as there weren't any hellhounds there—"

"There were," she lied.

Limos froze. "What? Are you sure?"

"Yes." Cara swallowed, feeling bad about the lie but not willing to risk Ares's safety. "Please. Help him."

"Fuck." Limos threw a gate, but before she stepped through, she stabbed a finger at Cara. "Stay here, and don't leave the house for anything."

*"Cara told you what?"* Ares snarled at Limos as he pinned the last demon to the ground with his sword as if it was an insect in a display case. All around them, Guardians were cleaning up from the battle, triaging their own. Looked like all were injured, two critically, and one was dead. Dead, along with several dozen demons that were already disintegrating.

The rest had fled when Cara escaped through the Harrowgate. Clearly, once their target was gone, they hadn't felt like sticking around to be slaughtered by Ares and his Aegis sidekicks.

Limos wiped her blade clean in the grass. "She lied. I'm going to kill her."

"Not if I get to her first." Her lie had left her without a Horseman to protect her. Ares yanked his sword out of the demon. "Has Than come out of his rage?"

"Yep. He's gone to New Zealand to follow up on a lead about a fallen angel."

"Help him," Ares said. "We need one. Now."

Limos popped a salute. "Yes, sir." Her sarcasm was tempered by an impish smile as she zapped a Harrowgate and stepped through.

Ares did the same, and came out in his great room, where there was no sign of the human.

"Cara!" he roared.

Torrent appeared from the kitchen with a steaming plate piled high with roast lamb and vegetables, Rath darting between his legs. "She was here a second ago," he said.

"Dammit!" Ares stalked through the house, fear spiking his anger. She wasn't in the master suite, or any of the other bedrooms. His anxiety grew as he checked rooms and kept coming up empty.

And then a sudden suspicion nearly laid him out.

*The* room.

With dread running like sludge in his veins, he charged to the end of the hall just past the storeroom. The door to the stairwell was ajar, confirming his suspicion. He took the stone steps down three at a time. The narrow, unfinished passageway was dark, but a light from the room at the bottom burned bright.

He insisted the room be lit. Twenty-four-seven.

He hit the bottom of the steps and skidded to a halt. Cara stood at the ancient bookcase, angled so he could partially see her profile. She'd opened the tiled box he kept there and was holding the items that had been inside. Irrational anger hitchhiked a ride with adrenaline and fear for Cara's safety, and he lashed out.

*"Get away from that."*

Cara jumped, whirled around, and nearly dropped the clay horse and dog. Jesus. If the toys had broken, he would have...just...Jesus.

"I'm sorry...I was—"

"You were going through my things."

Carefully, she placed the toy animals in the box, along with the wooden rattle. But she ran her thumb over the bronze ring and the milky green emerald set into it. "It's beautiful," she whispered.

His throat closed up. "It was my wife's."

She set it in the box. "And the other things?"

"They were my sons'. Now get out."

"The light was on—"

"Get. Out."

"I only wanted to know more about you."

"I told you my family was killed. What more do you need?" He stepped inside, and the room closed in on him. He hadn't been in here in decades. Vulgrim kept it clean and the light working, but Ares hadn't had the guts to visit. The knowledge that he'd been so cowardly ramped up his temper even more. "Get out."

Pity flashed in her eyes, and wasn't that just the icing on his shit cake? "I'm sorry about your family." She closed the box lid so softly he barely heard the click of the tiny latch slide into place. Her gaze traveled around the room, which held all of the possessions he'd been able to retrieve from the time he was human. "Why was the light on?"

How many times had he told her to get out, and she was still standing there, asking about the lights? He should toss her, but he didn't trust himself to touch her. He was too angry, and he wanted her too badly.

"I keep it on always. My youngest son was afraid of the dark." He'd thought it was stupid at the time, hadn't understood childish fears, because he'd never been afraid of anything as a child.

The room was getting seriously claustrophobic. He didn't bother telling Cara to leave again. He got the hell out of there. Sometimes, the best strategy was to retreat and regroup.

Cara called out to him, but he kept going, didn't stop until he was in the private, three-walled patio off his bedroom. He just wanted sixty seconds alone—

"Ares."

Fuck. He didn't turn around. Instead, he looked out over the sea as the last rays of sunlight cast a sparkling sheen on the water. This was his favorite time of day, when the sun-worshippers were winding down and the night-dwellers were just starting to stir. In this brief window of time, everything was quiet. Back in his military days, they'd called it the time of "peace shadows," because no matter how fierce the fighting had been, it slowed, for just a few minutes, as everyone adjusted their tactics.

"What happened?" she asked quietly. "I mean, how did it all go down?"

In the distance, the Greek shoreline began to light up, and wisps of smoke from kitchens and beach fires formed lazy, spiraling tendrils that reached for the handful of clouds. He figured that for this topic, there should be gale-force winds, driving rain, and maybe a tornado or two.

"I was twenty-eight. Home with my brother, my wife, and my sons. At the time, I thought I was human, and I didn't know the men who overran our city were creatures from hell in human skins. I sent my sons with my brother, and they escaped the city, but the demons captured me and my wife. They forced me to watch as they tortured and killed her. Afterward, they released me. Later, I learned that it was hell's calling card. Time for me and my brothers to come home."

"What did you do?" Her voice was as soft as the breeze, nonthreatening, and that was the only reason he continued.

"I found Ekkad and my sons, and we gathered my army

as demons poured out of hell in their true forms. Limos escaped from Sheoul during the upheaval, and when she found us, she explained the truth of our existence. That we were meant to join the forces of evil and use our knowledge about humans to destroy them. She warned me that the demons would do anything to get us on their side. That if I didn't join, my sons would die. I didn't listen. I believed I could protect my family."

He snorted, shook his head. "I was such a fool. For two years, my siblings and I battled demons. Ekkad was my right hand, my strategist, and I taught my sons to fight. They were like me, even as young as they were, they were strong, fast, and they healed quickly. One day, the fighting was worse than usual, we were badly outnumbered, and I sent my boys back to the command tent with Ekkad. When I returned, I found them." He closed his eyes, but the darkness didn't blot out the memories. "The hellhound had..."

"It's okay. You don't have to say any more."

"Yeah, I do." He blew out an unsteady breath. "My brother and sons died because of me. Because the demons knew exactly how to hurt me. And on that day, I turned as evil as I could have been without my Seal breaking. I went insane with rage. I gathered more humans for my army... bribed them, coerced them, forced them. Men, women, children. Didn't matter. All I wanted was for the demons to die. The humans were disposable to me. I rejected strategy that would take longer but save lives and instead went for quick victories by sheer numbers. In essence, I sent them to their deaths for my own needs. My brothers and sister helped, and it went on until we were brought to heel by angels and cursed."

He could practically feel revulsion wafting off Cara.

He definitely heard it in the rasp of her voice. "Why are there no records of this?"

"Because the angels fixed everything. They erased memories, created alternative scenarios, and destroyed all written evidence. Basically, the world started over from that point on."

The sound of ocean waves breaking on the rocks below filled a long silence. "If demons killed your family…"

"Why do I employ them?" He didn't wait for her to answer. "I found Vulgrim when he was a child. His herd had been wiped out by plague. The ones who weren't dead were dying. All except Vulgrim. Limos thinks his father was from another herd that had developed an immunity to the disease. He was too small to take care of himself. I don't know why I didn't leave him, I've never been fond of Ramreels, but I took him. Brought him home and nursed him back to health with goat milk."

"That was kind of you."

He shrugged, still looking out at the sea, which had darkened, though beneath the water, light-absorbing algae were glowing, little landing strips in the waves. "He turned out to be a good kid. Cranky teen. But a capable adult, and his loyalty to me can't be questioned. He looks upon me as a father."

"And now he's your… servant?"

Ares laughed. "He likes to act as if he's being forced into servitude, but he's not. I've treated him as an equal, offered to set him up in his own place, wherever he wants. Instead, he stays here. He lives with his mate on the other side of the island, and he's in charge of all the staff. The Ramreels here are all part of his herd, and his son, Torrent, is his second in command."

"You're very fond of him."

More than he would ever admit out loud. He remembered trying to teach Vulgrim to ride a horse, and only after a dozen falls did he realize that Ramreel physiology made it practically impossible for them to ride. Vulgrim liked to recount that story whenever he felt Ares needed to be humiliated, and Ares would act all irritable, but in truth, he liked the teasing that few others would dare.

"It's funny," he said. "Sometimes I wonder if he'd have gotten along with my sons." Had they not been . . . yeah.

There was another long silence, and then, "Did you love your wife?"

He smiled, but she couldn't have seen it. "Love was never part of our life. It was an arranged marriage. My wife knew what was expected of her, and she pleased me well enough."

"Well . . . *enough*? Sounds like it was fun to be her."

"She had a good life." It was her death that was the atrocity. "No need to be outraged on her behalf. I didn't beat her, I allowed her to spend coin on luxuries, and I didn't take mistresses."

"How considerate of you."

He turned to Cara, reached out to brush a wind-blown lock of hair off her face. "It had nothing to do with being considerate. Truly, I was a bastard. I simply had no interest in women. Fighting was my life." He waggled his brows. "The Greek god, Ares, is based on me."

She rolled her eyes. "That must have been an ego boost."

"I miss the days of the Greek empire. It was cool being a god." He sighed. "Then the single-deity religions came along and ruined everything."

"Gee, I'm so sorry."

He laughed at her sarcasm. "Makes things simpler for humans, I guess, but they've gotten most of it wrong. Today's population has no idea how much manipulation of facts has taken place over the centuries. Still amazes me that people spend more time researching a new vehicle than they do the religion they entrust their souls to. They should CARFAX their faiths. The history would shock the hell out of people."

One delicate eyebrow rose on her forehead. "I think someone's bitter about not being a Greek god anymore." Her mouth quirked in amusement, and she crossed her arms over her chest, which plumped her breasts out nicely. "But you and your brothers and sister must have had a blast, watching history happen and being part of it."

"At times," he admitted. He turned back to the sea and focused on some bobbing boat lights in the distance. "But mostly we spent our time watching events take place and wondering if they were portents that would bring about the breaking of our Seals. And unfortunately, we spent way too much time goofing off when we should have been trying harder to locate or protect our *agimorti*."

"I'm sorry," Cara said softly. "I've been a little selfish." He felt her palm on his back, and he was too stunned to move.

"Selfish? You've had everything taken away from you. How are you being selfish?"

"I didn't think about how awful this has to be for you. Your brother has turned against you, and it might be only a matter of time before you succumb to the same fate."

Jesus. She was serious. She actually gave a shit about how he felt. He wasn't sure if he liked that or not, but he did know he didn't want to talk about it. "Why did you lie to Limos?"

Her hand slid up to his neck and her strong, flexible fingers massaged the tense muscles there. After all he'd just told her about the evil he'd done, she still wanted to touch him. To soothe him. He didn't deserve it, but he didn't do anything to stop her.

"Cara? Why?"

"Because I was worried about you."

On some level, her admission pleased him. But on a much higher, much darker level, it pissed him the fuck off. Did she think he couldn't take care of himself? Did she not give a shit about her own life? He rounded on her. "That was stupid, Cara. You left yourself vulnerable. Do you like being attacked? Is that it?"

"N-no." She recoiled, and something desperate flashed in her eyes, a haunted shadow he had seen far too many times over the course of his life.

Shit. He reached for her, but a vicious snarl froze him to the ground, and hot, fetid breath against his ear sent his heart rate into a galloping speed even Battle would envy. He didn't need to look to know Hal was crouched on the wall, his teeth just inches from his throat.

"Hal." Cara spoke so calmly that no one could have guessed that just a moment earlier, she'd looked like she might break down. Damn... all this time, he'd wanted her to toughen up, but she was already there. She bounced back easily, fully, and most impressively. "He isn't going to hurt me."

Still the beast snarled, clearly not buying what Cara had to say. He lunged, and suddenly, his mouth was clamped down on Ares's throat. The teeth didn't puncture, but Ares couldn't move without being bitten or scratched.

"Cara," he gritted out. "What. The. Fuck."

She licked her lips. "Your anger scares him. He thinks you're tricking me."

"Convince him otherwise." After this, he was going to find a shaman, wizard, sorcerer...someone who could break a hellhound bond, because this asshole mutt needed to die, and his sire along with him.

Slowly, she eased up to them both. She curled one hand in Hal's scruff, and put her other hand around the back of Ares's neck. Her breasts became a soft pressure against his chest, and then she was on her toes, putting her lips on his. And what do you know, Hal's growls grew quieter.

"See, Hal," she whispered against his lips. "Ares won't hurt me." She squeezed his neck, her fingernails digging in so deep he hissed. In pleasure. "Will you?"

"No," he said against her mouth. "Never."

But he was a warrior, and if it came down to hurting her or saving the world, he knew what he'd choose. For the first time, the idea truly bothered him, and for the first time he actually felt like War.

# *Eighteen*

~

Cara really had no idea what was up with Hal, but he'd come out of nowhere, and no matter what she said to him, he was convinced Ares was going to hurt her.

*He could kill you.*

"He's not going to."

*He could. He is bad. He kills my pack. He tries to kill father.*

"I know," she whispered. The pain and death that Ares and Chaos had brought down on each other was staggering.

*I bite him.*

"No!" She stroked Hal's fur, desperate to calm him down. "I need him to protect me, like I need you. There are a lot of bad people who want me dead. You know that, right?"

Hal growled. *I kill them.*

All this talk of killing was seriously disturbing, and she didn't know if she'd ever get used to this world, these beings. Heck, she didn't want to get used to it. No one should ever grow numb to death.

"Hal, you must only harm those who mean *us* harm."

*Like War.*

"He means us no harm." No doubt the conversation seemed strange to Ares, who could hear only one side, and it didn't help that he kept tensing. Each twitch of his muscles made Hal's huge claws dig deeper into the stone wall. Scorch marks spread from beneath his paws, creating blackened veins in the rock. It was scary as hell, and she had to wonder what other surprises she was in for with the hellhound. Slowly, she ran her hand through Ares's silky hair and made sure Hal saw her nuzzle his cheek. "See? He likes me."

A dubious growl vibrated the air. She put her lips to Ares's again. "Kiss me," she murmured, and though she knew Ares could hardly move, he dipped his head, just slightly, to increase the pressure on her mouth. And while it might be crazy, the feel of him made her skin sizzle.

She kept kissing him, and gradually, Hal stopped growling. He released his hold on Ares's throat, and instantly, the tension drained from Ares's body. Wisely, though, he didn't move away from her. In fact, one arm came around her waist, and he hauled her tightly against him.

"You can go, Hal. Keep me safe by patrolling the island. Find rats."

*Tasty.* Hal's lips peeled back as he shot Ares a warning look. *He is danger.*

Yes, he was, but she didn't say anything, simply clung to Ares as Hal disappeared over the wall. She expected Ares to release her, but instead, he kissed her again. "I hate your dog," he muttered against her lips. "I want him to be stuffed and mounted on my wall. But I'm tired of fighting him, you, and myself."

Himself? "What does that mean?"

His long fingers swept over his throat, over that tiny crescent scar, and his armor melted away, leaving her crushed against his chest. His thigh parted hers, and she nearly moaned at the delicious pressure of his hard muscle against her core. "It means that sometimes, to win a war, you have to change tactics." He smiled against her mouth. "I'm flexible like that."

He swept her up, and before she could protest—or encourage him—he laid her out on the patio couch. The cushions sank deep under their weight. His calloused palm slid beneath her sweatshirt, and he shuddered when he reached her bare breasts.

"No bra," he said against her mouth. "Thank you. I hate those things. Dumbest human invention. Ever."

She captured his hand, encouraging his touch, loving the way he was both gentle and rough, a combination of long strokes over her flesh and stinging pinches on her nipples. Her breasts swelled, ached, and as if he knew she was wanting more, he stripped her sweatshirt off, tossed it to the ground, and took her in his mouth. He drew deep, his tongue rasping over her sensitive nipples, leaving her dazed, breathless, and oh so wet.

"Yesssss . . ." Her moan of pleasure floated into the twilight, joining the crash of waves and the distant call of sea birds. This was the most beautiful thing she'd ever experienced, a moment she'd remember forever.

Forever might be very short.

Flushing the depressing thought from her mind, she dug her nails into his shoulders and arched her back, needing to feel the entire length of his body against hers. His thighs parted her legs, putting his sex where she wanted it, and as she writhed and his hips rolled, heat built at her center, and lust intoxicated her.

It didn't take long before he was working her jeans' zipper, and her hands were just as frantic, tearing open his pants to release his massive length. The moment it sprang free, she took the shaft in her fist, reveling in the desperate male sound that broke from his throat.

His gaze gleamed with hunger as it locked with hers. Lips parted to allow for his panting breaths, he braced himself on one arm and slid his palm under her panties. His fingers slipped between her folds, and he groaned.

"You're so wet." One finger pushed inside her, and she nearly came. "So tight."

"I thought I was too weak for you." She squeezed his cock, rubbed her finger in the drop of wetness at the tip, and he hissed in pleasure.

"I was wrong," he rasped. "I've seen how you handle Battle, Hal . . . and me. I was so fucking wrong."

He leaped off the sofa, yanked her jeans from her legs, and then stripped out of his clothes. When he was done, he stood in front of her, a stunning work of masculinity. And, to her delight, he was as smooth and hairless between his legs as he was on his chest. Her heart jerked as he palmed his straining erection.

"I never do this." He squeezed himself, and she became glued to the motion he began—long, slow pumps of his fist down the length and back up to swallow the head as he delivered a little twist.

"Um . . . you never . . . masturbate?"

His eyes were slits behind his heavy lids, but the intensity was in no way diminished. "I never slow it down like this. It's always rough and hard with a female." He sank down between her legs, but he never stopped the erotic play with his penis. "It's always been about the release. The who-can-fuck-who-the-hardest."

Images of him pounding into other women—*females*, as he called them—wrung a nasty punch of jealousy out of her, but when she inserted herself into the picture, she flamed hot. To have all that undiluted sexual power ramming into her like a force of nature...*oh, God*.

"I want that."

Her declaration sent a shudder through him, and his strokes sped up. The idea excited him. "Not...now."

He still thought she was too weak. But if it were true that she was dying, she certainly wasn't going to get any stronger. "Ares—"

"No. You aren't like those other females. I want this to be different." He backed up, lowering his head between her legs. There was no warning, just his hot, wet tongue penetrating her slit.

She arched skyward, might have launched right off the cushion if he hadn't gripped her hips and held her firmly against his mouth. He alternated long passes of the flat of his tongue with lingering, gentle pulls on her clit and deep thrusts inside her.

"You taste like the ocean. Fuck..." Groaning, he lifted one leg over his shoulder and opened her wide, his thumbs spreading her to the night air and his sultry breath. She rolled her hips, encouraging him—not that he needed it. He pleasured her with a vengeance, his carnal timing keeping her at the edge of orgasm for endless, blissful minutes. Streams of erotic sensation made her mindless, light-headed, and before she knew it, her hands were tangled in his soft hair, guiding that magic tongue where she needed it most.

He didn't tease. He worked her with a goal, and when she began to buck, gasping for air, he growled against her core and latched on, sucking while plunging his tongue into her in a devastating rhythm. Her climax spun up like a storm, a whirlwind of ecstasy, and before it had fully tapered off, Ares lunged, mounting her, his closed fists coming down on either side of her head, the broad tip of his shaft nudging her center.

"I love the way you come," he whispered into her ear. "You're loud, the way a male likes it." Her breath caught at his words, but then he was rubbing his erection through her folds, sliding back and forth over sensitive tissues, and nothing mattered but getting him inside her.

"Wait." She slapped her palm on his chest. "Protection?"

He lifted his head, his brows drawn in confusion. "My guards are stationed nearby—ah, you mean for the sex." She nodded, and also really hoped his guards hadn't heard any of this. "I can't contract or transmit disease, and I take skullwort every two months to prevent my seed from planting."

Oddly phrased, for sure, but who cared? She was aching, her climax still throbbing, and she just wanted to get on with it. She stopped thinking, reached between them to guide him to her entrance. "Now," she said hoarsely.

"Now," he agreed, and rocked his hips, plunging into her. They both moaned.

His entire body undulated, his muscles bunching and flexing, and when he threw his head back, the corded tendons in his neck strained. They moved together, her legs wrapped around his waist and locked at the ankles over his butt.

"This," he breathed, "is so good. You're...still rippling."

The sea breeze wrapped around her, mingling with the scent of Ares's warm skin, the steamy sex, and the sweet flowers that lined the patio walls. Suddenly, he reared back, gripped her thighs, and watched their mating. It was such a turn-on, and she was so freaking into it. She braced herself on her feet and lifted her hips off the cushions so she could meet each of his powerful thrusts with one of her own.

The sight of him watching, the way it affected him so strongly, brought her to the very edge. His broad chest expanded in great, shuddering breaths, his eyes burned, and yet, she sensed he was holding back. He was driving into her with passion she'd never felt from the two lovers she'd had—the high school boyfriend she'd lost her virginity to, and then Jackson—but Ares's great power was restrained.

She. Was. Not. Weak!

An ancient, primal feminine instinct awakened in her, and she snarled, rose up, and dug her nails into his chest. He made a harsh noise, baring his teeth in surprise and pain. She didn't spare him. Ruthlessly, she raked her nails over him, dragging them over the rolling eight-pack of his abs. His roar of pleasure accompanied a mighty surge, and suddenly, she found herself lifted and her back pressed against the wall, with one of Ares's arms behind her as a buffer. Her knees were spread wide on the cushions, and Ares was kneeling between them, his hips pistoning urgently as he drilled her deep and fast.

Rocking his head, he sank his teeth into the juncture

between her throat and shoulder, and dear, sweet Lord, she was done for. His possession was swift and sure and she reveled in the animal mating. He was marking her with his teeth, with his body, and even the bruises she'd have later would be evidence of the savage fever that had taken him.

Her orgasm blazed through her with the intensity of the Greek sun, scorching her from the inside out. Her body clenched, the pleasure going on and on until he shouted a guttural curse, his body convulsing as a hot wash of seed jetted into her, touching off another orgasm for her, and maybe another for him.

Though he collapsed against her, his face buried in her neck, he kept moving inside her long after it was over. "Are you okay?" His voice was a wonderfully husky rasp against her hot skin.

"Never . . . better," she breathed.

With jerky movements, he eased her away from the wall and rolled them both onto the cushions so he was on his back and she was on her side, one leg and arm draped over him. His heavy sex lay glistening and spent on his stomach, and his chest rose and fell with gradually slowing breaths.

"We can't do that again, Cara." He trailed his fingers absently over her thigh.

"But I liked it." Loved it.

"You shouldn't have provoked me," he snapped. "And I shouldn't have let you." His voice tempered, went low and even. "You can't afford the energy expenditure or injuries, and I can't afford—"

"Can't afford what?"

"I can't afford to get too close to you. Even if you transfer the *agimortus*, you'll be a target for anyone who wants to hurt me or get to me by hurting you. My sons paid in blood because I loved them. That will never happen again."

"It's just sex, Ares."

His eyes flashed. "It's more than that, and you know it."

"No, I don't. I don't want to get attached to you any more than you want to be attached to me. But things are pretty intense all around us, and we could both use a break and a little pleasure. You asked if I'd ever been fucked, and I said no. Well, now I have. And I liked it. So quit being squeamish, and do it again."

*Spelunking* had to be the dumbest word in the English language. Limos supposed that what she and Thanatos were doing in central Oregon's underground lava tubes couldn't really be called spelunking, since they weren't doing much climbing or exploring, but Than seemed to delight in saying the word over and over just to irritate her. He had the oddest sense of humor.

She didn't know how deep they were inside the mountains of the Cascade range, but they'd been chasing the fallen angel for at least two hours now, and this was getting boring. Besides, she hated caves. Too claustrophobic, too dark, and way too much like the region of Sheoul where she'd grown up.

"Why did Zhreziel pick here to run to?" she muttered, as she picked her way over a pile of unstable rocks.

Than glanced over his shoulder at her. "Is that a rhetorical question? Because I hope you don't expect me to know the answer."

She sighed. "I just hope your spirits are holding him."

Li and Than had found Zhreziel in New Zealand, where they'd battled, and then had chased him to Japan, Turkey, Korea, and now, here. Finally, Than had released a couple of his souls from his armor and sent them after the angel. They couldn't kill Zhreziel, but their attempts would keep him grounded and unable to flash away.

"We're close." Than opened a Harrowgate to get them across a wide fissure. "I can feel them."

They stepped into the gate and came out on the other side of the bottomless expanse. "Do you really think we can repair Reseph's Seal?"

Accustomed to her rapid changes of subject, Than didn't miss a beat. "Yes." There wasn't even a question for Than, even though all he had to go on was an Aegis engraving in Deliverance's hilt, "From death will come life," which could mean anything.

Limos had always found Than's life of absolutes to be annoying, but in this case, she was glad to have him be so certain. She hated what Reseph had become, but she loved who he'd been. She just hoped they could repair the Seal before Deliverance was found.

Aegis bastards. She knew they had the dagger, knew because they'd taken it from her. Her brothers might believe that the Templars had lost it, but the truth was that she'd stolen it. It wasn't something she was proud of, but she'd been . . . different back then. Truth was, she had been relieved when they'd stolen it back after they'd incapacitated her back during the Great Famine.

"Think we'll see those two Guardian guys again?"

"Yes."

"The R-XR dude, Arik, was kind of hot, don't you think?"

"Never seen anyone hotter," Than said, his sarcastic delivery so deadpan that anyone who didn't know better might think he was serious. "He fills my dreams with his hotness."

"Now we're getting into TMI. Your wet dreams aren't something I want to know about." An agonized moan from deep inside the tunnel urged them on. Sounded like Zhreziel was getting his angelic butt kicked. She'd have had a little sympathy for him if he hadn't punched her in the face and given her a bloody nose in Korea. Bastard.

"Just don't be thinking the soldier is too hot. You need to stay away from guys like him."

Guys like him? She needed to stay away from *all* males. When it came to sex, she and Than both had to be careful, but for very different reasons, and while Than couldn't have intercourse, he could still enjoy someone else's body if he chose to. Li could only look.

"Duh." Than had a tendency to be a little overprotective. It was funny the way all her brothers were so different. Reseph had been her buddy, the one she'd party with. He'd always sit back and laugh when she got herself into trouble, not because he was laughing *at* her, but because he knew she could get herself out of it, and he got a kick out of the way she did it.

Thanatos was the overprotective one, always there to break heads if anyone pissed her off. He never gave her a chance to defend herself, because he wanted to be there to do it.

Ares took a stance somewhere in the middle. He let her handle her own issues, but if she asked for help—which was a rare occurence—he swooped in and struck fast, hard, and decisively.

They were all so cute and cuddly.

She wanted Reseph back, dammit.

They squeezed through an opening so narrow that Than nearly got stuck, and came out in a chamber where they found the fallen angel pinned to the cave floor, his struggles against the spirits failing.

Zhreziel snarled up at Limos—for some reason, he seemed to dislike her more than he disliked Thanatos—and called her a dozen or so unflattering names.

"Tsk-tsk," she admonished. "You're going to piss off my big bro—"

She didn't even have time to finish, because, as predicted, Thanatos went psycho on Z-boy's ass. It was all a bit unnecessary, but hey, the fallen angel really was a douche. How could any angel with a desire to earn his way back into Heaven not want the honor of bearing Ares's *agimortus*?

Dude was selfish.

Than bound Zhreziel's hands and feet, and then threw open a Harrowgate. "Time to go do your duty and save a human's life."

The angel glared. He seemed to have two expressions: glare and scowl.

Limos grinned. "Cheer up, dude. You'll really like Cara. But if you don't?" She leaned in, put her mouth right up to his ear. "Keep it to yourself, because Ares seems to have a thing for her, and right now, you *really* don't want to get on his bad side."

Well. *She'd* told *him*, hadn't she?

And they'd certainly done it again, and though Ares had

tried to go slow, to keep things leisurely, Cara would have none of it. Like the first time, she'd turned into a tigress who wasn't going to accept less than what she wanted. He'd been too engaged to retreat, and in that moment when she'd been marking him with her nails and her gaze that dared him to stop her, he'd wanted nothing more than to claim her in the most fundamental way possible. To make sure she felt this warrior on her and inside her for days.

He was pretty sure he'd accomplished that goal, and male pride made him puff up as he lay next to her, listening to her catch her breath after her eighth orgasm. He'd come almost as many times himself, but he could still go another round if she wanted to. The ability to have multiple orgasms was one of the few bennies he'd gotten from having a succubus for a mother.

Cara snuggled against him, twining their legs together and settling her palm on his chest. "Thank you."

"Sex with you isn't charity work."

She laughed, and the beautiful sound went straight to his heart. "I should hope not. But I wasn't talking about that. I was talking about everything."

"Everything?"

"Yeah, you know, for bringing me here. Showing me your world."

He shifted his gaze to the night sky so she wouldn't see the concern in his face. "Why would you be grateful to be here? You're in danger. You're dy—" He cut off with a curse.

"Dying. I know." She pressed a kiss into his pecs and lay her head on his shoulder. "And at first, as you know, I wasn't real happy about being in this situation. But then Reaver pointed out that I was stuck here, even if we can transfer the *agithingy-ma-bob*, and he's right. I mean, it's not just because of Hal. It's because I know too much to really integrate back into the life I had. Which brings me to my point." Her fingers drew random patterns on his chest as she spoke. Such a minor thing, but the intimacy in the skin doodles put a trickle of sweet warmth in his bloodstream. "I didn't have a life. There's nothing to go back to. Even if my time here is short, I've found something here that I'd lost."

"I don't understand."

"You said I was weak—"

He captured her hand. "God, Cara, I'm sorry."

Her full, sensual lips parted on a smile. "Don't be. You were right. But I've found my strength again." She pulled his hand to her and kissed his palm. The tender gesture laid him out, knocked his emotions into a tailspin that he doubted he was going to pull out of. "See, back home, I'd been in a bad place for a couple of years. I was about to lose my house, I'd lost confidence in myself, and my boyfriend left me."

He had to bite back a growl at the mention of the male. "What happened with your boyfriend?" Another long silence stretched, so long that he thought she'd fallen asleep. "Cara?"

"Yeah." She wriggled in tighter against him. "Jackson left. He couldn't deal with the attack."

"Attack?" The way she said it set off alarms inside him. She'd flipped out earlier when he'd asked if she... oh, fuck. He'd asked if she *liked* being attacked. Yeah, he was ready to kick his own ass.

"I'm sure you don't want to hear the gory details." She shifted to look up at the star-strewn sky. "I love this place. I'd spend all my time outside."

"That's why I live here." He feathered his fingers over her shoulder, loving how velvety smooth her skin was under his callouses. "And I do want to hear the gory details."

A tremor went through her, and he tugged her closer. "Jackson was my realtor when I moved to South Carolina. I was recovering from my father's death, and he was there for me. We dated, pretty whirlwind. He moved in after just a couple of months and helped me with my holistic vet business when the real estate market slowed down."

"And?"

"And one night I'd come home from taking care of a sick horse. I walked in on three men robbing my house." She swallowed audibly. "I tried to run, but they caught me and dragged me inside. They tied me up..."

"What did they do to you?" His mind worked overtime on the horrible scenarios.

"Nothing at first. They mainly just scared me. But then Jackson came home." She shivered, and he grabbed the blanket off the back of the sofa to cover her. "They beat him, and then they made him watch while they..."

Something in his chest tightened into a cold fist. "They *what*?"

She nibbled her lower lip thoughtfully, as if searching for the right words. A decent man wouldn't have pressed. But Ares wasn't decent. And he wanted to know what happened, because he wanted to know who he had to kill.

"Cara? *They. What?*" Silence. His gut turned inside out. "Did they violate you?"

"No." Her voice was small, and experience told him her trauma was big. "I think they were going to. They threatened me at first. Like they got off on my terror. It made them laugh to see me cringe when they pointed a gun at my face and threatened to blow my brains out. They slapped me around a little. Stuff like that. And Jackson had to sit there and watch."

Ares had to force himself to breathe. The bite of shackles cutting into his wrists as he was gutted by helplessness and horror came back to him in a rush. He could even smell the tang of blood in the dank dungeon air where he'd been chained so he could witness his wife being murdered.

"Then what?" He was pretty damned proud of the fact that his voice was level, even if his emotions weren't.

"My gift...the one I use to heal..."

*I've killed with it.* Oh, Jesus.

"One of them told me to strip. When I refused, he hit me. Fractured my cheekbone, I found out later at the hospital. The other men laughed." She covered her ears as though hearing the laughter, and shit, that was enough.

"Cara, hey, it's okay. You don't have to say any more."

But she was on a roll, as if she needed to spill it all before her time limit ran out. "He unzipped his pants and I...I...he died."

"How did he die?" he asked quietly.

"The other men ran." She didn't answer the question, but Ares let her keep going. "They were gone and Jackson called the police." Her breathing became ragged, and he ran his hand up and down her arm in a futile attempt to soothe her. "It's kind of all a blur."

"How did the man die?" he repeated, and she swallowed.

"The official report said heart attack."

"And unofficially?"

Her entire body trembled. "I felt my ability surface, but

it was different. It felt kind of...oily. When he grabbed me, I tried to push him away, and it just...happened. Like he'd touched a power line." She closed her eyes, but Ares knew from experience that doing so didn't block out the visions. "I killed him."

"You did what you had to do, Cara. When your life is at stake, you can't take any chances. Better him than you." When she said nothing, he had a feeling she was torn on that point. "There's something more, isn't there?"

"Yeah." She cleared her throat a couple of times. "Your brother, he asked if I got off on it."

Ares growled. "My brother is an asshole for saying that."

"No." Her fingernails dug into his chest, and he wondered if she even realized it. "You're going to think I'm awful."

"Never." He tipped her face up, forcing her to see the truth in his eyes. "There is nothing you could do to make me think badly of you. Understand?"

Her nod was full of uncertainty, and he wished he could do more to ease her fear. "Thanatos was right. It was horrible. But some part of me liked it. I can't ever do that again."

The guilt she'd been carrying around with her must have eaten her alive. "Cara, listen to me. What you felt was a rush of adrenaline, mixed with relief that the monster was dead."

"But it felt good," she whispered brokenly.

"Fuck yeah, it felt good. Felt good that the asshole was dead and never going to hurt you again. It's okay to feel that way." He doubted he was going to convince her that what he was saying was true, not in one five-minute counseling session, but he'd let her digest that for a while. "So what happened after that?"

Tension bled out of her body. She was obviously relieved to be off the subject of killing the guy. "The two other men ran off. Jackson and I did the police and hospital thing, but our relationship was never the same. He refused to talk about what he'd seen me do, and he couldn't ever deal with the fact that he'd been helpless and unable to save me."

Ares got that. But he also got the need for revenge-therapy. A sharp blade worked a lot faster than sessions with a shrink. "Did he find the assholes and kill them?"

In his arms, Cara jerked. "Of course not. The police caught them."

Jackson was a damned puss. Ares would have hunted those fuckers down and showed them how justice was served back in his day. Which was why Ares had sworn on his very soul that he would see Chaos die.

"Are they in prison?"

"They served their time," she said quietly, and he detected a note of bitterness. Ares made a mental note to do a little research into the crime and these guys. Maybe Hal would like in on the action too. Excellent way for them to bond. And Christ, he was thinking of getting buddy-buddy with the kind of creature he hated most?

*Let a woman too close, and while she sucked your cock, she sucked your brains and manhood right out of you, too.* An enemy had told him that, back in Ares's human days. They'd called a truce between their armies, had shared wine as they negotiated terms of battle. In truth, Ares had liked the guy, and had they not been fighting on opposite sides, he might have called him friend.

One week later, in the thick of the fighting, Ares had shoved a blade through the man's skull.

"So basically," he continued, "this Jackson asshole abandoned you, and the guys who tortured you spent a few months in jail?"

"Basically."

Damn, she'd taken a lot of blows in a short amount of time. "How long before the puss, ah, Jackson left?"

"He made it a couple of months. He couldn't look me in the face or deal with my issues."

Maybe Ares would hunt down Jackson after he found the punks who had traumatized Cara.

They sat in silence for a few minutes. The quiet was comfortable, though, something that had never happened between Ares and a female. It was nice.

Until Cara brought up the one thing he really didn't want to talk about. "Ares...you have a lot of guilt about your family, don't you?" She pushed up on one elbow so she was looking down at him. "Guilt that your wife and children died, and you never told them how you felt about them."

He tensed. "I loved my children."

"I don't doubt that you did." Her soothing voice brought him down a little, and then she traced her finger over his sternum, and he settled even more. How did she do that? He'd seen her turn a damned hellhound into a gentle ball of fur, had witnessed her charming Battle right down to his hooves. "But you're afraid they didn't know that. So you built a shrine to them, but you don't want to actually see it."

He seized her hand, stilling it. "Stop with the psychology bullshit. What makes you an expert on shrines, anyway?"

A breeze made her hair fan out over his skin. Felt good.

Too good. "After my mom died, I had all these things of hers...weird things, like ponytail holders. Her toothbrush. I packed them away, but I never looked at them."

He frowned. "Because you felt guilty about her death?"

"Because I don't remember telling her I loved her. I was little, so I probably did, but I don't remember. I guess I didn't want to keep her stuff where I would be reminded of that, you know?"

Yeah, he knew very well. But he didn't like that Cara saw so easily through him.

"Ares!" Ares jackknifed into a sit and twisted his body to shield Cara from Limos, who popped out of the open door between the patio and the bedroom. "Ares, we got—" She cut off, a blush coloring her tan cheeks. "Oh, um, hi, Cara."

"This had better be important," Ares said.

"Well, duh," Li huffed. Then she flashed a broad grin. "We nabbed a fallen angel."

Ares's heart skipped a beat. "Where?"

"He's hanging out in the great room. Thanatos popped *Armageddon* in the DVD player for him to watch. You know, a reminder."

"We'll be there in a minute."

Limos winked at Cara and flounced away.

"Does this mean what I think it does?" Cara asked, and it was Ares's turn to grin.

He'd been afraid to hope for this, for so many reasons. Yes, the end-of-the-world thing had been his primary concern, and it still would be; transferring the *agimortus* to the fallen angel didn't change the fact that Ares and his siblings would still have to go on the offensive to protect the guy. But transferring it meant that Cara would live.

And he would no longer weaken around her. His armor would shield him from emotion, which was exactly what he needed. Except he wouldn't need it, would he? If she was no longer his *agimortus*-bearer, he had to get rid of her, or she'd be a target for Pestilence.

The thought hit him like a blow to the solar plexus, knocking the wind right out of him. This was good news, so why did he feel like someone had died?

Dammit, he had to get his head on straight. His focus was to A, protect the world from a premature Armageddon, and B, destroy the hellhound he'd been after for centuries. The first problem wasn't going to be easy, but the second . . . for the first time in a long time, there was hope. Cara might be exactly what he needed to get Chaos's head mounted on his wall.

"Ares?"

He blinked, shaking himself out of the wreck of his tangled emotions. "Yeah," he rasped. "It means exactly what you think it does. Your life is saved."

# Nineteen

"One last push." Eidolon, Kynan's brother-in-law and head doctor at Underworld General Hospital, spoke in a comforting voice that joined the sound of Gem's panting breaths in the hospital's delivery room. His dark head was partially hidden beneath the drape of the sheet over Gem's legs, but when he looked up, his black eyes were bright with both confidence and exhilaration. He didn't normally deliver babies, but Gem wouldn't allow any other doctor to touch her. Kynan had been on board with that. He wanted only the best for his wife and child.

"I hate you all," Gem moaned, and Kynan smiled... then grimaced when she squeezed his hand so hard he heard joints crack.

Shade, Eidolon's brother, looked over from across Gem's swollen body, where he was gripping her wrist, the sleeve of glyphs on his arm glowing as he channeled his pain-killing Seminus demon gift into her. "E can heal your hand," he said, amusement threading into his voice. Shade's mate—Arik's sister—Runa, had given birth to triplets, so yeah, Shade had been through this.

Tayla was at Gem's knee, looking a little green. The Aegis warrior was six months pregnant with Eidolon's baby, and watching her twin sister give birth wasn't doing much for her bravery. He thought it was funny that she could hack a bloodthirsty demon to death, but something as natural as having a baby made her quake.

Not that Kynan blamed her. He'd happily choose taking a bullet to the gut over squeezing a bowling ball out of his ass. Women were amazing.

Gem's body jackknifed up as she bore down. A mixed shout and scream tore from her throat, and then the most beautiful sound in the world, the cry of a newborn baby, filled the room.

"It's a girl," Tayla breathed. "Gem, you have a girl!"

Gem fell backward, her hair matted to her face, but her green eyes glowed.

"Baby, you did it." Ky kissed his wife, and the next ten minutes were a blur as he cut the cord and watched Shade clean up the baby as Eidolon used his gift on Gem to heal tearing that normally would have required stitches.

Finally Shade brought over the squirming infant, bundled in a green blanket, and put her in Gem's arms. "She's beautiful," Gem whispered.

"Like her mom," he whispered back, a humiliating hitch in his voice. "So special."

"Extra special," Tayla murmured, and yeah, that was true. His daughter was the first person ever to be born a Marked Sentinel, a human charmed by angels so nothing save an angel could harm her. Kynan had been charmed nearly a year ago in order to be the keeper of Heofon, the necklace around his throat, and he'd been assured that his children would all be born with the same charm.

Cool.

"Did you guys finally decide on a name?" Eidolon asked.

Ky shook his head. "We wanted to see her first."

Tayla bent over, her burgundy hair obscuring her face as she kissed her sister on the forehead. "We'll leave you alone for a few minutes. And then you're going to get overrun. Wraith, Serena, Runa, Sin, Conall, Luc, Kar, and the kids are all in the waiting room."

"You called *everyone*?"

Tay grinned. "Well, duh. Making people wait in agony while someone is in labor is a hell of a lot more fun than a surprise. I'm so going to make you guys pace." She winced and grabbed her belly. "Probably for hours. I can already tell this kid has Eidolon's stubborn genes."

"Yes," Eidolon said flatly, "I'm the stubborn one of the two of us."

Tayla blinked innocently. "I'm sweet and malleable."

Shade coughed into his hand. "Bullshit."

The gaggle of demons argued as they shuffled out the door, leaving Kynan alone with Gem. "Well," she said, "what kind of name would fit her?"

Kynan brushed the back of his knuckle over the infant's cheek. She had his dark hair, his eyes, and Gem's perky nose and full lips.

"And remember, no demon names." Gem didn't want to honor the demon half of her at all, and Kynan didn't blame her. Time would tell what being a quarter Soulshredder would mean for their daughter.

His little girl smiled...at least, he was going to take that grimace as a smile, and man, the entire room lit up. *He* lit up. Warmth filled him, which seemed impossible, because he'd been whole and happy for so long and had no idea how his life could get any better. But it just had.

"You're my little angel," he murmured. "Your mom is my sunset, and you're my dawn."

Gem propped her head on his shoulder. "You always surprise me with how wonderful you are. You know, when you aren't being a jerk." At his chuckle, she smiled, and then her eyes flew open. "Dawn. That's it! It's perfect."

"Dawn." He looked down at the little bundle of calm, of sunshine, and yes, that was perfect. "Dawn it is."

His phone chirped, and as much as he didn't want to answer it right now...shit. He wasn't going to get it. Wasn't.

"Answer," Gem said.

"I can't."

"Ky, you're dealing with the potential end of the world. If you have to answer the phone to keep our daughter safe, do it."

"Man, I love you," he murmured.

"I know."

He grinned. They had gone through a lot to be together, and sometimes it still floored him to remember their journey.

An almost physical ache throbbed through him when he left Gem to step out into the hall. He'd make this quick. Regan's number popped up on the Caller ID, and he dialed. She answered on the first ring.

"Ky. We found it."

His breath caught in his throat. "The dagger?"

"Yep. The weird thing is that it wasn't in our chambers."

"We knew that. Every item at HQ has been numbered and catalogued, and there was no mystical Horseman killer."

She sighed. "I still figured we had to have it somewhere, maybe mislabeled or intentionally vague in its description."

Regan was an obsessive-compulsive control freak in an almost clinical sense, and he had a feeling she'd gone through every single item in their inventory. A couple of times. "Okay, so where is it?"

"A monastery in Spain. We need you to pick it up."

He scrubbed a hand over his face. "Why me?"

"Because our sneaky past colleagues hid it in a box that can only be opened by someone with angel blood."

And Kynan had an angel perched in his family tree. "This doesn't make sense, Regan. Why would The Aegis make the dagger inaccessible to most of its own people?"

"No idea. I'm lucky enough to have found it, let alone get an explanation for it."

Fuck. "Okay, but it's going to have to wait. Gem just had our baby."

"Boy or girl?"

"Girl. Her name is Dawn."

"Very pretty. The sooner you pick up the dagger, the sooner you can get back to her." Yeah, Regan was all heart.

"I'll get to it. Anything else going on?"

"We've intercepted more chatter that Arik has translated. It's not good. They're talking about how the human is dying, but then in the same breath, they're talking about Satan's bride."

"Do you think they're talking about Cara?"

"Maybe. I know if she dies, War's Seal will break, but I wonder if being handed over to Satan will do the same thing?"

"Dammit. I don't know. Just give me some time to be with my family, and I'll get on it."

"Okay. But Kynan, don't take too much. We're not looking at weeks or even days until War's Seal breaks. The way the underworld is buzzing, we might be talking hours."

Cara and Ares showered quickly. Well, it might have been quicker if Ares hadn't insisted on washing her, which led to another couple of orgasms for both of them. There had been a desperate, intense quality to what they'd done, as if Ares had been starving and was trying to fill up.

Or as if he'd been gorging because he didn't know if they'd ever do it again.

The thought niggled at her as she tugged on the jeans and blouse Ares had brought from her place. This transfer couldn't be anything but good, right? She would no longer be dying, so she and Ares could . . . could what? He wouldn't need to protect her, and they'd both admitted they didn't do "close," so why would she be around?

Despite the depressing thoughts, she watched Ares dress, admiring his body, the way his muscles rippled under tan, taut skin. Her own muscles ached, but in that lovely, well-used way that would remind her with every step that she'd had the best sex of her life.

He turned to her, his black tee stretching over shoulders so wide that with his armor on he had a hard time getting through doorways. He walked over to her, his gait purposeful but unhurried, and she felt her own body loosen in response, as if anticipating his touch. Sensuality oozed from him even when he wasn't trying—he was living, breathing, sex.

His smile was tense as he reached for her blouse and began to button it. "I'll help."

"I think I can manage," she said, but she let him.

He worked his way up, his nimble fingers brushing her skin—intentionally, she was sure, and despite all the sex they'd had, the thrum of desire began to buzz through her veins. He paused about halfway to trace the tip of his finger over the *agimortus*, which had faded again. They'd both noticed in the shower, and although she didn't feel any different, the mirror had told another story.

Raccoon circles framed her eyes, and her cheeks were gaunt, her skin pale. Even her ribs were showing, as if she were slowly starving to death.

"It'll be gone in a few minutes," Ares murmured.

"I can't wait. I know it's only been a few days, but it feels like I've been under a death watch for a year." She hadn't really admitted, even to herself, that she'd been terrified she'd never be rid of the mark, but now she could feel that pressure draining like a lanced blister. "It's weird though, because I'm only realizing how afraid I was right now."

"You've been in survival mode," Ares said, his expression taking on a serious cast. "I'm sorry, Cara. You should never have been dragged into this." He finished buttoning her up. "But it's almost over. If we can keep the fallen angel contained and safe, we can keep my Seal from breaking. And you're bonded to an immortal hellhound, so you should have several hundred years of life in you." A flush worked its way up his throat from his collar to his forehead. "I'll make sure you're taken care of and safe from Pestilence."

"Wait." Her fingers automatically went to the *agimortus*, which throbbed through the fabric of her shirt. "If I'm no longer branded with your mark, why would Pestilence be a danger?" And what did he mean by making sure she was taken care of?

"He might try to hurt me through you."

"Oh, great. So I still won't be safe."

He hauled her roughly against him, knocking the breath from her lungs. "You will be safe, Cara. If I have to hide you on the other side of the world, I swear you'll be safe." He kissed her, a hot pledge to back up his words.

Before she could even catch her breath, he took her hand and led her out of the bedroom.

They entered the great room, and Cara's optimistic mood faltered. The fallen angel sat on the floor, shoulders slumped, bloodied, his perfect skin bruised. Dark, stringy hair hung in his face. For all intents and purposes, he looked like a beaten dog. Except that his pewter eyes were molten with defiance.

On the television, explosions rocked the room through the stereo system. Every time someone screamed, the fallen angel jerked and bared his fangs.

Thanatos went down on his heels next to the angel. "Say hi to the nice lady, Zhreziel."

"Fuck you, Death."

Thanatos's smile was grim. "That could very well happen if I turn evil, so take the *agimortus* like a good servant of Heaven."

Cara put her hand to her belly, but that didn't stop the churning. "Why doesn't he want it?"

Zhreziel snarled. "Do *you* want it?"

"No, but—"

"But what? Are you completely stupid?"

In a flash, Ares had the fallen angel by the throat and was squeezing. "You do not speak to her that way." Loathing burned in Zhreziel's eyes, but he gave a reluctant nod, and Ares dropped him. "Cara, come here."

"No!" Zhreziel scrambled backward, but Thanatos caught him. The angel began to pant, his skin paling. "I don't want it. Don't . . . want . . . it."

Ares eyed the fallen angel with disgust. "You haven't entered Sheoul, which means you're redeemable. Taking the *agimortus* will be in service to humans. Don't you think that will be a good thing?"

"Good? Pestilence and his demons will be after me!"

"We'll protect you."

"The way you protected Batarel and Sestiel? Forgive me if I'm dubious about the quality of your *protection*."

"Idiot angel." Limos, who had been licking a blue lollipop, wagged it at him. "Those two thought they'd be better off on their own. That won't happen with you. We'll keep you nice and safe. And busy. Ares has a great video collection. Ooh, and a wet bar."

"What are you people not getting? I don't want the damned thing! If I have it and Pestilence kills me, my soul will belong to Satan. If he doesn't, and one of your other Seals breaks, then I will turn evil because I bear the *agimortus*. It's a lose-lose for me." He nodded to Cara. "She's human. Not meant to bear the *agimortus*, so she won't turn evil."

"You selfish shit." Ares's voice pulsed with mounting anger. "She's going to die if she doesn't transfer it. Do you *want* the Final Battle to begin?"

"Of course not," Zhreziel snapped. "But if I'm not carrying the *agimortus*, I can fight on the side of good and win my soul and wings back."

Oh, God. He was in a fight for his very soul. The nausea became a crashing wave that threatened to spill right out of Cara's stomach.

"Say it with me." Thanatos's voice was wintry as he spoke into the angel's ear. "Apocalypse. Armageddon. It will break in a matter of hours if Cara keeps the *agimortus*, because it's killing her."

"And if I take it," Zhreziel shot back, "it's only delayed. Either you or Limos will see the breaking of your Seal, and then you all turn evil. It's coming, you stupid fucks. No matter what, it's coming. And I'd rather fight against you than fight for you."

A soft "pop" rang out as Limos pulled the lollipop out of her mouth. "You realize we don't need your permission, right? So you should probably shut up now. We have to keep you safe, but we don't have to be nice to you." She gestured to the shelves of DVDs. "Ares has the complete collection of *Miami Vice*. We could torture you until you're begging for Pestilence to kill you."

"Release me!" Zhreziel brushed his hair away from his face, but it fell back, covering one eye as he swiveled around to Cara. "Please. Don't do this."

"Shut up." Limos slammed her candy down on the bar top and wrapped her hand around the back of the fallen angel's neck, forcing his gaze away from Cara. "Ares also has *Starsky and Hutch*."

This was not at all how Cara had envisioned this going, and she swallowed sickly. "Can we hold off? Find another fallen angel who would be willing?"

"Even if some mythical *willing* creature existed at some point in time," Limos said, "we're running out of even unwilling options."

Unable to bear looking at Zhreziel for one more second, Cara swung around to Ares. "So what *are* our other options?"

"There are none," Ares said. "Do it."

*Stall.* "I don't know how."

"Touch him with the intent of passing it. It should be automatic."

She shivered, suddenly chilled to the bone. "I can't."

"You can." Ares's hands clamped down on her shoulders, and he dipped his head to look her straight in the eye. "You have to."

"I won't do to him what was done to me." She took a bracing breath, steeling herself against what was probably a terrible decision. "I can't do this against his will."

Thanatos opened his mouth to say something—going by his thunderous expression, Cara could guess what—but Ares held up his hand to stay his brother. "Give us a minute."

She allowed Ares to lead her to a quiet corner. "Listen to me, Cara," he said slowly as if speaking to a child. "You're dying."

"Well aware of that."

"If you give it to him, you'll live. I can't—" He cut himself off with a curse.

"You can't what?" When he said nothing, she grabbed his chin and forced his eyes to meet hers. They were angry, but at the same time, sad.

"I can't lose you," he bit out. "I can't be with you, not with Pestilence around, but I can't lose you."

She didn't know what to say, but Ares did.

"*Please.*"

She knew how much it cost him to beg. "I wish I could," she said softly, and he stepped back as if she'd slapped him.

"Dammit, Cara." He thrust his fingers through his hair and paced for a dozen strides before returning to her. "We're in a war where there are no rules, no room for pity or kindness. The loser forfeits not just life, but the entire fucking *Earth*. Transfer the *agimortus*. Now."

"There is always room for kindness," she said. "Forcing this on Zhreziel would be an epic violation. I know this for a fact. This would be as bad as killing him. If I did it, I'd feel stained, Ares. Ruined."

Ares slammed his fist into the wall. "Do it, dammit!"

"No."

Ares regarded her with shuttered eyes, his calm more frightening than his rage. "Fine. Die. Bring about the end of the world. What's it matter to me? I'll be evil and won't give a shit."

"There's got to be another way."

"There's not," he roared.

She jammed her finger into his chest. "Yelling at me isn't going to do anything but make me dig my heels in deeper. You haven't learned a lot about women in your thousands of years, have you?" In the background, Limos snorted, and Ares pegged his sister with a glare. Cara snapped her fingers, bringing his head back around. The stunned expression on his face, the you-*dared*-to-snap-at-me look, might have made her laugh if the situation wasn't so we're-all-going-to-die. "You said you were some sort of military commander or general or something, and you have a kind of innate strategic knowledge. Well, use it and find another way out of this. Because I'm not transferring the *agimortus* to that fallen angel."

# Twenty

⌒

Ares needed a minute. No way could he stand in that room and look at Cara for another second. Too much emotion was tripping through him—anger, fear, hurt. It was all so unfamiliar, hitting him hard and all at once, that it was clouding his ability to think straight. His brain was working on ways to force her to transfer the *agimortus*, ranging from pleasant things like fucking her into capitulation, to dark, sinister ideas like blackmail or torture. Not her torture, but he'd bet he could get that fallen angel to beg her to transfer it.

She'd hate him forever for that. But she'd be alive. And the world would be whole.

He stepped outside, inhaled a lungful of sea air that was tinged with a smoky hint of hellhound. Hal was nearby. Maybe his sire would show up and give Ares the satisfaction of carving his heart out.

"Ares." Limos gripped his elbow just as he was about

to punch through the side of the building. "She isn't a warrior."

He ground his molars so viciously they hurt. "What's that supposed to mean?"

"It means she doesn't have your 'win at all costs' mind-set." The white flower in her hair slid out of place, and Limos grabbed it, tossed it to the ground in an uncharacteristic display of annoyance. "She wants to do the humane thing, and she isn't thinking beyond that."

"She should. She could bring about the end of the fucking world."

"I'm not happy about that, either," Limos said. "But we've got to give her time."

Frustration and anger hummed in his skull, spreading down his spine, into his organs, and all the way to his toes. "Time is a luxury we don't have."

"Well, duh. But we can't force her."

"Yeah, I can," he ground out.

"You are so stubborn." Limos stomped on the flower, smashing the thing flat in the sand. "Let me talk to her."

The hum became a buzz as dark energy coiled inside him. On his arm, Battle thrashed hard enough for him to feel a pinch. Odd. He snapped his gaze to Li's arm, and damn if Bones wasn't doing the same thing on his sister's skin.

"What the—" He broke off as a shock wave of energy hit him like a nuclear blast. He stumbled back a step, knocked off balance. "Limos . . ."

"I feel it," she gasped. "Oh, shit, what has Pestilence done?"

The tug of battle was like a million ropes attached to his organs, stretching tighter and tighter, until he wanted to blow apart. "War," he breathed. "A war just started."

The pound of Thanatos's footsteps turned to thunder as he burst from the doorway. "I—" Shadows swirled around him, and he groaned. A gate opened, sucked Than into it, and he was gone.

"No!" Limos grimaced, and then she was sucked through a similar portal.

*Cara.* This was a trick of Pestilence's and he knew it. The tug grew more powerful with each dragging step toward the house. His feet were leaden even though his body sang with the need to fight, the need to be engaged in whatever battle was going on.

As he went through the doorway, he felt as if claws had grabbed him, were spreading his rib cage, and agony clouded his senses. Laughter erupted, a hellhound snarled, and then Ares was sucked into the vortex that would drop him in the middle of a conflict and leave him powerless to leave until the worst of the blood had been shed.

Hal's pained cry rang in Cara's ears and vibrated through her entire body. A rapid drain of energy forced her to catch herself on the wall. She'd been standing in the great room, waiting for Ares and Limos to come back inside, while trying to avoid Thanatos's disapproving gaze. When he suddenly tore out of there, she hadn't been too concerned...not until Ares shouted for her and Hal yelped.

Legs trembling from the sudden weakness, she hurried outside and was instantly surrounded by Ares's demon guards. She couldn't tell most of them apart, but she knew Vulgrim by the silver ring that pierced his left horn, and Torrent by the slash of white on his broad snout.

Torrent backed her toward the entrance as Vulgrim

barked orders that had the other Ramreels shifting into various fighting stances.

"You need to get inside," Vulgrim shouted. "Now."

"But Hal—"

Torrent gripped her arm and dragged her toward the patio. "If your beast hasn't dematerialized to Sheoul already, our men will find him. You have to—" A spray of blood erupted from Torrent's mouth, splattering Cara's neck and chest. Horrified, she lurched back, her gaze glued to the arrowhead that jutted from his breastbone. Dear God, the weapon had punched through two layers of chain mail and his thick body. "Go . . . now . . ." He crashed to his knees.

*"Torr!"* Vulgrim's agonized bleat turned the warm night air into a chill shroud. He spun around and caught his son before he fell over, but even in the dark, Cara saw the death cloud that glazed over Torr's eyes.

The other Ramreels charged in the direction the arrow had come from, heading straight toward the glowing red eyes of a snowy demon horse and its unholy master perched on top. An arrow sailed out of the pitch black, nailing another of the Ramreels between the eyes. Strange demons charged from out of the dark. Humans . . . at least, they looked like humans . . . ran with them, their hands clutching wicked, bloodstained weapons.

The *agimortus* seared her chest, becoming a red-hot brand. The oily, slick feeling boiled up, feeding her terror as a hideous skeletal thing snared her by the hair and yanked her backward. She swung wildly, missing the creature. Remembering her self-defense training, she slowed. Concentrated. She swung again, this time landing a punch in the demon's hollowed-out belly.

Vulgrim was suddenly there, head bowed, ramming his great horns into the demon. The crack of bones and a pained screech rang out, and the force of Vulgrim's hit knocked her down. The silver flash of a blade glinted in the lights from the patio, and the demon's head rolled past her.

"Get inside." Vulgrim lifted her to her feet. "My *tesmon* cannot lose you."

*"Tesmon?"*

"Herd father." He tugged her toward the door. "Ares."

His furred arms closed around her protectively, and they stumbled onto the porch. A blade came from out of nowhere, slashing at Vulgrim's face. He deflected it with his horn, which sheared off like a carrot under a cleaver. The blond man who'd swung the weapon dove for Vulgrim, taking him down to the ground. Another man came from nowhere with an ax, and in horrible slow motion, Cara saw it coming down in an arc over Vulgrim's neck.

A million images flashed in her head, and she saw the face of the man she'd killed at her house in the expressions of the guys attacking Vulgrim.

*If you want to survive, if you want those you care about to survive, you may need to make sacrifices and do things you never thought you'd do. Things you might find distasteful, that go against everything you've ever believed.* Reaver's prophetic words were like a soundtrack that went along with the images, and without hesitating, Cara allowed her gift a full charge, nothing held back.

With a battle cry, she lunged, gripping one man on the shoulder and the other by the waist. Energy sizzled down her arm and through her fingers. The effect on the men was instantaneous; blood and tissue spurted from their eyes, noses, mouths, and ears. Their bodies swelled like balloons, and as they hit the ground, they broke open into steaming piles of gore.

There was no regret. Not. A. Bit. Ares had been right. It felt good to get rid of monsters, and hell if she was going to waste her life feeling bad about it.

Vulgrim, whose eyes had always seemed so tiny for his big head, stared at her, his eyes now the size of saucers. "That," he rumbled, "is one scary ability." He grunted. "I like it." He leaped to his feet. "Now go inside. Hide yourself!"

Cara careened off the doorjamb and the walls as she bolted toward the fallen angel. He'd somehow managed to roll under the coffee table, where he was working his bound wrists against the leg in a desperate attempt to fray the ropes. He saw her coming, and he hissed like a cornered lion.

"Behind you!"

Instinctively, Cara dove to the side, barely avoiding the swipe of a massive, clawed hand. Whatever was chasing her let out a pissed-off snarl. Hot breath blasted the back of her head, and she nearly gagged at the fumes. The door to the bedroom was just ahead—

"Don't touch her! She's mine." The voice froze her marrow. Pestilence. "And someone drag that angel to Sheoul."

The scaly thing chasing her ignored Ares's brother, and even as she stumbled through the bedroom door, she turned, saw the monster go down beneath the hooves of Pestilence's evil stallion. She slammed the door and locked it, but two seconds later, it crashed inward, and thousands of pounds of horse and warrior filled the room.

Somewhere in the house, Zhreziel screamed. Inside her head, Cara screamed, too. She should have transferred the *agimortus*, because the fallen angel was being dragged to Sheoul, where his soul was going to be ruined anyway.

The fear Cara had experienced at the hands of men who had robbed her house and the Guardians who had believed she was a demon paled in comparison to the sheer, icy terror that wracked her body now. She trembled as Pestilence swung down off the horse, his armor clanking and dripping a disgusting black substance as well as fresh Ramreel blood.

"Seems you're bonded to a hellhound," he said, his deep voice rumbling right through her soul. "That means that killing you isn't going to be as easy as running you through with a sword or slitting your delicate throat."

"Shame, that," she said, surprised at how she didn't sound nearly as afraid as she felt.

"I have him, you know. Your hellhound. He fought me and my men, but even now, he's being transferred to my lair."

She shook with fury so intense her teeth rattled. "Let him go, you soulless bastard."

Pestilence struck out, nailing her across the face with the back of his hand. "Do you kiss Ares with that mouth?" He smiled. "How does he feel about you being bonded to a hellhound, anyway?"

"That hellhound is keeping me alive."

"Stupid bitch. You're dying. All I need to do is chain you up and wait for it. But that's not nearly as satisfying as torturing you. And see, the strange thing about these pain-in-the-ass hellhound bonds is that I can't just chop off either your head or his. For some reason, you end up with the same protection we Horsemen have. No weapon can go through the spinal cord. Weird." He frowned. "I tried to chop off your hellhound's head, anyway. It's not fatal. But it hurts like a mother."

"You sick, twisted asshole," she rasped.

"Sticks and stones." He reached out and wrapped his gauntleted fingers around her throat, and even though her gift was still engaged and pumping enough power to light up a grid the size of New York City, Pestilence didn't even flinch as he lifted her off the ground. Her breath became searing whips of fire in her throat as she grabbed his wrists and tried furiously to fry him with her power. Nothing. The bastard was immune.

"Let's head to my place." His fangs flashed as he looked her up and down. "And then, little human, I'm going to see how sweet you are."

# Twenty-one

⌒

Ares, Limos, and Thanatos had fallen into a trap. One designed not to catch them, but to keep them busy.

Ares had known the moment he materialized in the war zone—the very place where the most recent plague had drawn Thanatos. Turned out that Pestilence and his demons had manipulated the governments of Croatia and Slovenia into war after convincing Slovenian leaders that the Croatian military had manufactured and distributed the disease that killed thousands of Slovenians.

Demons, all *ter'taceo* in positions of prominence, had incited things further by gathering thousands of Croatians and Slovenians into camps deep inside Hungary and taking away everything from clothes and water to food. They'd created a famine of *everything*. Their actions were an attempt not only to spark international war, but also to distract Limos.

It worked, and the thing that sucked was that large-scale

tragedies were like evil power plants for Ares and his siblings. As long as they remained on site, the juiced-up high rocked them like an orgasm mixed with cocaine, and no one could—or wanted to—unplug from that.

But Ares had to. Which meant taking out the people in charge of each side of the conflict.

Now, a day after Ares had been sucked to the bloody battlefields, he stood over the body of the Croatian general he'd killed and wondered how long it would be before he had to return to put down the guy's replacement. He'd already taken out Slovenian military leaders—both had been demons in human suits. Made him wonder how many of the military's upper echelon were Pestilence's bitches.

The tent flap peeled back, and speak of the asshole...

Pestilence sauntered inside, bloody fangs exposed in his creepy smile, Harvester on his heels. "Bet you were just thinking about me."

"Evil doesn't agree with you, brother."

"It absolutely agrees with me. You know what else agrees with me? Cara." He flicked his tongue over one fang. "Tapping that? Sweet."

Ares lunged, prepared to rip his brother's throat out. It wouldn't kill him, but it would hurt like fuck. He slammed his fist into Pestilence's neck, and his brother fell back, but he kept his feet under him. "If you hurt her—"

"Oh, I hurt her." Pestilence fired back with an industrial-strength slug to Ares's temple. Stars twinkled, birds tweeted, and bells rang to the tune of *I'm Getting My Ass Kicked*.

Pestilence was definitely drawing on the power of evil, was far stronger than he'd been before his Seal broke. Head still spinning, Ares grabbed the metal chair in the corner, spun, and brought it down on Pestilence's skull. The chair crumpled like a tin can, tearing one of the legs, and without missing a beat, Ares snapped off the hollow leg and jammed it into his brother's throat, taking a core sample out of Pestilence's flesh. Blood spewed out of the pipe, splashing the inside of the tent in gore, and Ares swore he saw Harvester smile.

A crimson tide bloomed in Pestilence's eyes, and he swept his arm in an arc, connecting with Ares's shoulder and sending him crashing through the side of the tent. Before Ares could get to his feet, Pestilence was there, kneeling on Ares's chest and digging his fingers into his throat. Agonizing pressure on his windpipe closed it off.

"You're coming with me, *brother*," Pestilence said, his voice a nasty snarl. "You're going to watch me break your Seal, but first, I'm going to make you very sorry that you tried to get in my way."

Pain shattered Ares's skull, and all went black.

⌒

*Man, Reseph loved a good party.*

*Jimmy Buffett was singing praises to the almighty margarita, the sun was hot, the ocean blue, a pig was roasting in a pit, and women were swinging their bikini-covered hips in an invitation that would give a blind man his sight back.*

*Limos worked the portable bar she brought out for the bashes she held at her Hawaiian beach house. She always invited the locals, who thought she was a Paris Hilton type, a young heiress living off her wealthy parents' money. Which explained why she was rarely at the beach house; Limos claimed she had a dozen homes all over the world and spent her time between them.*

*Reseph sat back against the palm tree, downed half his margarita, and wondered if he should take the hot blonde who was falling out of her swimsuit top into the water for a little below-the-waves action. Emmalee liked it the way he liked it...which was every way. But she got a little extra excited when there was a risk of getting caught, or when she knew someone was watching.*

*"Brought you a refill."*

*He looked up as Limos poured more margarita-on-the-rocks into his glass from a pitcher. "Thanks, sis." He popped his sunglasses up and scanned the crowd of around fifty, mostly humans. There were a few demons present, but as* ter'taceo, *they were disguised even to most other demons. "Wish Ares and Than were here."*

*Li sighed, plopped down beside him, and took a huge gulp from her pitcher. "Than said he'd be here, but Ares..." She shrugged.*

*Yeah, Ares rarely came to these get-togethers, and when he did, he had to hang out on the porch and watch from afar. Getting too close to the action caused too many fights to break out. "Did you even invite him?"*

*"No."*

*Ares probably knew about the party, but at least this way, he didn't have to go through the torture of refusing.*

*"Is someone going to start up a volleyball game soon?"*

*One black eyebrow arched. "You feeling the need to beat up a ball?"*

*He waggled his brows. "I want to watch all the bouncing boobs."*

*Limos slugged him in the shoulder. "You have not changed at all. Still the perverted playboy you were when you were human."*

*Yeah, he'd been that. The "son" of a powerful Akka-
dian priestess who claimed a virgin conception by a god,
Reseph had been raised to be a spoiled, irresponsible
bed-hopper. By the time Limos had found him at the age
of twenty-eight, he could have had fifty children by as
many women. Fortunately, his priestess "mother" had
been well-versed in mystical medicine...to the extent
that Reseph suspected that she'd possessed some demon
DNA in her background.*

*Thanks to skullwort, a demon herb that ended preg-
nancies in females and rendered males sterile for weeks
at a time, he'd never had to deal with losing a child the
way Ares had. Nor would he.*

*He could party all he wanted to.*

*A curvy brunette bent over and bared her breasts to
him, and nope, that never got old.*

*Limos just shook her head. "You're impossible."*

*"Hey." He assumed his best offended tone. "I can't
help it if the females love me."*

*"Whatever." Rolling her eyes, Li shoved to her feet,
brushed sand off her sundress, and gestured to the hog
pit. "It's time to carve. Make yourself useful."*

*He grinned as she tromped away, feet kicking in the
loose sand. Man, he loved his life. He really did. It sucked
that his siblings didn't have it as good as he did, though.
They were lonely, either by circumstance or by choice,
and though Reseph did his best to provide companion-
ship, it wasn't the same as being able to let loose with
someone who wasn't related.*

*Wishing he could do more for his sister and brothers,
he stood, turned, and nearly bumped into a breathtak-
ing redhead whose green eyes were windows to a good*

*time. She gave him a naughty smile, took his hand, and gestured into the lush forest. Well, the roast pig needed to cool anyway, right? Right. Cracking a grin of his own, he led the female to a private little cove, where he took them both as close to heaven as he'd probably ever get.*

Pestilence sat up with a hiss. Fuck, he hated sleeping. Hated how that sentimental idiot he'd been would leak into his dreams with memories of the good old days. Screw that. He was having so much more fun now. He winced at the tug in his groin, palmed his hard cock, and remembered he had a juicy little morsel of a human all chained up, tenderized, and ready, if not willing, to take care of the issue.

"My lord."

Pestilence groaned at his Neethul lieutenant's drawl and swung his legs over the side of the stone slab he slept on. He'd long since given up on beds, which got really fucking nasty when bloody, and he wasn't one for those rubber piss-protectors. Much easier to hose off rock, and really, comfort wasn't an issue, not when he only needed about an hour of rest a day.

"What?"

"Your brother is stirring."

"Good. And Cara?"

"The human is as you left her."

Which meant she was naked and huddling in a cage. Excellent. Time to grab her and show Ares why it was much, much better to be on the broken side of the Seal.

Ares came to in a fog, his muscles taut, joints stretched. His first attempt to lift his head was an epic failure. He might as well have tried to lift a bowling ball with a rubber band. The second try met with success, even if it took effort to keep from dropping his chin to his chest again. At least his eyes worked, well enough to allow him to see that he was in a small room that was clearly a crude, underground prison cell. Rolling his neck, he looked up at his bound wrists. The rope that held them together had been hooked to an iron ring in the ceiling.

He frowned. Rope couldn't hold him, so why would his brother even try? Smiling, he jerked his wrists.

Nothing happened. Okay, so the rope was definitely enhanced with demonic enchantments, but it still shouldn't be able to hold him.

Unless Cara was nearby.

His gut twisted even as he became aware that the familiar draining sensation gripped him. She was definitely very close, and as long as she was, he was severely handicapped. Making matters worse, a copper ring circled his horse glyph, preventing Battle from being released.

A scream rang out, chilling his blood, and he had to force himself to breathe.

The door flew open, and Pestilence entered, shoving Cara, who was naked and bruised, inside. She stumbled and fell to the straw-strewn dirt floor, and then she scrambled into a corner. Black, murderous rage scorched him from his skin to his bones.

"Bastard," Ares roared, before he could stop himself. *Breathe.* Now was not the time to let his temper reign. He had to stay cool if he wanted to find the chinks in his brother's armor.

"We're all bastards, really." Pestilence stripped off his muscle shirt, leaving him in leather pants. As Reseph, he'd spent more time in the nude than die-hard nudists did, and it seemed as though that quirk had survived the trip to the dark side. "Did I tell you I've been hanging with our mother? She's a hoot. You should have seen what we did to Tristelle a few hours ago at Lilith's temple. It was a real mother-son bonding thing."

Fuck. That stupid fallen angel. Ares had tried to warn her.

"The tales about our mother were accurate." Pestilence fingered the jagged edge of a dagger hanging on the wall. "She's a real whore. She even tried to seduce me. Want to know if I let her?"

Ares's stomach turned over. "I don't care about our mother."

"You will. She wants to meet you once your Seal is broken—which will happen shortly." Ares felt the seconds ticking by in the pounding of his heartbeat as Pestilence swung around to Cara, who did her best to become part of the wall. "I'm going to have my fun with her first. Remember Flail and Saw? Yeah, like that. Except that humans bleed so much better."

*"Do not touch her!"*

Pestilence shot Ares a glance dripping with false innocence. "Oh, I'm sorry. Is she yours? You don't want to share? After all we've been through?"

Ares's mind clicked through his options, and came up with pretty much nothing. Pestilence had the wheel right now, and Ares was the jackass who'd been shoved in the trunk.

Ripping open his pants, Pestilence stalked over to Cara, and Ares's cool evaporated and turned to scalding steam. He went crazy, kicking, jerking. Either the ceiling was coming down, or his arms were ripping from their sockets. Didn't matter. He had to get to Cara.

"Human." Pestilence's fangs punched down violently. "Did Ares ever tell you how he was forced to watch what happened to his wife?" He grabbed Cara by the throat and lifted her. She struggled in his grip, clawing at his hands. "Violated, tortured, killed. Right in front of him."

"Shut up," Cara croaked. Her knee came up, catching Pestilence in the thigh, but he didn't even flinch. Still, fierce pride welled up in Ares.

"Protective of Ares, aren't we?" Pestilence murmured, and for a split-second, maybe less, Ares could have sworn he glimpsed yearning in his brother's expression. Then the fucker flicked a fingernail against her cheek, drawing blood, and Ares knew he'd been mistaken, had allowed sentimentality and the brotherly bond to color his thoughts.

Never again. "If you do this, brother, I will find a way to torture you for eternity."

Pestilence shrugged. "After your Seal breaks, you won't care. I'll leave her corpse intact enough that you can get one last fuck out of her before we find Limos and Thanatos. Once we force our blood between their lips, their Seals will break, and we'll ride together again."

Helplessness would have brought Ares to his knees if he'd been standing. Plan. He needed a fucking plan. There would be no appealing to Reseph...he was clearly gone. Cara's terrified gaze caught his, and he did his damnedest to convey a message. *Fight him.*

Pestilence slammed her against the wall and squeezed her chin roughly. "How talented is that mouth? Ares?"

This was the break they needed. Ares hoped she'd play along. "Very. You'll not find a more clever tongue."

Pestilence swiveled his head around, eyes narrowed. "And you're telling me this, why? You *want* her to blow me?"

*Hell no.* Rage fogged his vision as that particular image burned into his brain. Through the growing fear that this might be a contest he wouldn't win, he forced himself to relax, but he couldn't clear the gravel out of his voice. "I would battle Satan himself to prevent it," he admitted, because his brother wouldn't buy anything less. "But I have no power. You're going to kill her. My hope is that if she pleases you, you'll make her death an easy one."

"I'll consider it." He shoved Cara to her knees in front of him. "Take it out. And if you do anything stupid, I'll cut off Ares's dick and make you eat it, do you understand?"

She paled, making her bruises and scrapes stand out starkly. Her hands shook as she reached into Pestilence's pants and removed his cock. The son of a bitch was hard already. Ares broke out in a fevered sweat.

*Come on, baby. Use your gift. Rip his fucking balls off.*

Her palm circled Pestilence's shaft and slid down. He cuffed her in the head. "Your mouth, bitch. Use your mouth."

Ares's chest cramped, his heart jackhammered, and fuck, he wouldn't survive this. Cara's lips parted, and he knew his brother could feel her warm breath on him. The demon in him went crazy. *Hold it together...*

Cara slid her hands around Pestilence's muscular thighs and pulled down his pants so the waistband circled his legs. Pestilence watched her, blue eyes glittering with anticipation and lust as she cupped his sac. Her tongue darted out, and Ares damn near screamed. No matter how evil he turned, he would somehow preserve the part of himself that had fallen for her, and he would avenge her.

He *would* destroy Pestilence for this.

Almost imperceptibly, Cara shifted, and just before her mouth made contact, she cranked her wrist so viciously that Ares heard the tear of flesh. Lightning quick, she dove toward Ares as Pestilence swung at her, blood flowing between his legs and a screech ripping from his throat.

"The bracelet," Ares yelled. "Move it off Battle!"

Cara scrambled to her feet and ran to him, barely avoiding Pestilence's second grab. She leaped, but her fingers only brushed the copper ring. "I...can't...reach!"

"Climb me. Hurry." He raised one leg, and she hopped on, straddling it as she shoved the bracelet up. "Out!"

Pestilence grabbed her by the hair and yanked her to the floor as Battle formed behind him. Cara screamed, flailed, kicked out. Pestilence's fist slammed into her jaw, and then he was smashed into the floor by Battle's giant hooves. The horse struck over and over.

"My power...it won't work on your brother." Stumbling, Cara came to her feet. Her voice was mushy, her words floating on blood, but her eyes were determined. Why he'd ever thought her weak, he had no idea.

"It's okay," he told her. "Battle's handling it. I need you to look for a lever."

She limped around behind him, and through the sound of the beating Pestilence was taking, he heard shouts outside the door. Pest's reinforcements.

"Hurry, Cara..."

"Got it!"

Something metallic clicked, and he dropped to his feet, hands still bound by the length of rope. She dashed over, her fingers making quick work of the knots. The door burst open, and demons swarmed inside. Ares threw a Harrowgate, using it as a weapon to shear two of them in half. "Battle!" The stallion whirled, stood still while Ares threw Cara into the saddle and then swung up.

Pestilence's body was ruined, his throat and face crushed, but he staggered to his feet and heaved a spiked club. It bounced off Ares's back, but the pain was forgotten as Battle charged the swarm of demons, plowing through them like a wrecking ball, and leaped through the gate.

The second the horse's hooves hit island sand, Ares whipped off his shirt and tugged it over Cara's head, shielding her nakedness from his staff, who were running to meet them.

"I'm sorry." Her voice trembled, her entire body shaking as the adrenaline rush that had gotten them out of there began to take its toll on her.

"I'm the one who should be sorry." Pressing kisses into her hair, he wrapped his arms around her, desperate to feel her warmth, her vitality, all the things she could have lost at his brother's hands. "He should never have gotten that close to you."

"Not that." She stared at the Ramreels stampeding toward them. "I'm so sorry, Ares." The scent of misery billowing from her set off his internal alarms.

The demons surrounded them, all sporting injuries. Vulgrim was there, limping, one horn sheared off. In his arms, he held a squirming little Rath. But Torrent wasn't with him.

"My lord." Vulgrim bowed. And when he unfurled to his full seven and a half feet, his red, watery eyes made Ares's gut plummet.

"Don't say it," he growled. "Don't. Even. Say it."

"We lost him, *tesmon*," Vulgrim said. "My son is gone."

# Twenty-two

After the news about Torrent, Ares dismounted, gathered Cara to his chest, and carried her to the bedroom. He didn't say a word, and neither did she. He started the shower for her, but when he began to strip, she asked for a moment alone. He needed time with Vulgrim, and though he protested, he finally relented, leaving Limos outside the door.

She washed carefully, her aches and pains slowing her down. Pestilence had worked her over pretty good during the hours before he captured Ares, and that last punch to the face had hurt like hell. She hoped his balls were throbbing as much as her jaw was. The bastard.

Ares returned as she stepped out of the shower, halting in the doorway. Her heartbeat had stuttered, almost painfully. The intensity in his bloodshot eyes froze her to the floor.

"You saved Vulgrim's life." His voice was strained.

"You killed for him." He crossed to her in three strides and hauled her against him. "I'm so sorry you had to do that."

"Ares," she whispered, "there wasn't any other option. I don't regret it, and I'd do it again."

He let out a ragged breath, scooped her up and took her to bed. As he laid her down, his gaze mapped and logged every one of her cuts and bruises, and smoldering anger joined his grief. "You need a doctor." He swallowed. "And the *agimortus*—"

"I know." It was dusky pink now, much lighter than it had been before Pestilence grabbed her. She patted the mattress. "Lie with me."

"I need to shower first."

She waited while he cleaned up, and then he joined her in bed, where, when he discovered her small gift, he stared at her. "A pillow?" He ran his hand over the silk cover, and she swore she saw a slight tremor in his fingers. "When? How?"

She braced herself on an elbow and watched him. She'd never tire of looking at him, of admiring his deeply tanned skin, his chiseled features, the ropey muscles that bunched and rolled as he moved. "After we rescued Hal. While you were fighting the demons with the Guardians. I asked Vulgrim to get a pillow for you." She put her hand over his. "It's not much, but I wanted to do something nice for you. You deserve to be comfortable when you sleep, Ares."

He grabbed her, had her tucked up against him so fast she didn't know what hit her. He said nothing, just held her, and instinct told her that was what he needed right now.

She drifted off, exhaustion and adrenaline crash making for a fine Valium. And if she could communicate with Hal...

She woke an hour later. She hadn't dreamed of Hal, and Ares was gone.

Instantly, she leaped out of bed, only to have her legs go wet noodle on her. She caught herself on the chair, sparing herself a nasty fall. Damn, she was getting weak. Her entire body ached, and at some point, her skull had become a giant juicer, turning her brain into a throbbing, liquid muck.

As quickly as she could, which meant she was turtle-slow, she dressed in a pair of olive-drab capris that were a lot looser than they used to be and a blue button-down blouse that didn't match; right now, fashion wasn't her biggest concern.

Barefoot, she padded out to the great room, where Ares was standing in front of the fireplace, one hand braced on the mantel, head bowed so deeply his chin touched his chest.

"Ares? Are you okay?"

He didn't look up, but he did let out a bitter laugh. "I should be asking you that."

"I'm fine."

Now he lifted his head, and she drew a startled breath at his red-rimmed eyes and his drawn expression. "You were taken prisoner, beaten, forced to kill, nearly forced to..." He trailed off, shook his head. "You are *not* fine."

No, her time with Pestilence had not been pleasant. But she'd survived. She'd even fought him without breaking down into a screaming, bawling puddle. "I think," she said softly, "that I should be the one to determine that." She moved toward Ares, but he stepped away. "What's wrong?"

He looked up at the ceiling fan, which was whirring madly. "I failed you. I failed Torrent."

"There's nothing you could have done for him. And maybe you don't remember, but you got me away from Pestilence."

"*Bull. Fucking. Shit.*" The venom in Ares's voice made her recoil. "*You* got us out of my brother's cell. I hung there like a slab of beef in a butcher's locker."

"I couldn't have gotten away without you." The *agimortus* etched into her chest joined the throbbing in her head, as if it wanted in on the conversation. "We did it together. And none of this would have happened if I'd transferred the *agimortus* in the first place." She should have done it, and she'd regret that decision for the rest of her life... short as it might be.

"Stop blowing smoke up my ass!"

"Why are you acting like this?" She reached for him, but he wheeled away, jamming his hands through his hair and leaving them there as he began to pace.

"What did he do to you?" His voice was flayed raw. "Before he brought you into the cell."

"It's not important, Ares." At his smoky growl, her heart skidded to a stop. "Oh... you think he raped me."

"Did he?" Still raw, as if his throat was bleeding.

"Would it matter?"

"Yes." This time, his voice was dead.

She shivered. Even though the men who broke into their house hadn't gotten the chance to rape her, Jackson could never see past what *might* have happened. Though he'd never said it, not outright, anyway, he'd viewed her as damaged goods. As ruined. Spoiled. When she'd touched him, he'd shrunk away, found some way to avoid intimacy with her. They hadn't made love even once after that night.

"So...if he raped me, would you think differently of me?"

Ares's head snapped back as if he'd been sucker punched. "No. Never." He regarded her from under the forbidding line of his dark brows, his gaze steely. "It matters because Pestilence tormented you while I was helpless to protect you. He knew exactly where to hit me, knowing I'd been through it once before with my wife. If he violated you on top of all that, I couldn't live with myself."

"He didn't, Ares." God, her heart was breaking for him, and she didn't know how to help except to reassure him. "I swear. He was too concerned with capturing you so you could watch."

Closing his eyes, he let out a long, relieved breath. But he still backed away when she reached for him.

"Ares, don't. Please don't pull away from me." This was Jackson all over again, but this time, it was much worse. Afraid of how Jackson would respond to knowing about her ability, she'd never given herself fully to him, had always held a part of herself away. But she'd bared everything to Ares. He'd made her stronger, while Jackson had only dragged her down.

He said nothing. Wouldn't even look at her. Not even as he strode from the room.

⌒

"You are a selfish piece of shit."

Ares jerked to a halt just inside his walled garden. "Excuse me?"

Limos came around from behind him and parked herself in his path. "Cara was tormented at the hands of our brother—"

"You think I don't know that?" Every single second of it was replaying in his head, and the only breaks he got in the show were when memories of Torrent popped in.

After Vulgrim and his mate, Sireth, Ares had been the first to hold Torr after his birth. Ares had watched the little guy learn to walk, had nearly come out of his skin while watching him negotiate rocky cliffs, had taught him to spar.

Vulgrim's pain now was Ares's, and for someone who had sworn to not allow emotion into his life, it felt as if Ares was drowning in it.

"Yeah, and you're making what Pestilence did about you. You, not her." Limos jammed her hands on her hips. "You feel helpless, impotent, because you couldn't protect your female. So to punish yourself for your guilt or your inadequacy or whatever, you're pulling away from her. Pestilence tortured her, but you aren't a hell of a lot better, because you're doing the same damned thing."

He wanted to tell Limos to go fuck herself, but she was right. He'd been convinced that Jackson was an asshole for how he'd treated Cara, and then Ares had gone and repeated one of the most painful times of her life.

The stone path that wound through the gardens became his racetrack as he started walking. Could he outrun his asshole self? Not likely.

The slap of Limos's bare feet fell into a steady beat behind him. "Hey, I'm sorry about Torrent." She grabbed his hand and pulled him to a halt. "I know how much you cared for him. Is there anything I can do?"

"Yeah," he said hoarsely. "Watch over Vulgrim and Rath. Pestilence knows how to hurt me." Overhead, a hawk drifted on a thermal, looking for prey. "Our brother is stronger than ever. He caught me off guard and bested me after I got myself free of the war. How did you get away from the starvation camps?"

"I alerted the media. Once they got wind of it, it was all over. I have a love-hate relationship with modern times, but today is true love."

"Where's Thanatos?"

"Gathering intel on where Pestilence might be building his army. When you took out those commanders and caused a cease-fire, it freed Than. He's putting his time to good use before Pestilence's plagues get worse. As it is, humans are starting to panic."

No doubt they were. He'd seen this so many times... humans were like freaking sheep who panicked at the first sign of trouble, buying up supplies, moving to isolated areas, building bomb shelters, taping windows. Humans imagined there was an Apocalypse around every corner.

This time, they were right.

Shit, he had to throw the king of Hail Marys. "Stay with Cara."

"Where are you going?"

He opened a Harrowgate. "To our mother."

"What?" Li snared his arm. "Why? Are you insane?"

Probably. Lilith was one of the few beings who was more powerful than him. She'd kept Limos captive, and if she got hold of Ares, she could very well hold him until Pestilence broke Ares's Seal.

"Lilith and Pestilence tortured Tristelle to learn where Unfallen are hiding. I'll give Lilith anything she wants if she'll tell me where to find one." He had to save Cara. Desperation was a lava flow in his veins.

"There are no more Unfallen."

Li and Ares whirled to Reaver, who stood just off the path near a fish pond, his expression as angry as Ares had ever seen it. "What do you mean, there are no more?" Ares ground out.

Reaver's blue eyes swirled with storm clouds, and lightning flashed in the pupils. "Just what I said. Either they have gone to Sheoul, or Pestilence has destroyed them. My brethren are gone, and we're out of time."

All the emotions Ares shouldn't be feeling—panic, fear, anger—distilled into poisonous fury, and Ares lost it. He didn't think. He reacted. Snagged Reaver's expensive-ass jacket by the lapels and slammed the angel into an olive tree. "*You lie.*"

"*You failed.*"

A five-bazillion jolt blast of pissed-off angel hit Ares like a freight train, throwing him a dozen yards across the gardens and through a pillar. Stone crashed down on him, he was pretty sure he'd be pissing blood soon, and he leaped to his feet with a roar.

"Ares, no!" Limos leaped in front of him at the same time Harvester flashed in, her shit-eating grin rocketing Ares right into orbit again.

"Evil is winning," she said, in a taunting, sing-song voice.

Reaver, a category five heavenly storm, shifted his focus from Ares to Harvester. She snarled, and they came together in a sonic fucking boom. Light flashed, and they were gone.

This couldn't be happening. Couldn't be happening. Couldn't *fucking* be happening! Ares wiped a stream of blood off his temple and cursed in a dozen different languages, but that didn't change the fact that they were so fucked his ass hurt. Though he guessed that could be the result of having a pillar shoved up it.

He shook stone dust out of his hair and rounded on Limos. "Contact Kynan. We need that damned dagger. It's Cara's only hope now. And I want the island's Harrowgate shut down. Pestilence isn't leading any more demons through it."

Limos whistled. "Won't be easy."

"I don't care," he snapped. "I'll pay whatever price I have to—"

"My lord! Ares!" Vulgrim ran toward them, gesturing back at the house. "The hellhound—"

Ares didn't wait for him to finish. Armoring up, he tore off across the garden, darted through the house, and found Cara on the bedroom patio. She had one hand on the scruff of Chaos's neck, the other scratching under his chin, and the only way this could be happening was if Cara had invited the hound in, which bypassed the ward. Limos came in behind Ares, her own armor creaking as she drew her weapons.

The hellhound swung his great head around, and Ares swore the beast was grinning. Ares could read it as clearly as he could a billboard. *Your female likes me.*

"Ares," Cara said quickly, "before you say anything—"

"Get away from him."

She ignored him. "Listen to me. For just a minute."

He was so not in the mood for this. "I want that monster dead."

Chaos snarled, and bullets of drool dropped from his mouth to splatter on the pavers.

"You need to call a truce," Cara said, and Limos made a strangled noise.

"You can't be serious," Ares rasped. "Never. Now get away from him before he hurts you."

Unbelievably, Cara wrapped her arm around the hellhound's neck, and through the red haze of hatred, he realized that she was wobbly and needed support. "He can't hurt me or he'll hurt his son. He needs my help to find Hal, Ares, and we need him."

"We don't need him. *I will never need him.*" He stepped forward, and the hound matched the move, putting one giant paw in front of Cara, holding her in place. If Ares didn't know better, he'd think Chaos was trying to protect her.

Which was ridiculous.

"I told you what he did to me, Cara. I can't forget that. I *won't* forget that."

Pain flashed in Cara's eyes. "Ares, if you kill him, you'll be fighting Hal for the rest of his life."

The cold, stark reality brought his temper back down to manageable levels. Fighting Hal very likely wouldn't be an issue. Hal would be dead soon, if Ares couldn't bury Deliverance in Pestilence's heart. And if he did, by some miracle, destroy his brother, how could Cara live with Hal and Ares wanting each other dead?

And damn...how could he let go of over forty-five hundred years of hatred?

But how could he not give Cara this, after all he'd put her through, and after what she'd sacrificed for him?

It was the hardest thing he'd ever done, but he lowered his sword, never taking his eyes off the evil son of a bitch.

Closing her eyes, Cara let out a relieved breath. "He says that as long as Hal lives, he'll honor the truce."

Honor. Not a word he'd associate with hellhounds. "Just one thing," Ares said thickly. "I need to know why he killed my brother and sons like that." There had been genuine hatred in Chaos's actions that went well beyond a normal kill.

Cara smoothed her hands along both sides of the beast's face. After a minute, maybe two, or ten...it was hard to say...Cara hung her head. "So much pain between you two." She lifted her gaze. "I can see his thoughts. Do you remember a battle in some mountains? There's a siege engine of some sort, ugly, with a boar head carved into it and"—she shuddered—"human skulls nailed all over the beams."

"Yeah. I remember." He, his sons, brother, and Ares's army had chased demon hordes all the way into the Ahaggar Mountains after his wife was killed, and once the demons were boxed in, the slaughter had begun.

"Chaos wasn't part of the demon-human war. He and his mate brought his pups out of Sheoul to teach them to hunt rats among the carnage. He was young, and it was his first litter. You killed them."

Ares swallowed. He'd done so much killing in his life, so much of it running together like thousands of rivers of blood into one massive sea. But he remembered his first hellhounds. He'd been so full of hatred after the death of his wife that he'd taken pleasure in slaughtering the female and her young. In Ares's eyes, they'd been nothing but evil beasts feeding on the corpses of his soldiers.

The ground shifted beneath him. They'd been hunting rats, not eating his men. Not fighting humans.

It was only days later that he'd come back to the command tent to find a giant hellhound standing over the remains of his sons and brother.

Oh, Jesus. Chaos hadn't started the feud between the two of them. *Ares had.* For so long, he'd believed Ekkad and his sons had died simply because he'd loved them, that they'd been targets for demons who were striking at Ares. But no, they'd died because Ares had destroyed a family.

"All this time I wanted revenge against him, and he wanted the same against me." He scrubbed his hand over his face. He still hated the damned thing, but Ares understood him now. "I'll honor the truce."

Chaos met his gaze, a mutual understanding passing between them. Neither wanted to cuddle or anything, but they'd give each other a wide berth and pass without swinging.

The hound dematerialized, and without the support, Cara hit the floor.

"Cara!" Ares dropped to his knees beside her and gathered her in his arms. She was unconscious.

Limos kneeled beside him. "Is she—"

"No," he croaked. "Her pulse is weak, though." He stood, keeping her close to his chest, and threw open a gate. "I'm taking her to Underworld General."

The hum of a tattoo gun was the sexiest sound Thanatos had ever heard. Well, not counting the sounds of actual sex, which he avoided like one of Pestilence's plagues. He loved the buzzing sensation and the bite of pain that vibrated deep into his muscles as the needle moved over the small of his back, and he forced himself not to shift so his aching erection could get a little comfort. That bastard deserved to hurt.

"Almost done." Orelia, a pale, eyeless Silas demon, wiped his sensitized skin with a cloth and went back to work.

She hadn't used a template and transfer for the design. She never did. The demon worked off images from her customers' minds, turning thoughts to art, and in Than's case, taking scenes of death out of his head and relocating them onto his skin, where they could no longer affect him so strongly. He remembered all the death and destruction he'd seen—and participated in—but once they'd been inked onto the canvas of his body, they no longer haunted.

As a bonus, he got off on the process, the pain, the pleasure. Tattoos and piercings were one of the few ecstasies he allowed himself.

"You're running out of room," Orelia said, as if he wasn't aware of that. Fortunately, her unique talent went beyond bringing thoughts to life. She could layer the images and somehow keep them from obliterating each other. The scenes bled together in harmony, each distinct, yet blended.

"Just finish."

Her long, bony fingers feathered over the design taken from his recent visit to the dying grounds of Pestilence's Slovenian epidemic. "This one was particularly bad. Your brother has been busy."

"What have you heard?" Questioning Orelia was his main reason for coming today. He could have held off getting the tat, but he needed intel, and this female, who got into the heads of her customers, had her finger on the underworld's pulse.

"You know I can't discuss things I shouldn't know."

Standard answer, standard bullshit, and Than didn't have time for it. "My brother is amassing an army. I want to know where."

"How would I know?"

Than whipped his arm around behind him and grabbed her thin wrist, wrenching the tattoo gun away from his skin. In one quick move, he flipped over on the table and dragged Orelia close. Like most Silas demons, her skin was so white the veins beneath were visible, her mouth was a mere slash that revealed black, pointed teeth, and her nose was little more than a bump that framed two gaping holes. Unlike most Silas demons, she had tattooed eyes onto her face.

He allowed his fangs to slice down—since she could snag images out of his mind, she was one of the few people who knew what he was and who he hadn't killed because of it. Not even his brothers and sister knew. This was a secret he'd kept well.

"I don't have to tell you what I'm capable of," he said. "You've tattooed it on my body for centuries."

"If I tell you what I know, my life will be in great danger."

"I guarantee that I'm more dangerous than any of your other customers."

The muscles in her throat bounced as she swallowed a few times. "But I don't want to stop the Apocalypse. I want out of Sheoul. The scenes I can draw on humans..." A gruesome smile split her oval face. She'd once said that on humans, her talent was prophetic. She had special, extra-painful tools for them, and once she tattooed their skin with a scene involving them, it came to pass. And Orelia was *very* creative. And cruel.

"Do you know what it's like to die at my hands? After the pain ends, your soul becomes part of me. You'll be trapped in the darkness of my armor with other souls, tormented with their pain and misery. If the Apocalypse happens, you're the first person I'm coming for, so you won't have a chance to play with the humans anyway." He tightened his grip until she whimpered. "So tell me what I want to know."

"Rumor has it that my people are flocking to the Horun region. But some of my clients have heard tales of growing excitement in Sithbludd."

"What else?"

"Pestilence has put out a call to all demons...anyone who brings him the head of an Aegi is promised a place at his side after the Apocalypse, and he's also started quietly paying a bounty for hellhound ears. That's all I know. I swear it."

Than released her and flipped over again. "Good. Now finish." He had some recon to do.

# Twenty-three

Ares stepped out of the Harrowgate into the emergency department at Underworld General Hospital, a facility run by demons to care for underworld creatures. Ares used to think it was crazy, but now he was pretty damned glad it existed.

His boots cracked on the obsidian floor as he crossed to the triage desk, where a sleek, catlike Trillah demon was shuffling papers. She sniffed the air and frowned as he approached. "Human?"

"Yes. She needs help. I want Eidolon."

"He's busy—"

"Get me the doctor, because if this human dies, I'm going to turn into your worst nightmare."

She hissed. "This hospital is protected by an antiviolence spell, so your threats are meaningless—"

"I'm not bound by antiviolence spells," he roared. "*Get. Eidolon.*"

"Threatening my staff will get you nothing." The calm voice came from behind him, and he wheeled around to the very demon doctor he'd been demanding to see.

"It wasn't a threat. If Cara dies, my Seal breaks. You get what I'm saying?"

Eidolon met Ares's gaze with a sharp, assessing stare few dared to give him, and Ares admitted to a grudging respect for the guy. This was Eidolon's turf, and he had to do what it took to keep the place safe. Right now, that meant saving Cara's life, and he knew that. The doctor, who looked as human as Ares, gestured to a nurse and immediately, two people—shapeshifters of some sort— rushed over and guided Ares to a cubicle.

Ares placed Cara gently on the exam table.

"What happened?" Eidolon snapped on some gloves, and the tribal tat that ran from his fingertips all the way to his neck began to glow. Seminus demons, a rare breed of incubi, possessed abilities that were somehow tied to their arm glyphs. Ares just hoped that whatever Eidolon's gift was, it would be enough to keep Cara alive.

"She's dying." Eidolon nodded as he checked her airway and breathing as one of the shapeshifters, a blonde whose name tag identified her as Vladlena, took Cara's pulse as the other listened to her heart. "Cara bears my *agimortus*, and it's killing her. Her death will break my Seal."

Frowning, Eidolon looked up. "But you said that if Sin had died, Pestilence's Seal *wouldn't* break."

"Different kind of *agimortus*." Ares gripped Cara's hand. "And you should know that she's bonded to a hellhound."

Eidolon paused as he reached for a pair of shears. "Interesting. Where's the hellhound?"

"I don't know."

"So the animal could be injured?" Eidolon sliced Cara's blouse up the middle, and a terrible, possessive pain rent Ares apart. Everyone froze, and he must have made some hellacious noise, because they were staring at him as if he'd just bitten the horns off a Croix viper.

"Ah...sorry." He clenched his fists at his sides, hoping that would keep them from striking out. This was weird, though; he'd never been so possessive of a female in his life. "I'm not usually...it's just..." God, he was never a stuttering fool, either.

"It's okay," Eidolon said wryly. "We get the don't-touch-my-mate thing around here."

"She's not my mate." Sure, he'd thought of her as his, but the word "mate" implied permanence. Something he and Cara wouldn't have.

"*Riiight.*" Eidolon nodded sagely, but real quick Ares figured out that the demon was being a sarcastic ass. "So you always tell doctors you're going to rip their heads off and decorate your mantel with them then?"

*He'd said that?* Jesus. Okay, he needed to clear his head, and fast. "Just do what you have to do."

Very slowly, Eidolon peeled open Cara's shirt, and Ares started to hyperventilate. Didn't matter that the guy was a medical professional. He was looking at Ares's woman. His...mate. Fuck.

He concentrated on stroking Cara's hand with his thumb, concentrated on not going all serial killer on everyone in the room. And it only got worse when Eidolon cut off her pants.

"She's got a lot of abrasions and contusions," Eidolon said, as he palpated her belly.

"Yeah." Ares's voice was scratchy. Wrecked. "She was...she took a beating." And fuck-oh-fuck, the *agimortus* had lightened more, was the pale pink of a healing scar.

Eidolon fingered one of the bruises, and his tattoo lit up. The bruise shrank and lightened, but Eidolon cursed. "That should have healed it completely." He stripped off his gloves. "She doesn't seem to have any serious injuries, but I'll call in my brother. Shade can check her organ functions." He covered her with a sheet. "I'll be right back."

The other staff members left with the doctor, leaving Ares alone with Cara. He didn't release her hand—wouldn't release it. "Cara? Sweetheart? Wake up."

Her eyelashes fluttered, but didn't open. "What happened?" Her voice was weak, barely there, and Ares wanted to both shout with excitement that at least she was awake, and scream with frustration that she sounded awful.

"You passed out. We're in a hospital. Cara, listen to me. I'm sorry about earlier. I shouldn't have walked away from you like that. I was being selfish, and you didn't deserve it."

Her eyes opened, and he hoped that all his years of military conditioning kept his shock from showing on his face. They were sunken, bloodshot, and the beautiful clear blue-green had gone murky, from sea-colored to something resembling a bog. "It's okay," she whispered. "I saw Hal. He was in a pit. There was blood. A lot of it. And...fighting."

"Shh." Ares squeezed her hand. "We'll get him. You need to rest. Conserve your energy."

She was going to argue; he knew it. But Eidolon

returned with a demon in a black paramedic uniform, one who resembled Eidolon so closely that Ares knew the guy was his brother.

"This is Shade," Eidolon said, and nodded at Cara. "Can he examine you?"

She slid Ares a glance, clearly unsure about all of this. He couldn't blame her. Human hospitals were unpleasant enough, but this one, with its black floors, gray walls covered with incantations scrawled in blood, and chains hanging from the ceiling, went well beyond unpleasant and right into disturbing. That was before you looked into the staff made up of demons, vampires, and shapeshifters.

"It's okay, Cara. These are good guys."

Utter trust eased her expression, and kicked him in the gut. "Okay, then." She offered Shade a trembly smile. "Do it."

Shade brushed back his shoulder-length dark hair and gently took her wrist. The markings on his right arm lit up, and his brow furrowed in concentration. Within a few seconds, Cara's color had started to come back, her cheeks pinking up, her lips plumping, and even her eyes had returned to normal. By the time Shade released her, she looked almost as healthy as she had when he'd first met her.

"What did you do?" Cara's voice was full of wonder as she looked down at her arms and hands.

"I can optimize bodily functions." He met Ares's gaze. "If you hadn't brought her in, she'd have been dead within the hour."

Ares swallowed. Hard. "And now?"

"Maybe we should talk outside."

"No." Cara eyed each of them in turn. "It's my life, and I deserve to know what's going on."

Shade shrugged. "Then I'll tell you that your organs are failing. It's as if you've got the plumbing of a hundred-and-fifty-year-old human. I was able to get everything working well again, but it's like you're a slow drain. I filled up the sink, but the plug's broken, so you're still leaking."

"How much time?" she asked, and thank God she had, because Ares hadn't found the strength to do it.

"Six hours. Give or take an hour." Shade jammed his hands in his pockets. "I can probably buy you another hour if I repeat what I just did, but after that . . ."

After that, Cara died, and Ares turned into the world's worst nightmare.

"We won't give up," Eidolon said. "We have the best staff and best researchers around. We'll look for a solution. Hit the call button if you need us." He left with Shade just as Limos and Thanatos arrived.

Limos waited until the two demons were out of earshot to talk. "I got a text from Kynan. No details, but he's on his way now. And Than might have a lead on where Pestilence is gathering his people. If we can find him, we might find the hellhound."

Cara struggled to sit up. "We have to help him."

"The good news," Ares said, as if any of this was good, "is that the boost Shade gave you will affect Hal, too. You bought him some time."

Near the triage desk, the Harrowgate flashed, and Kynan stepped out. In one hand he had a pink, frilly bag covered in teddy bears, and in his other hand was a leather-wrapped parcel. He strode over to Ares and planted the package in Ares's hand. "The dagger."

Ares exhaled in a relieved rush, but he couldn't let

himself get excited. They still had to find Pestilence, and they only had six hours to do it. "Thanks."

Kynan cleared his throat. "How's Cara doing?"

*Dying.* "We're taking care of her." The generic answer was all Ares could muster.

As Kynan shifted his weight, the rattle of a baby toy was very out of place. New life meeting impending death. "We've intercepted disturbing underworld chatter. The demons searching for Cara are talking about Satan's bride. Is she part of some prophecy we don't know about?"

Cara grabbed Ares's arm. "Is this true? Is there something you haven't told me?"

There was a lot Ares hadn't told her, but this wasn't one of those things. "You aren't Satan's bride."

"How do you know?" Kynan asked.

"Because I am." Limos adjusted the orange flower in her hair. "I mean, not right this second. We haven't gotten all tux and gowns and reserved a church or anything."

Kynan made the bag rattle again. It was the sound of family, and Ares's mouth went desert sand. "How?"

"It's none of your concern," she said lightly, which was deceptive, because the lighter Li got, the deadlier she could be. "I'm doing my best to prevent it, and that's all you need to know."

Kynan inclined his head. "Fair enough." He glanced at Cara and then back to Ares and lowered his voice. "I really need to speak with you privately."

The urgency in the human's eyes told Ares to listen. They stepped out of the room, Than and Li on his heels. All around them, doctors and nurses were scrambling to handle an influx of some kind of emergency coming through the sliding ambulance bay doors. And standing about forty feet away, her dark gaze focused on Ares, was Harvester. Bruises and burns marred her features—clearly, the battle with Reaver had been a fierce one. She remained focused but silent, apparently content to fulfill her role as Watcher. Since Reaver couldn't enter the demon hospital, anything she learned here would have to be shared with him before she could make use of it.

"Make it quick," Ares said.

"There was a scroll with the dagger." Kynan held out a rolled parchment, which Li grabbed. "The dagger was stolen from the Templars—"

"By who?" Than interrupted, and Li fumbled the scroll.

"That's unclear. But when The Aegis recovered it, they enhanced it. It'll still kill a Horseman, but it can also neutralize your *agimortus*."

Dread made Ares's heart pound against his rib cage. "What do you mean, *neutralize*?"

"I mean that if you plunge the dagger into your bearer's heart, you'll neutralize it," Kynan said. "You'll kill the host, but your Seal won't break."

Ares lost his ability to breathe. He now had a way to save the world—temporarily at least—but it wasn't acceptable. At all.

"Heads up, Aegi," Than said. "Pestilence put a price on dead Guardians. Watch your necks."

"Your brother is such an asshole." Kynan shifted his gaze to Ares. "I'll be in touch. Don't let us down." Kynan strode away, leaving Ares with a churning stomach as he looked over to Harvester, but the fallen angel was gone.

Numbly, he walked back into the room. His hand shook around the dagger, and he hated himself for it. Damn, the thing weighed more than he remembered. Kynan might as well have handed him an anvil. Limos and Thanatos closed in, staring at it as if it were a viper.

"We're not using that on Reseph," Than said, and Ares's hand jerked so hard he nearly dropped the weapon as he rounded on his brother.

"Damn you, Thanatos. This is *my* decision. He fucked with *my* woman, and I will do what I have to do." So much for the "*She's not my mate*" bullshit Eidolon had called him on. He'd fought against his feelings, but every general worth his salt knew when it was time to lay down arms and surrender. It was time.

Than's expression was somber, his voice as subdued as Ares had ever heard it. "Does that include killing the human?"

"Limos," Ares said, in a voice as cold as the winters where Thanatos lived. "Get him out of here before...just get him out of here."

Li dragged their brother out of the room, but not before Than had cast Ares an apologetic glance. Despite Ares's anger, he knew his brother wasn't being a dick. Reseph had been their brother for five thousand years. They'd known the human for a few days. The math added up to saving the family if they could.

Ares would probably feel the same if the situation were reversed. And, though Ares's strategic mind was scrambled this close to Cara, even he understood that there was risk in trying to end Pestilence. Cara...no risk.

Except to Ares.

"Ares." He took a deep, bracing breath and turned to Cara. Her gorgeous eyes were those of a warrior, and far too full of knowledge. "What did Thanatos mean by 'killing the human'?"

Ares had never wanted to beat his brother more than he did right then. Pain sliced through his hand; he'd gripped the dagger so hard that it had cut through the leather and into his skin.

"Ares. Tell me."

Tension flared in the sudden silence. "There's a way out of this," he began, as he twined his fingers with hers. "There's a way to ensure my Seal can't be broken until one of the others is. If I kill you with this dagger, my Seal remains intact, and Pestilence will have no way to turn me."

"Until another Seal breaks." Cara didn't hesitate. "Kill me."

Ares stepped back. "No," he whispered desperately. "I can't."

"You have to." A tear trickled down her cheek. "You know you do. Ares, I'm dying. It's happening. You have a chance to stop the Apocalypse, or at least delay it while you find a way to stop your brother."

"Cara..."

"But not here. Take me home. And make love to me one last time."

"Yeah," he croaked. "Yeah."

Pestilence was seriously pissed off. Funny how, when he'd been Reseph, he'd rarely gotten angry. Oh, no one wanted to be around when he finally did blow his stack, but it didn't happen often. Reseph had been such a... *insert something wimpy here*, because Pestilence was too pissed off to come up with anything clever or even crass.

He looked down at the bodies at his feet—three of his

minions who had allowed Ares and the human whore to escape. One of them had dared blame Pestilence ... he was missing a few organs, unlike the others, who had merely suffered broken necks.

"The best leaders don't terrorize their underlings." Harvester nudged one of the bodies with her foot while looking pointedly at Pestilence. "Ares always had the respect of his army. And their loyalty."

Steam built in his skull at her taunt. Fucking Harvester. Fucking Ares. How he wanted both of them to suffer. For now, though, he would have to be patient. Casually, he pushed off the post he was leaning against and stared at the bloody battle taking place in the pit below. The hellhound pup was ripping into a *khnive*, a creature about the size of the hound, but resembling a skinned opossum. The *khnive's* claws raked the hellhound, tearing a massive gash in its side. It was a blow delivered in desperation, and the *khnive* gave a final, gasping breath as it bled out through a gaping throat wound.

"Don't give the hound time to heal. Throw something else in there. Something big."

At his side, David, his Aegis spy-slash-gofer, nodded, his glazed eyes bouncing in his head. "Yes, my lord."

Pestilence rolled the vial of saliva they'd extracted from the hellhound between his palms. "Have you arranged for the venom delivery device?"

David dug a small metal ball out of his pocket. "The warlock assured me that once it's filled with the hound's saliva, it will be a potent weapon against your brother."

That was the first bit of good news he'd had in weeks. "Any chatter from The Aegis?"

"Deliverance has been found."

Sucking in a harsh breath, Pestilence swung around. "Are you certain?"

"I overheard my father talking about it."

"It's true," Harvester said. "And it has been modified by The Aegis. If Ares uses it to kill Cara, all hope for breaking his Seal is gone."

A trickle of sweat dripped down Pestilence's temple. "How long have you known about this modification?"

"Centuries. But it was forbidden to tell you until it was found."

Of course. Fucking Watcher rules. And now, if Ares killed Cara with the damned thing, it could be months, even years before he was able to break Limos's or Than's Seals, since he hadn't found Limos's yet, and Than seemed determined to hold on to his.

Pestilence needed that dagger.

Still rolling the vial in his palm, he carefully considered his options, and a plan began to form in his mind. "David, when I found you, you were pathetic. Hoping The Aegis would forgive you, that your father would love you again. You know that won't happen. You know you belong here with me, and that with me, you will receive rewards you never dreamed possible."

"Yes, my lord."

Pestilence wasn't sure how much agreement was the real David and how much came from the fact that Pestilence had borrowed his soul and left the human nothing more than a refillable vessel.

He'd brought a lot of humans to his side that way, and it was a great tradeoff for both of them. He sucked out their souls to give him more power, and evil filled the hole where their souls used to be, which gave them more strength and stamina than they'd had before. They could also use Harrowgates, which meant they could travel anywhere, any time.

Yes, most handy.

"Then, David, I have a mission for you." He threw his arm around the human's shoulders and walked him toward the Harrowgate, leaving Harvester to watch the hellhound fight. "There will probably be some pain involved, but afterward, you will be greatly rewarded." Assuming David didn't die, of course. He really hoped not. He hadn't been able to turn any other Aegi so far, and he'd found David to be quite useful.

"Just tell me what I need to do."

Pestilence smiled. "Let's plan."

Ares didn't allow Cara's feet to touch the floor. He carried her from the cubicle at the weird demon hospital all the way to his bedroom at his house. Limos and Thanatos had tried to follow, but Ares had snapped something harsh in a language she didn't know, and his brother and sister had backed off. And though things had been tense while they'd argued about Pestilence, she'd seen pain and sadness in Ares's siblings' eyes as Ares carried her through the Harrowgate.

There was a lot of love there, and she knew Limos and Thanatos would be at the house soon. Maybe they wouldn't come inside, but they'd be waiting outside for Ares.

They'd be there for him after Cara died.

Cara wrapped her arms around his neck, reveling in the security of being in his strong arms. But she couldn't resist a token protest. "I can walk, you know." Whatever the second demon with the glowy arm had done had given her a boost of energy that was just freakish.

"But if you walked, I'd miss out on holding you."

Both warmth and sadness washed over her, and she held tighter as he crossed the threshold into his bedroom.

"My lord..." The hesitant voice came from behind them, and Ares looked over his shoulder.

"What is it, Vulgrim?"

"Can I bring you anything?"

"No," he said softly. "But I want you to make it very clear that I'm not to be disturbed. For anything. Not even the end of the world."

The demon bowed. "Yes, sir."

"And Vulgrim? Never bow to me again. You're family, not staff."

The demon shot Ares and Cara a look of surprise, and then one corner of his mouth tipped up. "Yes, sir." He strode away, and Cara swore there was a little extra spring in his hooved step.

"Torrent looked so much like him," she murmured. Just days ago she had thought the Ramreels all looked alike, but now she recognized their individuality, from the slightly different shapes of their broad noses, to the kinks and striations in their horns and the varying shades of their fur.

"I know." He carried her to the bed, where slowly, reverently, he stripped her of the scrubs the demons had given her to wear home, and then she watched as he peeled out of his own clothes. He started to lower himself onto the bed, but she stopped him with a hand on his chest. "Just let me look at you for a second."

His mouth opened and closed, a pink blush rising up on his cheeks. With a nod, he stood up, his full, impressive height towering over her. Her mouth watered...literally watered, as she took him in. His muscles, so magnificently sculpted, were too perfect to be believed, and as she reached out to slide her palms over his pecs, she knew that even if they'd had centuries together, she'd never have tired of touching them.

With a soft moan of appreciation, she dragged her hand down to his abs, smiling at the roll of his eight-pack as they flexed under her caress. His cock, which had been flaccid only a moment ago, begin to swell, but she didn't go any lower. Not yet.

"Turn around," she whispered, surprising herself with the husky inflection in her voice.

"Cara, you should be lying down—"

"Don't," she said. "Don't treat me like I'm an invalid." She wanted him to remember her with strength, not as some helpless, frail sickling who was just waiting to die after he serviced her one last time. She would give as good as she got. "Don't hold anything back from me. Promise."

His throat convulsed, the tendons in his neck straining. "Yeah. Yeah, I promise." In a graceful flow of motion, he turned around, and her brain short-circuited.

*Nice. Ass.* Amused at how her fingers flexed involuntarily, she went up on her knees and eased the length of her body against him, planting her hands on his broad shoulders so she could caress at her leisure. The sound of his breath heaving out of his lungs blended with the distant crash of the waves, and she wished they could be out in those tidal surges, letting the water cool them as their bodies made heat.

So much time wasted, she thought, as she opened her mouth against the back of his neck. His skin tasted like salt and man, smelled like leather and spice. He groaned when she nipped him near a puckered scar and then soothed the spot with a lap of her tongue.

"Why the scars?" she asked, as she trailed her finger over a thin line. "Don't you heal completely?"

"They're from injuries before my curse."

She kissed one. Then another. "Touch yourself," she murmured against his skin, and he groaned again, his head falling back as the flex of muscles in his right biceps told her he'd obeyed. She pictured his big hand around his shaft, wondered if he liked to take long, slow strokes, or shorter ones that concentrated near the head. Well, she'd find out in a minute. First, she had some touching of her own to do.

Her heart raced, thudding so hard in her chest that she suspected Ares could feel it on his spine. Heat radiated from him, scorching her skin and making her burn all the way to her core. She smoothed her hands down his arms, loving the contraction of his muscles as he stroked his erection. The bed creaked as she scooted back a couple of inches so she could slide her hands down his back, and again, the roll of his firm flesh as he worked himself was a thing of beauty.

When her palms cupped his buttocks, he let out an erotic growl that sent a rush of liquid heat between her legs.

"You're ready for me." His voice was guttural, sexy, and she grew even wetter.

She licked between his shoulder blades. "How do you know?"

"My mother was a sex demon. I'm attuned to desire."

Why had he not mentioned the desire thing before? How many sensual tricks did he have up his sleeve from *that* kind of inheritance? Oh, her imagination could go wild.

She shifted, letting her tongue trail down Ares's spine, all the while enjoying the way his breathing grew more shallow the lower she went and the more deeply she kneaded the incredibly firm muscles of his butt and thighs. When her mouth reached the small of his back, he tensed. And when she planted an open-mouthed kiss on his right ass-cheek, he froze up completely.

"Woman, what are you doing?"

"Biting you." She sank her teeth into the place she'd kissed, and the sound that came out of him, a cross between a purr and a growl, punctuated by a gasp, made her shiver in delight. "What? No one has bitten your ass before?"

"I'll admit it's a first."

"Turn around."

He did, and because she was still on her hands and knees, she came eye level with his enormous erection. The tip glistened with a crystal bead, and without thinking, she licked it away.

Ares's entire body undulated, a spectacular arch of sinewy lines. She met his heavy-lidded gaze as she opened her mouth over the head of him, and then she closed her eyes and her lips, and savored his bold, smoky essence. His hands came up to tangle in her hair, his fingers sliding over her scalp as she sucked him deep and found a rhythm that soon had him pumping his hips. More...she needed more. Sliding her mouth up, she applied powerful suction at the cap, then swirled her tongue in smaller circles, moving from the rim to the weeping slit at the tip.

"Jesus, Cara," he gasped, his abs and thighs visibly tightening.

Smiling, she cupped his sac and lightly bounced his balls with her fingers, separating them, caressing them, and when she licked her way down his shaft and took his sac in her mouth, he shouted, grabbed his cock, and squeezed.

"Not. Yet." He panted hard. "So humiliating."

"Flattering."

She looked up, and no longer was his gaze heavy, lazy, dark. Now it burned with raw hunger, and it was her turn to gasp as he swept her up and threw her onto her back. "You make me insane, Cara." He mounted her, put himself between her legs so his shaft rubbed in her slick heat. His lips met hers in a kiss that was exquisitely gentle, despite the fierceness in his eyes. "I wish we had more time—"

"Shh." She framed his face in her hands, stilling him and putting every drop of intensity she had behind her stare. "There will be nothing but passion in this bed."

"And I swear on my father's name and his holy spirit that there will never be another in this bed," he ground out, and as tears sprang to her eyes, he dipped his head and took her breast in his mouth.

Instantly, the fire kindled again, roaring to the surface. She cried out and sank her nails into his back. God, that felt good. She tilted her hips, eager to have him inside her to ease the ache he'd sparked in her, but he backed up, denying her satisfaction.

She wanted to scream, but then he cupped her intimately, sliding one finger through her folds with maddeningly light strokes as he kissed his way down her belly. When he reared back to look at her...look at her *there*... she nearly closed up and covered herself. But now wasn't the time to be shy. Now was her last chance to be powerful. Beautiful. Seductive.

So she spread her thighs as wide as they would go, and her reward was his utter reverence. "So beautiful," he murmured.

And then he dove between her legs. His hands lifted her butt, his thumbs spread her folds, and his mouth captured her. Erotic pleasure swelled inside her until her skin grew tight with the pressure. Ares's tongue was magic, a hot, slippery wand that he swept up one side of her sex and down the other, sometimes using the entire flat surface to create broad strokes, sometimes focusing sensation with the firm tip.

"You taste...so...good." He flicked his tongue against her clit, and the orgasm that had been simmering just beneath the surface began to boil. "God, Cara..." His tongue pushed inside her, and her breath caught as she tried to hold back the detonation. She fisted the sheets, tugged at them, but all that did was give her leverage so she could pump against his mouth, pushing his tongue deeper, and when he smoothed it in circles inside her core...

Her body boiled over. The climax spiraled out of control, turned into a shattering, blinding ecstasy that went on and on. She felt him sucking on her, heard him moaning as he swallowed, and just as she began to come down, he mounted her. His thick length filled her, and she came again, locking her legs tight around his waist.

"That's it," he whispered against her throat. "Ride me, sweetheart. Ride me *hard*."

There had never been another option. She was caught up in a maelstrom of raw, animal lust and pure, soul-mending love, and for the first time in her life, she felt it all come together, as if she was finally whole. Finally happy with who and what she was, and had found the man who complemented her.

They rocked together, their bodies slapping as he pounded into her and she arched up to meet every impact. Sweat glistened on his skin, creating even more contrast and texture in the hills and valleys of his muscles, and when he threw his head back, teeth bared, tendons straining, the sight blew her last circuit. The most intense orgasm of her life tore through her with such power that she bucked her entire body off the mattress. Ares's arm went around her and pulled her up so he was sitting back on his heels and she was perched on his thighs, screaming as the pleasure popped along every nerve ending.

His roar of release joined hers, his hot semen splashing inside her and turning her orgasm into a fiery, stinging ecstasy that bordered on pain. Beneath her, Ares jerked, his muscles twitching, his breath coming in halting gasps. His pelvis continued to pump upward, though his movements were weak, uncontrolled, and after a few seconds, he fell forward with her, twisting so she wouldn't have to bear the bulk of his weight.

They lay like that, breathing heavy, sweating, trembling, for a long time. This should be the point where they drifted off to sleep in each other's arms or engaged in pillow talk, but instead, a terrible tension grew between them.

It was time, and there was no sense putting it off. Not when she could feel the energy Shade had given her seep away now that the sexual hunger had been sated.

"Ares?"

He squeezed her so tight she could barely breathe. "No."

For some reason, that made her smile. Then she reached across him to the dagger he'd set on the bedside table. It felt oddly warm in her hand. Seemed like it should be cold.

Carefully, she pushed against him, and he slid out of her, leaving her feeling empty. He propped himself up on one elbow and looked down at her, the expression on his handsome face laden with tragedy. "There's so much to say." His voice was halting, broken. Like her heart. "And yet..."

"And yet, what can be said?"

"Yeah."

Poor Hal. At least this was going to be a quick end for him, much better than being torn apart in a pit.

She put the tip of the dagger against her breastbone, took his hand, and placed it around the hilt. Then she wrapped her hands around his. They both shook as he moved the blade to the left, just under the swell of her breast, clearly knowing exactly where to shove it through to make the fastest, most lethal strike.

"Now," she said.

He gave a single, sharp nod, and his hand tightened beneath hers. "Now."

# Twenty-four

Now didn't always mean *now*.

How could Ares possibly do this? If Hal was reasonably healthy, Cara could suffer for a long time as his energy poured into her, keeping her heart beating even around the dagger's sharp blade. The pain would be excruciating.

His chest constricted. "I can't," he rasped. What if Kynan was wrong?

"You have to. You know you do." She tightened her grip around his, steadying it. How ironic was it that he was the battle-hardened warrior, part demon, part ruthless angel, and his hand was shaking, yet Cara, a mere human, was steady as a rock.

No, there was nothing *mere* about her.

They'd found each other too late. Way too late.

"We could wait. Just a little longer."

Her sad smile made his eyes sting. "You know we can't. I can feel myself getting weaker. Hal is getting weaker.

I could fade away at any minute, and then where would you be?"

Evil. He'd be evil. And not long after that, his brother and sister would be just as monstrous, and the end of days would be upon the human world. He knew that, and yet, he wanted every extra second with Cara that he could get. "I'll take you back to the hospital, and Shade can keep you alive for a little while longer."

"I don't want to live like that. In a bed, with some strange demon channeling energy into me? That's not life, and you know it." She pressed the tip of the knife into her skin, and a trickle of blood dripped down her rib cage. "Do it."

Ares was an expert at this. Had this been anyone else, he could shove the blade home and the victim would be dead before he knew what hit him.

But Cara would know. She would suffer. And he'd have to watch, knowing he'd caused it. Knowing he could do nothing about it.

Rearing up, he released the dagger. "Not yet. I can't. I can't do it. I need...a minute."

"Ares!"

In a near panic, he scrambled off the bed, opened the door, and fled out into the hall. Didn't matter that he was naked—he had no hang-ups, and his staff had seen him nude often enough. He heard thumping around in the bedroom, heard the telltale sounds of clothes ruffling. Cara was going to come after him. Dammit. He strode into the great room, cursing the return of the senses that tuned him in to global strife, and turned to the fireplace. It wasn't lit, was cold and empty, like his chest cavity.

The empty feeling was nothing new, given that it had

been that way his entire life. Hell, even when he'd had a family, had believed he was human, there had been something missing. And then Cara came into his life, and the cavern inside him had filled up. So he supposed it made sense that the sensation of emptiness was now so much more pronounced. Before, it had been normal. But now he knew what being warm felt like, and he was no longer used to the cold.

"Ares." Cara's voice was soft behind him. As she moved closer, all those battle vibrations melted away, and instead of feeling as if he wasn't whole without them . . . he felt at peace. The realization struck him like a blow. When he was with her, he didn't *lose* abilities . . . he *gained* peace.

How was he going to survive without her?

He didn't move as she padded up to him and plastered her body against his back, wrapping her arms around his waist. She'd brought him a towel, which she draped over his hips, and he would have smiled at her thoughtfulness if he wasn't on the verge of breaking down.

Her cheek rested on his shoulder blade, and her hot breath fanned over his skin.

This was so right. So terribly *right*. And it was all going to be gone soon.

"My lord?"

"What, Vulgrim?" His voice was harsher than he intended, but he had only minutes left with Cara, and he didn't want one second taken from him.

"An Aegi is here to see you. He says he may have a cure for Cara."

Afraid to hope, but his heart doing a backflip all the same, Ares wrapped the towel around his waist. With more calm than he felt, he turned, tucking Cara behind him. Vulgrim moved aside to reveal a man flanked by two of his guards.

"This is highly unusual," Ares said. "Who are you... wait... I saw you outside the Yorkshire headquarters."

The man nodded. "My name is David. Kynan and Arik were busy, so they sent me."

"Sent you? Why?" His eyes narrowed. "How did you get here?"

"Reaver." David opened his fist, and the Ramreels on either side of him reached for their weapons. He gulped, and very slowly held out his palm. "We found this in our archives. It was in a box marked with the *agimortus* symbol. We think that the *agimortus* can be transferred to this device and contained."

Ares scowled, but at the same time, his heart leaped. "I've never heard of such a thing."

"We hadn't either. We don't know much about it. We were hoping you would know what to do with it. In any case, it's better off in your hands than ours."

Ares nodded to Vulgrim, who took the object from David and brought it over. He placed it in Ares's hand. It was round, metallic, about the size of a golf ball. He didn't recognize the etchings on it... some kind of demonic language, he thought. But why would there be demonic symbols on something meant to contain an *agimortus*—

*Fuck!*

He flicked his hand to hurl it to the floor, but it burst open, shooting tiny needles into his skin. The familiar burning sensation of being bitten by a hellhound shot up his arm and into his body. Every muscle and joint locked up, but his mind spun, and he tried to warn Cara, to tell her to run, but the poison was already affecting his mouth and tongue.

"Ares!" Her panic rang loud in her voice, and then the sounds of battle rang out even louder.

The two Ramreels pounded the human, knocking him to the ground as Vulgrim made a shield of himself in front of Ares and Cara. "Take the human to the dungeon," Vulgrim snarled. "Find out what's happening outside!"

But Ares knew. Pestilence was out there, and the only thing he could do now was pray that Than and Limos had arrived.

Cara's hand closed around his, warm and comforting.

He should have killed her when he had the chance. God help him, he should have. Now she was going to suffer at Pestilence's hand, and all because he was too weak to let go of the woman he loved. Everything he'd always believed, that loving someone made you weak, was true.

⌒

Limos and Than ran toward the house, the sound of Vulgrim's shout hitting them as they'd stepped out of their individual portals.

"We're too late," Than barked.

Dammit! Limos had wanted to give Ares and Cara some time together, so they'd followed up on Thanatos's lead regarding Pestilence's whereabouts. They hadn't found him, but they'd found one of his minions who had been all too gleeful about some plan Pestilence had to retrieve Deliverance from Ares.

She and Than had come straight here, but by the sound of things, they hadn't been fast enough.

They burst through the front door and ran into the great room, where Ares was frozen in front of the fireplace, Vulgrim standing protectively in front of him, and Cara looking fierce despite the fact that she was pale, gaunt, and probably on the verge of collapse.

"He's been poisoned with hellhound venom," Vulgrim grunted. "My boys took the male responsible downstairs."

"I heard a horse," Cara said. "But I don't know where. Outside, I think." A crash of broken glass had Limos wheeling toward the hallway. "The dagger!" Cara started after Li, but Thanatos grabbed her.

Limos sprinted to the bedroom, drew short when she saw Pestilence standing there in his armor, Deliverance in his fist.

"Ah, Limos. So good to see you." He frowned. "Sort of. Your presence ruins my plan to kill Cara, but hey, she's near death anyway."

Disgust bubbled up, completely destroying all the leftover happy-happy-joy-joy sentiments about him she'd held on to. Like Thanatos, she wanted to believe that there was some good left in the creature standing before her, but unlike Than, she knew they couldn't bank on it. "Just so you know, I fully support the idea of ramming that dagger into your black heart."

"Really?" Pestilence hefted the dagger in his palm, feeling its weight. "I saw the Dark Lord the other day. He asked about you."

Limos snorted. "Did you tell him to go fuck himself?"

"I told him how you can't wait to spread your legs for him."

"Never."

"You can't fight him, sister. And once your Seal is broken, you won't want to. But either way, he'll take you. He's getting impatient. He wants children."

She shuddered, unable to imagine carrying Satan's

spawn in her belly. "You always swore you'd protect me from that fate. How a little thing like a broken Seal has changed you."

His laughter grated on every nerve. "It isn't the Seal. I'd have left you to your fate even if my Seal hadn't broken once I learned what a lying, scheming bitch you were." She stiffened as he leaned in, brushed his lips across her ear. "I know your secret."

"You've always known that The Aegis didn't lose Deliverance. You helped me cover the whole thing up." After he'd rescued her from The Aegis's grip, she'd fessed up, and he'd helped her do some creative rearranging of Aegi memories and promised to keep her secret from their brothers.

Thing was, she'd lied to Reseph, too. Even he hadn't known the true reason she'd stolen the dagger.

"But now I know *why* you stole it," he said, and her gut knotted. "But that's not the secret I'm talking about. I'm talking about the other one. The big one."

Her breath left her, her muscles went rubbery, and her blood congealed in her veins. When Pestilence stepped into his Harrowgate and disappeared, she nearly crumpled on legs that wouldn't work anymore.

He knew. Dear God, *he knew*.

And if he spilled her secret to Thanatos and Ares, she'd lose everything.

# Twenty-five

Cara's legs gave out. She'd tried to stay on her feet as the battle raged around them, but as Ares's muscles began to twitch as though thawing, hers turned to mush. She hit the floor hard, and instantly, Vulgrim lifted her into his furry arms.

"Cara," Ares rasped.

Vulgrim shifted her close to Ares, and she reached out to cup his cheek. He quieted, though his eyes gleamed with pain.

Thanatos, who had remained in the great room to defend them, cursed when Limos returned, her expression troubled.

"Reseph has the dagger."

"Dammit," Thanatos snarled. "Ares, you were supposed to—" He cut himself off when he looked over at Cara, and she finished the sentence for him.

"Kill me. We're both well aware of that. And it isn't

easy on either one of us, so I'd appreciate it if you kept your damned mouth shut."

Limos's violet eyes shot wide, and she casually sidled up to Thanatos as if thinking she'd need to restrain him. Several tense heartbeats passed. A rumble came up from deep in Ares's chest, and dark shadows passed over Thanatos's face. Finally, Thanatos's lips quirked into a half-smile.

"You are either brave or foolish."

"Neither," she said. "I figure I'm going to die anyway, so I have nothing to lose by telling you what a jerk you're being."

"Thank God," Limos sighed. "Someone else besides us who is willing to tell Than when to shove it. You're a keeper, Cara." Well, *that* made the room fall silent again, and Limos turned bright red. "Um, I, ah—"

"It's okay." Cara wriggled as best as she could in Vulgrim's arms. "Ares?"

Ares's head fell forward. His hand opened, and the little ball fell out.

Thanatos crouched and nudged it with the back of his gauntlet. "Son of a bitch. Handy little hellhound spit delivery device. Reseph always was inventive."

"We have his minion in the basement," Vulgrim said. "Maybe he can offer up some intel?"

"Oh, he'll offer it up," Thanatos said, as he strode away. "Give me five."

Vulgrim placed Cara on the couch, and then he dragged Ares over and sank him next to her. Gradually, Ares regained the use of his body, and the first thing he did was take her in his arms.

"I'm sorry," he whispered. "I am so sorry."

She nearly laughed. "What is there to be sorry for? Not killing me?"

"I hesitated. And because of that..."

"You could turn evil. The world could end. I know. I get it."

His hand came up and turned her face to him. "No. I failed to make sure you went quickly. Even if you were to suffer, at least you wouldn't suffer in the afterlife, knowing that because of your death, Armageddon broke the world."

Her eyes stung. They were on the verge of the end of the world, and he was worried about her soul. "You're amazing, you know that?"

"I'm a fool. For so many reasons."

The pound of footsteps coming up the stairs drew their attention, and they all turned to the stairwell. Thanatos emerged, wiping his bloody hands on a towel. "That Guardian is toast."

"He's dead?"

"No. I pulped him, but I meant that he's no longer human. Pestilence did something to him. Not sure what, but he's not...right."

"What did you get from him?" Ares asked.

"Obviously, he lied about Reaver bringing him here. And he gave up the location where they're keeping Hal."

Ares narrowed his eyes. "You think he's telling the truth?"

"Even if I wasn't sure of my methods, what he said matches up with what I got from Orelia. We need to head to Sithbludd."

Cara perked up as much as she could. "We can save him before they kill him." They all exchanged looks. "What? What is it?"

"Probably a trap," Ares said. "If Pestilence knows we have his boy, he'll know we'll get information out of him. Which means he knows we'll go after the dog in order to buy you some time. He's well aware that we need to keep you alive as long as possible while we try to retrieve the dagger."

"Of course we go after Hal," Cara said.

"You're not going anywhere."

"Yes, I am. I'm dying, Ares. Whether it happens here or there makes no difference. So if there's any way I can help—"

"How can you help?" Thanatos interrupted. His words were soft, not meant to be rude, and she didn't take offense. "You're weakened, barely able to stand. You'll only get in our way if we have to worry about you."

"Than..." Ares's dangerous growl filled the room.

Cara squeezed his hand. "He's right." She arched an eyebrow at Than. "But not entirely. If my dream was any indication, Hal is crazed right now. He won't allow any of you to help him. I can get close. Free him so he can flash away or call to his family to help fight. If you can't get the dagger, saving Hal will buy us a few hours if he's not being torn up in the pit. If you do retrieve the dagger, I'll be right there." In which case, saving Hal would be pointless, because he was going to die anyway. "We might not have even seconds to lose. You know I'm right."

Yeah, they did. She could see it in their eyes.

"If I get the dagger," Ares said, "I'm using it on Pestilence."

The tension in the room quadrupled, but when Than inclined his head in a slow nod, the house breathed a slow sigh of relief.

But Cara wasn't holding out for hope. If Ares got the dagger, Pestilence wasn't going to stand still while his brother shoved a blade into his chest. No, Deliverance had her name on it, and she knew it. This mission was a one-way ticket for her.

Ares stood, all commander and military bearing. "Than, get as many of your vamps to fight as you can. I'll send my Ramreels. Limos, call in every favor you've got in the underworld—"

"No." She crossed her arms over her chest. "I'm not sending anyone in my place. I'm going with you."

"Li, you can't," Ares said.

Cara looked between them, confused. "Why can't she?"

"As long as she's in the human realm, she's relatively safe from Satan. He can't enter the human realm to get her, and thanks to an agreement our mother made long ago, he can't send his minions to get her unless she gets cozy with a male—"

"Hey!" Limos jammed her fists on her hips. "Private much? Yes, I'm a proud member of the hymen club. So what?" She turned to Cara. "What he's saying, in that doltish way of his, is that I'm safe up here. But all bets are off if I enter Sheoul. Some parts are safer than others for me, which is why I can go to the Horsemen every once in a while, even if I can't stay for long."

Ares scowled. "And only if all three of us are there with you." He cursed. "Two of us. Doesn't matter. You're not going, Limos."

"I have to. You need all the help you can get," she argued. "And let's face it...if we fail, I'll end up there anyway."

The foul words that fell from Ares's and Thanatos's

mouths made Cara blush all the way to her hair follicles. Limos just crossed her arms over her chest, tapped her foot, and waited for the tirades to end.

"No amount of planning is going to make this battle go any better, Ares." Thanatos's yellow gaze was somber, and the shadows that seemed to perpetually follow him had gone still. "Reseph knows every trick up your sleeve, every play in your book."

"We can't rely on chaos and luck to defeat him," Ares said.

"But that's how Pestilence operates," Limos said quietly. "It'll be an even playing field."

"Hardly. He has the high ground and a lot larger army."

"Then," came Reaver's deep, ringing voice from the doorway, "we bring the element of surprise."

# Twenty-six

Ares did not want to do this. Oh, his body was alive with excitement—it craved battle. Craved the feel of flesh rending and bone crunching under his blade. But his heart and head weren't in it. Not when he knew that one way or the other, Cara wasn't coming back from their foray into Sheoul.

Reaver, who Ares owed an apology and who had been as battered as Harvester, had agreed to assist as much as he could, and though he couldn't set foot in the region they were traveling to, he'd brought help in the form of Kynan, who was untouchable, and a blond Seminus demon named Wraith, who was apparently just as untouchable, part vampire, and the brother of Eidolon and Shade. Sin, their sister, and her vampire mate, Con, had come as well, since Sin was ultimately responsible for Pestilence's Seal breaking in the first place.

And Shade had come to give Cara a power boost. It had improved her color and taken the cloudiness out of her eyes, but her lungs were rattling, and over the top of her head, Shade had given Ares the universal shake of the head that meant *not much longer*.

Fuck.

They exited the Harrowgate, which had been crammed full of people and three warhorses. Eerie silence greeted them. The only sound was that of the stallions' hooves thudding on the hard-packed Sithbludd dirt.

Ares tightened his arm around Cara's waist as she sat in front of him. "I've never been in this region before."

Thanatos glanced around. "Me either."

"Maybe because this place sucks." Wraith flipped a throwing knife from hand to hand. "I thought we were going to get to fight. Talk about lame. I'm seriously disappointed in you Horsemen people."

"Kynan?" Limos said sweetly. "Could you maybe have found a more annoying demon to bring with us?"

"Nope." Kynan drew a stang from the harness beneath his leather bomber. "They don't get more annoying than Wraith."

"If you're going to do something, you might as well be the best," Wraith muttered, as he moved off toward an area of shadows. Not even the ever-present hazy light that permeated the land seemed to penetrate the murky darkness.

"What's going on?" Cara's voice was quiet, but whether it was because she was fading or because she was afraid, he didn't know. "Where's Hal?"

"Does any of this look familiar? From your dream?"

"Not really. When I saw it, there were lots of demons. It was smoky. There were big cliffs and vines. There's nothing here. It's like a gray desert."

"I think we were duped by the Aegi," Than growled.

Kynan peered up where reddish, cloudlike wisps floated, providing a sense of depth. "Thanks for letting Reaver take David back to The Aegis. He'll never be released again."

Limos let out a dubious snort as Cara sniffed the air. "It's weird. It smells the same. And I swear, I can feel Hal. Give me a second." She leaned back against Ares, resting her head against his softened armor. He held her protectively as her lids closed over eyes that were far too dull.

Desperation, sadness, and anger all combined to create an emotional cocktail that threatened to knock Ares on his ass. He'd never felt this way about another person, and his heart was in foreign territory. He wanted to scream at the unfairness of this situation, but he had to get a grip, keep the wall up, because he needed to be stronger now than he'd ever been.

"I can hear him." Cara kept her eyes closed, but pointed directly ahead. "That way. He's snarling. He says... he says they're here." She frowned. "I don't understand. Something about a wraith. And a veil. A... whisper veil?"

"Shit!" Ares wheeled Battle around. "Open the gate! Open the fucking gate!"

Sin and Con sprinted toward the Harrowgate. An ear-shattering boom rocked the area, and everyone stumbled, including the horses. The whisper veil, a concealment enchantment, lifted to reveal the true area, which was a sea of demons and weapons, and in front of the Harrowgate, a creature rose out of the ground, all wisps of mist, sharklike teeth, and claws as long as Ares was tall.

"Fucking vapor wraith!" Con grabbed Sin, yanking her off her feet to snatch her out of the way of the beast's snapping jaws in the nick of time.

Ares hated vapor wraiths. They could be bound to

Harrowgates, and while a single beast couldn't screw much with Ares and his siblings, the three more that materialized, each progressively larger than the first twelve-footer, could put a hurting on them if they tried to get out through the gate.

And he didn't have to attempt to throw his own portable gate to know that Pestilence had neutralized that ability.

Swarms of demons rushed them from all sides, including from above.

"Watch the arrows!" Than shouted, even as he knocked one out of the air with his sword.

No doubt the tips were coated with hellhound saliva.

"Get me to Hal—" Cara cut off as a raptor horror, a man-sized, eyeless thing with bat wings, swept down and nearly knocked her out of the saddle. Ares caught her by the wrist, tried to haul her back up, but an ax caught Battle in the chest. He screamed, reared up, and Cara plummeted to the ground.

"*Cara!*"

"Go," she gasped. "I'll get to Hal." Her gaze shifted. "Behind you!"

He twisted around in time to barely avoid being skewered by a sword twice the size of his, wielded by a troll. And yet, in the middle of the battle taking place, everything went slow motion, and he locked gazes with Cara.

*Go*, she mouthed. *I love you.*

He tried to say it back, but all that came out was, "Get to Hal!"

Cara's life was more important than his feelings.

---

"Get to Hal!" Ares had shouted, but he didn't need to. Cara was desperate to get to the hound, whose cries rose above even the shriek and thunder of hundreds, maybe thousands, of demons.

Ares said Hal would be kept in the pits by the same symbols that had imprisoned him in the cage Sestiel had put him in. All she had to do was destroy the symbols, and Hal would be free.

Crawling, she avoided being chopped in half by a huge ax blade. The creature wound up for another swing, but Kynan took its head off with something that looked like a sharp Frisbee. Blood showered her, a gruesome rain of blackish-crimson that splashed into her mouth and nearly made her vomit. *Don't think about it. Don't think about it...*

Adrenaline gave her waning strength a much-needed boost as she scrambled on her hands and knees beneath the feet of some horrible winged thing, and then rolled between the legs of another. On either side of her, Ares and Thanatos fought, shielding her from the worst of the horde. In front of her, Wraith cleared the way. Like Kynan, nothing touched him. If she hadn't been so busy trying to avoid being skewered, she'd have been fascinated by the way things would swing at the two men, but at the last minute, the enemy would stumble or fall, or something else would randomly strike them down.

When she reached the pit, her heart stopped. Huge ivory spikes lined the twenty-foot-deep hole, all angled inward to keep Hal—and any other creature that got tossed in—from getting out. Blood, both dried and fresh, splattered the walls and pooled on the dirt floor. Dear God, it was barbaric. She'd love to shove the scumbags who'd done this in the pit with Hal and see how they liked being torn apart.

Except...Hal wasn't in any condition to fight.

He lay against the wall, his panting, labored breaths spraying pink froth. His tail thumped once, and then he went back to just trying to survive.

"Oh, my God," she whispered. "Get me down there." She grabbed Wraith's pant leg. "Get me down there."

The demon scooped her up, and in one easy, nimble leap, sailed over the spikes to land, feather-lightly, in the pit. Hal growled, but it was a feeble attempt, the sound fading to a whimper, and her heart broke.

Still in Wraith's arms, she gestured to the stone walls, which were covered in strange markings. "We've got to destroy them."

"Those aren't containment markings." Wraith whirled so fast she shrieked. He hurled a morning star upward, and a batlike demon that had been diving into the pit tumbled in the air and landed in a heap at Wraith's feet. "Bastard."

"I hate this place," she muttered.

"Ditto." Wraith turned back to Hal. "His collar. It's got the containment symbols on it."

"Put me down. You watch my back."

Wraith eased her to the floor. On her first step, she wobbled. On the second, her legs gave out. Wraith caught her before she hit the ground. Very gently, he placed her next to Hal.

"Hey, buddy," she murmured. Hal licked her hand without lifting his head.

With the rumble of battle going on above her, and even inside the pit as demons leaped in but were dispatched by Wraith before they landed, she worked the collar. Her vision blurred with tears, and her fingers shook, all of which made for painfully slow progress as she manipulated the mechanisms on the series of tiny pins that held the collar in place. Removal had to be excruciating, but Hal took it like a trouper. When the last one popped free, the collar fell to the ground.

Hal didn't move. His chest rose and fell in uneven fits and starts, and Cara realized that her own breathing had become shallow and raspy. The world spun and tilted as she wrapped herself around Hal and gave in to the exhaustion that rode her hard.

She was going to die in a pit of evil, wasn't she? This... sucked.

"Wraith." Her mouth was as dry as the hot air here, and she had to pause to work up some saliva so she could talk. "Help the others. Need the dagger."

"Not without you two." Palming a bone from some long-dead creature, he scratched out the markings on the walls. When every one of them was gone, the spikes at the top of the pit retracted.

"Let's get topside before demons make a run on this place."

Fear was a spike right in her heart. Wraith's scenario would be a disaster. He might be untouchable, but he'd be overrun, and it would only take one demon to slip past him for Cara and Hal to be toast.

Wraith scooped them both up, grunting under their combined weight, and then he leaped, landing once again in a smooth crouch. Even though her energy and thought processes were flagging, she assessed the situation in a heartbeat.

With the exception of Kynan, everyone who had come to fight for the home team was bathed in blood, and a lot of it was their own. Their clothes—or armor—were torn, bashed, or broken.

The fighting raged, but as Wraith placed Cara and Hal on the ground, Ares was right there, and everyone else closed ranks, forming a protective circle around Hal and Cara even as they continued to fight. The demon horde, despite all the bloody, broken bodies on the ground, didn't seem to have thinned at all.

"*Cease!*" The demons all froze as Pestilence rode through the masses, smashing demons who weren't quick enough to get out of his way. "I call a five-minute truce." He inclined his head at Ares. "Don't say I never did anything for you." He gestured in the direction of the Harrowgate.

"Hey there, Horsemen!"

Cara folded her legs under her and cradled Hal's head in her lap as she squinted into the smoky darkness. A massive man with a dark blue mohawk broke through the ocean of creatures. He might have been handsome, if not for the extreme paleness of his skin, which revealed a pattern of black veins beneath. Protruding from his bare back were a set of black, leathery wings, which extended to his calves. She had no idea what kind of pants he was wearing, but they were silvery, form-fitting, and they kept shifting, as though they were constantly rearranging themselves on his body.

Demons bowed and fell to their knees as he passed, and the ones in front of him knocked into each other and fell all over themselves to get out of his way. If his smile was any indication, he was getting a kick out of it.

Thanatos's split lips stretched into a big grin. "Hades. It's about fucking time."

Hades? *The* Hades?

"Fuck off." Hades ran his palm up his hairless chest. "Try negotiating with Azagoth to stop the flood of souls into Sheoul-gra so you can take a break, and see how long it takes *you*."

Wraith bent over and whispered in her ear, "Azagoth is the Grim Reaper. I'm kind of related to him. How cool is that?"

Kynan shoved his stang into a holster. "You're such a name-dropper."

"Why are you here?" Ares wiped blood from his eyes with the back of his hand. "Tell me you're not working with Pestilence."

"That's the thanks I get?" He spun around. "Guess you don't need me."

"Hades, stop being a baby." Limos leveled a grave look at Ares, one that even had Battle stilling, though his muscles twitched. "He's here because you said to call in favors. Cara needed a favor."

Ares's entire body jerked. "Oh, hell. I didn't...think of that."

"Think of what?" Cara craned her neck to look up at him.

Hades turned around, his wings spreading and folding again with a soft whoosh. "You are human. If you die in Sheoul, your soul will be trapped here forever. I'm here to escort your soul aboveground."

Oh, God. "Thank you," she whispered.

He shrugged. "It's my good deed for the millennium. And Limos promised to send me Baskin-Robbins."

"Time's up," Pestilence shouted. "And did I mention my secret weapon? No? Ah, well, I'm forgetful some-times." He swept his arm in a dramatic gesture, and out of the sky, three dozen winged men dropped in front of Pestilence's horse.

"Fuck," Wraith breathed. "Fallen angels."

"Well," Kynan said grimly, "you said you wanted to fight."

"I don't understand." Cara peeled her eyes away from one of the winged newcomers—Zhreziel, whose expression said he had an ax to grind, and probably on the Horsemen's bones.

"The only beings that can harm me and Wraith are angels. Which includes the fallen variety."

"And they're hard as fuck to kill, unless you're another angel. Or a Horseman. Even better, Pestilence probably knows about our charmed status, thanks to David." Wraith's fangs flashed. "Man, if I get killed, not even the fact that David is Serena's brother is going to save him from her." For some reason, he smiled at that. "My mate can be a total badass. It's so hot."

"Okay, boys." Pestilence's grating voice rang out. "Kill the human and the mutt, and let's get this Apocalypse started!"

Thanatos released his souls, and they screeched as they shot toward the evil army. As if rejuvenated by the brief break, the demons swarmed, more vicious than ever. It was a nightmare of teeth, claws, and weapons. Helplessness splintered what bravery Cara held in her reserves, and somehow Ares knew. He tossed her a dagger, a last-resort weapon to be sure, but at least she had something with which she could strike a blow to any demon that made it through the wall of her defenders.

Assuming she had the strength to use it.

Everyone, including Hades—who made demons explode

with a mere touch—fought hard, but one by one, the horses went down, and the Horsemen were crushed under the wave of monsters. Despair and fear became the air Cara breathed, so thick she couldn't even scream when the rain of blows fell on Cara and Hal. Wraith and Kynan leaped on top of them, shielded them with their bodies, but somehow, blades found their way through the pile.

Pain ripped into her, as razor sharp as the weapons piercing her flesh and organs. Deep inside, a weird tugging sensation grabbed at her, and she felt as if she was being peeled like a banana. When the realization hit her, she cried out.

The tugging and peeling was her soul trying to leave her body.

Snarls rang out. Screams. Warm blood splashed on her face. A weight came off her as Wraith and Kynan pushed away. *Ares.* Where was Ares?

"Holy shit," Kynan murmured. "Damn."

Cara couldn't move, could barely breathe as she lay on her side in a fetal position, wrapped around Hal. She figured she had about five breaths' worth of life remaining, but dammit, she was going to watch the end come. With effort, she opened the one eye that still functioned, though it felt as if her eyelid was made of steel wool. Through uneven blurs and blood, she saw massive black paws. Teeth. Red, glowing eyes.

Hellhounds.

"There has to be thousands of them," Wraith said.

The forest of black legs milled and parted. Something massive moved toward them, and before Cara could even blink, a monstrous, three-headed hellhound stood before them, easily twice as big as the largest of the others.

"Hey, Cerberus," Hades said.

"Cerberus?" Kynan gasped.

"Yeah." Hades scrubbed his hand over his mohawk. "This can't be good."

"And why is that?"

"He hates me for binding him to Sheoul-gra. He only gets to leave when I do. He's probably here to rip me to shreds. Again."

The beast shouldered aside Hades, and finally, Cara caught sight of Ares. His armor was mangled, his left hand mashed, and his legs impossibly broken, but he was using his one good hand to drag himself to Cara. She wanted to cry, but that tugging sensation had overcome her, and tears, it seemed, stayed with the body, not the soul.

Ares pulled himself against her as everyone else moved to block Cerberus, who was on a path directly for her and Hal.

Cerberus's three heads snarled as one.

"S'okay." Cara's voice was reed-thin, barely there, but apparently it was enough, because everyone shifted, allowing Cerberus to pass.

The big beast sniffed at her, and then one of the heads licked Hal. Hal opened his eyes, and a single word came to her. *Grandfather.* He hadn't said it to her, but somehow, she intercepted the transmission to the three-headed hound.

One of the heads turned to her, its crimson eyes glowing. *You are* reoush, *beast-healer. Rare. You will not die.*

Not dying didn't seem like an option. She sucked in a gurgling breath...and it didn't leave her. Blackness swallowed her whole even as she felt the warm stroke of a tongue over her lips.

# Twenty-seven

Cara wasn't sure what happened. All she knew was that she'd come wide awake in Ares's arms, Hal was bouncing around in the demon remains and happily tossing things like arms and legs into the air, while off in the distance, other hellhounds were...she squinted, and then wished she hadn't. Ares wasn't kidding when he said hellhounds liked their prey a little too much. Swallowing sourly, she jerked her gaze away from the hellhound playground to see medical people in scrubs patching up the home team.

Eidolon and Shade were doing the glow-thing to Sin, while Con held her hand, his own wounds so extensive Cara was surprised he was sitting up without help. Kynan was patching up Wraith, who kept yelling obscenities, and some black-haired guy Con had called Luc was trying, unsuccessfully, to work on Ares.

Ares, who kept shoving the guy away even as he

spoke gently to Cara. "You're awake. Thank God, you're awake."

"Where..." She cleared her throat to rid it of the scratchiness that made her voice sound as if she hadn't used it in decades. "Where are the demons? Pestilence?" She frowned. "Cerberus. Or did I dream it all?" Even as she said it, she knew she hadn't dreamed it.

"The hellhounds broke Pestilence's army. He had to retreat. Cerberus and most of the hounds gave chase. Shade brought help from Underworld General."

"How am I alive?" And damn, she felt really freaking great, too. As if she'd been plugged into a battery the size of Mount Everest.

"It seems," Ares said, "that you received Hell's Kiss from the hellhound king."

Okay, that was...significant, she was guessing. Tail wagging, Hal romped over. *All of us. You belong to all of us now. All bonded to you. Except for those bonded to others. You are* reoush, *our healer.*

"Oh," she breathed. "Oh, wow."

Ares's eyes bored into her. "What is it?"

"It um...seems that I'm bonded to all of them. They've adopted me as their official physician of sorts."

Luc froze as he reached into the medic bag next to him. "*All* hellhounds?"

"As in, every hellhound in existence?" Ares added.

"That's what Hal says."

"Holy shit." Limos's voice came from behind Ares, but Cara couldn't twist around to see her. "That would make you—"

"Immortal." Ares blew out a long, shaky breath. "You're immortal."

"It's beyond that." Hades strolled over, picked up what Cara thought might be the leg of some creature, and tossed it for Hal. "Fetch!" He turned to Cara as Hal bounded off. "Any injury you sustain would be spread evenly throughout the hellhound population, so you'll heal instantly. Only Cerberus himself...and God...can kill you now." He frowned. "I can't believe that fucker did that. He never does that. I asked him to do it to my girlfriend once, and he refused. Ripped my arm off." He snorted. "Course, she fucked me over later anyway. The bitch."

This was all so strange, and yet, it was all becoming normal. "Wait, why would they need a healer, if I'm bonded to them? An injured hound would take energy from me, right?"

Hades shook his head. "Cerberus's bond doesn't work that way. It's against natural law to alter an entire species. You reap the benefits of taking from them, and they get you as a healer."

Didn't seem like a fair tradeoff to her, but she wasn't going to complain. "Ares, are you okay? Your legs..."

"They're fine. Eidolon gave me a quick zap when he first got here, and I'm regenerating to heal the rest. So I really don't need any medical help." The last bit was aimed at Luc, who gave Ares the finger.

Hiding a smile, Cara reached for Ares's hand...and noticed that Battle wasn't on his arm. Instant alarm lanced her. "The horses. How are the horses?"

"They could use your help," Ares said softly.

"You should have told me!" She leaped to her feet, and she had to cover her mouth with her hand to contain her gasp of horror. Now she understood why Ares had held her the way he had, angled away from the animals.

The carnage was...unbelievable. Thanatos was kneeling next to Styx, who was a mass of bone erupting from muscle. His legs were twisted in awkward angles, and he had so many blades and arrows sticking out of him that he looked like a porcupine.

Battle and Bones bore similar injuries, and all of the horses were surrounded by people in scrubs, who were working frantically to save the stallions.

Cara scrambled over to Styx, who appeared to be in the worst shape—though the amount of play in *that* distinction could be measured in a thimble.

Styx's eyes were closed, his nostrils flaring as he breathed. Blood bubbled up through the multiple wounds in his chest, and nothing the medical people were doing seemed to help.

"Oh, no," she breathed, as she kneeled at the stallion's head.

Thanatos's hand captured her wrist. His yellow gaze was tortured, and fear had drawn deep lines in his handsome face. "Can you help him? Please? I know I've been harsh with you—"

"I understand." He had the fate of the human world resting on his shoulders, and he'd been justifiably more concerned with that than her feelings.

Gently, she extracted herself from his grip to lay both her hands on Styx. Closing her eyes, she summoned her healing energy. A blast of power slammed into her, and her head snapped back so hard her hands came off the horse.

"What is it?" Ares gripped her shoulders from behind, bracing her as she blinked out of the stunned fog she was in. Thanatos was staring at her with concern, and Limos had twisted around from where she was caring for Bones to watch with just as much worry.

"I don't know." Cara shook her head, clearing it of the last of the fuzzy feeling. "Usually I feel a trickle of power, but this was like a river. Like a dam had burst. Let me try again." Once more, she placed her hands on the stallion, but this time, she opened herself up more gradually.

Energy sang through her with a hundred times the strength she was used to, and that was on the lowest setting she could manage. Tentatively, she let it out through her hands, and all around her, people gasped.

Cara didn't open her eyes. In her mind, she could see everything. There was no pain for her, but the horse's wounds were closing, weapons were being pushed out of flesh, and bone was knitting together. A great surge of affection hit her as Styx's health improved, and within minutes, he was communicating his gratitude to her in words and images and little nuzzles of his velvety nose against her thigh.

Gradually, there was nothing left to heal, and she pulled back her power and opened her eyes. The medical people were watching her in awe, and even Eidolon, who seemed to have a similar ability, was eyeing her with speculation.

"Can you do that with people?"

She shook her head. "Only animals." Eidolon looked disappointed. Thanatos offered his hand to her, and though she didn't need his help to stand, she took it, sensing that he needed to do this. Ares stepped back, apparently sensing the same thing. When she was standing before the giant warrior, he kneeled at her feet, head bowed.

"In my time, totem priestesses were honored. Revered as descendants of the *aos si*."

*"Aos si?"*

"The folk. You'd call them...fairies. They possessed the gift of healing animals and killing people when angered. They're long dead, but you obviously carry their blood." He looked up at her and placed his fist over his heart. "You have my gratitude and my respect forever."

Somehow, Cara knew she'd just been elevated to an equal in Thanatos's eyes. Warmth seeped through her, but she didn't spend time doing anything more than offering him a thank you. She'd have to ask more about the *aos si* later. She had two more horses to heal.

The process was the same with both Bones and Battle, and when she was finished, she wasn't worn out at all.

And there'd been no pain.

"You were drawing on the power of the hellhound pack," Limos said. "That. Is. Awesome."

Ares pulled Cara to her feet as Battle came to his. Nearby, Hal and Hades were still playing their gruesome game of fetch, and the medical staff were packing up and preparing the dead for transport.

Cara wrapped herself around Ares and held tight. "I just wish my power worked on more than animals. I might have been able to save some of your staff."

Thanatos nodded grimly. "I lost twelve vampires."

"I'll have to tell Vulgrim that fourteen of his herd are dead." Ares pressed a kiss to the top of Cara's head. "But you're safe. You still bear my *agimortus*, but since you can't be killed, you're no longer a target for Pestilence or his minions. Which means you're coming home with me." He cleared his throat. "If you, you know, want to."

How adorable was he? "Of course I want to. But...the *agimortus*...I'll drain you."

Than snorted. "Something tells me he'll be happy for you to *drain* him."

"Hell yeah." Ares sifted her hair through his fingers, so simple, but so intimate. "Not even a question." Her concern must have shown like a neon sign, because he cut her a serious look. "The effect is temporary, and the tradeoff is worth it a thousand times over."

"Gag." Limos studied her chipped nails. "Get a room."

"It's not all good news, though," Than warned. "Pestilence is going to come after Limos and me now. And if one our Seals breaks, the other two will fall soon after."

"And he still has Deliverance," Limos pointed out.

Usually bringing up the dagger made Than irritable, but he merely nodded. "Let's get out of here."

"I never want to come here again," Cara muttered.

"You never will." Ares lifted her into Battle's saddle and swung up behind her. "Hades handled the vapor wraiths at the Harrowgate, so let's get the hell out of here. Pun intended. Where do you want to go?"

"First, your shower. Second, your bed."

Instantly, she felt the nudge of his erection against her butt. "Anything you want."

"Anything?" She twisted around in the saddle, hooked her hand behind his head, and pulled his mouth to her lips. "Because now that I'm immortal, you have no excuses to avoid the full-on rough stuff."

He groaned. "We're so out of here."

They didn't make it to the bedroom. Hell, they didn't even make it to the house. Ares had wanted to inform Vulgrim privately of his herd-mates' valiant deaths, so, at Cara's request, he'd left her on the beach near his house, where she could wash in the waves and relax.

Now Ares was stripping off his clothes as he walked across the white expanse of sand toward Cara, who was splashing in the sea, her eyes sparkling like the water around her. He admired her graceful, sleek lines as she rose up, exposing her high, firm breasts and the shadowed juncture between her legs. The sea swells licked at her the way he planned to do when he got her onto land.

He was hard, hungry, and ready before he hit the first wave. By the second, his body was straining for her, his blood running like lava through his veins. By the third, she was wrapped around him, her silky sex rubbing against his, her lips sucking on his neck.

He groaned as she ground against him, working her entrance over the tip of his shaft. "Give me thirty seconds to wash off the demon blood—"

Her throaty growl both turned him on and told him what she thought of that idea. Granted, blood and gore had never bothered him, but this was Cara, and although he knew damned good and well that she could handle whatever he threw at her, she deserved him to be clean, at least.

With more effort than he would have believed he'd need, he peeled her off of him, but not before she fisted his cock and gave him a couple firm pumps that nearly had him spilling in her hand.

"I want what you promised me," she said, and yeah, she'd get it.

He fell backward in the water, scrubbed his hands over his face and hair while he was beneath the waves. When he breached the surface, prepared to drag her to him... she was gone. Instant, ice-cold fear stabbed him, but when he saw her on the beach, backing toward the craggy trees on the coastline and crooking her finger in a playful come-and-get-me gesture, his worry veered straight to lust.

Oh, he was going to get her, all right. And he was going to come. Several times.

On fire for her, he surged out of the water with the single-minded focus of a starving predator. The little minx squealed, turned and ran, but she didn't have a prayer. He was faster, and he was going to take her down like a wolf on a deer.

What he didn't count on was her ability to climb trees like a cat.

He caught up with her deep in the northern grove, where she was standing above him on the thick branch of an ancient, gnarled olive tree.

"Woman, what are you doing?" His voice was rough, his breathing rapid, but not from exertion. The chase had revved him, stoked his craving for either battle or sex, and he was no longer afraid to give Cara both.

"Since you made me wait, I'm making you work for it." She shifted her stance, allowing him a tantalizing view of her glistening center, and a carnal sound escaped him. He was riveted by the sight, knew how she felt, tasted, smelled, and the list of things he wanted to do to her was endless.

"You think I won't climb that tree?"

"This branch won't support you."

He exhaled slowly through his nose, an age-old tactic he employed during the thickest part of a battle when rash decisions lost wars. And right now, a rash decision would have him tearing that tree up by the roots to get at his female.

His gaze fell on the surrounding foliage, and his strategy fell into place. Smiling triumphantly, victory already singing in his heated veins, he stalked a few feet away to one of the many wild grape vines that had overtaken the island. He tore a thick vine from the plant and wrapped one end around his fist.

Cara eyed him warily as he stalked back to the tree. "Are you ready, Cara?" he asked silkily, and her eyes narrowed.

"What do you have planned—" She cut off as he snapped the vine like a whip, catching her around one slim ankle. He jerked the vine, yanking her feet out from under her.

Her shriek of surprise rang out, followed by a grunt as the backs of her knees caught a lower branch. In an instant, she was hanging upside down from the tree and hurling curses that would make a hardened soldier blush. Ares puffed up with pride.

"What did I tell you about challenging me?"

With a snarl, she reached for him, and he let her catch him around the thighs because they were now in the perfect position for what he'd been wanting to do to her from the moment he'd first seen her naked. Sure, in his fantasies they'd been horizontal, but vertical worked too. Maybe even better.

He stepped into her so they were skin on skin, her plump breasts pressing into his abs. Breathing deeply, he took in the heady scent of her desire as he bent his head slightly to put his mouth level with her sex. A delicious sting urged him closer as her fingernails dug into the backs of his thighs and her hot breath fanned over his shaft and balls.

Two could play at that game. Though he scarcely had

the patience to tease, he took the time to blow on her damp curls as he spread the lips of her sex with his thumbs. The sight of her slick, pink flesh, open and exposed to him, almost made him weak in the knees.

Swimming in need, he licked her from her clit to her core, loving the way she squirmed helplessly against him as he did it again. And again.

Almost vengefully, she dragged her lips up his shaft and closed her mouth over the head of him. His cock kicked, pulsing as her wet heat sucked him deep. She wasn't gentle as she worked him, using her teeth to pinch his flesh and her fingernails to score it. Her tongue lashed at him and her lips rasped over sensitive spots, and the blend of sensations had him pumping his hips, fucking her mouth.

But he didn't forget what he was doing. Pushing his tongue fully inside her, he began a thrusting motion in time with his pelvic action. The peaches-and-cream taste of her, mingled with the salty essence of the sea, drove him harder, and her sweet moans buzzed through him, vibrating his cock and spreading through every nerve ending.

He slid his thumbs inward to massage her clit between them as he tongued her. Her juices flooded his mouth, and he groaned, swallowing her hungrily.

"Ares." She gasped his name around the cap of his penis, and damn, he loved feeling her lips move like that, turning his name into an erotic caress.

Sensing the orgasm coiling within her, he doubled his efforts, rolling her swollen nub with the pads of his thumbs and whirling his tongue inside her. Faster and faster, he circled the rim of her opening and then buried his tongue deep. Cara bucked and thrashed, and this time when she called his name, it was in the throes of ecstasy.

He tasted her climax, an extra zing of sweetness on his lips. As she panted through the waning pleasure, he dragged his tongue back to feather it over her quivering clit, and she went off again, her hands gripping his buttocks so hard he knew he'd be bruised, even if only for a few minutes.

"Need . . . you . . . now," he said hoarsely.

Spurred on by pain, passion, and the elemental need to mate, he lifted her, unhooking her legs from the branch. In one smooth move, he flipped her, planting her on her hands and knees on the sandy ground. Pure animal desire compelled him now, and he went to his knees behind her, gripped her hips, and drove his cock inside her. He gave her what she'd asked for, sparing her nothing. He pounded into her with everything he had, scooting them both forward and leaving deep grooves in the ground.

"Yes," she rasped, reaching one hand behind her to gouge his thigh with her nails. "More."

He hissed, the pleasure-pain building another layer onto his ecstasy, her demand fueling his lust. Growling like something straight out of Sheoul, he snared her wrist, tucked it under her as he grabbed her other arm so she fell forward. Even though the sex haze engulfed him, he was aware that this was his mate, his treasure, and he popped his forearm out so her cheek rested on it instead of the ground.

She thanked him for his courtesy by biting him.

Ah, damn, he loved her. Roughly, he gripped both her wrists in one of his hands and held them prisoner against her flat belly so her ass was in the air and he was covering her. In this position, she was totally at his mercy, completely dominated, and as her moans mingled with the slap of his thighs against her butt, she was also completely lost to pleasure.

His climax boiled in his balls, tingled at the base of his spine, and as it erupted, he sank his teeth into her shoulder, and she shouted in her own release. Pain shot through him as she bit down again on his arm, and fuck that was good, propelling him to another orgasm that hitch-hiked onto the first, the most intense, soul-shattering sexual experience of his life.

Her core squeezed around him, dragging out the pleasurable spasms as they waned. They were both panting, damp with sweat, and every one of Ares's muscles was quivering. So. Damn. Good.

It took several minutes for his senses to reboot, and then he realized he was crushing Cara, his teeth still buried in her skin, and he scrambled off her. "Shit...Cara... are you okay?"

A lazy smile curved her mouth as she rolled, catlike, onto her back and stretched, exposing her long, beautiful body to him. "That," she purred, "was what I've been wanting all along."

He swept her into his arms, amazed at his good fortune. "Any time, sweetheart."

"Good." She licked his throat, a lingering, hot stroke that jumpstarted him again. "Remember all those things you said to me in the shower?"

His mouth went dry. He remembered. He'd been an ass, describing things he knew she hadn't done. But they'd just crossed two of them off the list. "Yeah," he croaked.

"Well, I want to do the rest. Today. So I hope you have candles, honey, a riding crop, and a whole lot of stamina."

Oh, he had all of those things.

God, he loved this woman.

# Twenty-eight

Ares stood in the sand near the sea's edge, a warm breeze caressing his face. The secluded cove was several hundred yards from his house, at the base of a trail Cara would be trekking down right now. He'd told her he wanted to have a picnic to celebrate their month anniversary, so he'd come ahead of her, had laid out a blanket and a basket containing chocolate, fruit, and champagne. In his hand, he clutched a box with a white-knuckled grip.

He heard Cara's soft footfalls behind him, and he smiled when she wound her arm around his waist and leaned against his back. "Where's your mutt? I half expected him to come with you."

"He made it about a third of the way before he took off after a rabbit."

"Damned thing is supposed to be hunting rats," he muttered, but his gruffness was feigned. With the exception of one accident when Hal played a little too rough and nipped Ares, freezing him up for about fifteen minutes, they got along well. They both understood that Cara's safety and happiness were paramount, and that was perfect common ground.

Ares did get a little nervous when too many other hellhounds roamed the island, however. On the plus side, Pestilence hadn't returned. The presence of so many of the beasts was a huge deterrent. Especially since he'd made mortal enemies of them by putting a bounty on their heads.

*Bad move, brother.* One hellhound hating you sucked enough, and Ares knew that for a fact. Having them all hate you? Yeah, Ares wouldn't want to be in Pestilence's boots right now.

Ares turned around, devouring the sight of his little hellhound queen. Though he could probably call her a horse queen, given how Battle, Styx, and even Bones worshipped her, and definitely a Ramreel queen.

While Cara was feeding Rath, whom they'd brought into their home, they'd discovered that Cara's gift worked on animal-based demons. The Ramreels were all over that, and he suspected some of them were intentionally banging themselves up just so Cara would heal them.

She looked down and curled her toes in the sand. "I love being barefoot."

"Limos must be rubbing off on you."

Cara grinned. "She gave me this dress, too."

"Her taste is questionable sometimes, but you look damned fine in ancient Greek fashion." He trailed his finger over the curve of her one bare shoulder. "Like a goddess." Unable to resist, he bent and kissed her there, tasting the tang of salt air and the warmth of the sun.

"Mmm... you can keep doing that."

He smiled against her skin. "Oh, I plan to."

"So, what were you doing staring out into the sea?"

"Thinking about how lucky I am."

"Yeah?"

"Yeah." He lifted his head, feeling nervous and weird and flustered. Definitely not like him, but since meeting Cara, he'd felt a lot of things he wasn't used to. "This has been the best month of my life." Even though they were still seeking Limos's *agimortus* while putting out Pestilence's fires all over the globe, he and Cara had made this island their paradise, their sanctuary.

And Cara had turned his life upside down in the best way possible.

"I've never been this happy," Cara murmured.

"Good. Because I have something to ask you." His mouth was so dry he barely got that last part out. Before she could say anything, he dropped to one knee. "I always thought this was a stupid custom, but I want to do it. I want to honor your time and traditions."

Her hand came up to her mouth, and her eyes glistened, and he hoped to hell it wasn't because she was horrified or upset.

He flipped the box open with his thumb. "Will you marry me?"

Cara's sharp breath filled him with terror. Absolute, mind-numbing terror. He'd rather be bitten by one of her hellhounds than have her say no.

"Ares... oh, that's a beautiful ring."

It was a three-carat diamond set into the only thing he had of his human mother's—a bronze band he'd had coated in platinum to strengthen it while keeping the original, uneven character. "I can get a different setting, or a bigger stone—"

"No." She sank to her knees to face him. "It's perfect."

He swallowed. "Is that a yes?"

She threw her arms around him and planted a big one on his lips. "Yes. Absolutely yes!"

"Thank you, God," he breathed, as she pulled back just enough to allow him to take the ring from the box and slip it onto her finger. It fit perfectly and looked right on her. So right.

Cara wiggled her fingers, admiring the diamond as it glinted in the golden sunlight. Then she gave him a smile infused with sinfulness. "How secluded is this cove?"

"Very."

"Then make love to me."

"So demanding," he murmured, but he pushed aside her shoulder strap and licked her there, intending to work his way down.

"I can be demanding," she sighed, "when I know what I want."

"And what you want is me."

She pushed her dress down, exposing her breasts, and his breath caught. He doubted that would ever stop. "Here's your answer."

"Good answer." He groaned when she cupped his cock through his cargos.

"It'll always be my answer."

"Mine, too." He framed her face in his hands and held her with his gaze. "Cara, you maneuvered your way into my life. My heart. I always believed that love crippled a warrior, but I fought harder for you than I've fought for anything else. You made me stronger. You conquered me, and now I want it all with you."

She gave him a naughty smile. "Checkmate. I win."

"Always." He was lost to her.

And he'd never been so happy to concede a battle.

Half angel, half demon…
She's not for just any man.

Please turn this page
for a preview of

# *Immortal Rider*

Available in December 2011.

# One

⟨ornament⟩

Arik Wagner had to hand it to the Four Horsemen of the Apocalypse; they threw one hell of a party.

Three of them, did, anyway. The fourth, whose name had been Reseph before his Seal broke and he became Pestilence, had been laying low since his defeat at the hands of his siblings a month earlier. The asshole and his demon army were regrouping, no doubt, but for now, everyone was breathing a sigh of relief.

Hence the party, which was part celebration for the victory, and part engagement party for Ares, also known as War, second Horseman of the Apocalypse, and his fiancée, Cara. Everyone who'd survived the battle had been invited to Ares's Greek mansion, and Ares had also extended an invitation to the Underworld General staff, so most of Arik's demon in-laws were here.

Thanatos, the fourth Horseman—who would be Death when his Seal broke—bumped into Arik as he dove for a football someone had tossed from across the huge great room. "Watch it, asshole," Arik muttered.

"What's the matter, human?" Thanatos punched him in the shoulder with the ball hard enough to make Arik step back. "Ping-Pong more your speed?"

Arik shot Kynan Morgan, an old Army buddy who was now in charge of The Aegis, an ancient demon-slaying organization, a you-ready-to-go-or-what look, and Ky, who was deep in conversation with Ares, held up his finger. He and Arik had intended to stay no more than ten minutes, since Ky wanted to be with his wife, Gem, and their new baby. That was more than fine with Arik.

If Arik spent another minute inside with these supernatural, superior asshats, he was going to slit his own throat. Also, if Limos, the drop-dead-gorgeous female Horseman, caught him leering at her one more time, she'd likely slit his throat for him.

No one seemed to be paying any attention to him, so he strolled out of the house and into the cool night air. He'd always liked Greece, had visited a couple of times on military assignments. The food was good, the weather perfect, and the people weren't assholes to Americans. Sure, the Greeks had a high concentration of demons living among them, but some of the oldest countries did. Demons, being extremely long-lived, if not immortal, had a tendency to stay in the places they knew well.

They really weren't all that adventurous. Pussies.

He parked himself on a stone bench overlooking the sea. He could feel the piggy eyes of Ares's Ramreel demon guards on him, but he ignored them and looked up into the heavens. The stars were bright tonight, their lights glittering against the pitch black sky. He smelled

Limos before he heard her; the scent of coconut drifted in on a breeze and made his blood pump a little faster. Coconuts had never turned him on before, but then, the smell had never been attached to a red-hot female with hair the color of the midnight sky, either.

"What are you doing?" Her soft, feminine voice was at odds with the warrior he knew she was, and he wondered how she sounded in bed. Did she hold on to her female side, or did she play rough, dominant, letting the fighter in her take over?

"Just needed some fresh air."

"Why?"

*Because you were making me crazy.* "Just did."

"Wanna fight?"

He blinked. "What?"

She came around in front of him. Her knees touched his, and her Hawaiian dress, violet, to match her eyes, swirled around her shapely ankles, flapping at his boots. "I sense agitation in you. Want to let some out? A little hand-to-hand?"

Jesus. Okay, yeah, she might sense some tension in him, but it wasn't because he wanted to draw blood. He wanted to get naked, and the weird thing was, he imagined getting that way with her. All he'd have to do would be to fist that dress, hike it up over her hips, and he'd be at eye level with her most private place. Would she let him go down on her? What would she taste like? Did that coconut scent permeate everything? Because he fucking loved coconut.

Somehow, he scrounged up enough self-control to put his hands on her waist and set her aside so he could stand. "I don't want to let anything out." *Except my dick.* She'd probably kill him if she knew what he was thinking.

He started for the house, because he was going to drag Kynan out of there if he had to, but naturally, Limos would have none of that. These Horsemen seemed to have a huge sense of entitlement.

"Stop." She grabbed his elbow and swung him around. "I'll let you throw the first punch," she cajoled, with a waggle of raven brows.

He leaned down and stared her in the eyes. "I don't hit girls."

It was the wrong thing to say . . . which was why he said it. Half a second later, he found himself flat on his back, with her flip-flopped foot on his neck. "See," she said brightly, "that is why I was offering to give you the first throw. At least this time I didn't break your ribs."

"Wow," he said. "Do you emasculate all the men, or am I special?"

Her sensual lips curved into an amused smile. "Oh, you're special, but I wouldn't take that as a compliment."

"I can see up your dress." It wasn't true, but the way her eyes went wide, and she started to sputter . . . totally worth the way she scrambled to gather her dress and squash his windpipe a little more. He brought his hands up to grasp her ankle, his intention to lift it to give him some room to breathe, but her skin was so soft he ended up just lingering like that.

"What are you doing?" she gasped, and he smiled.

"Nothing." He smoothed his thumb up and down the side of her leg, in the sensitive place where the ankle met the calf. Her muscles were firm, her skin silky, and man, he wanted to slide his hands up more. But he had her where he wanted her—off guard. Now to take it one step further . . .

"You," he purred, "are a HILF."

"A what?"

"Horseman I'd like to fuck."

With a yank, he tugged her leg out from under her, and at the same time, he twisted so she came down on top of him instead of on the ground, breaking her fall. She looked so startled, so utterly disbelieving that he'd bested her, that she lay motionless on his chest, mouth open, staring at him.

God, she was gorgeous. And that mouth...made to make a man beg for mercy. So he kissed her. Didn't even realize he'd done it until his lips were on hers. He hadn't thought she could be any more shocked, but her eyebrows shot up so far it would have been comical if he hadn't been rocking his head up to put them into a more serious kiss. That was the thing about him—no half-measures. He might not have realized he was kissing her, but once he did? He was taking it as far as she'd let him go.

Command and conquer.

For a brief, sweet moment, she kissed him back. Her lips softened and her tongue met his, hesitantly, as though she wasn't sure what she was doing but wanted to take what she could as fast as she could. And then, his world turned upside down.

Limos reared back, and with what he was pretty sure was all her strength, she slammed her fist into his cheek. Pain spiderwebbed across his face, along every bone, through every tooth. He'd been tasting her, and now he was tasting his own blood.

"What the hell?" he shouted...or at least, he tried to shout. His words were mushy, thanks to his mashed lips, cut tongue, and, likely, badly fractured jaw and cheekbones. He heard something more like, "*Nut da bell.*"

"You kissed me." She backed away so fast she lost her flip-flops. "You fucking bastard, you *kissed me*!"

Son-of-a—

All around him, the ground began to rumble, and then there were giant, spiny arms punching up out of the dirt. Hands seized him, a dozen maybe. Agony wrenched through him as his limbs were twisted and pulled, and his skin was shredded.

Consciousness became a fluid thing, something he couldn't quite reach. His vision went dark, but his ears still worked, and before they shut down, he heard Limos's panicked voice, but what she said made no sense.

*"Don't say my name, Arik. No matter what they do to you, don't speak my name!"*

―――

Limos was utterly frozen, terrified in a way she had never, ever been. And given that she was five thousand years old, that was saying something.

Her brothers and Kynan charged out of the house, weapons drawn, and then they skidded to a halt.

"Jesus Christ," Kynan shouted. "What the fuck? Arik!"

"Limos!" Thanatos tugged her against him, and she realized she'd been moving toward the behemoths that had grabbed Arik and were dragging him down into the earth.

"He kissed me." She said the same thing over and over, her voice a high-pitched, terrified wail.

Wordlessly, Ares produced a blade, and in one smooth motion, launched it at Arik. Limos's first instinct was to stop him, but the blade was already in the air, on a course for Arik's heart.

The whistle of an arrow cut the night, and Ares's dagger shattered. Pestilence, his ice-blue eyes glowing in the light of the moon, stood near the cliff, his bow in hand, a satisfied smile on his face. "You'll thank me later, sis."

Thanatos roared in fury, and a black, furry blur streaked past them both. Before Hal, Cara's hellhound protector, reached Pestilence, he opened a portable Harrowgate and stepped through it.

He was gone, and when Limos turned back to Arik, he was gone, too. The only sign that he'd been there was blood in the sand.

"What the fuck just happened?" Kynan rounded on Ares. "Why did you try to kill him, you cocksucker?"

Limos couldn't speak. Funny how she'd been screaming incoherently, but now she couldn't dredge up a single word. Ares, for his part, stayed calm despite the fact that Kynan had called him a cocksucker and was now fisting his shirt and snarling in his face.

"He kissed Limos," Ares said, his voice rough as sandpaper. Maybe he wasn't as calm as she thought. "She wasn't allowed to give her affections to a male in any way."

Kynan released Ares to turn his murderous glare on Limos. "Explain."

There were still no words. None. The night, which she'd always hated because it reminded her so much of Sheoul, closed in on her. How could Arik have done that? How dare he think it was okay to kiss *her*, one of the Four Horsemen of the Apocalypse? And how long could she go on blaming him, when she had wanted it just as badly?

"Goddammit, someone fucking answer me!"

"We told you that Limos is to become Satan's bride," Thanatos said. "But not until her Seal breaks, she's captured in Sheoul, or until she does something to make him jealous."

"Okay," Kynan growled, "so the big guy is jealous. Why is she still here but Arik is gone?"

"Because it's not that simple. The Dark Lord can't have her until the male who incited the jealousy utters her name while in agony."

Kynan swallowed loud enough for her to hear. "So he's still alive? Where?"

"Hell," Limos rasped. "Arik is in hell."

# VISIT US ONLINE

@ WWW.HACHETTEBOOKGROUP.COM.

## AT THE HACHETTE BOOK GROUP WEB SITE YOU'LL FIND:

**CHAPTER EXCERPTS FROM SELECTED NEW RELEASES**
•
**ORIGINAL AUTHOR AND EDITOR ARTICLES**
•
**AUDIO EXCERPTS**
•
**BESTSELLER NEWS**
•
**ELECTRONIC NEWSLETTERS**
•
**AUTHOR TOUR INFORMATION**
•
**CONTESTS, QUIZZES, AND POLLS**
•
**FUN, QUIRKY RECOMMENDATION CENTER**
•
**PLUS MUCH MORE!**

BOOKMARK HACHETTE BOOK GROUP
@ WWW.HACHETTEBOOKGROUP.COM.